LITTLE WOMEN AND WEREWOLVES

Jo would shut herself up in her room, put on her scribbling suit, and "fall into a vortex."

Little Women and *Werewolves*

LOUISA MAY ALCOTT

and PORTER GRAND

BALLANTINE BOOKS | NEW YORK

A Del Rey Trade Paperback Original

Copyright © 2010 by Porter Grand
Illustrations copyright © 2010 by Random House, Inc.

Published in the United States by Del Rey,
an imprint of The Random House Publishing Group,
a division of Random House, Inc., New York.

DEL REY is a registered trademark and the
Del Rey colophon is a trademark of Random House, Inc.

ISBN 978-0-345-52260-3

eBook ISBN 978-0-345-52262-7

Printed in the United States of America

www.delreybooks.com

2 4 6 8 10 9 7 5 3 1

Illustrations by L. Bark'karie

Book design by Barbara M. Bachman

Illustrations

...

FROM THE OFFICE OF

WELLS PUBLICATIONS

New York, New York

APRIL 1, 1868

My Dear Miss Alcott,

This novel, as is, has a peculiar flavor, which I do not think will suit the frail palates of women readers. Your vibrant description of war amputees being pursued and felled by salivating, monstrous creatures was nearly enough to send this hale man into a swoon; I can little imagine there to be many women with the vigor and stamina necessary to survive this tale of *Little Women and Werewolves*.

I do, however, find the story of the sisters to be pleasing, appealing, and appropriate. Should you care to have this manuscript reconsidered for publication, expand upon the sisters and extract the werewolves and other unsavory themes.

One last note: If this has been submitted in jest, I heartily applaud your humor.

Very Truly Yours,
MANDRAKE WELLS

...

*M*S. BARNARD WAS ODD; A SEVERE AND RIGID LADY with a great deal of hair who read rabidly and usually devoured several books a week. She obviously preferred books to people, blustering into and out of the library with a mute scowl, and as we shared a passion for literary and historical fiction, I was the only librarian to whom she spoke, and then, only about books. Even though librarians often receive small tokens of appreciation from patrons, I was immensely surprised when, before moving to a nursing facility, Ms. Barnard bequeathed to me a smelly cardboard box full of yellowed books. Actually, there were books on top, but below the crumbling volumes nestled a very old manuscript, tied together with a faded, ancient blue ribbon. Below that was an assortment of dried insect husks and a mummified mouse.

I very much enjoyed the manuscript, but I did not believe *Little Women and Werewolves* was really Louisa May Alcott's original version of *Little Women* until I finished it, turned the last page, and found the rejection letter from Mandrake Wells. It was then I remembered having read that Louisa May Alcott preferred writing Gothic pieces and mysteries. *Little Women* was ultimately published by Thomas Niles of Roberts Brothers, so Louisa May obviously did not approve of Mr. Wells's condescending tone, and so took his advice but sent the rewritten book to a different editor.

Sadly, as the box had sat in my car and then the garage for months before I dug through it, Ms. Barnard was deceased by the time I found the manuscript. And so I dedicate this book to the memory of Ms. A. M. Barnard, and of Blitzkrieg, who was my own handsome, loyal, and beloved werewolf.

LITTLE WOMEN AND WEREWOLVES

...

CHAPTER 1

Pouting Pilgrims

"CHRISTMAS NIGHT WILL HAVE A FULL MOON, SO ON TOP of no presents, we can't go out," grumbled Jo, lying on the rug. "It's fortunate we thought to have a Christmas play, so we could invite friends to stay overnight, or it would have been completely ruined."

"It's so dreadful to be poor! And it's a horror to have no father or brothers about to do heavy chores and protect us from the werewolves," sighed Meg, rubbing at a spot on her old dress with her thumb.

"Yes, I don't think it's fair for some girls to have lots of pretty things and other girls nothing at all," declared little Amy, with an injured sniff.

"We've got Mother, and each other, anyhow," said Beth contentedly from her corner. "And we can protect ourselves. Besides, Father is as sad as we that he cannot be here with us. And what does it matter that some girls have lovely clothes when they, just like us, must stay inside during a full moon? Remember that many of them don't even have sisters, so they must shiver all alone in their pretty boots as they listen to the werewolves howl."

Elizabeth, or Beth, as everyone called her, was a rosy, smooth-haired, bright-eyed girl of thirteen who spoke in a soft voice, had a shy manner, a timid voice, and a peaceful expression. Her father called her just that, "Little Tranquility," since she kept herself happy and safe, beyond the boundaries where harsh reality could invade, within her own little world.

The four young faces on which the firelight shone brightened at the cheerful words but darkened again when Jo said sadly: "No matter where he wants to be, the fact is we will have no father here for Christmas, and we shall not have him as long as this terrible war goes on."

"He would want us to be merry," Beth pointed out. "And we each have a dollar to spend for the occasion."

"We can do little with that, and I would hardly want to, with such suffering going on all around us," Meg said, trying to push from her mind all the pretty things she wanted. Meg, or Margaret, was the oldest sister: sixteen, and very pretty, being plump and fair, with plenty of soft brown hair, a sweet mouth, and white hands of which she was rather vain.

"I can do a lot with it. I can buy a new book, maybe two," Jo said. She was fifteen, very tall, thin, and brown, and brought to mind a new colt trying to learn how to use its long limbs. Her features battled with one another: a firm, set mouth, a comical nose, and sharp gray eyes that were by turns fierce, funny, or thoughtful. Her long, thick chestnut hair was her one beauty, but it was usually bundled into a net, to be out of her way.

"I planned to spend mine on new music," said Beth with a smile, a lovely tune playing in her head.

"I shall get a nice box of Faber's drawing pencils; I really need them," said Amy decidedly. Amy was the youngest. She had icy blue eyes and yellow hair that curled on her shoulders; pale and slender, she always carried herself like a young lady mindful of her manners.

"I have earned a treat, spending my days teaching those dreadful children," began Meg, in the complaining tone again.

"You don't have half such a hard time as I do," said Jo. "How would you like to be shut up for hours with a nervous, fussy old lady, who keeps you trotting, is never satisfied, and worries you till you're ready to fly out of the window or box her ears?" It was her lot to spend her days reading to Aunt March, her father's wealthy and grouchy widowed aunt.

"It's naughty to fret, but I do think washing and cleaning is the worst work of all. It makes me cross, and my hands are as rough as a man's. I would so like to have soft hands when I sit at the piano and play," Beth said, looking down at her work-reddened hands.

"I don't believe that any of you suffer as I do," cried Amy; "for you don't have to go to school with impertinent girls, who tease me when I don't know my lessons, injure me because my coat is worn, stare at my ugly nose, and think their father better than mine because of the contents of his wallet," cried Amy.

"You certainly mean insult rather than injure, don't you?" Jo laughed. "It isn't as if they blacken your eyes, or rip the flesh from your bones like the werewolves would if they could get their sharp teeth around your throat."

"I know what I mean, and I am correct in saying they injure me. It is in the figurative sense. It's proper to use good words, and improve your *vocabulary*," returned Amy with dignity.

"Don't fight your own war within these walls when true war rages outside them," scolded Meg.

"But Jo does use such slang words, as if she were from the lowest of classes," observed Amy. Hearing that, Jo sat up and began to whistle.

"Don't, Jo; it's so boyish!"

"That's why I do it."

"I suppose you also howl like the werewolves."

Jo raised her face to the ceiling and let out a low and fierce howl.

"I detest rude, unladylike girls."

"I hate affected, niminy-piminy chits."

"Foxes sharing a den agree," sang Beth, the peacemaker, with such a fearsome but funny face that both sharp voices softened to a laugh.

"Really, girls, you are both to be blamed," said Meg, beginning to lecture in her elder-sisterly fashion. "Jo, you could be concentrating on being a young lady, especially as you have grown so tall and look like one with your hair worn up."

"I ain't one! And if I look like a lady with my hair up, I shall wear it down till I'm twenty," Jo cried, pulling down her hair so the chestnut-colored locks fell over her shoulders and down her back. "It's bad enough to be a girl, anyway, when I like the work and play of boys, and have little time to worry about such things as manners. Why, I should be off fighting with Father, but instead have to stay home and knit like a poky old drooling woman. At least my socks get to see battle." She shook the blue army sock hanging from the end of her knitting needle till the needles rattled like castanets.

"It is your burden to bear, so make the best of it," said Beth, stroking her sister's hair. "Fight werewolves, not your own sister, if you want to fight so badly."

"As for you, Amy, you are altogether too particular and prim," continued Meg. "Jo may assume the part of the wolf in our family, but you'll grow up an affected little goose if you don't take care."

"If we have a wolf and a goose, then what am I, please?" Beth asked.

"A dear, and nothing more," answered Meg warmly; and no one contradicted her. Nobody mentioned aloud that Beth was their mouse, the meek pet of the family, kept carefully caged for her own safety.

The snow fell softly outside as the sisters knit their blue socks for the fighting soldiers. The girls' father had once been wealthy but had lost a great deal of money, so they were not fully accepted by either the rich or the poor young people in town, but the sisters had, in one another, all the friendship, diversion, and caring they needed. The carpet and furniture in the house were old and well worn, yet it was a comfortable home filled with the warmth of the fire and the scent of Christmas roses that bloomed on the windowsill.

The clock struck the hour of six, and Beth put a pair of slippers by the fire so their mother would have a warm pair to slip into when she returned home. "These are so worn," she said, holding them out toward her sisters. "I think I'll buy Marmee a new pair with my dollar."

"No, I shall!" cried Amy.

"I'm the oldest," Meg began.

"But I am the man of the family, with our dear father gone, so *I* shall provide the slippers. It was me that Father asked to take care of Mother while he was away," Jo said.

"Let's each get her something for Christmas!" Beth exclaimed. "We don't really need to get anything for ourselves."

"But what would we get?" asked Jo.

They thought for a moment, and then suddenly began spilling out ideas.

"A pair of gloves!" Meg announced.

"Army shoes, or perhaps boots, for the nights she insists on standing guard defending us against werewolves," Jo said. "Or, even better for those nights, a pocket knife with a sharp and ready blade made of real silver."

"A small bottle of cologne doesn't cost much, so I could also buy myself a few pencils," Amy added.

"We can shop tomorrow afternoon. Marmee will think we're going to buy things for ourselves. There is so much to do yet for our Christmas play, but I can think about it and plan it in my head while we walk," Jo said, pacing the room, back and forth, back and forth.

"This is my last year acting. I am really too old, even now, to be doing so," observed Meg, who was as much a child as ever about "dressing up" frolics.

"I'll believe you are stopping when I see it," Jo said. "You are our best actress, and our productions will end if you quit the boards."

"What play will we do, Jo?"

"Mine," Jo replied, trying not to appear too boastful. "The one I wrote. *The Werewolf Curse: An Operatic Tragedy* is perfect for the occasion."

"Oh, yes, Jo! It will be perfect." Beth sighed, thinking her sister gifted with wonderful genius in all things.

"And I shall play the fiercest werewolf that ever lived!" Jo marched about the room, teeth bared and fingers curled into claws, as her sisters shrieked and laughed.

"How nice to see my girls so merry!" Marmee said, stepping into the room. Although not elegantly dressed, she was tall, had a noble air, and her girls thought her the most splendid mother on earth.

"You look tired, or sad, Marmee," Meg said.

"I was helping at the clinic, as you know, and the Brigade stormed in and took three women, three patients away."

"The Brigade!" Jo cried. "I thought they disbanded due to the war."

"When the men went off to fight, it certainly appeared that way. But now there are women rising up to fight, as they call it, 'the threat of werewolves among us,' and a war hero leads them, one who was injured and sent home, but with a hunger for battle still in his heart. He and others returning from the war are reviving the Brigade with alarming swiftness."

"Did they accuse all three of those women of being werewolves?" Amy asked, eyes wide.

"They said two were werewolves and the other a werewolf sympathizer. One had an infected wound, and they produced a knife said to have cut into a werewolf as it attacked, and they swore it a perfect match to her wound, although I did not think it was, and I said as much."

"I'm glad the clinic is so far from us if that's where werewolves take refuge," Amy said with a sigh.

"But there is no proof they are what they are accused of being. And you're safe here, Amy, just as we have always told you. I know you fear the werewolves more than anything else on this earth, but you are well protected, my child," Marmee said as she smoothed her youngest daughter's hair.

"And the other women?" Jo asked. "What was the Brigade's case against them?"

"The other accused of being a werewolf had a weak infant, and we all know pure werewolves, those born of both werewolf mothers and fathers, languish during their first few years. But hunger and poverty also cause infant weakness, a fact the Brigade chose to ignore completely."

"What of the sympathizer?"

"I have no idea what evidence they had against that woman.

They took her out by her hair as she kicked, cried, and screamed; but what is saddest is that sometime during the mêlée, the ailing infant perished. It is so unfair that they continue to lay blame only at the feet of the poor; I cannot recall a time that a wealthy person was executed as either a werewolf or a werewolf sympathizer. Oh, but the Brigade frightened us all, stomping about in those horrible breastplates and helmets, and I saw absolutely that some of them were women. The whole affair was surely as brutal and inhuman as anything on the war's battlefields."

"We are all so helpless against that foul Brigade, it's a wonder they have amassed such great support," Meg said.

"People are afraid, and they are selfish. They cannot see what it's like to be another, to live as a werewolf with a need for human meat. And because they are the werewolves' prey, they vilify the poor creatures and view them as purely evil. I think, although most citizens disapprove of the Brigade's tactics, they yet view it as necessary."

"If only the whole world had Father's generous outlook!" Beth exclaimed.

"If that were the case, he would be here by our sides because there would be no war either against werewolves or against each other," said Marmee.

"Come warm yourself by the fire, Mother," Meg suggested.

Marmee nodded and held her hands out toward the comforting flames of the hearth. "I reminded the Brigade that it was nearly Christmas, but they turned the table and reminded me of the woman slaughtered and eaten last month who had children of her own left behind and alone for Christmas. But I then spoke up once more to add that they would be quite busy if they wished to rid us of werewolves completely, for with so many gone in the war, a full one-quarter of our population are now werewolves, rich as well as poor; of all ages and both men and women."

"And what was their reaction then, Marmee?" asked Jo, inching forward to better hear and memorize her mother's tale of confrontation.

"They differed, as expected, saying that nowhere near that many werewolves exist, but there were many others present who believed my figures accurate. No one in that room could remember a time when there were no werewolves among us; some recalled even long-dead forebears relating their childhood memories of bolting their doors on nights with full moons."

"I overheard Father, just before he left, estimating that it was close to one-third of this town's population who are werewolves," said Beth.

"It can't be that many!" Amy exclaimed.

Marmee glanced at her other daughters, and they all quickly assured Amy that the quoted numbers were inflated, although in their hearts they feared the numbers to be even higher.

"And the werewolves all live far from us, don't they?" Amy questioned.

"They do, indeed," Marmee said with a smile. "Just as we have always told you."

"What happened then, Marmee?" Jo asked, wanting sorely to hear the remaining details of the story.

"The Brigade declared before everyone present that their newly formed band is true to the original goals established nearly one hundred years ago, and that they will hunt any and all werewolves, that privilege carries no weight in their eyes."

"Privilege always carries weight," said Meg with a heavy sigh as she looked down at the threadbare carpet.

"I like Father's idea to school the werewolves in self-control so they might dampen their urges, just as we all learn to resist sin," Jo said. "I believe it is an innovative concept, one that would prove meritorious, and might allow others to trust them more readily. As Father always said, man slaughters as swiftly as any werewolf. I feel the good sense of his words each time I walk past a butcher shop and see the hapless animal heads and body parts displayed and awaiting some family's supper table. After all, everyone knows the unfortunate truth that werewolves must, occasionally, eat human meat and blood to be healthy and strong. Eating only animals, they will eventually wither and languish, sicken and die. Some allowances must surely be made for that."

"Anyone who opens his mind and heart could see as much," Marmee agreed, "and I am thankful your father is not here now to witness the Brigade's atrocities. The dear man respects all life equally. He always did, and for that rare, compassionate stripe, I fell in love with him. For there have been instances when werewolves stopped suddenly in mid-attack, and we can only assume it was because they recognized their victim. They, like us, become what they are taught, so I, too, think education is essential."

"But what of those victims not born werewolves? Those whom if they are bitten, but their hearts are not eaten, then become werewolves?"

"Well, they still live, so can learn. Live and pray and work and love, as we all do, except for that one short night each month. This wrathful contempt for werewolves is impious."

"Speak no more of this, Marmee. Rather sit and relax," Beth urged.

"Yes, I should." Obviously fatigued, she sank into her chair as the girls bustled about and got the tea table ready. "We are all so tired out by this war, that little concern has been paid to the werewolves of late, yet the attacks are now greatly slowed. I much prefer to apply my efforts to helping the poor, not condemning them."

Once everyone was sitting with tea or toast in hand, Mrs. March produced her prize—a letter from Mr. March.

"Father is quite a saint to go to war as a chaplain, although too old and weak to serve as a soldier," Meg said.

"I would happily go as a drummer. Or perhaps a nurse, to cut off ruined limbs and throw them to the battlefield werewolves," Jo said, sawing the air with her butter knife.

"Jo!" Four voices wailed in unison, pretty noses wrinkled with disgust.

Jo sighed. As usual, she had said the wrong thing.

Mr. March's letter was filled with hope and cheer, and he sent his love to each of his "little women"; and each resolved in her soul to be all that Mr. March hoped to find in his girls when the year brought around the happy coming-home.

They all sat silently, sad and dismal, until Mrs. March broke the silence by reminding them of the *Pilgrim's Progress* game they used to play, where they would put packs on their backs and pretend to travel the world. They would work their way up from the City of Destruction, which was in the cellar, to the Celestial City, which represented heaven, or eternal reward, on the roof, where a treat of cake and milk awaited the good pilgrims who had survived the valley of the hobgoblins, fighting Apollyon and sneaking past the two roaring lions who tested their faith.

"Now, my little pilgrims," said Mrs. March, "suppose you begin again, not in play, but in earnest, and see how far on you can get before Father comes home. Look under your pillows in the morning, my dears, and you will find your guidebooks," she added mysteriously, and would say no more.

They worked a couple of hours on their boring, but necessary, sewing, and then stood around the old, out-of-tune piano as Beth coaxed music from the yellowed keys. They sang together, as was their household custom each evening, Marmee's rich, beautiful voice leading her girls through the tunes, and then they all went contently off to bed with their lullaby yet wafting through their heads.

...

CHAPTER 2

A Christmas Show

J O WAS THE FIRST TO WAKE IN THE GRAY DAWN OF CHRIST-mas morning. No stockings hung at the fireplace, and she should have anticipated as much, but her memory still teased her with Christmases past when they each received a sock crammed with goodies. Things were very different now.

Jo suddenly recalled Marmee's words and dug beneath her pillow, unearthing a crimson-covered book. *Pilgrim's Progress!* It was a wonderful old story about the best life ever lived, and a true guide for any and all pilgrims during their life's journey. When the girls were younger, the book was their daily focus, but as they grew older, they referred to it less and less. Jo understood Marmee's intent in gifting them each with a copy, for one should not grow too far from righteousness. Meg woke next to find a green-covered edition, Beth found hers dove-colored, and Amy's was bound in blue. They sat discussing the story while the east grew rosy with the coming day. When they trudged downstairs to wish a merry Christmas to their dear mother, they found only Hannah, who had lived with the family since Meg was born and was considered more a friend than a servant. She told them their mother had rushed off to help some poor creature who had come begging. "She run straight off to see what was needed."

They decided to have everything ready for her return and assembled a basket with all their presents. They heard the door slam and quickly hid it, but found it was only Amy, who, after reading a bit of *Pilgrim's Progress*, felt guilty and went to exchange the small bottle of cologne she had purchased for a larger size for her dearest Marmee.

The street door slammed again and they all hurried to greet their mother, eager for the breakfast whose aroma made their stomachs rumble with want. "Merry Christmas, Marmee! Thank you for the books!" they all cried.

"Merry Christmas, little daughters! Before we sit down, I want to tell you about a poor woman with a brand-new baby and six hungry children not far from here. They are cold and in need, and my only wish for Christmas is that you give them your fine breakfast as a Christmas present and content yourselves with our usual milk and bread for your own Christmas feast."

The hungry girls wanted to protest, but knew their mother only wanted them to do what was right. For a minute no one spoke; then Jo exclaimed impetuously, "I'm so glad you came before we began to eat!"

All the girls began to pack up the food to carry it, in a small, ragged procession, to the hungry family.

As they started down the path from their home, Jo looked to one side and saw a handsome young man, the Laurence boy, the grandson of the man who owned the fine estate next to their house. She lifted her chin in greeting, her hands being too full to wave. A lovely smile blossomed across the boy's face and the others called out wishes of a merry Christmas to him.

"I wonder why such a handsome boy keeps so much to himself," Jo mused aloud.

"He and his grandfather have always done so," said Marmee.

"The old man keeps his mind on his business and a strict rein on his grandson. Those are people with much to lose, for, as we well know, it is hard work not just in making a fortune, but also in the keeping of it."

"It's our poor luck to live next to such a pair of hermits," said Amy with a frown.

"I have often felt an aloof neighbor is preferable to a nosy one," Marmee said, laughing.

The little parade reached their destination, and their hearts ached when they saw the bare, miserable room and the pale, wide-eyed children dressed in dingy, torn clothes.

Without a moment's hesitation, Hannah, who had carried wood, made a fire and stopped up the broken windowpanes with some of her old clothing that she had brought. The girls spread the table while Mrs. March fed the sickly mother tea and gruel. The children called the March family angels as they ate, stuffing food into their chattering blue lips with cold, chapped, purple hands.

The March women walked back home, feeling content and merry for giving away their breakfasts to neighbors in want.

"That woman," said Jo, "should make a Christmas gift of a few of her children to the werewolves. The youngest, as the older ones may be able to work and help around the house."

"That's a terrible thing to say, Jo, even for you!" Amy exclaimed.

"But it would leave more for the rest of them," Jo argued.

"Enough, Jo. I worry much about the Brigade's growing strength. Werewolves should not be a topic of frivolous conversation. And you know well that a mother could never do such a thing as feed her child to wolves," Mrs. March stated, shaking her head.

"Marmee, are you saying you would not sacrifice Amy in order to feed more to me?" Jo teased, looking out of the corner of her eye to watch Amy's reaction.

Realizing her sister's game, Amy grinned, grabbed up some snow, and threw it at Jo.

After giving Marmee her presents, the girls dedicated the rest of the day to getting ready for the evening's festivities, as nobody could leave the house that night once the moon appeared, full and round in the sky. Every blanket and quilt the family owned had been gathered from drawers and trunks. Some would be used for the stage; others would serve to warm guests through the night once the production had ended.

There was no money to spend on props and décor for the stage, but the resourceful March sisters found scraps and bits throughout the town. They searched trash piles constantly, often venturing as far as the pickle factory, where they knew bits of spangling tin could be scavenged. No gentlemen were admitted to their shows, so Jo played the male parts, and more than one of their guests in the audience that Christmas night sighed heavily at the sight of Jo, dressed as a handsome villain with clanking sword, slouched hat, black beard, mysterious cloak, and her favorite russet-colored boots.

The introduction was a tremendous success, and the dozen girls in the audience hooted, clapped, and stomped in anticipation of a thrilling production. Jo, behind the scenes, pulled on her fearsome wolf mask, made from scraps of sheep hide rubbed to gray with hearth ashes. The lights were turned down to begin the second production, *The Werewolf's Curse*. As a light came on to illuminate Jo, wearing her horrible mask, she raised her head to howl, but from outside came the cry of a real werewolf, long and sorrowful, and bloodcurdling enough to inject terror into the very marrow of the girls' delicate bones. Trembling, the girls huddled together. Jo could not have asked for a more fitting start to her play, and the result was that her audience was captive and awed throughout the entire production. At the end, they cheered even louder than they had after the first play.

"Do you think there are girl werewolves as well as boys?" one girl asked.

"There must be," another responded. "There have certainly been women, as well as men, who have been bitten by them and thus cursed to become one."

"But people here are not bitten by werewolves, they are devoured by them!"

"Yes, they are torn to pieces and eaten, with only a skull, and perhaps a foot or an elbow, left of them to bury and mourn."

"Once the heart or brain is destroyed, the werewolf dies, so anyone eaten thus would not survive," Jo informed them all.

"Still, some must be merely bitten or scratched, and survive to become werewolves themselves each full moon."

"There can't be any that are girls," Jo cried, and then in a complaining voice added, "There are no girls allowed outside when the moon is full, so none can be bitten and turned into werewolves."

"We are only kept in for our protection," Beth said with a smile.

"Well, I can protect myself," Jo said, rising up and taking her foil in hand. "And I can protect all of you as well. Back, werewolf, back!" she cried merrily, dancing about and thrusting her sword through the air.

"The Brigade is gaining strength and numbers, I hear," said one dark-haired girl.

"I find the Brigade every bit as frightening as the were-wolves," another confessed.

"As they intend," Jo said with a snort. "For they have no other reason to wear those terrifying breastplates and helmets now than to scare the citizens. Long ago, when the Brigade once hunted werewolves under the full moon, they were justified in wearing thick leather and chain mail as protection against the bites and scratches. Back then, there was no error in who was hunted, for the werewolf wore its pelt as proof of who it was; today, they extract whomever they choose, in the safety of day-light and multiple witnesses, and seem to only condemn the poorest among us."

"But the group has been around as long as the werewolves themselves—as far back as any living person can recall, and be-yond. Does that not mean they serve a purpose?"

"Not as they once did, I tell you!" Jo insisted. "Although, sadly, most people think them essential. The Brigade was origi-nally founded out of what had been viewed as necessity, when people lived in frightfully frail shelters, but now we have sturdy homes in which we can wait for the moon's cycle to pass."

"Then you don't believe the Brigade keeps us safe from were-wolves, Jo?"

"Once, but no longer. I would join the Brigade immediately if they yet hunted under the fullness of the moon and wore that thick studded leather and chain mail."

"I doubt there are women in the Brigade."

"But there are, I assure you. Marmee saw. You well know that since the war began and the men followed it off, women have had to step in to do everything."

"Do you suppose, when the men return from the war, that they will slaughter all the werewolves because they have slaughtered some of our people?" one girl asked nobody in particular. "Perhaps they will all be killed off then."

"There are a lot of them to kill!" said Jo. "Have they ever not been among us in great numbers?"

"I think not," answered one girl. "My grandfather once told me that when he was my age, his grandfather told him stories of large packs of werewolves from his childhood, and that at that time, most of the population were werewolves."

"Do you mean from the childhood of your grandfather's grandfather?"

"Yes!"

"That was a very, very long time ago!"

"Yes, decades and decades."

"It hardly sounds possible."

"But it is," Jo said immediately. "Father has always told us that our families have lived with the werewolves in this area for many generations. He said we must welcome them as we would any other neighbor, but to just be careful and never tempt fate when the moon is full."

"But we seldom know who they are. It's hard to protect one-self against enemies you cannot name," Amy said.

"Then, as Father would suggest," said Beth, "treat everyone with kindness, but be well aware that the devil knows how to tempt us all."

"Not everyone is as kind and forgiving as your father, though," one girl reminded them all. "Most people in this town applaud those helmeted men who happily hunt and kill the werewolves."

"Yes, and I imagine, once the others get back from their war, their bloodlust will be boiling over for the want of spilling more."

"I would much rather become a werewolf than be eaten by one," said one girl.

"I would rather go to my eternal reward than reside as a being who had to hide itself from the world," said Amy assuredly.

"A werewolf sympathizer must hide just as well," Jo reminded her. "They are forced to live in as great a fear as the werewolves, as the penalty for being such is far too similar. Is this war not producing enough blood for them? Why must they also don uniforms and declare enemies?"

"Well, they could never accuse me of sympathizing with werewolves," the dark-haired girl declared. "I would like to see them all dead."

"No need for that," Jo fumed. "We have learned well to coexist."

"Coexist? You believe that?"

"Absolutely. Once each month, we barricade ourselves against them, and the rest of the time we put them out of our minds," said Jo, widening her stance for effect.

"I want to hear no more of werewolves!" Amy cried, pale and trembling. "I cannot bear another word, or I shall not sleep a wink tonight for fear of dreaming of enormous packs of them circling this house."

Hannah appeared suddenly, announcing that supper awaited them below. The sisters looked at one another questioningly as their guests followed Hannah downstairs. There had been no money for supper. What could Marmee have found to serve?

"You two go on ahead while we get out of our costumes," Jo told Amy and Meg, who made short work of bounding from the room and down the stairs.

Jo scratched her chin where the beard was glued on, as she

peered out the window. The window looked down into Mr. Laurence's large, lovely house. She inhaled with a gasp as she saw Mr. Laurence's handsome dark-haired grandson standing in the moonlight. He wore no shirt. The view did not allow her to see if he wore trousers, for the angle down cut him off at midchest, but the sight of his muscled shoulders and chest made her heart twirl.

"Beth! Come see!" she whispered.

The sisters stood, watching breathlessly, as the moonlight caught his eyes, which shone like jewels as he stared with longing at the moon. His head jerked once, and then again, as his face distorted and lengthened. His neck stretched, thickened, and darkened with sprouting hair. He stared up to the ceiling as his nose and mouth stretched out into a muzzle, and his ears grew up and out. Dripping, pointed teeth pushed out from his open mouth as he writhed in what appeared to be intense pain. Hair began to grow and fall quickly over his skin as his shoulders thrust forward. And then he dropped down and could be seen no longer.

Jo stood transfixed, a chill running up her spine. It was not a chill of terror, as one might think, but rather one of excitement and desire. It had been thrilling merely to watch, but her hands itched also to stroke the hair that covered the youth's body, to feel the animal breath in her face, and to stare into the eyes that had glinted golden in the moonlight.

"The Laurence men are werewolves!" Beth exclaimed.

"It explains the old man's reluctance to befriend others," Jo said. "But Beth, we cannot tell anyone. Swear to me you will not tell a soul. Not Marmee, not Meg, not Amy. And not even our father when he returns." Jo looked at her sister and knew that Beth, sweet, odd Beth, would never tell. She would savor this secret and hide it away deep in the forest of her pretend kingdom, where her cats were queens and her soiled old dolls their subjects.

"I swear, Jo. I would not care to be responsible for their fate if anyone was to know. We have lived alongside that family our entire lives without a problem. Werewolves or not, they are our neighbors. I could not turn on them, no matter that they seldom speak to us; I could not bear having their blood on my hands."

"There is one matter more to consider," said Jo. "Our Amy. Think of her reaction if she knew werewolves lived in the house next to ours."

"She would never sleep through another night!" Beth cried. "She believes they all live far off, beyond the borders of the town, in their own community."

"Yes," Jo said. She thought it a wise falsehood invented by Father when Amy was small and suffered so severely from nightmares. She remembered how Marmee and Meg sat up many a night with the weeping child; Father could no longer stand seeing them so exhausted, and so created stories to soothe her."

"There is only one thing to do. Let us add this knowledge to our burdens and we two, alone, shall carry it," said Beth decidedly.

"Then we agree to be eternally silent in this matter," Jo said, holding out her hand so Beth could shake it to solidify their oath.

Flushed and aroused with the thrill of what they had witnessed, the sisters ran downstairs, stopping short at the sight of a feast of ice cream both pink and white, cake, fruit, French bonbons, and, in the middle of the table, four enormous vases filled with hothouse flowers.

"Marmee! Where?" Beth asked.

"You could never guess. The others certainly couldn't. So I

will tell you right off. Old Mr. Laurence sent it all," Mrs. March said with a wide smile.

Beth and Jo stared at each other for a moment, happier than ever for the pledge of silence they had made.

"Did he say why he sent it?" Jo asked.

"Hannah told one of his servants about your breakfast party. He was so impressed with your charity that he felt he had to do something pleasant for you in return."

"I bet his grandson put him up to it," Jo said. "He looks as if he'd like to know us, but he's bashful. I wish we could get acquainted."

"But Mr. Laurence seems like a nice enough man himself. Even if he doesn't care to speak much with girls," Amy said.

"His house is so big and rich-looking," one of the guests said with a sigh.

"I think he keeps his grandson locked up, like a captive, and makes him study constantly," Meg added.

"The boy brought this all over himself. I asked him in, but he said he could not stay, even though he looked wistful at hearing the frolic upstairs, and evidently having none of his own," Mrs. March said. "And then, after he brought the last of it, he hurried away as if on fire."

Jo felt herself warm at the mention of the boy, and she recalled the sight of him, first with no shirt, his strong, lean arms and shoulders exposed, and then as he transformed from boy to wolf. She exhaled heavily to calm herself.

...

CHAPTER 3

The Laurence Werewolf

"HOW DO WE LOOK?" JO ASKED, AS SHE AND MEG STOOD dressed and ready to go to Mrs. Gardiner's New Year's Eve party.

"Beautiful!" Beth exclaimed, being ever blind to the poorer details, such as where Jo had burned off Meg's hair trying to curl it, or that Jo's gloves had to be held balled in her hands to hide the lemonade stains on them.

"I have a burn mark on the back of my dress, but I don't plan to dance, so I'll stand all night with my back to the wall," Jo said, looking back and pulling her skirt forward to eye the miserable stain.

Before entering the party, Jo asked Meg to kindly point it out to her if she lapsed into behavior that was less than ladylike.

"I will nod if you are fine, and lift my eyebrows if anything is wrong. Now hold your shoulders straight, stand tall, take short steps, and, above all, don't shake hands when you are introduced to somebody. Only boys do that."

"How can one ever remember all the proper ways to act?"

Meg was asked to dance immediately, and readily accepted the offer, though her slippers were too small and pinched her feet terribly. Jo sidled along the wall. She saw a tall red-haired boy advancing toward her, undoubtedly wanting to ask her to dance, so she fled, forgetting about hiding the burn on the back of her skirt. She went from one group of people to the next, ducking behind the tallest of them, and peering out to find the boy following her each time. She was finally able to lose him by slipping behind a hanging drape. She watched the boy continue on and breathed a sigh of relief.

She turned around and saw she was in a man's study of sorts. A curtain blew inward on the other side of the room, so she stepped through it and onto a long balcony. She took a deep breath of crisp night air, turned, and found herself face-to-face with the Laurence boy. Her heart fluttered in her chest like a newly caged bird, and her feet itched to turn and carry her far away from the boy she knew to be a werewolf, but manners had to be respected, werewolf or no.

"Dear me," she stammered. "I had no idea anyone was here."

The boy laughed. "Don't mind me. Stay, if you like."

"Shan't I disturb you?" Jo asked, her heart thumping even harder and her nerves tingling as she stared at his suit jacket and recalled his bared shoulders and chest.

"From whom are you hiding?"

"A dreadful boy who was determined to ask me to dance. And you?" she asked, stepping back as he approached. She looked behind her and took comfort in a group of boys standing just outside the open door of the study.

"From everyone. The stench of all the different perfumes and pomades turns my stomach. I fear I'm sensitive like that."

"Well, I wear no perfume, so unless I speak carelessly, I shouldn't turn your stomach."

The boy laughed. When their eyes met, they both looked quickly away. From under her lashes Jo took in his brown skin, curly black hair, handsome nose, fine teeth, and small hands and feet. She concentrated on his hands, and imagined those fingers touching her, running down her arm, or holding her cheek.

"I have had the pleasure of seeing you before. You live near us, don't you?" he asked, interrupting her fantasy.

"Yes. Next door," Jo replied. She was nervous but realized she was a bit more at ease than she had expected to be in the presence of the first werewolf she'd ever personally known.

"Do you care for a bite?" He held out his plate of food, but she declined his offer when she saw it held no tarts, fruit, bonbons, or cakes, only mutton, sausages, and slices of what looked like pork. She might have taken a bonbon or cake if there had been one, but it was just as well there were none, for her hands trembled noticeably.

"I suppose you are going away to college soon?" she said. "I often see you with your books."

"Not for a year or two. Not until I'm seventeen."

"Aren't you but fifteen?" asked Jo, looking at the tall lad, whom she had imagined seventeen already. "I'm fifteen, too."

"I will be sixteen next month."

"I wish I could go to college."

"I hate the thought of it."

"What would you like to do?"

"Live in Italy and enjoy myself in my own way."

"My mother told me you were born there. In Italy."

"Yes, I was young when I came here to live with my grandfather, but I miss Italy yet."

An Italian werewolf! How utterly romantic! Jo's heart pounded. "You don't enjoy living with your grandfather?"

"Not really. The master and the slave."

"He can't be as bad as all that. He seems kindly, as he sent us that great feast. Or was that your idea?"

"He can be, and often is, that bad. He's very stern. Believe me, the gift was his idea. I can put very little into his head, since what I say he cannot absorb, Miss March."

"I ain't Miss March, I'm only Jo."

"Then call me Laurie."

"Laurie Laurence. What an odd name."

"My first name is Theodore. The boys called me Dora, so I made them call me Laurie."

"And how did you make them?"

"I thrashed 'em."

"I wish I could thrash my Aunt March! She forever calls me Josephine instead of Jo, and insists I forever read the same tiresome books to her over and over again, while an entire library of thrilling books sit at the ready."

"Are they her books?"

"They were her husband's. He died some time ago. He used to build railroads and bridges, and he always had fine tales, and cards of gingerbread for me. The moment Aunt March falls asleep, or sees to company, I run to find another book. There are books on poetry, romance, history, travels, and some with glorious pictures of places all over the world, and some places that lie only in someone's imagination."

The two smiled, and then Jo asked, "So do you and your grandfather share no interests at all?"

"One. We share one."

"What is it?"

"Just something of gentlemanly interest."

"And do you engage in this interest together often?"

"Oh, yes. Monthly."

Jo felt the hair on the nape of her neck stand out and a quiver shake her spine as the knowledge that she was actually speaking with a werewolf surfaced anew. Yet she was surprised to realize that she was greatly at ease with this young man, much more so than with any of the stuffy, pretentious young men loitering around the dance floor and refreshment tables. Never before had she felt such an immediate kinship with anyone upon first meeting.

"You're shaking. We could go inside if you're cold."

"No, I'm fine. I'm actually quite warm. Someone must have walked across my grave just then," Jo said, allowing superstition to explain away her shiver.

"Let's go inside anyway."

They had just settled into chairs when Meg's head appeared in the doorway and she beckoned Jo out.

"There you are! I searched everywhere, simply everywhere, for you," she cried, throwing herself down on the hallway sofa. "I've sprained my ankle. That stupid high heel turned, and gave me a sad wrench. It aches so I can hardly stand, and I can't see how I will be able to get home."

"I knew you'd hurt your feet in those silly shoes. I'm sorry, Meg, but we must either sleep here tonight or hobble home. It isn't as if we can afford to hire a carriage. Besides, it's past nine and dark as Egypt out there."

"I can offer a solution," Laurie said, stepping out from the room.

Meg gasped and looked from his face to Jo's.

"I have my grandfather's carriage. It isn't as if I'll have to drive out of my way to take you home."

"I couldn't ask that of you. It's so early," Meg protested.

"I always go home early. Truly, I do. And I'm bored with this party."

Jo could think of no reason to refuse his kindness. The moon was not full, and she would not be able to tell her sister the truth about the boy, so the young women graciously accepted young Mr. Laurence's offer.

Meg felt quite festive and elegant in the luxurious closed carriage while Laurie and Jo rode up in the box to guide the horses. Jo thought she would certainly remember this night for the rest of her life, as she had never before taken a moonlit ride with a werewolf and probably never would again.

Jo came up with a mischievous plan to see how Laurie would react to a conversation about werewolves.

"Let's pretend it's a night of the full moon and that werewolves hide everywhere along our route."

Laurie glanced at her queerly and then smiled. "So you hope to meet a werewolf?"

"I hope to know many—to have them as friends."

"Even during a full moon?"

"Especially during a full moon."

"And would you strip down to your bloomers, or beyond, to run through the night with them?"

Jo was flustered, but she regained her composure quickly. "That is a question that a little woman should not be asked by a young gentleman. A true gentleman would never make reference to what a lady wears beneath her garments."

"Jo, you're right. I apologize most profusely, and of course I expect no answer to my wicked question."

Something in the way he held himself, in the very way he breathed, and in his animal alertness made Jo want to sit nearer to him. She knew she would feel safe nestled against him, inhaling the intoxicating musk of his skin, but she fought the urge and stayed where she was. She sat crookedly, though, to face him, and she breathed deeply, hoping to swallow the very same air he was exhaling as he recited an amusing story he had heard.

They chatted easily the rest of the way home. Meg and Jo thrilled their mother and sisters with tales of the party, the mishap, and the handsome and gallant boy who rescued them and guided them home safely.

Jo had laid a hand on Laurie's arm when she thanked him for the ride home. A jolt had run up her arm, and she could feel the cloth of his sleeve on her fingertips until she fell asleep that night.

...

CHAPTER 4

Befriending Werewolves

THE HOLIDAYS WERE OVER, AND THE SISTERS HAD TROUBLE returning from their week of merry-making to their daily tasks. Meg was especially cross one morning as she prepared for the day; trying to decide which of two shabby dresses was least shabby, she bewailed her situation, railing about all she did not have and the life of luxury she was not living.

"It could be much worse," Beth consoled her. "You could have no home or clothes at all."

"Or you could be a werewolf," Amy added.

"You don't imagine there are any rich or happy werewolves?" Jo inquired, laughing.

"I only know I would hate it," Amy sniffed. "Turning into an animal and eating off the ground."

"But then, at least, you would have a solution to your flat nose. It would grow out into a lovely, long snout," Jo teased as Meg and Beth chuckled.

"I will keep my nose and my body as they are. Nothing could possibly be worth even associating with werewolves," Amy said, feeling her nose with her fingers.

Jo and Beth exchanged a quick glance. Jo began whistling, which swiftly earned her a scolding.

"Let's go down and see to breakfast," Jo said to Beth. "It will be so much kinder to our ears down here," she added when they reached the kitchen.

But their poor ears had short respite, as Meg was soon downstairs complaining about almost falling over one of Beth's kittens. She railed on and on, and Beth soon retreated to lie on the couch. Jo went to check on her a short time later, and found her with tears running down her cheeks.

"Dear Beth, don't let her sour mood ruin your day."

"I can tolerate complaints, so long as they're not directed at me," Beth sobbed.

"Well, you have no time for this. You have six little ones to ready for the day."

Beth cheered up a bit and allowed Jo to lead her over to the six dolls she tended as carefully as if they were living children. There was not one whole or handsome doll among them; all were old and ugly outcasts. But Beth cherished them even more for that very reason and set up a hospital for infirm dolls where they were all nursed, caressed, fed, and clothed with unfailing affection. It was unnerving for the other household members to walk into the room and have eleven little eyes (one doll was missing an eye) instantly upon them. The worst doll of the lot had no top to her head and hadn't any arms or legs, but Beth wrapped her in blankets and put a bonnet on to cover her head wound. This doll made Jo most uncomfortable, for it was she who had reduced the poor thing to such a condition and then tossed her into the ragbag to be discarded. The doll seemed to awaken to Jo's presence the moment she entered the room, and its sharp blue eyes flung constant accusations at the girl.

Beth began to sing to the dolls, and the cats gathered around like nursing assistants, rubbing up against the girl and the dolls to administer their own feline doses of healing care. Jo took one last glance at her sister, who would spend her day cleaning, cooking, and tending to the imaginary friends who peopled her world. Perhaps Beth would one day outgrow this life, but Jo suspected, as time went on, it was more likely that she would move further and further into this safe, pretend land she had created.

Jo drank some milk, trying to think of other things so she did not have to absorb the complaints of Meg and Amy, who were comparing their lives to those of girls from more affluent families. She tried to think of what her mother would say if she heard her daughters going on so and decided that Marmee would probably invent a story that would show her daughters their sins and weaknesses. Jo opened her mouth to begin such a tale but closed it again after deciding her time could be better spent clearing snow. She donned rubber boots, an old sack and hood, and grabbed a broom and the shovel.

"What in the world are you going to do now, Jo?" Meg asked as Jo passed through the hall.

"Going out for exercise," Jo replied with a mischievous twinkle in her gray eyes. "I don't like to doze by the fire like a pussycat. I'm going to find some adventure."

She went outside and began to dig paths with great energy. The snow was light, and with her broom, she soon had a path all around the garden for Beth to walk in to give her invalid dolls some air. She stopped and found herself facing the Laurence house, which was separated from theirs by this garden. The stately stone mansion had always been mysterious to the March girls, as none of them had ever seen the inside, but they often played games, when Marmee was absent, where they guessed at the house's contents and secrets. It seemed a lonely, lifeless sort of house.

Jo's eye glided up the stone wall to Laurie's window. She did not see him, so made a snowball and lobbed it up. Laurie's surprised and handsome face appeared, losing its listless stare the moment he spotted Jo. His big eyes brightened, and his soft lips spread out into a smile. Jo laughed and called out, "How do you do? Are you sick?"

Laurie opened the window and croaked out as hoarsely as a raven, "Better, thank you. I've had a horrid cold, and been shut up a week."

"So you can't come out?" Jo frowned.

Laurie shook his head and coughed into his hand.

"What do you do to amuse yourself?"

"Nothing; it's dull as tombs up here."

"Don't you read?"

"Not much. They won't let me."

"Maybe a visitor could read to you," Jo said. "Maybe I could read to you." She thought her idea brilliant, for being with a werewolf in daylight would be perfectly safe, and she would finally have the privilege of seeing the interior of that stately mansion.

"Would you?" Laurie croaked.

"Shut that window, and wait till I come."

With that, Jo marched into the house to get ready, and Laurie flew about his own house, preparing for his guest.

A surprised servant announced Jo, and she entered and presented Laurie with a blancmange decorated with a garland of leaves and the scarlet flowers of Amy's pet geranium. She next unearthed from her pocket one of Beth's kittens, on loan. The moment she woke the poor thing, it began to hiss and claw as if feral. She held tight to the tiny, frail body and tried to explain away the creature's reaction.

"Please, it isn't the kitten. Cats don't react well to me or to this house," Laurie said, dropping his eyes.

Jo saw a red welt form on her hand where the kitten struggled desperately to free itself. As she watched blood well up along the scratch and spill over onto her wrist, she said, "I . . . I better take him home."

"You will come back, won't you?"

"The moment I drop him in the door I'll run back," Jo promised. Once she returned, neither of them mentioned the kitten again.

Jo looked around the room, memorizing the lush furnishings so she could relate every detail to her sisters, and wondering how the home of werewolves could so closely resemble that of any other wealthy family. She laughed to herself, for what had she expected—piles of bones and straw furniture?

"You know, I watch your family sometimes. When you forget to put down the curtain in the window where the flowers are," Laurie said. "I suppose you find that terribly rude, but I can't help myself. You always seem to be having such good times. I have no mother, so watching yours, well, it warms me."

Why, this werewolf lad was the same as any other! "Why don't you come over instead of watching? You and your grandfather both. Mother is so splendid, she'll do you heaps of good."

"I would like to, but my grandfather says I shouldn't be a bother to strangers."

"We ain't strangers, we are neighbors. We *want* to know you, and I've been trying to do this ever so long. My father, he's in the war right now serving as a Union chaplain, but when he's home, we always have a house full of people. So many people need help, and he thinks he can, by his will alone, help them all."

"I'm sorry. But do you have much to spare?"

"Oh, there's always some to spare! But try to tell my sisters as much. They worry so over money."

"And you, Jo. Do you fret about money as well?"

"No need," she said, grinning proudly. "I shall be a famous writer, and will have more than enough money to care for myself and my family. Of course, it must be hard for Meg. She remembers the luxury in which we once resided, when her life was all ease and pleasure, and want of any kind was unknown. The mourning of that life turns her bitter at times, especially if she sits considering the four cross midgets under her charge. You see, she tends the cantankerous children of a wealthy family. Their name is King, and they apparently take the name too much to heart, and feel and act superior to others."

"What do your other sisters do?"

"Amy goes to school and worries about her flat nose and shabby clothes. Her teacher, Mr. Davis, is cruel and seems to enjoy any opportunity he can find to humiliate members of his class. All too often, Amy makes that far too simple for him, and she comes home in tears."

"What an ogre! He sounds like a terrible man."

"Oh, yes, he is. Everyone thinks so. Beth stays home," continued Jo. "She's terribly shy. But as Mother is always out performing charitable acts, Beth keeps the house in order. Mother is a fine example for us, but we are still selfish and always wishing for more than we have."

"You seem very dear to each other."

"We are. Every night at the table, we tell each other stories about our day. Last night, Mother told us about a poor man who had four sons in the war: two dead, one missing, and one injured. She said we could easily bear the burden of giving one man to the war if that unfortunate soul she met could shoulder giving four sons. But Beth's story was the most interesting of all last night. She told me she saw your grandfather at the fish market. A poor woman there was begging to work for scraps for her children, and being refused. So your grandfather hooked a large fish on the end of his walking cane and gave it to the pitiful woman just like that. He seems like a very kind man."

"So you have told me." Laurie nodded.

"You and your grandfather are not close at all?"

"He doesn't think I should waste my energy on my musical aspirations. Rather, he wants me to follow him in business."

"Are you musically talented?"

"Very much so. I have a fine ear."

"Please. Play for me," Jo said, nodding toward the piano. She listened to Laurie play, and felt quite refined with her nose luxuriously buried in heliotrope and tea roses. He played remarkably well, and when he finished, she stood and applauded. Caught up in the moment, she let out a sharp whistle of appreciation. "If you were a girl, I believe your grandfather would be quite proud of your abilities," she gushed.

"But I'm not a girl, and he's not at all proud of me."

"Well, I am! Extremely proud! And I suspect he is but doesn't know how to tell you as much."

Mr. Laurence watched the friendship build between Jo and his grandson, and in a short space of time the March family was freely paying visits to the grand estate. Mrs. March loved to talk with Mr. Laurence about her father, who had known him; Meg walked the conservatory for hours, losing herself in the majestic surroundings; and Amy was always eager to admire the fine paintings and statues. She was so stirred and enlightened by the art that she felt, absolutely, that one could reach the Celestial

City not only standing in dirt fields and on humble floors but also through the lushness of art's beauty, and it was this majesty she vowed to always have in her life.

Beth at first was too afraid to venture into the house of a werewolf she did not know, and she sighed for the grand piano, closing her eyes and imagining her fingers playing across the ivory keys. Eventually she did venture into the house, once she saw her family do so and felt it was safe. When she finally laid her fingers upon the piano keys, she played with a beauty that gave Mr. Laurence unspeakable delight. He listened secretly, with his study door opened, to the old-fashioned airs he liked, and between her visits, he made certain that new exercise and songbooks were supplied. Occasionally, he stepped out to say a word or two to her, but they did not much converse, for the poor girl stammered and blushed and could not meet his eyes.

Beth, being the generous soul that she was, wanted to thank Mr. Laurence for giving her this gift of music, so decided to work him a pair of slippers, for even werewolves must suffer when the winter chill reaches their toes. She chose the material and pattern with grave care—a cluster of cheerful pansies on a deeper purple ground—and was finished with them quickly. She fingered her work and closed her eyes, imagining herself slipping them onto the old werewolf's feet and then planting a firm kiss on his cheek. She wrote a short, simple note and, with Laurie's help, got them smuggled onto the old gentleman's study table.

Nearly two full days later Beth returned home to waving hands and joyful, screaming voices after running an errand and giving her invalid doll its daily exercise.

"It's a letter from the old gentleman. Come quick and read it!"

Beth's sisters steered her into the parlour in a triumphant procession, and her mouth fell open when she saw a little cabinet piano with a letter lying on the glossy lid.

"Look, Beth, look! There are cunning brackets to hold candles, and green silk, puckered to hold a gold rose in the middle. Even a rack and stool!"

Beth read the letter with tears in her eyes, and realized she had to march over to the Laurence house, right then, before she grew frightened thinking about it. She decided to think of the old man as another of her pets, not a cat, not a dog, but a larger, nobler creature that knows its mistress and would never harm her. She hurried across the lawn, followed by her sisters, and was admitted to the house. The moment she laid eyes on the old gentleman, all fear fell away from her; she ran to him, put both arms around his neck, and kissed him. She clung, not wanting to release him, but realized there were curious eyes watching her, so willed her arms to unwind from around him and stepped back. The glow of joy on Mr. Laurence's face made her nearly as happy as the gift of the piano.

If the roof of the house had blown off, Mr. Laurence could not have been more astonished; but he liked it—oh dear, yes! He liked it amazingly. He set Beth on his knee and laid his wrinkled cheek against her rosy one, and all his crustiness vanished. He closed his eyes and thought of his son and the Italian lady the boy had married. He had not liked the woman, had not thought her worthy of his son, even though she was a gifted musician, and because of her, he never saw his son again. They both died, and he took in their only child, Laurie, who had inherited his mother's musical talents; but he could not allow the boy such a feminine pursuit. Now he had this sweet young girl to play for him. With tears in his eyes, he looked at the girl's sisters, who stood watching the scene: the small, pretty little blonde, the plump one with the large eyes, and the tall, outspoken one with the temper, pluck, and spirit of a boy. He wished his lap was big enough to hold them all.

As Jo stood watching Beth and Mr. Laurence sitting together and whispering, she couldn't help but wonder what type of reaction her mother and sisters would have to learning that the Laurences were werewolves. It hadn't bothered her or Beth, and she liked to think her mother would view them no differently, but she did suspect that Meg and Amy would have a volatile reaction to such news.

...

CHAPTER 5

Educating the Educator

As AMY RAN TO SCHOOL, KNOWING SHE WOULD BE TARDY, she stopped short when four members of the Brigade strode down the street wearing the traditional helmets and breast-plates cut from thick leather and studded with metal. Each man was as big as a bear, and nearly as hairy, and they donned sour expressions as they examined, from head to toe, each person they passed. Their breastplates were belted in place, and shiny daggers made of pure silver flashed at their sides; their helmets were really more headpieces, as they swept down in three parts, one covering noses and the other two sweeping across cheeks, so the wearers appeared otherworldly and uncivilized. The people on the streets parted widely to allow the fearsome men to pass, looking down or away, lest they each be declared a werewolf and get dragged unhappily away. Amy shivered in her little shoes at the sight of the four of them as they passed her, and they left a cold gust of air and the heavy smell of leather in their wake. But that unnerving sight was not to be the worst part of her day.

Hours later, a tearful Amy ran through the house, looking for someone to comfort her. She glanced out into the backyard and saw Laurie astride his horse with her sisters and mother looking on. She ran outside, almost colliding with Mr. Laurence.

"What's the trouble, young lady? What can be worth so many of your tears?" he asked, wiping away her tears with the crisp handkerchief he pulled from his breast pocket.

Amy was unable to speak as she held out her palm to show an angry red welt.

"What is this?" Mr. Laurence roared.

"I showed off the pickled limes I bought for my classmates. Jenny Snow told on me because Mr. Davis, our teacher, had declared limes a contraband article. But I owed them to some of the others and had to pay off my debt." She began to sob anew.

"Where did you get money to buy limes?" Mrs. March asked.

Amy looked down, but Meg admitted that she had given Amy the money, feeling her sister should clear her debt.

"Even after they were forbidden?"

"I . . . I didn't tell her that part!" Amy wailed. "I was afraid she wouldn't give me the money for them if she knew."

"And I wouldn't have!" Meg said, annoyed.

"So what happened to your hand?" Jo asked, stroking Laurie's horse as the boy listened gravely to the conversation.

"Mr. Davis made me throw the limes out the window, and then slapped my hand with a ruler. He delivered blow after blow, until I felt I would never again have full use of my hand."

Mr. Laurence sucked in his cheeks to hide his smile, amused at Amy's dramatics, but he and Laurie exchanged a long and serious look and nodded in some unspoken agreement.

"Jo told me about that cruel man before. He sounds awful," Laurie said.

"Perhaps his morning coffee was too strong, or there was an east wind to aggravate his neuralgia," Mrs. March mused.

"He was nervous as a witch and cross as a bear all day. The word *limes* was like fire to powder," Amy said.

"Well, that seems unfair," said Mr. Laurence. "Part of the man's job is to exercise patience, dealing with children all day. We better have a treat and some tea, to soothe our poor Amy."

"Amy will have no treats," Mrs. March said. "She was in the wrong, and it cost her classmates time when they could have been learning. We will take tea, but Amy will go home and help Hannah in the kitchen."

Jo felt a tug of pity for Amy, for she understood, as she also felt the pain of customs that made one girl popular and another an outcast. Amy was merely trying to hold her own against the wealthy and spoiled girls in her class. She waved to Laurie and ran after Amy. Amy heard her advancing and turned to see Laurie riding away on his horse.

"He is a perfect Cyclops, isn't he?"

"How dare you say so," Jo cried. "He has both his eyes, and very handsome ones at that, might I add."

"I didn't say a thing about his eyes, and I don't see why you need fire up when I admire his riding."

Jo started to laugh. "You silly goose! You mean centaur. A Cyclops is a fearsome monster of myth with one huge eye in the middle of his forehead. Centaurs are those delightful creatures with the back end of a horse and the front end of a handsome man. That is what you intended to say, isn't it?"

Amy nodded, then frowned. "I wish I had a little of the money Laurie spends on that horse."

"Well, you don't," Jo said, putting an end to that line of thought.

Amy told her tale of the day's woe anew and found a sympathetic ear in Hannah, who shook her meaty fist at the "villain," and pounded potatoes for dinner as if she had Mr. Davis himself under her pestle.

The next night, the moon hung full and bright in the sky, reflecting the snowy landscape so it was nearly as bright as day. Mr. Davis sat in his house, reading papers written by his students and marking them with thick red marks and comments in the many places he perceived errors. Suddenly, there was a noise on his porch, and he rose and drew the curtain aside to peer out the window. He saw nothing and decided it was perhaps a gust of wind, or a miscreant raccoon. Hearing it again, he was convinced it was an intruding animal. He slipped on his coat and sighed. There was no end to the classes he must deliver. Now, on his time off, he had yet another lesson to teach, and so he grabbed a walking cane with which to thrash the creature so it would learn to stay away from his home. They were vandals, always raiding for food with amazing cunning and dexterity.

He walked outside and stood staring. He tiptoed across the porch boards and examined every corner but found them all empty. Although the moon was full, he didn't fear the werewolves, as he had not heard them bay even once that evening. They were, undoubtedly, reveling far on the other side of town that night.

A sudden clanging from near his carriage house announced the interloper's whereabouts, so he went down the stairs and rushed around the side of the house. He flattened himself against the building, hiding in the shadows while he peered out and tried to see exactly where the scamp stood. Seeing nothing, he started away, slowly, from his haven. Halfway to the carriage house, he thought to look down and follow the animal's tracks. He stopped, seeing not the small, delicate footprints of a raccoon but huge, canine imprints that chilled the blood in his veins. He began to back up, slowly at first, but a fearsome low growl compelled him to throw his cane in the direction of the noise and then turn and run.

The naughty, playful werewolves allowed Mr. Davis the false security of reaching his house and actually placing one foot on his porch step before pouncing. They knocked him hard and flat, and all the air was pushed from his lungs, so he lay gasping as he tried to right himself. He wished he still had his cane in hand, with which to defend his life and limb.

He turned over onto his back, and the larger of the two werewolves stepped up and stood astride him. The beast's enormous teeth were bared and dripped foam that was hot when it fell onto his skin. The gazes of hunter and prey were locked, and Mr. Davis could not look away from the gleaming golden eyes. The scent of wet fur and stale musk suddenly overwhelmed him, turning his stomach. He forced himself to look away. He gazed, numbly, out to one side and saw long, curled, eager claws growing out from one massive paw. He shrieked and looked away. The moonlight was completely blocked by the pure mass of the creature, so he could stare only into the darkness of the growling face, or at the wide and powerful black heaving chest of the astounding brute that now owned his life.

The smaller werewolf approached from one side and sniffed the frightened, supine man's outstretched hand. In one smooth arc, the snarling beast grabbed, tore, and released the hand.

Mr. Davis held his trembling hand up but could not see it as he was swallowed by the shadows of the two werewolves. His mind snapped to images of his students' open palms growing redder and redder as he enthusiastically struck them, again and again. He felt blood flow down his arm and allowed the limb to drop to his side. He wished to be able to die right then, and be

The beast's enormous teeth were bared and dripped foam
that was hot when it fell onto his skin.

spared the experience of a painful and horrible death. But it was not to be. Poor, unfortunate Mr. Davis felt most of the flesh torn from his bones before the larger werewolf plucked his beating heart from the cavity of his chest, devoured it with great relish, and sent the suffering man's soul away into eternity.

...

CHAPTER 6

Jo's Demons

IT TOOK A FEW WEEKS FOR THE SHOCK OF MR. DAVIS'S death to wane and the community to return to normal. Werewolf attacks were not uncommon, but whenever a renowned member of the town was harmed, the ripples were felt throughout the population. To many of the young, who did not fully absorb the finality of the victim's death, the werewolf attacks were exciting; even some older people, with lives lacking satisfaction, viewed them as a fantastic source of conversation and a welcome diversion from the staleness of their own existence.

The March girls were, of course, horrified, but Marmee reminded them that God did not take a soul until their purpose on this earth had been fulfilled, and so they worked through their grief and were soon back to their normal routines.

In fact, shortly afterward, Laurie invited Jo and Meg to the theater. Meg quickly and enthusiastically accepted, but Jo's mind raced as she stood behind her gushing sister and wondered if Laurie had been the werewolf who attacked Mr. Davis. Then she thought herself foolish, for there were a great many werewolves, and any of them could have been responsible for Mr. Davis's demise. But she recalled the exchanged stares and decisive nods the boy had exchanged with his grandfather when Amy told her tale of Mr. Davis's cruelty, and she suddenly thought that the two werewolves might have executed the man to avenge Amy. What lucky girls they all were if they had were-wolves to protect them!

A few days later, when Jo and Meg prepared to leave the house, Amy begged to go with them, but Jo would have none of it; Amy wasn't well enough, and as she pointed out, she hadn't been invited. Jo's tone and manner angered Amy, who began to put her boots on, saying in her most aggravating way, "I *shall* go!"

But Jo scolded, "You shan't stir a step; so you may just stay where you are."

Sitting on the floor with one boot on, Amy began to cry. Meg tried to reason with her, but Laurie called from below and the two girls hurried down, leaving their sister wailing; for now and again she forgot her grown-up ways and acted like a spoilt child. Just as the party was setting out, Amy called over the banisters in a threatening tone, "You'll be sorry for this, Jo March! See if you ain't."

"Fiddlesticks!" returned Jo, slamming the door.

It was the smirk on Jo's face as she dismissed her that ignited the angry flame inside Amy. She raged through the house, to Jo's bureau, where she turned the top drawer upside down on the floor, just as she had during their last quarrel. Staring at the pile on the floor, she formulated the perfect revenge, and her hands shook slightly as she picked up the manuscript. It was a book of perhaps half a dozen fairy tales that Jo had worked over, pa-tiently, for years. She had put her whole heart into it and hoped to one day make them something good enough to print. Amy set the book aside and returned everything else to the drawer, ar-ranging the contents carefully so there was no empty gap where the manuscript had been.

Amy slipped into the parlour, looking about carefully to be

certain neither Beth, Hannah, nor Marmee were near enough to witness her actions. She fed the papers, one by one, to the hungry fire, delighting as the flames danced and reached eagerly for each fresh sheet. She stirred the fire so the ashes of the manuscript blended into the wood ashes. There. It was as if Jo's book had never existed.

Meanwhile, Meg, Jo, and Laurie had a charming time watching the brilliant and wonderful production filled with comical red imps, sparkling elves, and gorgeous princes and princesses. Jo's pleasure was slightly spoiled when the fairy queen's yellow curls reminded her of Amy's; and between the acts she wondered what Amy would do to make her sorry. The girl, as she had promised, was certain to wreak some sort of revenge.

When Jo and Meg returned, Amy was reading quietly in the parlour. She assumed an injured air, never lifting her eyes from her book to ask a single question about the performance. Curiosity might have conquered her resentment if Beth had not been there to inquire and receive a glowing review of the play.

Jo went first to her room, to put away her hat and to see if Amy had soothed her feelings by upsetting something of hers. After a hasty glance in her various closets, bags, and boxes, she decided that Amy must have found something else with which to entertain herself and forgotten about the theater.

There Jo was mistaken; for the next day she made a discovery that produced a tempest. Meg, Beth, and Amy were sitting together, late in the afternoon, when Jo burst into the room, looking excited, and demanding to know if anyone had seen her book.

Meg and Beth said "No" at once, and looked surprised. Amy poked at the fire and said nothing. Jo saw her color rise, and was down upon her in a moment.

"Amy, you've got it!"

"No, I haven't."

"You know where it is, then!"

"No, I don't."

"That's a fib!" cried Jo, taking her by the shoulders and looking fierce enough to frighten a much braver child than Amy.

"It isn't. I haven't got it, don't know where it is now, and don't care."

"You know something about it, and you'd better tell at once, or I'll make you," Jo said, giving her a slight shake.

"Scold as much as you like, you'll never get your silly old book again," Amy said, forgetting, in the excitement, to stay mute, as she had planned.

"Why not?"

"I burnt it up."

"What? My little book I was going to have finished for Father when he returned home? Have you really burnt it?"

"Yes, I did! I told you I'd make you pay for being so cross yesterday, and I have, so—"

Amy got no farther, for Jo's hot temper mastered her, and she shook Amy till her teeth chattered in her head. "You wicked, wicked little beast! You greedy little demon! I can never write that book again. I will never forgive you for taking it from me— and from Father. Never! Not for as long as I live. You are not my sister anymore."

Meg flew to rescue Amy, and Beth to pacify Jo, but Jo was beside herself; and, with a parting box on her sister's ear, she rushed out of the room up to the old sofa in the garret to mourn her departed fairy tales.

Jo paced her attic sanctuary, not knowing how to act or what to do to relieve her pain and anger. She felt her little sister a far greater monster than any werewolf, even the one who had torn Mr. Davis limb from limb and eaten him. How fitting a joke God had played by placing such a beast in Amy's pretty body.

When Mrs. March came home, she brought Amy to a sense of the wrong she had done her sister. Jo's book was the pride of her heart, and was regarded by her family as a literary sprout of great promise. The entire family had hoped the stories would someday be good enough to print, and that the sale of them would help ease the family's burdens. Amy began to understand that she had done something to harm them all, and that no one would ever love her again until she asked for pardon for her act. Mrs. March looked grave and grieved, Beth mourned as for a departed pet, and Meg refused to defend or comfort Amy in the least.

When the tea bell rang, Jo appeared, looking so grim that it took all Amy's courage to say meekly, "Please forgive me, Jo; I'm very, very sorry."

"I shall never forgive you," was Jo's stern answer.

The next day, to escape Amy's presence, Jo asked Laurie to go ice-skating with her. Amy heard the clash of skates and was offended, as Jo had previously promised to take her along the next time she went skating.

Meg suggested that Amy tag quietly along and wait to appear until Jo and Laurie were laughing and having fun. In a better mood, Jo might soften toward her. Amy hurried to ready herself, but Jo and Laurie were already out on the ice by the time she got to the nearby river.

Jo saw Amy coming and skated off as quickly as she could. She heard Amy panting after her and laughed to herself when the little girl fell, taking a bitter, unhappy sort of satisfaction in her sister's troubles.

As Laurie turned the bend, he called back to Jo, "Keep near the shore; it isn't safe in the middle after the recent warm spell."

Jo heard him, but Amy was struggling to her feet and did not catch a word. Jo glanced over her shoulder, and the little demon she was harboring said in her ear: "No matter whether she heard or not, let her take care of herself."

Laurie had vanished around the bend; Jo was just on the turn, and Amy, far behind, was striking out toward the smoother ice in the middle of the river. For a moment, Jo stood still, a strange feeling creeping through her; then she resolved to go on, but something forced her to turn around just as Amy threw up her hands and went down, with a sudden crash, through the rotten ice. She tried to call Laurie but had no voice. She tried to rush forward, but there was no strength in her feet to propel them. She stood staring at the blue hood above the black water. She inched closer and watched Amy's greedy little hands reaching out to her; the very same hands that had destroyed her manuscript, her gift to her father and family that she had worked on so terribly hard. She realized that she was quite prepared to watch her sister perish.

Something rushed quickly past her, and Laurie cried out.

She wanted to scream for him to leave Amy where she flailed, but her tongue was thick in her dry mouth and would not form words. Leave her, she thought desperately; leave her so there would be one less mouth to feed. There would be so much more for the rest of the family with selfish Amy gone.

Laurie had Amy out of the water, and he wrapped his coat tightly around her. He tore off his skates, ordered Jo to collect their things, and walked the dripping, coughing, and crying girl home. Jo watched the boy performing so capably while she simply stood dumbstruck, but it was best she could not move, for as Amy shivered and leaned into him, Jo wanted to pull her out of his brown, able hands and refill them with her own arm and shoulder.

Once home, and after an excited time and much fuss, Amy fell asleep, rolled in blankets, before a hot fire. During the calm, Mrs. March called Jo to her side and told her how sensible she had been to cover her little sister and get her home so quickly.

Jo reddened with guilt, afraid to tell her kindhearted mother that she had been ready and willing to watch the girl drown. "Laurie saved her. I froze, not knowing what to do, and feeble with shock. Just as I always say the wrong thing, I thought and did the wrong thing. I was so very angry with her."

"You have my temper, Jo. But you'll learn to control it."

"I can't imagine you ever angry, Marmee."

"I am. I'm angry every day of my life, Jo; but I have learned not to show it; and I still hope to learn how not to feel it, though it may take me another forty years to do so. My good mother used to help me, but I lost her when I was just a little older than you. Then your father came along. He is so full of patience, forgiveness, and goodness that I knew I had to struggle as hard as I must to always be kind."

"Oh, Mother! I hope to someday be as good as you," Jo cried.

"I hope you will be a great deal better." Marmee laughed. "You must not let this bitterness take root between you and Amy, your 'bosom enemy' as Father calls it, or it may sadden and spoil your entire life."

Jo held her mother close, thankful that Laurie had been on the ice to act, when she had allowed herself to be completely stilled and conquered by evil thoughts. How unusual a turn of events, that she should watch her sister nearly die while a werewolf ultimately saved her!

She went to Amy, who lay with her wet hair scattered on the pillow, and stared into the angelic sleeping face. Maybe she would be able to love her again. For now, she was content that she no longer hated her.

...

CHAPTER 7

Of Monsters

MR. LAURENCE WOULD BE HUNTING UNDER THAT night's full moon with an old friend he had known since boyhood. Harrison Adams was a wealthy landowner with whom Mr. Laurence had always shared life's best and worst moments: they had gotten into mischief as lads, exchanged advice and experiences while courting, watched each other's children grow up, mourned each other's losses, and shared the secrets and the burdens of the werewolf life.

The two men changed to wolves when the moon rose and glowed golden, and Mr. Laurence noticed the predominance of silver hair in his friend's muzzle, silver that spread across his nose and mouth, ran up his snout and around his yellow eyes. It had been some time since he had seen Adams in his wolf body. He also quickly discovered that his friend's hearing was much diminished, for as they prowled, he noticed he had to either be very close or raise his voice to be heard when he yelped a call to him.

They were not out very long when Mr. Adams rushed ahead, intent on the scent of what was obviously very tempting prey. Mr. Laurence was just catching up to his friend, having been distracted by a scent in the air, when he heard footsteps. He rotated his ears and discerned that the footsteps were those of two-legged creatures. He yipped to alert his friend, but the old were-wolf had his nose deep in a fallen log and did not hear him. Suddenly, the footsteps were upon them, and Mr. Laurence stepped back into some undergrowth, hoping his friend was hidden by his crouching posture.

An arrow whizzed through the air, planting itself in the side of Harrison Adams, whose high yelp of pain rang out into the night before he fell over onto his side. Mr. Laurence could see the red stain spreading on his friend's pelt, and their eyes met through the underbrush. Mr. Laurence wanted to rush to his side to comfort him, but he knew he must not if he wished to escape with his own life. He worried that he would be forced to witness the Brigade skin Adams alive to collect his pelt, and willed his friend to pass on quickly and peacefully while he widened his nostrils to identify and memorize the scent of the approaching men.

Mr. Laurence was flattened onto his belly, looking out through the leaves and twigs of the bushes that harbored him, as the men arrived to survey the fallen beast. He inhaled the scent of their excitement and of their massive leather boots and breastplates while they exclaimed and whooped over their prize. Adams tried to crawl off, but his leg was caught by one of the men and he was yanked up and fiercely slammed down. A low whimper escaped the abused body, and the men began, all of them at once, kicking at it with gleeful enthusiasm. One hearty kick turned the body over so Mr. Laurence could no longer see his friend's face, but a few well-placed blows returned him in the other direction, and as he was jostled from side to side, the arrow painfully worked its way deeper and deeper into his body.

"Lowly werewolf!" one man cried out before driving the toe of his boot into the fallen creature's jaw. "Eat the leather of this boot if you hunger!"

Mr. Laurence stared hard and was grateful to see the light of life leave his friend's eyes and be replaced by a hollow, glazed stare. Adams's body withered then, and reshaped into the sad image of a naked, wrinkled old man.

"Good God! Do you see who this is?" the one man cried out to the others. "It's Harrison Adams."

"Adams? The landowner?"

"Yes."

"What a wonderful prize!" another man proclaimed. "And there can be no recrimination against us, for we caught him in his wolf form."

"This will show one and all that the Brigade does not hunt only the poor. Why, he must be the wealthiest man in this town!"

From his safe haven in the bushes, Mr. Laurence disagreed silently knowing his own wealth exceeded that of Harrison Adams. Then he scolded himself for becoming distracted by such inane thoughts and moaned inwardly at the thought that his once proud and powerful friend would now be a spectacle hanging in town for all to see. The men called to one another to be careful in carrying the body away, for they needed it as their new symbol, a trophy to offer proof of the Brigade's harsh serving of justice to the rich as well as the poor.

Mr. Laurence waited for some time after the men had walked off with their prize hoisted high above their heads as they sang loudly, intoxicated by their stroke of luck. Little did they know that an equally valuable trophy was close within their reach, and Mr. Laurence wondered what lucky charm had protected him and failed Adams so miserably. Halfheartedly, knowing he must "feed his wolf," he caught and devoured a fox and a raccoon and then went home, where he paced and whined for the remainder of the night.

He knew he shouldn't, that he didn't need to see Adams's body ripped open and hanging on display to know what had happened to it, but he went into town the next day nonetheless. A crowd was assembled, staring with disbelief at the dangling corpse of a man who had been one of the most influential members of their town.

"We caught him in full wolf form, prowling about the woods. Seeking one of you—one of us—to devour!" a large man dressed in the uniform of the Brigade was saying, his eyes shining with delight within the leather helmet.

Mr. Laurence looked into the ashen face of his dead friend and had to lean his full weight onto his cane to keep himself upright. Adams's chest had been ripped open and his heart removed and burned. A stray piece of the flaccid skin around the hole in his chest wafted slightly, caught by the breeze, and Mr. Laurence kept his eyes glued to its dance.

"We shot a wolf to protect all of you and found a man of immense wealth and power. No longer can it be said that we harass and hunt only the poor!" the helmeted man continued.

"You didn't know he was rich when you shot him. You may not have, had you known," an anonymous voice from the crowd called out.

"Nonsense," the large Brigade member scoffed. "We shot one who was preying on the good citizens of this town. We don't care who they are or what they do while human. We care only that they will tear out any of our throats, given the chance, one night each month. The deed is done, and here hangs one werewolf from whom you are all forever safe."

The other members of the Brigade began a cheer, and most of the people in the crowd joined in. Mr. Laurence was sickened, and he stumbled around the corner and leaned his weight against the brick side of a building. It was just then that Beth appeared. She had run, as fast as she could, past the spectacle of the slain werewolf and had also rounded the corner to put any traces of the horror out of her sight.

"Mr. Laurence. Are you all right? Are you ill?" She laid one hand on his shoulder, as he had given no indication that he'd heard her.

"Beth," he said, the corners of his lips gathering up slightly at the sight of his friend. "Beth. I saw my friend there. Harrison Adams. My oldest, my dearest friend. Accused and slain. I saw it all, Beth. I am weak with grief."

"Come. I'll take you home," she said, glancing about nervously with the worry that someone had seen Mr. Laurence upset over the werewolf slaying.

"He's gone. They killed him."

"That was him back there?"

"It was." He nodded grimly.

"Let me take you home."

"My errands," he said weakly. "They are yet undone."

"And they will forever be undone," she reminded him in an uncharacteristically stern voice, "if you are seen and accused as a sympathizer."

The old man nodded at the wisdom of her words and allowed himself to be taken back to his mansion. Beth ran home only long enough to leave word of where she was with Hannah, and then rushed back to the Laurence mansion, where she sat the old man in his chair, tucked a woolen throw around his lap, and stoked the fire. She ran to the kitchen to order a pot of tea and then settled in to sit with her friend for the rest of the day.

"Tell me about your friend if you feel so compelled," she said, sitting at his feet and taking his hand in both of hers. "Tell me what he was like, what he did, and why you loved him."

So Mr. Laurence purged himself and told Beth about his departed friend.

"A man never walked this earth who was so quick to appear when a friend needed him," he began. "When my wife, and then my son died, it was Harrison Adams who pulled me through my grief. He was caring and giving, much like you, my dearest Beth."

He talked on and on, reliving his friend's life, and Beth hung on his every word. After hours of relating his memories, after three pots of tea and a full plate of bread, he breathed out heavily, spent. It was then that Beth led him upstairs to his bed, laid him down, covered him with a spare blanket, and closed the drapes against the day's diminishing light. With tears streaming down her face, she descended the stairs and crossed the garden to home.

Meanwhile, Jo had returned from Aunt March's in a low and foul temper, for the old woman had chided and scolded her incessantly the entire day. Jo had noticed, the moment she arrived home, that Beth was absent, and so asked after her.

"She's been all day with the Laurences. It seems some tragedy struck, and she's there to give comfort," said Meg.

Jo's cheeks colored with anger. How nice for Beth to pass her time in a beautiful mansion while others had to sit with ill-tempered old women and nipping, spoiled dogs all day! She tried to read, but her head pounded as Aunt March's bitter complaints echoed through her mind. Rage blurred her vision, so she spent most of the day pacing her attic room and staring out the window to catch sight of Beth, or any movement in what Meg called the "mansion of bliss." She considered going over there, but she didn't know what she might do if she walked in to discover Beth and Laurie sitting close together.

Jo went from angry to furious. She nibbled little of her supper, and stomped through her daily walk practicing what she would do and say at the first sight of Beth. Strong words, she thought, for it was clear, though quite unfair, that Beth had set her mind on winning Laurie, the only person with whom Jo had ever formed an instant friendship.

When Beth finally came home, well after dinner, Jo greeted her with silence. She saw that Beth was fretful over something, so finally asked, "Which Laurence were you comforting? Was it Laurie?"

"Laurie?" Beth asked absentmindedly. "No, no, Jo. It was Mr. Laurence." And Jo's heart softened to see the tears fall hot and heavy from her sorrowful wide eyes. "Oh, Jo. His dear friend was slain by the Brigade, and this pitiful old man's body hangs on display in town. And he saw it! He saw the friend with whom he had grown up torn apart by those, those . . . butchers!"

"Was the friend truly a werewolf?" Jo asked softly so no one else could hear.

"He was, I admit. But think of Mr. Laurence. He is kind, he is gentle. I cannot believe he does not have God's favor. He lives a virtuous life and does not deserve to dwell in the City of Destruction. Must he truly be judged as a servant of Beelzebub simply because he was born a werewolf? Was it not by God's choice that he is one?"

Jo embraced her sister and smoothed her hair as she spoke

softly in her ear. "God does not judge the hunter who takes the buck or the drake from his family to feed his own, and the were-wolves hunt for sustenance. Remember Father's lessons, dear Beth. The werewolves suffer in being who they are, and must be judged only by how they treat others in their daily lives."

"But that is not how others judge them."

"Then it is for God to judge those others."

Beth cried for a while longer, and it hurt Jo to see her sister worry so severely over someone else, but she knew that to be Beth's nature; she felt the pain of others and took it upon herself to suffer for them. Of course she would hurt over the old man's loss, for Beth had grown very fond of Mr. Laurence. Jo could lit-tle believe that she had suspected her sister of being at the man-sion with the intent of flirting with Laurie.

Jo lay awake all night listening to her sister sniffle, and star-ing out at the brightness of the moon, for she could not sleep after having had envy of her sister lodged so deeply and sharply in her heart. And over a werewolf! A creature that would happily snap her in half and dine on her very flesh, on her aching, beat-ing heart, and on the blood that coursed, at that moment, hot with shame through her veins. That beautiful shining moon might change some from men to beasts, but the vile jealousy within her had turned her into a monster just as quickly.

...

CHAPTER 8

Meg Dresses Up
at Vanity Fair

ONE MERRY APRIL DAY, MEG AND HER SISTERS STOOD packing her "go abroady" trunk in her room. Meg was gushing about how fortunate it was for her that the King children should have the measles, and that Annie Moffat did not forget her promise to have Meg over for a fortnight of novelty and pleasure.

Meg knew she did not own the proper attire, but her clothes were clean, presentable, and freshly trimmed. Accessories were borrowed from her sisters or gifted to her by her mother, and so she knew she ought not to complain, even though she expected she would reach a point of feeling great shame. Mrs. March hoped she enjoyed herself, but hoped even more that she did not come back more discontent than she went.

The next day, Meg departed. At first she was daunted by the splendor of the house and the elegance of its occupants, but the Moffats were kindly and quickly put her at ease. Meg noted that they were not particularly cultivated or intelligent people, and that all their gilding could not quite conceal the ordinary material of which they were made; but the more she saw of the house and Annie's possessions, the more she envied her, and thought her own home terribly bare and dismal.

So she was delighted to discover a bouquet of flowers sent to her by Laurie, with an accompanying note from her mother; they cheered her considerably and made her forget how shabby her party dress was next to the other girls' rich and crisp new gowns, and she now actually looked forward to attending the "small party" wearing the fragrant and beautiful blooms. The other girls so admired the lovely flowers that she set some aside for herself, and then made up dainty bouquets to share with them. The girls accepted them with quiet surprise.

She enjoyed herself very much that evening, and forgot all about the old dress she wore, until overhearing the others discuss how they simply must loan her a gown for the upcoming "grand party," and that her mother was obviously trying to marry her off into the wealthy Laurence house. Mortified, angry, and disgusted, she had a restless night and was tempted to feign illness and return home, but Belle, Annie's sister, who was engaged to be married, told her first thing in the morning that she had sent an invitation to Mr. Laurence for the large affair on Thursday.

Meg hardly knew how to respond, but felt mischievous, and thought of a lovely way to tease the Moffats. "I'm afraid he won't come," she said.

"Why ever not?"

"He's far too old."

"How old is he?"

"Nearly seventy, I believe."

"No, he's a youth!" one said.

Her merry eyes gave her away.

"She means the grandfather! She's toying with us!"

The others tittered and scolded her. She felt at ease once more, and a member of the group, until the topic of dressing for the grand party arose.

"I have the perfect dress for you to wear, Meg," said Sallie Moffat.

"I thought I would wear my white one again."

"Don't be foolish. I have a sweet blue silk laid away that I wore only once and have now outgrown. You shall wear it, won't you? To please me?"

When Meg saw the beautiful sky-blue gown, she weakened and agreed, enthusiastically, to wear it. The girls immediately dressed her to see how she looked in it.

"It's perfect on you. But I insist on putting new ribbons on it. These are frayed in spots," Sallie said. She handed it off to a maid with orders that it be made up with fresh trimmings.

There were muffled giggles behind her. Meg turned to see what the joke was, but the girls were all turned away from her, so she assumed it was simply one bit of silliness among many.

On the night of the party, the girls made Meg close her eyes while they slipped the dress over her head. When she was permitted to open them, she was surprised to see that the dress had been trimmed in red ribbons, a color she would not have considered to accompany the delicate blue of the silk. But the red ribbons teamed with the red roses Laurie had sent looked right, and the colors seemed to complement each other. The girls fussed over her, promising they would make her into a little beauty, crimping and curling her hair, polishing her neck and arms with fragrant powder, and touching her lips with coralline salve to make them redder. She was laced so tightly into the sky-blue dress that she could hardly breathe. She blushed at herself in the mirror when she noticed how low the dress dipped at the neck, but then a rosy glow of pride covered the tint of embarrassment in Meg's cheeks when the mirror told her that she was, indeed, a little beauty. Accessories were thrust at her: a cluster of red tea roses pinned at the bosom and sides to display her pretty white shoulders, a pair of high-heeled blue silk boots for her feet, a lace handkerchief, a plumy fan, and a bouquet of bloodred roses to carry in a silver holder.

Walking through the party, Meg recognized Mrs. Moffat's voice.

"Her father is a colonel in the army. They're one of our first families, but reverses of fortune, you know—intimate friends of the Laurences. She's a sweet creature, and my Ned is wild about her."

Meg knew that to be a fib, since Ned Moffat never even glanced in her direction, but she paid it little mind. She had worse things to think about when she overheard Major Lincoln comment to his mother, "They have made a fool of the March girl. I wanted you to see her, but she is entirely spoiled, nothing but a painted doll tonight."

That is exactly what she deserved for trying to be someone other than herself, she thought as she laid her head against the cool glass of the windowpane and stood half hidden by the curtain. She breathed deeply and resolved that she would not allow these gossips to ruin her evening; her father had lost his fortune trying to help others, and there was no shame in that, and if she wanted to overdress for a party, then that was her privilege.

She recovered and forced herself to walk through the crowd. She noticed other girls had red ribbons trimming their dresses, and they all seemed to be interested in her. They smiled as she passed them, lightly touching the ribbons on their dresses and staring directly into her eyes. She thought them friendly, but something in their expressions made her hesitant to stop and chat. The girls without red ribbons in their dresses also looked at her, but not as warmly.

She was delighted to suddenly see Laurie standing before her, but the expression on his face was grim. She smiled, waiting for him to grin widely and tell her how nice she looked. Instead, he snarled and called her foolish to allow others to embellish her with so much fuss and feathers.

"You . . . you don't like it then?" she stammered.

"No, not a bit. It isn't you. It isn't you at all. And I don't suppose you realize that you are also living a lie this night. At least I think you are, unless you have been hiding a great secret from us all."

"What do you so go on about? I can't understand what you're trying to tell me."

"The red ribbons in your dress," Laurie said, face dark with severity.

"What of them? They complement the roses you sent. And thank you so much."

"Meg, you know you are very welcome, but, hear me, please. Have you not noticed others reacting to your red ribbons?"

"I did notice, but I don't understand."

"No, of course not. The ribbons are a sign to others."

"A sign?"

"They tell the world that you are a member of the Lycanthrope Society, a werewolf."

Meg's jaw dropped open, and her head swung around the room as she looked for the other girls who wore red ribbons braided through their gowns.

"But why? Why would they dare openly reveal such a secret?"

"Well, they wouldn't, of course, do so on the streets, but here, among their own and their peers, they can be quite proud of who they are. Being a member of the society is an honor, and only the best families of werewolves are welcome."

Meg simply stared at Laurie as he took the bright red hand-kerchief from his breast pocket, mopped his brow, and stuffed it back in so one end of it draped out.

"I . . . I suppose they should be proud of who they are. Anyone should," Meg said in a small and uncertain voice. "But if the Brigade were to find out . . ."

"The Brigade does not delve into the private matters of certain members of society," Laurie said evenly.

"Mr. Adams's death proved to us all that the newly formed Brigade has no qualms about defying and prosecuting wealthy and poor werewolves alike, as they feel the wealthy ones have long been held unaccountable. It seems foolhardy to put on such a display, although I admit I have never seen these red ribbons before, or perhaps I simply never noticed."

"You never saw it. It is something high society enjoys, but only at the most formal functions or meetings. There was no red trim at the small party, was there? This is a small ritual reserved for only the grandest of affairs."

"Why, Laurie? So they can recognize and befriend one another? I did see that those with red ribbons seemed much friendlier and sweeter than the other girls."

"That is part of it, but it makes the girls, especially, more desirable. Boys who are not werewolves feel daring for escorting a werewolf."

"That is why I had so many offers to dance and had so much attention paid to me."

"No, Meg. It is because you are lovely and witty, even if you are dripping with your silly fuss and feathers."

"Whatever should I do, Laurie? I don't know what to do."

Laurie sighed. "I should never have told you tonight. Can you act as if you don't know? Just be pleasant and go about as you were."

"I want to rip the ribbons off this dress immediately."

"That would be rude. It would be a mockery to the werewolves to reveal that their sign had been used as nothing more than a cruel joke."

Meg wondered for a moment how much she cared about the feelings of werewolves, but then thought that the girls who wore the werewolf sign were probably from wealthy families, and as pretty as any of the others. They each had lives, friends, families, and favored pastimes. She watched them as they laughed, danced, drank, flirted, and smiled. They were different from her only one night each month. Her father had tried very hard to instill such ideas concerning the werewolves in his daughters' heads. She stretched up to stand tall, for this was her night to display the tact and empathy that her good father had taught her.

When Meg returned home, she told everyone all about her adventures in high society, describing for Amy, in great detail, the dresses and accessories the women wore. Amy retired to bed that night with images of decadent food, décor, and clothing dancing through her head. Once Meg was secure the little blond head was settled on the pillow for the night, she gathered her mother and two sisters around her and told them the stunning revelation that there was an entire high society of werewolves. Jo and Beth sat listening with wide eyes as she described the smiling girls with the red ribbons laced through their dresses and the eager boys who sought to escort them.

"I didn't dare reveal this with our little Amy's ears opened wide; her fear of werewolves is so keen. We have always allowed her to believe that werewolves are from far-off clans, and I think she would be terrified to learn that they are among us at every turn."

"That was wise of you," Mrs. March said. "I have always believed we are correct in keeping her safe from that knowledge. I am also proud that you held your head up and did not openly respond to the cruel trick those girls played on you. Your father always said we must treat even werewolves as we would wish to be treated, and he would be as proud of you as I am for the way you handled that situation, for you considered the feelings of others above your own hurt and fear."

Meg looked into her mother's face, swallowed hard, and then revealed overhearing the gossip that Marmee had a grand plan to marry Meg to wealth. Mrs. March sighed and called all her daughters to her side.

"The Moffats are correct that I have a plan. I have a great many," Marmee said. "All mothers do. I want my daughters to be beautiful, accomplished, and good; to be admired, loved, and respected; to have a happy youth, to be well and wisely married, and to lead good, useful, pleasant lives, and I want you to be chosen by good men. I am ambitious for you, but not to marry rich men simply because they are rich and have splendid houses that are not homes because love is wanting. Money is a needful and precious thing—and when well used, a noble thing—but I never want you to think it is the first or only prize to strive for. I'd rather see you poor men's wives, if you were happy, beloved, contented, than queens on thrones, without self-respect and peace."

"Poor girls don't stand any chance," Meg sighed, "unless they put themselves forward."

"Then we'll be old maids. That would sit fine with me," said Jo stoutly.

"It is so much better to be happy old maids than unhappy wives," Marmee instructed. "Always remember that your mother is ready to be your confidante, father to be your friend, and both of us trust and hope that our daughters, whether married or single, will be the pride and comfort of our lives."

"We will, Marmee!" the girls sang out. "Just you wait and see. We will."

...

CHAPTER 9

Pickwick Publications

*E*VER SINCE THE GIRLS HAD HEARD ABOUT THE thrilling Lycanthrope Society, their imaginations had been tickled. The three sisters who knew of it wanted, more than ever, to form a secret society of their own, and Amy, although ignorant of the werewolves' chapter, had always longed to be in one as well. These societies were all the rage among the wealthy, but the March sisters, being outcasts, well knew they would not be invited into any of the other high-society clubs.

All four may have wished for high-society trimmings and affairs, but in every other way, they were as different in taste as they were in age. Even the flower garden they planted had to be divided into quarters so each could plant the flowers she most loved. Meg planted roses, myrtle, and heliotrope, and a little orange tree; Jo planted something different each season, this year choosing sunflowers to feed her family of chicks; Beth opted for old-fashioned, fragrant flowers—sweet peas, mignonette, larkspur, pinks, pansies, southernwood, chickweed for the birds, and catnip for the pussies. Amy had a bower in hers, rather small and earwiggy but pretty to look at, with honeysuckles and morning glories hanging their colored horns and bells in graceful wreaths all over it, and tall white lilies and delicate ferns growing below.

The happy spring days were filled with gardening, walks, rows on the river, and flower hunts. But the rainy days brought a need for original diversions and fresh arguments about the type of society they wished to form. Finally, agreeing that they all admired Dickens, they called themselves the Pickwick Club. With only a few interruptions, for a year they met every Saturday evening at seven o'clock in the big garret to conduct their ceremonies, solemnly wearing their big badges tied about their heads and meeting to discuss *The Pickwick Portfolio*, a paper to which they each contributed something. Jo, who reveled in pens and ink, was the editor. Meg, as the eldest, was Samuel Pickwick; Jo, being of a literary turn, Augustus Snodgrass; Beth, because she was round and rosy, Tracy Tupman; and Amy, who was always trying to do what she couldn't, was Nathaniel Winkle. Pickwick, the president, read the paper, which was filled with original tales, poetry, local news, funny advertisements, and hints, in which they good-naturedly reminded one another of their faults and shortcomings. On one occasion Mr. Pickwick put on a pair of spectacles (without the glass), rapped upon the table, stared hard at Mr. Snodgrass, who was tilting back in his chair till he arranged himself properly, and then began to read:

"The May twentieth edition of *The Pickwick Portfolio*. We begin with the Poet's Corner and a poem by our own A. Snodgrass.

" *Again we meet to celebrate*
With badge and solemn rite,
Our fifty-second anniversary,
In Pickwick Hall, to-night,

" 'We all are here in perfect health,
None gone from our small band;
Again we see each well-known face,
And press each friendly hand.

" 'Our Pickwick, always at his post,
With reverence we greet,
As, spectacles on nose, he reads
Our well-filled weekly sheet.

" 'Although he suffers from a cold,
We joy to hear him speak,
For words of wisdom from him fall,
In spite of croak or squeak.

" 'Old six-foot Snodgrass looms on high,
With elephantine grace,
And beams upon the company,
With brown and jovial face.

" 'Poetic fire lights up his eye,
He struggles 'gainst his lot.
Behold ambition on his brow,
And on his nose a blot!

" 'Next our peaceful Tupman comes,
So rosy, plump and sweet,
Who chokes with laughter at the puns,
And tumbles off his seat.

" 'Prim little Winkle too is here,
With every hair in place,
A model of propriety,
Though he hates to wash his face.
The year is gone, we still unite
To joke and laugh and read,
And tread the path of literature
That doth to glory lead.

" 'Long may our paper prosper well,
Our club unbroken be,
And coming years their blessings pour
On the useful, gay "P.C." ' "

The president allowed a moment for the members to laugh, applaud, and finally contain themselves, and then read the tale of *The Masked Marriage: A Tale of Venice* written by S. Pickwick, followed by T. Tupman's *History of a Squash.*

"Now," the president continued, turning his eye to the next page. " 'Mr. Pickwick, sir: I address you upon the subject of sin the sinner I mean is a man named Winkle who makes trouble in his club by laughing and sometimes won't write his piece in this fine paper I hope you will pardon his badness and let him send a French fable because he can't write out of his head as he has so many lessons to do and no brains in future I will try to take time by the fetlock and prepare some work which will be all *commy la fo* that means all right I am in haste as it is nearly school time. Yours respectably, N. Winkle.' (The above is a manly and handsome acknowledgment of past misdemeanors. If our young friend studied punctuation, it would be well.)"

A bit of giggling was heard, but stopped quickly when the president issued a severe look to the audience.

"This will bring no laughter," he warned, and then proceeded to read: " '*A Sad Accident*. On Friday last, we were startled by a violent shock in our basement, followed by cries of distress. On rushing, in a body, to the cellar, we discovered our beloved President prostrate on the floor, having tripped and fallen while getting wood for domestic purposes. A perfect scene of ruin met our eyes; for in his fall Mr. Pickwick had plunged his head and shoulders into a tub of water, upset a keg of soft soap upon his manly form, and torn his garments badly. On being removed from his perilous situation, it was discovered that he had suffered no injury but several bruises; and, we are happy to add, is now doing well. ED.'

"This is followed by even more sad news, I'm afraid," the president said, wiping under his eyes for effect. " '*The Public Bereavement*. It is our painful duty to record the sudden and mysterious disappearance of our cherished friend, Mrs. Snowball Pat Paw. This lovely and beloved cat was the pet of a large circle of warm and admiring friends; for her beauty attracted all eyes, her graces and virtues endeared her to all hearts, and her loss is deeply felt by the whole community.

" 'When last seen, she was sitting at the gate, watching the butcher's cart; and it is feared that some villain, tempted by her charms, basely stole her, or that she stayed out past dark and was consumed by voracious werewolves. Weeks have passed, but no trace of her has been discovered; and we relinquish all hope, tie a black ribbon to her basket, set aside her dish, and weep for her as one lost to us forever.' "

They sat quietly, each remembering Mrs. Snowball Pat Paw

in her own way, and the president allowed this moment of respectful silence.

"A sympathizing friend sends the following gem:—'A Lament,' for S. B. Pat Paw,

" '*We mourn the loss of our little pet,*
And sigh o'er her hapless fate,
For never more by the fire she'll sit,
Nor play by the old green gate.

" '*The little grave where her infant sleeps*
Is 'neath the chestnut tree;
But o'er her *grave we may not weep,*
We know not where it may be.

" '*Her empty bed, her idle ball,*
Will never see her more;
No gentle tap, no loving purr
Is heard at the parlour door.

" '*Another cat comes after her mice,*
A cat with a dirty face;
But she does not hunt as our darling did,
Nor play with her airy grace.

" '*Her stealthy paws tread the very hall*
Where Snowball used to play,
But she only spits at the werewolves our pet
So gallantly drove away.

" *'She is useful and mild, and does her best,*
But she is not fair to see;
And we cannot give her your place, dear,
Nor worship her as we worship thee.'

"That was contributed by A. S.," the president informed the teary members.

They moved on to the advertisements, which the president read swiftly.

"Miss Oranthy Bluggage, the accomplished Strong-Minded Lecturer, will deliver her famous Lecture on WOMAN AND HER POSITION, at Pickwick Hall, next Saturday evening, after the usual performances.

"A weekly meeting will be held at Kitchen Place, to teach young ladies how to cook. Hannah Brown will preside; and all are invited to attend.

"The Dustpan Society will meet on Wednesday next, and parade in the upper story of the Club House. All members to appear in uniform and shoulder their brooms at nine precisely.

"Mrs. Beth Bouncer will open her new assortment of dolls' millinery next week. The latest Paris fashions have arrived, and orders are respectfully solicited.

"A new play will appear at the Barnville Theater, in the course of a few weeks, which will surpass anything ever seen on the American stage. THE GREEK SLAVE, OR CONSTANTINE THE WEREWOLF AVENGER, is the name of this thrilling drama!

"Hints: If S. P. didn't use so much soap on his hands, he wouldn't always be late at breakfast. A. S. is requested not to whistle in the street. T. T., please don't forget Amy's napkin. N. W. must not fret because his dress has not nine tucks.

"Weekly Report: Meg—Good. Jo–Bad. Beth—Very good. Amy—Middling."

The president finished reading the paper, and a round of applause followed. Mr. Snodgrass rose to make a proposition.

"Mr. President and gentlemen," he began, assuming a parliamentary attitude and tone, "I wish to propose the admission of a new member, one who highly deserves the honor, and would be deeply grateful for it, and would add immensely to the spirit of the club, the literary value of the paper, and be no end jolly and nice. I propose Mr. Theodore Laurence as an honorary member of the P.C. Come now, do have him."

Jo's sudden change of tone had made the girls laugh; but all looked rather anxious, and no one said a word as Snodgrass took his seat. Jo had considered adding the fact that Laurie would be a true asset due to his experience in a secret high-society club, the Lycanthrope Society, but knew she could not reveal his secret. She imagined Beth would realize as much, however, and would vote for him.

"We'll put it to vote," said the president. "All in favor of this motion, please to manifest it by saying 'Aye.' "

A loud response from Snodgrass, followed, to everybody's surprise, by a timid one from Beth.

"Contrary-minded, say 'no.' "

Meg and Amy were contrary-minded; and Mr. Winkle rose to say, with great elegance, "We don't wish any boys; they only joke and bounce about. This is a ladies' club, and we wish to be private and proper."

"I'm afraid he'll laugh at our paper, and make fun of us afterward," observed Pickwick, pulling the little curl on her forehead, as she always did when doubtful.

Up rose Snodgrass, very much in earnest. "Sir! I give you my word as a gentleman, Laurie won't do anything of the sort. He likes to write, and will give a tone to our contributions, and keep us from being sentimental, don't you see? We can do so little for him, and he does so much for us, I think the least we can do is offer him a place here, and make him welcome, if he comes."

Tupman rose to his feet. "Yes; we ought to do it, even if we *are* afraid. I say he may come, and his grandpa too, if he likes."

This spirited outburst from Beth electrified the club, and another vote was taken.

"Ay! Ay! Ay! Ay!" they all cried at once.

"Good! Now allow me to present our new member," Jo exclaimed, throwing open the closet door to display Laurie sitting on a ragbag, flushed and twinkling with suppressed laughter.

"You rogue! You traitor! Jo, how could you?" the three sisters whined.

"The coolness of you two rascals is amazing," said Mr. Pickwick, trying to frown but instead producing an amiable smile.

Laurie and Jo each tried to take the blame for formulating and initiating the plan. The sisters forgot and forgave immediately once Laurie made his acceptance speech. "As a token of my gratitude for the honor done me, and to promote friendly relations between adjoining nations, I have set up a post office in the hedge in the lower corner of the garden; a fine, spacious building, with padlocks on the doors. It's the old martin-house, but I stopped up the door, and made the roof open, so it will hold all sorts of things and save us valuable time. Letters, manuscripts, books, and bundles can be passed in there; and as each nation has a key, it will be uncommonly nice. Allow me to present the club key; and, with many thanks for your favor, take my seat."

The newest member, Sam Weller, deposited the little key on the table and received his applause. No one ever regretted his admittance, for a more devoted, jovial member no club could have. He added great "spirit" to the meetings, and a "tone" to the paper; for his orations convulsed his hearers, and his contributions were excellent, being patriotic, classical, comical, or dramatic, but never sentimental.

Many queer things passed through the little post office: tragedies and cravats, poetry and pickles, garden seeds and long letters, music and gingerbread, rubbers, invitations, scoldings, and puppies. The old Mr. Laurence liked the fun, when he learned of it, and amused himself by sending odd bundles, mysterious messages, and funny telegrams; and his gardener, who was smitten with Hannah's charms, actually sent a love letter. How they all laughed when that secret came out, never dreaming how many love letters that little post office would hold in the years to come!

...

CHAPTER 10

The
Laurences' Famished Visitors

THE GIRLS WERE DISCUSSING HOW TO SPEND WHATEVER idle summer time they had. The Kings and Aunt March were off, freeing Meg and Jo. Jo, however, was exhausted from helping the old woman pack up and sending her off that morning, and her sisters comforted her.

"Aunt March is a regular samphire, is she not?" Amy asked, sampling the lemonade she was making for sweetness.

"You mean *vampire*, not a seaweed; but it don't matter; it's too warm to be particular about one's parts of speech," Jo murmured.

The sisters planned to lay abed, rest, read, row on the river, and dream of pretty dresses they could never afford. As the days went on, tempers soared with the temperature, and household chores were sorely neglected. By the end of it, the girls all agreed that the experiment in leisure had proven that larking and lounging didn't pay. They would have regular hours for work and play, and prove they understood the worth of time by employing it well; thereby, they would make their next leisure sweet when it came.

One July day, Meg checked the postbox Laurie had contributed, and was dismayed to find a single glove from the pair she had lost and sorely missed. There was also a German song, translated by Laurie's tutor, Mr. Brooke, and an invitation to a picnic from Laurie. He wanted them to meet his friends the Vaughns, who were visiting from England. The girls knew only that there were four of them. Kate Vaughn was older than Meg; the twins, Fred and Frank, were near Jo's age. Frank was lame and used a crutch. The little girl, Grace, was nine or ten.

The morning of the picnic, the girls took great care in preparing themselves, especially since watching from the window that a huge tent was erected, carriages were arriving, and hampers and baskets were being filled with food.

They all enjoyed the morning rowing, but Jo caught Fred cheating at croquet and informed him that he had been seen nudging the ball with his foot. He was smug and haughty, but Jo managed to be a good little woman and keep her temper in check, which made her sisters proud.

The next day, the Vaughns were leaving to go to Canada, but that night the full moon would hang low in the sky. Jo wondered if they, too, were werewolves. If not, how could they possibly be planning to stay with Laurie and his grandfather? Perhaps they would lock themselves up, or the Laurences would be locked out of their house that night. She sat by the window to watch any comings and goings, but exhausted by the day's events, she fell asleep with her cheek on the windowsill.

Meanwhile, the Vaughns and Laurences, all six transformed into panting, hungry werewolves, left the Laurence mansion to prowl the night. Fred led the pack, nose in the air and sensing a meal. Laurie was on his heels, ready to protect or defend, as he must, as Fred did not know the town or its people. Frank kept up well, prancing steadily on three legs, and Mr. Laurence carefully brought up the rear, allowing the younger pups the folly of the hunt, but he was well prepared to act if necessary. The pack leapt through fields, around gardens, and over lawns until they stopped in the middle of town. Laurie paced nervously and growled, but stopped when his sharp ear turned to pick up voices in the air. The males looked back at the others, whose long tongues ran across their lips with expectations of feeding. The two young males crouched low, careful to be as quiet, yet as swift as possible.

From out of the tavern two men emerged, tripping over their own feet and laughing at their own clumsiness. Behind them came two women, each reaching out to take the men's arms. Their shrill voices were grating, and their smell sweet on top and rank underneath. One of the men stopped and reached for a woman, trying to lift her skirts.

"Not here, fool!" she shrieked. "We'd be wise to move inside and not linger under this full moon."

"Afraid to be eaten?" The man laughed. "What makes you think you won't be eaten indoors?" He lunged and bit her shoulder, which made her and the other woman screech with delight.

"Here, we're just around this corner," the woman said.

The werewolves knew they had to be quick. They padded up slowly, carefully cutting off their prey's path to the doorway just ahead of them. They inched forward slowly, and then Grace, the youngest and most impatient among them, suddenly pounced.

She advanced upon one of the women and thrust her to the ground, where she ripped off the bodice of her dress and one of her breasts in one efficient bite. The other woman screamed, and the men stood in a shocked stupor. One man was taken quickly in a skillful blow, thrown down, and pinned neatly. The werewolves bit through his flailing legs and gaping mouth, harming him just enough to keep him supine and completely mute. The second woman and the other man collected themselves and ran toward escape. But Frank intercepted the woman and cast her brutally against the hard brick of the building. To silence her squawking, he ripped her throat so deeply that her trachea came away, dangling from his bloody jaws. He spit the thing out so he could lap up the warm blood that spurted from the woman's throat as she tried to scream. She little realized that she was already finished and so still fought to save herself.

This energy excited the werewolves, and they turned to the running man, who was quite corpulent and pitifully slow. Laurie stepped back so his guest, Fred, could do the honors. Fred smote him from behind, flinging him prone onto the ground. The others approached, abandoning the dead women and the injured man, whose bodies they would clean up later, at their leisure. They rolled the portly man over and bit into the meat of his protruding belly. He gasped for breath, grasping his chest with plump fingers extending from a burly hand. His mouth opened in a silent scream, and his eyes rolled wildly. Tearing with their hungry teeth, they dined on the yellow fat of his stomach and then devoured the wet and waiting organs. Last, they dragged the bodies to one shadowed spot and gathered around them, stripping the meat from bones as if at a dinner party.

The Vaughns were gone by the time word of the killings reached the March house the next day. It had been a grisly scene for those who arose early and discovered the bodies. Little was left of the victims' meat, and nothing was left of their organs, but scraps of clothing and bloody bones confirmed absolutely what had happened. The greatest shock of the matter, for a community that was accustomed to werewolves, was that it had taken place in the thick of the town, something that had never before occurred.

The girls found Laurie in his hammock outside and ran to him to discuss the slaughter and the Brigade's vengeance. The boy paled, wondering what these girls, these new friends, would think of him if they knew he was one of those responsible for the event. He quickly changed the subject and soon had them all inventing a lovely Celestial City and each constructing her own imaginative castle complete with furniture, staff, horses, books, and wonderful food and clothes. They discussed their goals and hopes for the future. Laurie wanted to be a musician, Jo a famous author, Amy a famous artist. Meg wanted only to be rich, and dear, sweet Beth only cared that everyone was together and happy.

As Laurie watched the girls walk back to their house to attend to their afternoon chores, he thought how simple their lives were, with no deep, dark secrets they were forced to hide. He thought it must be a delight to live so freely, openly, and easily. But remembering the afternoon's conversation, the boy said to himself, with the resolve to make the sacrifice cheerfully, "I'll let my castle go, and stay with my dear old grandfather while he needs me, for I am all he has."

Meanwhile, as the summer passed and the October days began to grow chilly and the afternoons short, Jo was very busy up in her garret. Realizing she very well could be a breadwinner for the household, she had soon finished the manuscripts for two stories and brought them to a newspaperman in town. As she walked out of the office, she ran, most unexpectedly, into Laurie on the street.

"You look flushed. Did you have a bad time just now?" he asked, examining her red face.

"Not very."

"What did you do in there?"

She tried not to tell him, to hurry on ahead, but he was ravenous in his curiosity, and agreed to tell her a secret he knew if she would tell hers. She finally confessed, once they were out of the city and well on their way home, that she had left two stories with the newspaper for consideration.

"Hurrah for Miss March, the celebrated American authoress!" he sang, throwing his hat in the air and catching it again, to the great delight of two ducks, four cats, five hens, and half a dozen Irish children who were lingering about the yard of their farmhouse.

"Hush! It won't come to anything, I dare say; but I couldn't rest till I had tried, and I said nothing about it, because I don't want anyone else to be disappointed."

"It won't fail! Why, Jo, your stories are works of Shakespeare, compared to half the rubbish that's published every day. Won't it be fun to see them in print; and shan't we feel proud of our authoress?"

Jo's eyes sparkled, for it's always pleasant to be believed in; and a friend's praise is always sweeter than a dozen newspaper puffs.

"Where's *your* secret? Play fair, Teddy, or I'll never believe you again," she said.

"Very well, but you must promise never to reveal this secret to another soul."

Jo stood tensed. Would he confess that he was a werewolf? Perhaps his friends were also werewolves, and he'd admit that he and the Vaughns killed those four people on the night of the last full moon. More exciting, he might confide that it was he who had done away with nasty Mr. Davis. Her imagination trotted wildly, inventing stories that grew increasingly wild, and she smiled coyly, raising her ear up toward his awaiting lips.

"I know where Meg's glove is."

"Is that all?" a disappointed Jo said. "That's your grand secret?"

"It's quite enough, as you'll agree when I tell you."

"Tell, then."

Laurie bent and whispered three words into Jo's ear. Jo frowned, surprised and displeased. "How do you know?"

"I saw it."

"Where?"

"Pocket."

"All this time?"

"Yes; isn't that romantic?"

"No, it's horrid!"

"But you promised to keep this between us. You are not to tell anyone. Even Meg."

"But this is another matter entirely. Why, it isn't even your secret, is it?"

And although Jo didn't reveal the secret just then, she harbored it within her, which gave her an ill temper. Realistically, she knew it would be horrifying to discover that the werewolf Laurie had killed actual people, but were he and she not friends? Should he not trust her with his deepest secrets? She fluctuated between wanting Laurie to confess that he was a vicious killer who ate the meat and drank the blood of people just like her, and wanting only the sweet side of him she so admired to exist. So torn and confused was she that she remained rankled and sour for days.

One day, after being chased all over the garden by Laurie, Jo bounced inside, laid herself on the sofa, and affected to read.

"Have you anything interesting there?" asked Meg with condescension.

"Nothing but a story; don't amount to much, I guess," returned Jo, carefully keeping the name of the paper out of sight.

"You'd better read it aloud; that will amuse us, and keep you out of mischief," said Amy in her most grown-up tone.

"What's the name?" asked Beth, wondering why Jo kept her face behind the sheet.

" 'The Rival Painters.' "

"That sounds well; read it," said Meg.

With a loud "Hem!" and a long breath, Jo began to read very fast. The girls listened with interest, for the tale was romantic, and somewhat pathetic, as most of the characters died in the end.

"Who wrote it?" asked Beth, who had caught a glimpse of Jo's face.

Jo sat up very straight, cast the paper aside, and answered, "Your sister!"

"You?" cried Meg, dropping her work.

"It's very good," said Amy critically.

"I knew it! I knew it! Oh, my Jo, I *am* so proud!" And Beth ran to hug her sister and exult over this splendid success.

"The success is limited," Jo admitted. "I gave two stories to the newspaperman, and he said he liked them both and that I should write more. But there was no pay this time, because he said he doesn't pay beginners. Although the next time, he assured me, there would be. In time, I may be able to support myself, support us, with my stories."

The house exploded with congratulations and proud murmurs. The girls wanted to hear the whole story of Jo's going to see the newspaperman. They all spoke at once, exclaiming about how excited Father would be to hear about his little woman being recognized for her talent. Beth grabbed and smoothed the newspaper, insisting that they save it so their father could see it the moment he came home from the war.

"We will save them all, Jo," Beth said. "We'll create a massive book filled with the clippings of every single thing you get published."

Jo hugged each sister in turn, biting down on her tongue to keep it from wagging the secret Laurie had revealed as she stood embracing Meg.

...

CHAPTER 11

Shorn and Separated

"NOVEMBER IS THE MOST DISAGREEABLE MONTH IN THE whole year!" Meg complained, staring out the window at the frostbitten garden.

"Exactly why I chose to be born in it," observed Jo pensively.

"This dullness was terrible enough, but now we have that horrible telegram telling us Father is ill. And we have no way to get to him," Amy cried.

"The list of things Marmee needs for the trip is beyond our means: food, nursing supplies, clothing," Meg said, counting off the list on her fingers.

"We will find a way," said Beth, throwing a shawl over her head and shoulders. "Just you wait and see. I'll be back soon. Marmee asked me to go over to ask Mr. Laurence for some old wine for Father." The other girls began to plan how they could help their mother. Jo, seeing the efforts her sisters were making, stole out of the house.

Mr. Laurence came hurrying back with Beth, bringing every comfort he could think of for the invalid, and offering himself as Marmee's escort.

"I won't hear of it," Mrs. March replied, knowing it would be a long, sad journey.

Rushing through the entry with a cup of tea in one hand and

a pair of rubbers in the other, Meg ran straight into Mr. Brooke, who had heard the news and came to offer his company and protection to Mrs. March on her difficult trip. Meg lost herself in the gentleman's brown eyes for some moments, found reason once more, and invited him into the parlour.

The short afternoon wore away, and all the errands were done. Supplies had been gathered, and money was borrowed from Aunt March. Meg and her mother were busy at some needlework, Beth and Amy made tea, and Hannah finished her ironing with what she called a "slap and a bang." But Jo had been gone for hours, and they began to worry. Just as Laurie was about to go off to find her, she stomped into the house with an odd look on her reddened face. She pushed a roll of money into her mother's hand and said, "This is my contribution toward making my father comfortable, and bringing him home!"

"Twenty-five dollars! Jo! Where did you get this?" Mrs. March asked, fingering the money as if assessing if it were real. "I hope you haven't done anything rash."

"Or illegal," Amy taunted.

"No. It's mine. I earned it fairly. I only sold what was mine to sell."

"A story?" Beth, ever the optimist, asked.

"No," Jo said, pulling off her bonnet to show a closely cropped head where her abundant locks had once been.

Everyone exclaimed at once, but it was Amy's biting words that found her ears, crawled inside, and burrowed down in a peevish little knot. "Oh, Jo," Amy wailed. "Your hair! Your one beauty."

Beth hugged the shorn head, kissing its crown and weeping. Jo shrugged her off with an air of indifference that deceived no one.

"It will do my brain good to have that mop taken off; my head feels deliciously light and cool, and the barber said it would grow back quickly. Besides, now I have less dressing to do to act out male roles in our productions," Jo said. "And here, Marmee, I saved you a lock." She folded the long chestnut tress into her mother's hand.

That night, as Beth and Amy slept, Meg lay awake in the dark and listened to Jo weep for her lost crowning glory.

With funds and supplies in place, the girls were left to their own resources as Marmee and Mr. Brooke hurried off to be by Mr. March's side. For a week the amount of virtue in the old house would have supplied the neighborhood, but they soon began to spend more and more time on their personal pursuits. They did remain faithful in writing to their mother; as they missed her so terribly, it was the only way they could console themselves. Laurie, Hannah, and Mr. Laurence enclosed letters of their own with the girls' nearly every week, so the plump envelopes had to be carefully flattened and poked into the letter box for mailing. Mrs. March had all the news—of spoiled dinners made by poor cooks, Jo's constantly changing head as her hair grew back, wardrobe woes and victories, werewolf attacks and fatalities, and Amy's mastery of the French language. In return she sent news that Mr. March was improving and loved and missed all his little women.

Mother had asked the girls to look in on the Hummel family, the poor widow with the many children to whom the family had donated their Christmas breakfast, and to offer help where needed. Beth had been there every day since her mother left, and was trying to talk one of her sisters into going in her place.

"Oh, please, Beth, not me," cried Amy. "I simply can't bear to go the Hummels' awful hovel. It must be the most dreadful thing in the world to be so poor and know you will remain that way for the rest of your life."

"The baby is sick, and I have no idea what to do for it," Beth said. "It seems sicker and sicker every day. I think you should go, Meg, or Hannah. Besides, I have a terrible headache and need the relief today."

Meg promised that she would go tomorrow.

Jo reminded Beth that she had a cold and shouldn't go, and Beth lay on the sofa to rest. Soon she fell asleep. When she awoke an hour later, she found that Jo had become absorbed in her work of writing, and Amy was nowhere to be found. Meg was trying on clothes, and Beth could see her older sister would not be soon distracted from her diversion; and so, with a sigh, she put on her hood, filled her basket with odds and ends for the children, and went out into the chilly air. It was late when she returned, a grave look on her face. Jo ran up to her immediately.

"Stay back, Jo."

"Why? Beth, what's the matter?"

"Have you had scarlet fever?" Beth asked with a shaky voice.

"Years ago, when Meg did. Why?"

"Oh, Jo! The baby's dead!" Beth burst into tears and told her tale of how Mrs. Hummel's baby died in her lap. "It seemed asleep as I held it, but it suddenly gave out a small cry, shuddered, and then lay very still. I just sat and held the poor thing. When the doctor came, he said it was scarlet fever and scolded Mrs. Hummel for not calling him sooner. She tried to explain that she was too poor. That softened him a bit, and he said he would not charge her for his call. He told me to go home, and to take belladonna right away, or I'd have the fever."

"No, you won't have it. I won't allow it!" Jo cried, taking her anguished sister in her arms so she couldn't see the frightened look on her face.

"Don't let Amy come; she never had it," Beth said. "You and Meg can't catch it again, can you?"

"I guess not; don't care if I do; serve me right, selfish pig, to let you go, and stay writing rubbish myself!" muttered Jo, as she went to consult Hannah.

Hannah decided they would send Amy off to Aunt March's for a spell, until Dr. Bangs could come to take a look at Beth, who was suffering a headache and sore throat.

Amy wept, rebelling, when told she had to go. Laurie dropped by and found the youngest sister weeping in the parlour. Laurie offered her a jolly plan; he would come and take her out every day, driving or walking.

"But they're sending me off as if I was in the way!" Amy protested.

"Bless your heart, child! It's to keep you well. You don't want to be sick, do you?"

"No, but it's dull at Aunt March's, and she is so cross."

"It won't be dull with me popping in every day to tell you how Beth is, and take you out gallivanting," Laurie said with a laugh. "Bring your best dress. We can go to the theater. And I promise to bring you back home the moment we know Beth is well."

As Amy suffered under the torment of crabby Aunt March and her insolent parrot, Polly, who called her a fright and echoed back to her whatever she said, Beth was, indeed, afflicted with scarlet fever. She wore an angry red rash on her skin and a thick yellow coating on her tongue. She suffered with headaches and groaned with nausea, flailing about in her bed, streaming with perspiration one moment and begging for more covers the next. Meg and Jo considered sending for Marmee but decided to wait, to see if Beth's fever would break.

The moon was full, and in the thick of the night, Jo arose to see half a dozen or more werewolves circling the house, sniffing the air where the aroma of near death hung. One of them lifted its muzzle to the sky and sent out a frightful baying that pierced her through to the very marrow of her bones. Terrified, she ran to her sister's side and found Beth asleep, though fitfully. She cried out in her sleep, and Jo was shocked to hear what sounded like a howl rise up out of Beth's throat. Jo curled up in the rocking chair across from the bed and watched her sister for a time, and then peered out the window to observe the prowling werewolves. The moonlight caught their sleek, dark fur, igniting it into alternating shades of red, black, brown, and gold as they paced. When they raised their heads, that same light inflamed the golden orbs of their eyes to match the brilliance of the moon.

"My sister is ill because I was too lazy to share in the chore of helping the Hummels," she whispered into the window. "So I will protect her, werewolves, from you or from whatever life sends, and I will gladly trade my very breath for hers."

While Jo watched over her, Beth was aware that she was there. She felt paralyzed, not awake and not asleep, and as if she was not within her body. A part of her was in that bed, but another part was somewhere outside with the werewolves. She was running through the green of the Laurences' lawn wearing not a single stitch of clothing. Moon rays touched her skin, and its whiteness glowed with kindled warmth. She held her arms out, allowing the werewolves to inhale and memorize her scent. She followed them, running until she was panting with exhaustion, and caught up to them as they tore into the flesh of a stray per-

son who had been foolish enough to wander outside. From an instinct she never knew she possessed, she dropped to the ground
and rolled in the blood that had spattered, and when the werewolves were finished with their meal, they licked every drop of
blood from Beth's soft milky skin.

CHAPTER 12

...

March of Darkness

"HA! HA! NEVER SAY DIE, TAKE A PINCH OF SNUFF, GOOD-BYE, good-bye," Polly, the surly parrot, called out to Amy every time she entered the room.

Aunt March thought Polly delightful and would say with a laugh, "Hold your tongue, you disrespectful old bird!"

Polly would repeat gruffly, "Hold your tongue, you disrespectful old bird," tumble off Aunt March's chair with a bounce, and run to peck at Amy.

"Why does she peck at me? She didn't go near Laurie when he was here."

"She has never taken to the boy," Aunt March replied. "She goes nowhere near him, ignores him completely."

It didn't take Amy a full day to wish she could feed the discourteous creature to the werewolves. Sadly, the full moon had just passed, but she entertained herself with fantasies of tying the bird outside as a werewolf appetizer during the next. And then she nearly wept at the thought of having to be at Aunt March's for that long a time.

At home, how dark the days seemed as Beth suffered fever fits, her pitiful fingers playing on her coverlet as if on her beloved piano while she tried to sing from a throat so swollen there was no music left in it. She did not know the familiar faces around her, and addressed them by the wrong names. She longed for her cats but would not have them brought to her, fearing they, too, would get sick. Jo stayed always in the darkened room, at her sister's side, meditating on the sweetness of Beth's nature. The girl filled a deep and tender place in all their hearts and had such unselfish ambition to live for others. Jo thought with regret of how seldom she herself exercised those simple virtues with which Beth made their home so happy.

Outside the March home, Beth was sorely missed. Laurie haunted the house like a restless ghost, and Mr. Laurence had locked the grand piano, unable to bear the reminder of the young neighbor who used to make the twilight so pleasant for him. The milkman, the baker, the grocer, and the butcher inquired how she did; poor Mrs. Hummel came to beg pardon for her thoughtlessness, and to get a shroud for her darling little daughter, who had joined the baby in death. The neighbors sent all sorts of comforts and good wishes, and even those who knew her best were surprised to discover how many friends shy little Beth had made.

The first of December was a bitter, snowy day, and the year seemed to be preparing for its death. For days Hannah had sat up at night, Meg had kept a telegram in her desk all ready to send off to her mother at any minute, and Jo had remained steadfast at Beth's side as she lay hour after hour, tossing to and fro with incoherent words on her lips, or sank into a heavy sleep that brought no refreshment. When Dr. Bangs came that morning, he looked long at Beth, held her hot hand in both his own for a minute, and laid it gently down, saying, in a low tone, to Hannah—

"If Mrs. March *can* leave her husband, she'd better be sent for."

When Laurie came over soon after, he took one glance at Jo's face and asked, "What is it? Is Beth worse?"

"We must send for Mother," she said, then burst into tears. "She don't look like my Beth, and there's nobody to help us bear it, with Mother and Father both gone, and God seems so far away that I can't find Him."

Laurie, with a lump in his throat, sat with her, hoping his friendly hand could comfort his friend's sore heart. She could not speak, but she held on tight. Soon she dried the tears, which had relieved her, and looked at him with a grateful face.

"Thank you, Teddy. I'm better now and will try to bear it if it comes." Then her head went down again into her handkerchief and she cried despairingly, "I can't give her up. Beth is my conscience. I *can't* give her up. I can't."

"I don't think she will die," Laurie said. He drew his hand across his eyes and could not speak until he had subdued the choky feeling in his throat and steadied his lips. It was unmanly, but he couldn't help it. "She's so good, and we all love her so much, I don't believe God will take her away yet."

"The good and the dear people always do die," groaned Jo, but she stopped crying, for Laurie's words had cheered her up.

Laurie had brought some wine and urged Jo to drink a glass. She took it with a smile, Laurie poured a glass for himself, and they drank to Beth's health.

"I have something that will warm the cockles of your heart better than quarts of wine," said Laurie, beaming at her with a face of suppressed satisfaction.

"What is it?" cried Jo.

"I telegraphed your mother yesterday. Brooke answered that she'd come at once, and she'll be here tonight, and everything will be all right."

Laurie spoke very fast, and turned red and excited, but Jo grew quite white, flew out of her chair, and embraced her friend, laughing rather than crying as she clung to him. "Laurie, you're an angel! How shall I ever thank you?"

Jo thought of all the foul things she had heard about werewolves, and all the idle threats directed at them by ignorant people who were determined to harm them. She vowed to herself that she would repay Laurie and his grandfather their many kind acts by helping to make others see werewolves as beings, like people, who had many facets in their nature. Others needed to know that, except when the moon was full, they acted like anyone else. Like a lightning bolt, she was struck with the sudden realization that, through her writing, she could accomplish this; she could tell the werewolves' stories for them. She felt a sense of the enormous power she possessed.

The girls never forgot that night, for no sleep came to them as they kept their watch with a dreadful weight of powerlessness. Beth howled in her sleep like a she-wolf, and her body tossed from one side of the bed to the other. Her skin was ice cold, but they could not keep the covers over her, as her hands and feet wheeled in the air as if she was running through the woods, stalking prey like a starving werewolf.

"If God spares Beth, I never will complain again," Meg whispered earnestly.

"If God spares Beth, I'll try to love and serve Him all my life," Jo responded.

"I wish I had no heart, mine aches so," sighed Meg after a pause.

"How shall we ever get through life if it is as hard as this?" Jo asked despondently.

The clock struck twelve and they looked outside to see that

the snow still fell and the bitter wind still raged. An hour later, Laurie departed for the station. They were haunted by anxious fears of delay in the storm, or accidents along the way.

It was past two when Jo awoke to find Meg kneeling before their mother's easy chair, with her face hidden. A dreadful fear passed coldly over Jo as she thought, "Beth is dead, and Meg is afraid to tell me." She rushed to Beth's side, and seeing that the fever flush and the look of pain were gone, she kissed her sister's pale and peaceful face and bid her goodbye.

Hannah, started out of her sleep, rushed to the bed, felt Beth's hands, listened at her lips, and then threw her apron over her head. "She's sleepin' nat'ral. Praise be given! She breathes easy!"

The doctor came to confirm it, and though a homely man, the girls thought his face the most heavenly they had ever seen when he said, "Yes, my dears, I think the little girl will pull through this time. Keep the house quiet, let her sleep, and when she wakes, give her—"

What they were to give, neither heard; for both crept into the dark hall, and, sitting on the stairs, held each other close, rejoicing with hearts too full for words.

Never had the sun risen so beautifully, and never had the world seemed so lovely, as it did to the heavy eyes of Meg and Jo, as they looked out in the early morning, when their long, sad vigil was done.

"It looks like a fairy world," said Meg.

"Hark!" cried Jo, starting to her feet.

Yes, there was a sound of bells at the door below, a cry from Hannah, and then Laurie's voice, saying, in a joyful whisper, "Girls, she's come! She's come! Your mother is home!"

Once she was greeted and warmed, Mrs. March sat like a hen

on her nest at Beth's side. The girls had to wait upon their mother, for she would not unclasp the thin hand that clung to hers even in sleep. When Beth woke from that long, healing sleep, the first thing her eyes took in was her dear mother's face. Too weak to wonder at anything, she only smiled, and nestled in close to the loving arms about her.

Meg and Jo finally closed their weary eyes and lay at rest, like storm-beaten boats, safe at anchor in a quiet harbor. Mrs. March would not leave Beth's side, but rested in the big chair, waking often to look at, touch, and brood over her child, like a miser over some recovered treasure.

CHAPTER 13

Amy's Altar

POOR AMY WAS HAVING HARD TIMES AT AUNT MARCH'S. She felt her exile deeply, and realized how much she was beloved and petted at home. But Aunt March had a soft spot for her nephew's children, and though she didn't think it proper to confess it, the well-behaved little girl pleased her very much. She tried to make Amy happy, but she had her rules and orders, her prim ways, and long, prosy speeches to deliver, and succeeded only in making Amy feel like a fly in the web of a very strict spider.

Aunt March thought there had been bad effects from the freedom and indulgences the girl enjoyed at home, so had her wash cups every morning, polish up the old-fashioned spoons and fat silver teapot, dust the room, feed Polly, comb the lap dog, and fetch and deliver this and that the entire day long. After her lessons, she was allowed only one hour for exercise or play, and after dinner, she had to read aloud, sew, and then listen to Aunt March's utterly dull tales of her long-past youth.

If it hadn't been for Laurie popping up each day to wheedle Aunt March into allowing him to take Amy out for a walk or a ride, Amy would have gone mad. They spent afternoons walking or riding, and Amy noticed that, in this part of town, the Brigade did not parade about flaunting their powers; rather, they were totally absent. When she mentioned as much to Laurie, he shrugged and said he thought it fine he was not forced to look at their puffed leather chests and the unkempt hair trailing out from the bottoms of their helmets. "They're a brigade of bullies, not protectors, if you ask me," he added.

But despite Laurie's visits and outings, Amy always had to return, far too soon, to Aunt March's enormous house and grounds. The parrot alone was enough to drive her to distraction. He pulled her hair, upset his bread and milk in his newly cleaned cage to plague her, and teased the dog to barking the moment Aunt March dropped off to sleep in her chair. She could not endure the dog, either, for the fat, cross beast snarled and yelped at her when she made his toilet, and lay on his back with his legs in the air and an idiotic expression when he wanted to eat, which was about a dozen times a day. The cook was bad-tempered, and the old coachman deaf.

But the maid, Esther, was a Frenchwoman who amused Amy with odd stories of her life in France. Her real name was Estelle, but she had complied when "Madame," as she called Aunt March, ordered her to change it. Esther allowed Amy to roam the house, and showed her where curious and pretty things were stored away in big wardrobes and ancient chests; for Aunt March hoarded like a magpie.

Amy's chief delight was an Indian cabinet full of queer drawers, little pigeonholes, and secret places that hid an array of ornaments. She found great satisfaction in examining and arranging these objects, especially the jewelry, some pieces of which had reposed on their velvet cushions for forty years. There was the garnet set Aunt March wore the day she came out, the pearls her father gave her on her wedding day, her lover's diamonds, jet mourning rings and pins, queer lockets, with portraits of dead friends, weeping willows made of hair, baby bracelets, Uncle March's big watch, and Aunt March's wedding ring, which laid in a box because it was now too small to fit on her fat finger.

"Which would Mademoiselle choose if she had her will?" asked Esther, who always sat near to watch over and lock up the valuables.

"I like the diamonds best, but there is no necklace, and I'm fond of necklaces, they are so becoming. I should choose this if I like," Amy replied, admiring a string of gold and ebony beads, from which hung a heavy cross of the same.

"I, too, covet it, but not as a necklace; ah, no! To me it is a rosary, and as such I should use it like a good Catholic," said Esther, eyeing the handsome thing wistfully.

"Is it to use as you use the string of good-smelling wooden beads hanging over your glass?"

"Truly, yes, to pray with. It would please the saints if one used so fine a rosary as this, instead of wearing it as a vain bijou."

"You seem to take a deal of comfort in your prayers, Esther. I wish I could feel as good, quiet, and satisfied as you look."

"If Mademoiselle was a Catholic, she would find true comfort; but as that is not to be, it would be well if you went apart each day to meditate, and pray, as did the good mistress whom I served before Madame. She had a little chapel, and in it found solace for much trouble."

"Would it be right for me to do so too?" asked Amy, who, in her loneliness, felt the need of help of some sort. "I could pray for my sisters, and my father, who is away at war, and for all those who have fallen victim to the werewolves. Why, I could even pray for the werewolves themselves, as even God's beasts need blessings."

"It would be excellent and charming; and I shall gladly arrange the little dressing room as your chapel if you like. Say nothing to Madame, but when she sleeps, go to it and sit. Think good thoughts and pray to God to preserve your dear sister."

Amy liked the idea, and the pious and sincere Esther affectionately promised to fix up the space.

"This piece," Esther said, holding up a silver pin in the shape of a cross that was braided with vines, "is meant to keep werewolves away. Ah, and here we have the matching ring."

"I wish I knew where all these pretty things will go when Aunt March dies," Amy said, watching Esther lock up the jewel cases.

"To you and your sisters. I know it; I witnessed her will," whispered Esther, smiling.

"How nice! But I wish she would let us have them now."

"It is too soon yet for the young ladies to wear these things. But there are some that are proper for young ladies to wear. I have a fancy that the little turquoise ring will be given to you when you go, for she approves your good behavior and charming manners."

"Do you think so? Oh, I'll be a lamb!" Amy tried on the ring with a delighted face and a firm resolve to earn it. "I do like Aunt March, after all!" she exclaimed.

From that day she was a model of obedience, and the old lady complacently admired the success of her training.

Esther fitted up the closet with a little table, placed a footstool before it, and over it a picture of the Madonna and child, taken from one of the shut-up rooms. Esther thought the picture was of no great value; it was, however, a valuable copy of one of the world's most famous pictures, and Amy's beauty-loving eyes never tired of looking up at the sweet face of the divine mother, while tender thoughts of her own softened her heart. On the table she laid her little Testament and hymn-book, kept a vase always full of the best flowers Laurie brought her, and came every day to sit alone thinking good thoughts, and praying for her precious sister. Esther had given her a rosary of black beads with a silver cross, but Amy hung it up and did not use it, doubtful as to its fitness for Protestant prayers.

Every day Amy prayed, and she found her prayers turning more and more to the people who had been consumed by the werewolves with no bodies to bury, and, inexplicably, to the werewolves themselves, whose heavy trials she was beginning to recognize. Just the thought of the Brigade breaking into her home and casting accusations about made her worry for her family, so she could barely imagine what thoughts raced through the minds of the werewolves as they attended to their daily duties under the tall, threatening shadows of the members of the Brigade.

Outside the safe nest of her home, Amy was quite sincere in her need for prayer and goodness. She felt herself a young pilgrim with a very heavy burden. She tried to forget herself, to keep cheerful and be satisfied with doing right, though no one saw or praised her for it. In her first effort at being very, very good, she decided to make her will, as Aunt March had done, so if she *did* fall ill and die, her possessions might be justly and generously divided. It cost her a pang even to think of giving up the little treasures that in her eyes were as precious as the old lady's jewels.

One rainy afternoon, during her play hour, she had taken

Polly upstairs and was amusing herself in one of the large chambers that held a wardrobe full of old-fashioned costumes. She liked to parade up and down in front of the long mirror dressed in faded brocades, quilted petticoats, large turbans, and high-heeled shoes. She was tossing her head and flirting with her fan when Laurie appeared at the door. The bird squawked at the sight of the werewolf, and nervously sidled behind a flounced petticoat.

"That bird is the trial of my life. She talks so large and bold, but yesterday was frightened away by a spider," Amy said.

"That's a lie! Oh lor!" the bird called out, but refused to emerge.

"I'd wring your neck if you were mine," Laurie called back, but the bird did not respond.

"I'm glad you dropped by," Amy said, taking a paper out of her pocket. "I want you to read this, please, and tell me if it is legal and right. I felt I must do it, for life is uncertain and I want no ill feeling over my tomb."

Laurie bit his lip to contain his laughter and read the document with praiseworthy gravity, considering the spelling:

—

MY LAST WILL AND TESTIMENT.

I, Amy Curtis March, being in my sane mind, do give and bequeethe all my earthly property—viz. to wit:—namely

To my father, my best pictures, sketches, maps, and works of art, including frames. Also my $100, to do what he likes with.

To my mother, all my clothes, except the blue apron

with pockets,—also my likeness, and my medal, with much love.

To my dear sister Margaret, I give my turkuoise ring (if I get it), also my green box with the doves on it, also my piece of real lace for her neck, and my sketch of her as a memorial of her "little girl."

To Jo I leave my breast-pin, the one mended with sealing wax, also my bronze inkstand—she lost the cover,—and my most precious plaster rabbit, because I am sorry I burnt up her story.

To Beth (if she lives after me) I give my dolls and the little bureau, my fan, my linen collars and my new slippers if she can wear them being thin when she gets well. And I herewith also leave her my regret that I ever made fun of old Joanna.

To my friend and neighbor Theodore Laurence I bequeethe my paper marshay portfolio, my clay model of a horse though he did say it hadn't any neck. Also in return for his great kindness in the hour of affliction any one of my artistic works he likes, Noter Dame is the best.

To our venerable benefactor Mr. Laurence I leave my purple box with a looking glass in the cover which will be nice for his pens and remind him of the departed girl who thanks him for his favors to her family, specially Beth.

I wish my favorite playmate Kitty Bryant to have the blue silk apron and my gold-bead ring with a kiss.

To Hannah I give the band-box she wanted and all the patchwork I leave hoping she "will remember me, when it you see."

And now having disposed of my most valuable property I hope all will be satisfied and not blame the dead. I forgive everyone, and trust we may all meet when the trump shall sound. Amen.

To this will and testment I set my hand and seal on this 20th day of Nov. Anni Domino 1861.

AMY CURTIS MARCH.

WITNESSES:

ESTELLE VALNOR, THEODORE LAURENCE.

"What put this into your head?" asked Laurie soberly.

Amy looked at him and lay a bit of red tape, sealing wax, a taper, and a standish before him for him to sign and deal the document with.

"It's Beth, isn't it?"

"Is there real danger for her?"

"I'm afraid there is, but we must hope for the best," he said, comforting her by placing a hand on her shoulder in a brotherly fashion.

Amy looked away. "I almost forgot. Don't people sometimes add to their wills?"

"Yes; codicils, they call them."

"I want one in mine—that I wish *all* my curls cut off, and given round to my friends. I forgot it, but I want it done, even though it will spoil my looks. And anything that is left, I want to be donated to the legal fund that helps those accused by the Brigade."

"You realize most never live to see their trial," Laurie said, suddenly pale and grim.

"That doesn't matter," she replied softly.

Once Laurie had left, Amy went to her little chapel and, sitting in the twilight, prayed for Beth. She pretended she could hear her sister playing the piano for old Mr. Laurence, as this was the time of day she did so. Her eyes streamed with tears, and she felt that a million turquoise rings would not console her for the loss of her gentle sister.

...

CHAPTER 14

Raging Against Change

L AURIE RUSHED TO AUNT MARCH'S TO TELL AMY THAT
Beth was recovering and that her mother had returned home.
Her little pink lips curled up into a smile, as she was certain that
her good thoughts in the little chapel had begun to bear fruit.

"I have yet more happy news. You have a visitor," he said,
stepping aside so Mrs. March could enter the room.

With a cry of joy Amy rushed to her mother, and sat on her
lap, and told her trials, receiving consolation and compensation in
Marmee's approving smiles and fond caresses. Marmee gave her
the sad news of another werewolf attack, and of four people who
had been taken into custody by the Brigade and were scheduled
for execution in the usual manner—hanged with their hearts extracted from their chests and burned. Marmee complained that
she was certain the poor and unlucky farmers and peddlers ar-
rested were innocent, and so Amy decided to pray for them, and
then was reminded to show her mother the little chapel.

"I like it very much, dear," Mrs. March said, looking from the
dusty rosary to the well-worn little book, and the lovely
Madonna picture with its garland of evergreen. "It is an excellent plan to have some place where we can go to be quiet, when
things vex or grieve us. Could it be that you are learning that

even though life gives us a good many hard times, we can always bear them if we ask help in the right way?"

"Yes, Mother; and when I go home I mean to have a corner in the big closet to put my books and the copy of that picture which I've tried to make. The woman's face is not good. I cannot draw anything that beautiful. But I have done the baby well, and I love it very much." As Amy pointed, Mrs. March noticed something on her lifted hand. Amy followed her gaze. "Yes, I wanted to tell you about this. Aunt March gave me this ring. She called me to her, kissed me, and put it on my finger. She even had a funny guard made, a smaller ring to keep the turquoise on, as it's too big. May I wear them?"

"You are rather young for such ornaments," Mrs. March said, looking at the plump little hand with the band of sky-blue stones on the forefinger, and the quaint guard formed of two, tiny, golden hands clasped together.

"I promise to try not to be vain, and I wish to wear them most to remind me of something."

"To remind you of Aunt March?"

"No, to remind me not to be selfish. I've thought a lot lately about 'my bundle of naughties,' and being selfish is the largest one. I hope to cure it if I can. Beth is so well loved because she isn't selfish at all. I worry that nobody would feel bad if I fell ill as she has, and I may not even deserve to have anyone feel bad about my being sick. I want to be more like Beth. I'm apt to forget my resolutions, but this can remind me. May I try?"

"Yes. Wear your ring, dear. The sincere wish to be good is half the battle, so I think you will prosper. Now, I must return home to my Beth. Keep up your heart, little daughter, and we will soon have you home again."

"What of Father? Will he be home soon? Who is caring for him?"

"Mr. Brooke was kind enough to stay to nurse him, and I am certain he will see him on to good health."

Later that night, Marmee was back at home and sitting with Beth when Jo entered the room and said she had something to discuss.

"Is it about Meg?"

"How quickly you guessed! Yes, it's about her, and though it's a little thing, it fidgets me," Jo said.

"Speak low," Mrs. March whispered. "Beth is asleep. Tell me all about it."

Jo settled herself at her mother's feet. "Last summer Meg left a pair of gloves over at the Laurences', and only one was returned. We forgot all about it, till Teddy told me that Mr. Brooke had it. He kept it in his waistcoat pocket, and once it fell out and Teddy joked him about it, and Mr. Brooke owned that he liked Meg, but didn't dare say so, she was so young and he was so poor. Now isn't that a *dreadful* state of things?"

"Do you think Meg cares for him?" asked Mrs. March with an anxious look.

"I don't know anything about love, and such nonsense!" cried Jo. "In novels, the girls show it by blushing, fainting away, growing thin, and acting like fools. Meg does nothing of the sort; she eats and drinks, and sleeps, like a sensible creature; she looks straight in my face when I talk about that man, and only blushes a bit when Teddy jokes about lovers. I forbid him to do it, but he don't mind me."

"Then you fancy Meg is *not* interested in John?"

"Who?"

"Mr. Brooke. I call him John now. We fell into the way of doing so at the hospital."

"Oh, dear! I know you'll take his part. Mean thing! To go petting Papa and truckling to you, just to wheedle you into liking him."

"John went with me at Mr. Laurence's request, and was so devoted to poor Father, that we couldn't help getting fond of him. He told us he loved Meg, so he was perfectly open and honorable. He promised not to ask for her hand until he could offer a comfortable home. He is an excellent young man, Jo. We could not refuse to listen to him, but I will not consent to Meg's engaging herself so young."

"Of course not! It would be idiotic!"

"Jo, remember to keep your voice low," Marmee said, looking over at Beth, who had turned in her sleep. "I have confided in you," Mrs. March said, "and I want you to say nothing to Meg about this. I am waiting until John comes back so I can see the two together and better judge her feelings toward him."

"She'll see his in those handsome eyes that she talks about, and then it will be all up with her," Jo raged. "She's got such a soft heart, it will melt like butter in the sun if anyone looks sentimentally at her. Why, she read the short reports he sent more than she read your letters, and pinched me when I spoke of it, and she likes brown eyes, and don't think John an ugly name, and she'll go and fall in love, and there's an end of peace and fun, and cozy times together. I see it all! They'll go lovering around the house, and we shall have to dodge; Brooke will scratch up a fortune somehow, carry her off, and make a hole in our family; and I shall break my heart."

"I do want to keep my girls as long as I can. Take heart. Meg is only seventeen, and your father and I agreed she should not bind herself in any way, nor be married, before she is twenty. If she and John love each other, they can wait."

"But wouldn't you rather she marry a rich man?"

"Money is a good and useful thing; and I hope my girls will never feel the need of it too bitterly, nor be tempted by too much. If rank and money come with love and virtue, I should accept them gratefully, and enjoy your good fortune; but I know, by experience, how much genuine happiness can be had in a plain little house, where the daily bread is earned. I am content to see Meg begin humbly, for if I am not mistaken, she will be rich in the possession of a good man's heart. It is better than fortune to own that, whether it be the heart of a poor man, the heart of a rich man, or even the heart of a werewolf."

Jo gave her mother a shocked look, and Marmee's smile told her she had added that last part more for effect than as a true expression of her mind. But it made Jo pause and think that perhaps happiness could be found with a werewolf—if it was one, as Marmee had said, who owned a good heart. "I'd planned for Meg to marry Teddy, and sit in the lap of luxury all her days," she said boldly, biting her tongue to keep from telling her mother the boy's secret.

"I'm afraid Teddy is hardly grown-up enough for Meg, and too much of a weathercock, just now, for anyone to depend upon. Don't make plans, Jo; but let time and their own hearts mate your friends."

Jo sighed. "I hate to see things go all crisscross and getting snarled up, when a pull here, and a snip there, would straighten it out. I wish wearing flatirons on our heads would keep us from growing up. But buds will be roses, and kittens, cats."

"Flatirons and cats?" Meg asked, entering the room.

"Only one of my stupid speeches," Jo said. She thought, as she glanced at her sister, that she did, absolutely, believe that she would prefer to see Meg marry a wealthy werewolf than a poor and boring man.

"I finished my letter to Father," Meg said, handing it to her mother for approval.

Marmee read it over and pronounced it lovely. "Perfect, in fact, and beautifully written. But please add that I send my love to John."

"You call him John?" Meg asked with an innocent smile.

"Yes. He's been like a son to us. We're quite fond of him."

"I'm glad of that; he is so lonely. Good night, Mother."

Marmee gave Meg a tender kiss and watched her leave the room. With a mixture of satisfaction and regret, she whispered, "She does not love him yet, but will soon learn to."

...

CHAPTER 15

Amy Hunts Werewolves

AMY'S NIGHT OF THE FULL MOON AT AUNT MARCH'S WAS destined to be the most exciting of her visit, as Esther promised the estate would literally swarm with werewolves. She was uncertain if they were attracted by a plant or bush growing in abundance on the property or by the scent of Madame's old, dry skin, but she firmly asserted that if there was a full moon in the sky, there would be werewolves aplenty on the grounds. Amy and Esther planned to stay up and "hunt werewolf" from the upstairs window. At first Amy refused, and her blood surged through her veins with blind desperation at the mere thought of werewolves; but Esther explained that by *hunt*, she meant only to catch sight of one, and she assured the little girl that they were perfectly safe and secure from their perch in the upstairs of Aunt March's great house. They had paper at hand to keep a tally of each they saw, and for the victor there awaited a thick peppermint stick snatched from Aunt March's hidden supply.

"What does one wear to hunt werewolves?" Amy asked.

"Were I on the ground with them, certainly not these skirts. I think I might wear a gentleman's trousers, so I could stretch my legs to run, and be ready to climb trees, scale fences, and flee in a moment at great speed," Esther replied.

"My sister Jo has trousers. But they are part of her stage

wardrobe. She often has to assume the male roles because we haven't a brother to act those parts, although Laurie is loved by us all enough to be a brother. But he is a poor actor. Jo says he emotes too often, overacting the part, and standing in front of the speaker when he should be in back, so she seldom allows him a role. Especially if it is one of her plays."

"Your sister writes plays?"

"My sister writes everything," Amy said, rummaging through a drawer to find a scarf to wear about her neck to protect it from werewolf bites. "It's what she loves to do. She hopes to make a living of it."

"It would be fine if she did," Esther said. "There is too much written by men. They like to air their opinions and tell everyone else how to act. Of course, I trust you will not repeat I said that."

"I may repeat the words, but I'll assume them as my own, if you don't mind," Amy said as she slipped a bracelet on her wrist and held her arm up to admire it.

"I don't mind at all, mademoiselle," Esther said with a smile. "Rather, I would be flattered. I am going down for a moment to put Madame and her dog to bed. I've no doubt that she still sits asleep in her chair with the dog in her lap. I'll bring back some tea and biscuits, if there are any left. If not, perhaps some bread."

"Bring Polly, too, if you will," Amy called out. She stopped and shook her head, having surprised herself by longing for the company of the atrocious bird.

Amy found an old fur coat in the back of the wardrobe. She examined it·and found a space in one of the cuffs where the fur overlapped. She carefully snipped off a piece of the gray fur and was glad to see, old and shabby as it was, that she had not spoiled the coat in the least. She could take the fur home and show it to everyone as a bit of werewolf fur obtained on a hunt. She struggled to return the coat to its place deep in the dusty, black, forgotten realm in the very back corner of the wardrobe.

The two women were well into their pot of tea when they heard the first baying of the werewolves. Amy froze, her heart thumping wildly in her chest. She didn't believe she had ever heard their cry so close. It was a sound that burrowed through one's skin and chilled the blood that flowed through one's veins, and Amy knew that haunting call would remain lodged forever in her memory, alongside the worst of her childhood nightmares where werewolves prowled and lurked and killed.

Another howl arose. Polly shrieked, "Abandon all hope," and hid so deeply in the wardrobe that she was probably well behind the long-abandoned gray coat from which Amy had cut her swatch of werewolf fur.

"And, now," Esther said, extinguishing the lamp, "we hunt."

Each chose a window overlooking the gardens and watched as nearly a dozen werewolves milled about, as if at a social event. When Amy said as much, Esther laughed and said, "Oh, but they do attend grand parties, only as people, not as wolves. Where I am from, high society accepts them, and it is quite fashionable and bold to be the escort to a werewolf."

"You mean, of course, when the moon isn't full."

"Yes. Of course."

"How can one possibly know who is and is not a werewolf?"

"They give signs. They have their ways," said Esther in a most mysterious fashion.

Amy realized she had forgotten to take tally of the werewolves she saw prowling the gardens, but she no longer cared if she won the peppermint stick. Esther could have it. Her prize was in watching the sleek beasts as they lounged and socialized between hunts. They looked much like a picture of wolves she

If there was a full moon in the sky, there would be
werewolves aplenty on the grounds.

had once seen, but broader and fiercer, and much more energetic. Even as they seemed to repose, a paw or tail constantly
twitched, and the glowing eyes carefully took in every movement in the vicinity. Pointed ears stood alert, and massive chests
heaved with the breath of excited hunger.

"This must be the place the most popular werewolves come
to meet," Amy said.

"I like to think as much," Esther agreed. "It's where they con-
verge. Where they come to see and be seen."

"Does Aunt March mind them being out there?"

"I doubt she has any idea. Madame's always asleep well before dark, despite the season, and can't be woken by baying,
screaming, or shrieking. I never told her how they roam the
grounds because I so enjoy watching them. Depending upon her
turn of temperament, she could report them to the Brigade."

"What if the Brigade discovers them and accuses her of being
a sympathizer?"

"Such problems haunt mainly the poor. The wealthy families
in this town have not been jailed or executed very often for
being either a werewolf or a werewolf sympathizer, although
that's changed with the death of Harrison Adams at the hands of
this newly formed Brigade. Right now, the werewolves know
they can come here for a haven. They can relax and be free from
the threat of the Brigade, for that band of men would not dare
tramp about on this property uninvited. Do you ever think, on
the nights with full moons, that the werewolves may also be in
danger?"

"I give it no thought, as they all reside far from my home."

Esther eyed the girl, considered correcting her, but decided
against it. Instead, she said, "See how majestic they are?"

"Yes. They walk about as if they take a great pride in doing so," Amy marveled, face pressed against the windowpane to better observe the fascinating creatures. "I thought werewolves spent the night hunting for meat. I never dreamed they spent it playing."

"The night is long, mademoiselle. They have time for both. The ones you see there now may not be there in the next hour, and there will be others to take their place."

"So they come and go from here throughout the entire night, and you have no idea why?"

"I think they may know Madame. You know, when they aren't in wolf form."

"Know her?"

"Yes, of course. We all know werewolves. They come from all places and all classes. Did you not know that?"

Amy shook her head. "I always thought they lived in their own space, all together."

"No, they are just like us. Rich, poor, happy, sad."

"So do you think, then, that these would be the popular werewolves if they know Aunt March?"

"Well, they would at least be the wealthiest."

Amy watched out the window as she absorbed this information. She wondered if she knew anyone who turned into a beast when the full moon rose every month. A fight began between two of the larger werewolves. They snarled and growled so fervently, the noise could be heard from behind the closed windows, and although the sound aggrieved Amy, it also excited her, and she strained her ears to catch every intonation. The werewolves lunged at each other, biting each other's neck ruffs and rising up to impressive heights on their sturdy back legs. Their lips were pulled back, and in the moon's bright light, she could see the razor sharpness of their dangerous teeth.

"I hope they don't draw blood. I don't care much for the sight of blood," Amy said, blanching.

"They won't. It's merely a game. They do it all the time. See the she-wolf who sits to the side watching?"

"I see the werewolf, but I don't know how you can tell it's a girl."

"It must be because I have watched them for so long. It is a girl, believe me, and she is the prize for the winner of the game."

"The prize?" Amy gasped. "But what if she doesn't care for the winner?"

"I think she likes them both and will be happy for whoever wins."

"Do the girls play games to win a boy?"

"No. At least I have never seen them do so. It's something the males seem to very much enjoy, just as in the rest of mixed society."

"It's all for the men," Polly called out from her hiding place deep in the wardrobe. "It's all for the men."

CHAPTER 16

A Werewolf's Mischief

JO'S SECRET WEIGHED UPON HER, AND SHE FOUND IT HARD not to go about looking mysterious and important. Meg, having learned that the best way to manage Jo was by the law of contraries, refrained from asking Jo what she was withholding, believing her sister would reveal all. But Jo held her air of dignified reserve, although she rather dreaded the company of Laurie, for he was an incorrigible tease, and she feared he would coax from her every word her mother had said about John Brooke and Meg.

She was quite right, for the mischief-loving lad no sooner suspected a mystery than he set himself to finding it. He wheedled, bribed, ridiculed, threatened, and scolded; affected indifference, hoping to surprise the truth from her; declared he knew, then that he didn't care; and at last, by dint of perseverance, he satisfied himself that it concerned Meg and Mr. Brooke. Feeling indignant that he had not been taken into his tutor's confidence, he set his wits to work to devise some proper retaliation for the slight.

Meg absorbed herself in preparations for her father's eventual return, but a change had come over her and she was quite unlike herself. She started when spoken to, blushed when looked at, sat quietly over her sewing with a timid, troubled expression on her face. To her mother's inquiries she simply answered that she was quite well, and Jo's she silenced by begging to be left alone.

Jo feared that Meg felt love in the air, for she was twittery and cross, failed to eat, lay awake, and moped in corners. She heard her sister sing the song Mr. Brooke had given her, and once, Meg said "John," then blushed red as a poppy. "Whatever shall we do?" Jo asked Marmee in alarm.

"Nothing but wait. Let her alone, be kind and patient. Father's coming will settle everything," Marmee replied.

The next day, Jo handed Meg a sealed note that had been left in the postbox. She thought it odd, however, as Teddy never sealed them.

Jo and Marmee were deep in their own affairs when a sound from Meg made them look up to see her staring at the note with a frightened look on her face.

"My child, what is it?" cried her mother, running to her, while Jo tried to take the paper that had done the mischief.

"It's all a mistake—he didn't send it—oh, Jo, how could you do it?" And Meg hid her face in her hands, crying as if her heart was quite broken.

"Me! I've done nothing! What's she talking about?" cried Jo, bewildered.

Marmee took the crumpled note Meg had pulled from her pocket and read it. "It's from John, declaring unrestrained passion and asking that she not tell me and Father."

"It was Teddy who wrote it! That little villain! That's the way he meant to pay me for keeping my word to Mother," Jo howled.

"Jo," Marmee said. "You have played so many pranks, that I am afraid you had a hand in this."

"On my word, Mother!" She grabbed the note and scanned it. "If I *had* taken a part in it, I would have done better than these flat words."

"Oh, dear," Meg cried. "It's so like his writing."

"Oh, Meg, you didn't answer the first note?" cried Mrs. March, quickly.

When Meg confessed that she had, Jo ran to the Laurence house to summon Laurie. He came quickly, received his dressing-down from the women with humble apology, and made his way quickly back home, tail between his legs like a scolded dog. As soon as he had gone, Jo wished she had been less severe and more forgiving; Meg had quickly forgiven his folly.

While Jo battled her conscience, Mr. Laurence and Laurie were engaged in their own skirmish, fueled by Laurie's staunch refusal to tell his grandfather the details of the drama played out at the March house. The topic quickly drifted awry and burrowed into the habitual nettles that resurfaced over and over again in the Laurence men's relationship.

"You wonder why I don't strive to do everything according to your codes and principles," exploded Laurie. "But it would be wasted effort on my part. My father did everything you asked of him, and it was yet short to please you. He went to school, into the family business, and married a werewolf, all in accord with your wishes. But his fault was that he did not marry the werewolf you wanted him to, rather marrying one whom he dearly loved, but who was not good enough in your eyes. Nobody is good enough for you, sir, and I certainly can never be, having come from that 'Italian werewolf,' as you call my mother."

"Your mother was lovely, and one of the most accomplished musicians I have ever had the honor of hearing," countered Mr. Laurence.

"I, too, am a musician, yet you deny me honing this one gift I have from my dear mother simply because you have no respect for it, or for her."

"I had the utmost respect for the woman, her music, and her husband."

"Then why did you disown my father simply for marrying a beautiful and talented Italian woman?"

"There are things that you, at your age and lacking experience, cannot understand, boy, so leave it at that."

"I understand enough. I understand your stubbornness broke up our family and that my father was begrudged the luxury of dying on his home soil, instead perishing in a foreign land!"

"Stop dredging up the past! This is none of your business!" Mr. Laurence raged, grasping and shaking the stunned boy until his eyes snapped shut and his teeth rattled in his skull. "Is this why you defy me, you think you avenge your father? You'd do well to check yourself, young man."

"I'd do better to disappear, if only to deny you the pleasure of expelling me from your house!" Laurie spat, breaking away from the old man and rushing pell-mell up the stairs just as Jo stepped onto the garden path leading from her house to theirs.

Once admitted to the house, Jo had to pound on the door of Laurie's little study, as he refused to come out. He made threats of all sorts if the pounding did not stop but finally yanked the door open, and acted surprised to see Jo.

"Whatever is the matter? Surely our little lecture did not put you into this dark state of mind."

"No. I've been shaken and I won't bear it," he growled indignantly.

"Who did it?" demanded Jo.

"Grandfather. For refusing to tell him why you summoned me over."

"Go make up with him. I'm certain he's sorry."

"Hanged if I do! I'd rather run away. Come on then. Why not? We can run off to Washington to see Brooke, and you can surprise your father."

For a moment it looked as if Jo would agree, for as wild as the plan was, it suited her. Her eyes kindled as they turned wistfully toward the window and she dreamed shortly of a life on the road with a werewolf companion. She was tired of care and confinement and longed for a change, but her eyes fell on the old house opposite, and she shook her head with sorrowful decision.

"If I was a boy, we'd run away together, and have a capital time. But I'm a miserable girl, and I must be proper. Please don't tempt me more, Teddy."

"I thought you had more spirit than this!" Laurie sniffed.

Jo walked away, feeling defeated and helpless, leaving Laurie bent over an old railroad map, with his head propped in both hands.

Jo went to Mr. Laurence's study. Her knees shook a bit when she realized she was going to be alone in the room with the elder werewolf; she was more than accustomed to Laurie by now, but the old man was sterner and far more mysterious. She reminded herself that he needed the moon to turn into a beast, and was no threat in the soft daylight of the afternoon. The shaggy eyebrows unbent a little when he saw her, and he rolled the library ladder over and pretended to search for a book.

"Are you here to tell me what the boy did?"

"He did do wrong, but we forgave him. We promised, all around, to never speak a word about it to anyone," she said, hoping her voice was even and that it did not expose her fear.

"He shall not shelter himself behind a promise from you soft-hearted girls. Out with it, Jo!"

"I cannot tell, sir. My mother forbade it."

The old man sighed so deeply, his shoulders dropped. "I'll forgive the boy if he held his tongue because he promised, rather than from obstinacy. I suppose you think me unkind to him."

"Oh, dear, no, sir. You are rather too kind sometimes, then just a trifle hasty when he tries your patience. Don't you think you are?"

"You're right, girl, I am! I love the boy, but he tries my patience past bearing, and I don't know how it will end, if we go on so."

"I'll tell you," Jo said, gazing straight at him to gain his full attention. "He'll run away."

Mr. Laurence's ruddy face changed suddenly, and he sat down, casting a troubled glance at the picture of a handsome man that hung over his table. It was Laurie's father, who *had* run away in his youth. Jo fancied the old werewolf remembered and regretted the past, and she wished she had held her tongue.

Mr. Laurence gave her a sharp look and put on his spectacles, saying slowly, "You are a sly puss, but I don't mind being managed by you and Beth. Here, let's be done with this nonsense." He wrote a note, using terms one gentleman would use to another after offering some deep insult. He sent Jo upstairs with it, along with orders to bring the boy down for dinner. Laurie did relent and went to partake of humble pie dutifully with his grandfather, who was quite saintly in temper, and overwhelmingly respectful in manner, all the rest of the day.

Everyone thought the matter ended, and the little cloud blown over; but the mischief was done, for though others forgot it, Meg remembered. She never alluded to a certain person, but she thought of him a good deal, dreamed dreams more than ever; and once, Jo, rummaging her sister's desk for stamps, found a bit of paper with the words "Mrs. John Brooke" scribbled over it again and again. She groaned tragically and cast it into the fire.

...

CHAPTER 17

Home for Christmas

LIKE SUNSHINE AFTER A STORM WERE THE PEACEFUL weeks that followed. Beth was soon able to lie on the study sofa all day, amusing herself with her beloved cats and sewing for her dolls. Her once active limbs were stiff and feeble, so Jo took her for daily airings about the house in her strong arms. Meg cooked delicate messes for "the dear," and Amy, a loyal slave of her turquoise ring, celebrated her return by giving away as many of her treasures as she could prevail on her sisters to accept.

As Christmas approached, the usual mysteries began to haunt the house, and Jo frequently convulsed the family by proposing utterly impossible or magnificently absurd ceremonies in honor of this unusually merry Christmas. Laurie was equally impracticable, and would have had bonfires, sky-rockets, and triumphal arches, if given his way. After many skirmishes and snubbings, the ambitious pair were quenched, and went about with forlorn faces, which were rather belied by explosions of laughter when the two got together.

Several days of unusually mild weather finally ushered in a splendid Christmas day. Hannah "felt in her bones" that it was going to be "an uncommonly plummy day," and she proved herself a true prophetess, for everybody and everything seemed to abound with grand success.

Laurie and Jo, like elves, had worked by night, and conjured up a comical surprise. Out in the garden stood a stately snow maiden, crowned with holly, bearing a basket of fruit and flowers in one hand, a great roll of new music in the other, a perfect rainbow of an afghan around her chilly shoulders, and a Christmas carol to Beth, issuing from her lips, on a pink paper streamer. How Beth laughed when she saw it! How Laurie ran up and down to bring in the gifts, and what ridiculous speeches Jo made as she presented them!

"I'm so full of happiness, that, if Father was only here, I couldn't hold one drop more," said Beth, sighing with contentment as she huddled in the soft, crimson merino wrap from her mother.

"So am I," added Jo.

"I'm sure I am," echoed Amy, poring over her engraved copy of the Madonna and Child, which her mother had given her in a pretty frame.

"Of course I am," Meg added, smoothing the silvery folds of her first silk dress, a gift that Mr. Laurence had insisted on giving her.

"How can *I* be otherwise?" said Mrs. March, holding her husband's letter that said he would soon be with them. Her hand went up to caress the brooch made of gray and golden, chestnut and dark brown hair, which the girls had just fastened on her breast.

Now and then, in this workaday world, things do happen in delightful storybook fashion. Half an hour after everyone had declared herself almost too happy to hold even one drop more of joy, Laurie opened the parlour door and popped his head in very quietly. In a queer, breathless voice, he said, "Here's another Christmas present for the March family."

Before the women could protest the generosity of the Laurences, he stepped aside, and in his place stood a tall man, muffled up to the eyes, leaning on the arm of another. There was a stampede as Mr. March became invisible in the embrace of four pairs of loving arms; Jo disgraced herself by nearly fainting away, and had to be doctored by Laurie in the china-closet; Mr. Brooke kissed Meg entirely by mistake, as he somewhat incoherently explained; and Amy, the dignified, tumbled over a stool, and, never stopping to get up, hugged and cried over her father's boots in a most touching manner. Mrs. March was the first to recover herself, and held up her hand with a warning, "Hush! Remember Beth is resting."

But it was too late. The study door flew open, and joy put strength into the feeble limbs as the crimson-clad Beth ran straight into her father's arms. Full hearts overflowed with the sweetness of the moment.

Mr. Brooke suddenly insisted that Mr. March needed his rest, so both invalids were ordered to repose, which they did, by both sitting in one big chair, and talking hard. Meg was violently poking the fire, the warmth of the flames unable to disguise the flush of her cheeks. Jo saw, and understood, and she stalked grimly away to get wine and beef tea, muttering to herself as she slammed the door, "I hate estimable young men with brown eyes!"

There never was such a Christmas dinner as they had that day. The fat turkey was stuffed, browned, and decorated; so was the plum pudding, which melted deliciously in one's mouth; likewise the jellies, in which Amy reveled like a fly in a honey pot. Everything turned out well, which was a mercy, Hannah said, "for my mind was so flustered it's a merrycle I didn't roast the pudding and stuff the turkey with raisins."

Mr. Laurence and his grandson dined with them; also Mr. Brooke—at whom Jo glowered darkly, to Laurie's infinite amusement. At the head of the table, two easy chairs stood side by side, in which sat Beth and her father, feasting modestly on chicken and a little fruit.

Jo did not stare at the plates but wondered what would have happened if the Brigade had, at that very moment, stormed into their house to examine the Christmas dinner each had chosen and placed on their dish, for the Laurence men ate only the meat, skin, and fat of the turkey.

Everyone drank to good health, told stories, sang songs, "reminisced," as the old folks say, and had a thoroughly wonderful time. A sleigh ride had been planned, but the girls refused to leave their father; so the guests departed early, and, as twilight gathered, the happy family sat together around the fire.

"Do you remember?" Jo asked. "Just one year ago we were groaning over the dismal Christmas we expected to have."

"A rather pleasant year on the whole!" said Meg, smiling at the fire and secretly congratulating herself on having treated Mr. Brooke with dignity.

"I think it's been a pretty hard one," said Amy, watching the ring shine on her hand with thoughtful eyes. "Except for the werewolves, who seem to have found plenty to eat in Mr. Davis and other assorted poor souls."

"Ah, you should see all the werewolves at the battlefields. I can barely count them. At least they eat well once a month, which is more than can be said, more often than not, for the other soldiers." Mr. March sighed.

"All that matters is that we have you back," whispered Beth, who sat on her father's knee.

"Rather a rough road for you to travel, my little pilgrims, but you have got on bravely, and I think the burdens are bound to tumble off very soon," said Mr. March, looking with fatherly satisfaction at the four young faces gathered around him.

"It's singing time now," Beth said, slipping from her father's lap and seating herself at the dear little piano. She touched the keys, and in the sweet voice the others never dared to think they would hear again, sang a quaint and fitting hymn.

Like bees swarming after their queen, mother and daughters hovered about Mr. March the next day, neglecting everything to look at, wait upon, and listen to the new invalid, whose greatest danger was now to be killed by kindness.

Jo had just scolded Meg for her absentmindedness, which she suspected was caused by that virus John Brooke, and Meg was responding in kind, by arguing, when there came a soft rap at the door.

"Good afternoon, I came to get my umbrella—that is, I came to see how your father finds himself today," said Mr. Brooke, staring beyond Jo, who had answered the door.

Jo glared at the man. She so wished that Laurie had confided in her, told her that he was a werewolf. Then she would be able to ask him, to beg him, to rip this man into the tiniest of pieces during the next full moon so that he could not infect her loving family and take her sister away. Strong words sat on the tip of her tongue, but before Jo could spit out her reply, Meg appeared and said, "Mother will like to see you. Pray, sit down. I'll call her."

"Don't go; are you afraid of me, Margaret?"

Jo stomped off as Meg smiled and sat. She wet her lips and said, "How can I be afraid when you have been so kind to Father? I only wish I could thank you."

"Shall I tell you how?" said Mr. Brooke, taking her small

hand suddenly in both of his. There was so much love in his brown eyes as he stared at her that Meg's heart began to flutter.

"I'm too young," Meg faltered, wondering why she was so flustered, yet rather enjoying it.

"I'll wait. As long as I must."

It was at this interesting moment that Aunt March hobbled in. "Bless me, what's all this?" she cried with a rap of her cane as she glanced from the pale young gentleman to the scarlet-faced young woman.

"This is a friend of Father's," Meg stammered.

"Well, I insist on knowing what your father's friend was saying to make you as red as a peony. I know mischief when I see it."

"We were merely talking. Mr. Brooke came for his umbrella—"

"Yes, and I shall go fetch it now," Mr. Brooke said, hastening into the other room.

"Brooke? You mean that Laurence boy's tutor? Now I see it all. You haven't gone and accepted him, have you, child?"

"Hush! He'll hear you!"

"If you mean to marry him, not one penny of my money ever goes to you. Remember that, and be a sensible girl."

"I shall marry whom I please, Aunt March, and you are free to leave your money to whomever you like."

"Get off your high horse, girl. You'll be sorry, by and by, for not taking my advice. You'll be sorry when you've tried love in a cottage and found it a failure."

"It can't be a worse one than the loneliness some people find in their big houses!"

Aunt March put on her glasses and looked at the girl, for she had never heard her speak in such a manner. She felt it best to start anew, in a better spirit. "Now, Meg. Be reasonable. I mean my advice kindly. You ought to marry well and help your family. It's your duty to make a rich match."

"Father and Mother don't think so. They like John."

"Your parents, my dear girl, have all the worldly wisdom of two infants."

"I'm glad of that!" Meg declared stoutly. "I couldn't find a better, kinder man if I waited half my life. He is good and wise. He's got heaps of talent, and he's energetic and brave. Everyone likes and respects him, and I'm proud to think he cares for me, even though I'm poor and young and silly."

"Well, I wash my hands of the whole affair! You are a willful child, and you've lost more than you know by this bit of folly. I'm so disappointed in you, I haven't the strength or will to see your father now. Don't expect anything from me when you are married. I'm done with you forever."

Slamming the door in Meg's face, Aunt March drove off. Meg turned around to find Mr. Brooke standing there. He had heard it all. So had Amy, who gave a small shudder. Surely, marrying a poor man was the worst match a woman could make. She agreed with Aunt March, but her sister needed her support— now more than ever. She went and took her sister's arm on one side and John Brooke's on the other and led them, together, into the parlour.

Soon after, Jo came downstairs, and hearing no sound at the parlour door, was satisfied that Meg had sent Mr. Brooke away. She was about to begin the celebration when she turned and found the objectionable man and her sister embracing.

A warm domestic scene in the parlour followed. A glum Jo listened, with the grave, quiet look that best became her, as the family exclaimed excitedly that Meg and Mr. Brooke planned to marry in a few years. Her father and mother sat together, quietly reliving the first chapter of the romance that, for them, had begun some twenty years ago. Amy was drawing the lovers, who sat apart in a beautiful world of their own, and Beth lay on her sofa, talking cheerily with Laurie as he leaned on the back of her chair.

CHAPTER 18

Mr. March's Calling

THREE YEARS PASSED, BRINGING FEW CHANGES TO THE quiet March family. The war was over, and Mr. March safely at home, busy with his books and his small parish, which admired his studiousness, wisdom, and charity, and found in him a minister. Earnest young men found the gray-headed scholar as young at heart as they, despite his fifty years of hard experience, for those years had distilled no bitter drop. Thoughtful or troubled women instinctively brought to him their doubts and sorrows, assured of finding gentle sympathy and wise counsel. Sinners told their sins to the pure-hearted old man and found salvation; gifted men found a companion in him, and ambitious men caught glimpses of nobler ambitions than their own.

He prayed constantly: for the war fallen, for those taken by the werewolves, and for the werewolves themselves, for the Brigade was strong now, their numbers bloated by the returned soldiers, and a week did not pass that there was not a werewolf accusation.

War widows and their families and war veterans with grave injuries were of particular concern to Mr. March, and more and more amputees and disfigured soldiers traveled long distances to find him. He did what he could to shelter them, feed them, clothe them, and comfort them, but longed to find a way to help them make their own way in the post-war world. He awoke one morning charged with an energy that sent him spinning away from his family without one bite of breakfast, for a dream had been sent to him and he could spare no time before setting out to turn that dream into a reality.

He went out and called before him all the amputees and injured men he could find and told them to go off and seek others in their same sad situation. He toiled the long day through, and at nightfall, Jo went to him to bring him back home.

"Mother sent me for you," Jo said. "You missed every meal today, and she is keeping a plate warm for you."

"My soul is well fed," he said with a smile. "I have a divine plan, one sent to me from heaven above, one that will assist the most horribly wounded of my soldiers."

"Your soldiers?" Jo asked with some trepidation, for she and her sisters wanted some of their father's attention, and it sounded as if he was diverting the little bit they got of it elsewhere.

"My soldiers," he said, nodding. "My injured and maimed, my disfigured and unsightly. I have a way to help them thrive, to show them that they can conquer life's demand for basic needs despite their loss of limbs, hope, and love."

"What is your plan, then, Father?"

"An exhibit. An exhibit of their wounds."

"You risk having others shun them and mock them. It would be a cruel display!"

"Not cruel at all. It can remind us all of the sacrifices that have been made. It can lead to the poor men earning some money of their own, for the exhibition would not be free. Perhaps they can find homes and jobs from those who pay to see them. If nothing else, it will educate the public, show them the results of war, and force them to think of what sacrifice they can make to repay those already made."

"Then you will need nourishment," Jo said, seeing the fire in her father's eyes and knowing no man or woman on earth would quench what he had made up his mind to accomplish. "Come home and eat, rest, see your family, and start afresh the day after tomorrow with vigor. Tomorrow you have a daughter to marry off, and you must be at your best for that."

Jo knew that to outsiders it appeared that the five energetic women ruled the March household, and so they did in many things, but her father, the quiet scholar sitting among his books, was still the head of the family, the household conscience, anchor, and comforter. If Mr. March had a goal set in place, the women had no choice but to step aside or offer their own sweat to help him accomplish it.

"I thought perhaps John would like to be involved, too," Mr. March said as he and Jo walked home. "Poor boy, he received no stars and bars, although he deserved them for his war service and his injury. His bookkeeping job is not totally fulfilling, although he seems satisfied in an honestly earned salary."

"Far better than running risks with borrowed money."

"Yes, the boy has good sense and sturdy independence," Mr. March said. "But he needs additional stimulation."

"I'm sure my dear sister will stimulate him sufficiently," Jo said with a frown. "We could have offered him a place in planning the wedding. Mother doesn't even make her missionary visits to the wounded boys and soldiers' widows, being too absorbed with Meg's affairs."

"I wish I could give your sister as grand a wedding as Sallie Gardner and Ned Moffat's was, but she told me she feels that John's patient love can offer her such a splendid future, and she feels the happiest, richest girl in the world. She is content with the little brown house he found for them, finds it altogether charming from garret to cellar."

"It is all they need, and more. There is simple but sturdy furniture, plenty of books, a few fine pictures, and a stand of flowers in the bay window. We sisters did what we could to refresh and cheer it, and artistic Amy even arranged different-colored soaps to match the different-colored rooms," Jo pointed out.

"I pray more that her cupboard always has food, her back clothing, and her hearth fire, than worrying if one color matches another."

Jo said nothing, so Mr. March patted her hand that held his arm and continued, "No man will have to worry about support for you, my little woman, already earning a full dollar a column for your romance stories."

"You mean for my rubbish?"

"There are people who enjoy them. They lift their spirits, so you enhance their day. There is no nobler way to spend one's time than in making others glad."

Jo shrugged. "Aunt March doesn't seem any worse off for the lack of me."

"She and Amy get on just fine. You better serve by being home and reading to Beth."

Poor Beth. The fever had left her delicate, with a weakened heart. Not an invalid exactly, but no longer the rosy, healthy creature she had once been; yet always hopeful, happy, and serene, busy with the quiet duties she loved. She had made enough dusters, holders, dishcloths and piece bags to last Meg until her silver wedding anniversary.

"I hear Laurie is bringing home a college friend to attend the wedding," Jo said, wanting to change the subject.

"How did you hear?"

"I didn't have to be told. Amy is rushing to prepare herself so she can bask in the smiles of adoration. She's quite a belle among them."

"She has always been endowed with the gift of fascination. She is just beginning to learn how to best use it. You yourself seem quite in your element around those college boys."

"Yes. But they don't fall in love with me as they do with Amy."

"What good does it do to hold many hearts when you can only be true to one?"

The pair arrived home to find Laurie just going up the path to their house.

"Where is your friend? Did you come back alone?" Jo asked immediately.

"Yes, sad story. The fellow fell ill and is convalescing at school."

Inside, Laurie pulled Amy's hair ribbon and handed Meg a parcel containing a watchman's rattle.

"It's a useful thing to have in the house in case of fire or thieves," observed Laurie amid the laughter of the girls. "Any time John is away, and you get frightened, just swing that out the window and it will rouse the neighborhood in a jiffy." Laurie gave them a sample of its powers that made them cover up their ears.

"That will certainly scare even the werewolves away!" Amy said with a giggle.

Beth and Jo both glanced at Laurie, but he showed no reaction.

In his love of jokes, this boy gentleman, though nearly through college, was as much a boy as ever. His latest whim had been to bring, each time he came home, some new, useful, and ingenious article for the young housekeeper. So Meg had received a bag of remarkable clothespins; next, a wonderful nutmeg grater, which fell to pieces at its first trial; a knife cleaner that spoilt all the knives; a sweeper that took the nap off the carpet and left the dirt; labor-saving soap that took the skin off one's hands; infallible cements that stuck firmly to nothing but the fingers of the deluded buyer; and every kind of tinware, from a savings bank for odd pennies to a wonderful boiler that would wash articles in its own steam, with every prospect of exploding in the process.

In vain, Meg had begged him to stop, but he was possessed with a mania for patronizing Yankee ingenuity, and seeing his friends fully furnished forth, so each week held some fresh absurdity.

As Laurie was leaving for home, Jo offered to walk him out and said, "Now, Teddy, I want to talk seriously to you about tomorrow. You must promise to behave well, and not cut up any pranks and spoil our plans. I know you always save yourself at school through frank confession and honorable atonement when you pull pranks there, but this is to be Meg's only wedding ceremony, so we must remain sober throughout."

"Not a prank," Laurie vowed.

"And I implore you not to look at me during the ceremony; I shall certainly laugh if you do."

"You won't see me; you'll be crying so hard that the thick fog around you will obscure any view of me."

"I never cry unless for some great affliction!"

"Such as old fellows going away to college, hey?" cut in Laurie with a suggestive laugh.

"Don't be a peacock. I only moaned a bit to keep my sisters company."

"Jo, don't lecture me anymore, there's a good soul. I have enough all through the week, and I like to enjoy myself when I come home. Oh, by the way, my friend Parker is really getting desperate about Amy. He talks about her constantly, writes her poetry, and moons about in a most suspicious manner. He'd better nip his little passion in the bud, hadn't he?" asked Laurie, in a confidential, elder-brotherly tone after a minute's silence.

"Of course he had; we don't want any more marrying in this family for years and years to come!"

"It's a fast age, and I don't know what we are coming to, but you'll go next, Jo, and we'll be left lamenting," said Laurie, shaking his head over the degeneracy of the times.

"Me! Don't be alarmed; I'm not one of the agreeable sort," Jo said with a forced laugh. "Nobody will want me, and it's a mercy, for there should always be one old maid in a family."

"You won't give anyone a chance," said Laurie with a sidelong glance and a little more color than before in his sunburnt face. "You won't show the soft side of your character; and if a fellow gets a look at it by accident, and can't help showing that he likes it, you throw cold water over him and get so thorny no one dares touch or look at you."

"Well, I don't like that sort of thing; I'm too busy to be worried with such nonsense, and I think it's dreadful to break up families so. Now, don't say any more about it; Meg's wedding has turned all our heads, and we talk of nothing but lovers and such absurdities. I don't wish to get cross, so let's change the subject"; and Jo looked quite ready to fling cold water on the slightest provocation.

Whatever his feelings might have been, Laurie found a vent for them in a long low whistle, and the fearful prediction, as they parted at the gate, "Mark my words, Jo, you'll go next."

CHAPTER 19

A Happy, Humble Wedding

HE JUNE ROSES OVER THE PORCH WERE AWAKE BRIGHT
and early on that morning, rejoicing with all their hearts in the
cloudless sunshine. Their ruddy little faces were flushed with
excitement as they swung in the wind, whispering to one another what they had seen; for some peeped in at the dining room
windows, where the feast was spread, some climbed up to nod
and smile at the sisters as they dressed the bride, others waved a
welcome to those who came and went on various errands in garden, porch, and hall. All of them, from the rosiest full-blown
flower to the palest baby bud, offered their tribute of beauty and
fragrance to the gentle mistress who had loved and tended them
for so long.

Meg looked very like a rose herself; for all that was best and
sweetest in her heart and soul seemed to have bloomed into her
face that day, making it fair and tender, with a charm more beautiful than beauty. She would have neither silk, lace, nor orange
flowers. "I don't want to look strange or fixed up today," she
said. "I don't want a fashionable wedding, but only those about
me whom I love, and to them I wish to look and be my familiar
self."

So she made her wedding gown herself, sewing into it tender
hopes and innocent romances of a girlish heart. Her sisters

braided up her pretty hair, and the only ornaments she wore were the lilies of the valley, which "her John" liked best of all the flowers that grew.

"You *do* look like our own dear Meg, only so sweet and lovely that I should hug you if it wouldn't crumple your dress," cried Amy, surveying her with delight, when all was done.

"Then I am satisfied. But please hug and kiss me, everyone, and don't mind my dress; I want a great many crumples put into it today!" And Meg opened her arms to her sisters, who clung about her with childish, innocent faces for a minute, feeling that the new love had not changed the old.

"Now I am going to tie John's cravat for him, and then stay with Father for a few minutes, quietly in his study." Meg ran down to perform these little ceremonies, and then to follow her mother wherever she went, conscious that, in spite of the smiles on her motherly face, there was a secret sorrow hidden in the motherly heart at the flight of the first bird from the nest.

As the younger girls stood together, giving the last touches to their simple toilet, they saw themselves older and changed. Jo's angles had softened, and she had learned to carry herself with ease, if not grace. Her curly crop had lengthened into a thick coil, more becoming to the small head atop the tall figure. There was a fresh color to her brown cheeks, a soft shine in her eyes, and only gentle words fell, this day, from her sharp tongue.

Beth had grown slender, pale, and quieter than ever. Her beautiful, kind eyes were larger, and in them dwelt an expression that saddened, although it was not sad in itself. It was the shadow of pain that touched the young face with such pathetic patience. She never complained, rather always spoke hopefully of "being better soon."

Amy was the "flower of the family," for at sixteen she had the air and bearing of a full-grown woman—not beautiful, but possessed of that indescribable charm called grace. One could see it in the lines of her figure, the make and motion of her hands, the flow of her dress, the droop of her hair—unconscious, yet harmonious, and as attractive to most as beauty itself. Amy's nose still afflicted her, for it never *would* grow Grecian; so did her mouth, being too wide, and having a decided chin beneath it. These offending features gave character to her whole face, but she never could see it, and consoled herself with her wonderfully fair complexion, keen blue eyes, and curls, more golden and abundant than ever.

All three wore suits of thin silvery gray (their best gowns for the summer), with blush roses in their hair and bosoms; and all three looked just what they were—fresh-faced, happy-hearted girls, pausing a moment in their busy lives to read with wistful eyes the sweetest chapter in the romance of womanhood.

There were to be no ceremonious performances; everything was to be as natural and homelike as possible. So when Aunt March arrived, she was scandalized to see the bride come running to welcome and lead her in, to find the bridegroom fastening up a garland that had fallen down, and to catch a glimpse of the paternal minister marching upstairs with a grave countenance and a wine bottle under each arm.

"Upon my word! Such a state of things!" cried the old lady, taking the seat of honor prepared for her, and settling the folds of her lavender *moiré* with great rustle. "You shouldn't be seen until the last minute, child."

"I'm not a show, Aunty, and no one is coming to stare at me, to criticize my dress or count the cost of my luncheon. I'm too happy to care what anyone says or thinks, and I'm going to have my little wedding just as I like it. John, dear, here's your hammer." And away Meg went to help "that man" in his highly improper employment.

Mr. Brooke didn't even say "Thank you," but as he stooped for the unromantic tool, he kissed his little bride behind the folding door, with a look that made Aunt March whisk out her pocket handkerchief, with a sudden dew in her sharp old eyes.

A flock of cousins arrived, or, as Beth used to say when a child, "The party came in." Aunt March eyed them disapprovingly, and then her glance fell on Laurie. "Don't let him come near me; he worries me worse than a flock of mosquitoes," whispered the old lady to Amy, as the room filled and Laurie's head towered above the rest.

"He has promised to be very good today, and he can be perfectly elegant if he likes," returned Amy with a sly smile she hid beneath a sweet one. She would later tell him of the old aunt's statement, which assured he would haunt the old lady with a devotion that would nearly distract her.

There was no bridal procession, but a sudden silence fell upon the room as Mr. March and the young pair took their places under the green arch. Mother and sisters gathered close, as if loath to give Meg up. The fatherly voice broke more than once, which only seemed to make the service more beautiful and solemn. The bridegroom's hand trembled visibly, and no one heard his soft replies, but Meg looked straight up into her husband's eyes and said, "I will!" with such tender trust in her own face and voice that her mother's heart rejoiced and Aunt March sniffed audibly.

Jo did *not* cry, although she was near to it once, and was only saved when Laurie stared fixedly at her with a comical mixture of merriment and emotion in his wicked black eyes. Beth kept her face hidden on her mother's shoulder, but Amy stood like a graceful statue, with a most becoming ray of sunshine touching her white forehead and the flower in her hair.

It wasn't at all the thing, but the moment she was fairly married, Meg cried, "The first kiss for Marmee!" and, turning, gave it with her heart on her lips. The next fifteen minutes, she shared her joy with everyone, from Mr. Laurence, who stood with wet eyes shining proudly, to old Hannah, who, adorned with a headdress fearfully and wonderfully made, fell upon her in the hall, crying, with a sob and a chuckle fighting in her throat, "Bless you, deary, a hundred times!"

Speeches were made, everyone trying to say something brilliant. Laughter was ready and hearts were light. But for drink, only water, lemonade, and coffee were found, and Laurie, wishing to serve the bride, appeared before her and asked, "Has Jo smashed all the wine bottles by accident? I am certain I saw some lying about this morning."

"No; your grandfather kindly offered us his best, and Aunt March sent some, but Father put away a little for Beth and dispatched the rest to the Soldiers' Home. You know he thinks wine should be used only in illness, and he is much obsessed with injured soldiers of late."

"I, too, have noticed that, and he said he wanted to talk to me about an idea that came to him in a dream that could much benefit our war heroes."

"He itches to get on with his cause, and this day torments him," Meg said with a sad smile.

"No matter his goals, his heart is here, where it belongs and where he wishes it to be. Don't for even a moment think otherwise."

After lunch, all the married people danced around the new-made husband and wife with joined hands, as the Germans do, while bachelors and spinsters pranced in couples outside. Laurie promenaded down the path with Amy, showing such infectious spirit and skill that everyone else followed their example without a murmur. The crowning joke was Mr. Laurence and Aunt March, for when the stately old gentleman *chasséed* solemnly up to the old lady, she just tucked her cane under her arm and hopped briskly away to join hands with the rest and dance around the bridal pair, while the young folks pervaded the garden like butterflies on a midsummer day.

Beth paled, sad at seeing Mr. Laurence dancing about so gleefully when she felt too weak to join in, and Jo led her away to sit down, and covered her with a lovely flowered quilt perfect for the occasion.

"I have not been so active since well before my illness," Beth said, breathing heavily.

"It's a lovely wedding, is it not?" Jo smiled, smoothing her sister's skirt and pulling the quilt over to cover her feet.

"I believe Meg and John will be very happy. Do you know why?"

"No. Why?"

"I recently heard that it is rumored to be very good luck to have a werewolf attend your wedding. And we know there are at least two here."

"Where did you hear that?" Jo asked, never having heard it herself but liking it and wanting to believe it.

"From a friend."

"Which friend?"

Beth shrugged. "Perhaps it was one of the cats who told me."

Jo exploded with laughter. "And how, pray tell, would the cats know?"

"Why, they hear things from the many other cats who wander this way. A great deal can be learned from them, for they know how to sit very, very quietly and listen."

"Well then, I imagine they can tell us a great deal we are too loud and busy to discover on our own," Jo said with a thoughtful nod.

When everyone was out of breath and leaving for home, Aunt March told Meg, "I wish you well, dear. I heartily wish you well, but I think you'll be sorry for it." As for the bridegroom, she warned, "You've got a treasure, young man. See that you deserve it."

Meg and John's little house was not far away, and the only bridal journey Meg had was the quiet walk with John from the old house to the new.

Before they left, the family gathered around Meg. She took her mother in her arms. "Don't feel I am separated from you, Marmee, dear, or that I love you any less for loving John so much." She promised to visit every day, and expected each of them to come to see her and her new husband often, if for no other reason than to laugh at her housekeeping struggles.

The March family stood watching her, with faces full of love and hope and tender pride, as she walked away, leaning on her husband's arm, with her hands full of flowers and the June sunshine brightening her happy face. And so Meg's married life began.

...

CHAPTER 20

Amy's Howling Humiliation

AS IF A SECRET SOCIETY OF TWO, BETH AND MR. MARCH nestled together and hatched a fabulous plot to produce the Exhibit of Amputees. Together, they approached Jo and Amy, asking that they contribute their skills.

"Jo, we need your expertise for staging. How should we present the men and their injuries? Should they be brought out together or one at a time? Should the injuries be displayed from simplest to worst? And against what backdrop?" Mr. March asked. "And Amy, your artistic talents are needed, so that all may see and be instantly impressed. How the men dress, and how the stage is prepared, is of paramount importance, for we have only one chance to catch the attention of the audience, and from there we have the challenge of holding it."

With wide, frightened eyes, Amy looked to Jo, who nodded.

"I would be happy to help in any way I can, Father," Amy replied.

"And I," said Jo.

"We also need your assistance with the fliers and posters. We thought Jo could write them and Amy draw them," Beth added. "I would be happy to color in the designs or copy the script once everything is written out clearly and effectively."

"Of course," both sisters said, almost in unison.

"When will this take place?" Jo asked.

"Not as soon as I'd like," Mr. March admitted. "We need time to prepare, and we must allow ample opportunity to spread the word. But first we have to gather our amputees. I am also hoping to have a guest speaker. Mr. James Edward Hanger, from Virginia, who was the war's first amputee. While recovering, he invented limbs that replace those lost. Imagine, a cane that actually slips on the leg and allows one to walk again! I am corresponding with him, and we both feel that many of those in attendance may be willing to purchase these limbs for some of the wounded men."

"That's wonderful, Father. Just let me know what to do and when," Jo said.

Later, alone together in the garret, where they could not be overheard, Amy ranted that she wanted no part of the sickening display her father and sister planned. "What will people think? What will they say?"

"What does it matter?" Jo shrugged. "The more I think of this, the more sense I see in it. Only through education will we be able to open people's eyes to the plight of these men."

"You are as bad as they are!" Amy cried, her face reddened with outrage. "I have no contributions to offer. I want to be nowhere near these men and their stumps, lesions, and gashes."

"They can't help their condition. I'm certain they wish they were still complete and unmarred. Let me remind you, dear sister, that they lost parts of themselves fighting for a noble cause."

"Is madness a disease as infectious as scarlet fever? Beth's madness comes from her fever, and Father's from the war, but you are beginning to sound every bit as mad."

"How can you say that?" Jo said angrily. "They are free thinkers, but I would hardly call them mad."

"Beth speaks to her dolls and cats all day, claiming to share secrets and wisdom. Father is obsessed not with people but rather with the hideous injuries to their flesh. I am quite justified in calling this a madness!"

"Call it that all you care to, within these walls, but I never want to hear you accuse either of them of such in earshot of another living soul."

"Even Beth's cats?"

Jo glowered at her sister and tried to sort out the myriad of sharp replies that ran through her head, so she could spit out the most scathing. But she was unable to separate the swirling words one from another, so simply stood there mute.

"Oh, that's right. I can't say anything they would overhear, or they'd tell all the other cats," Amy taunted.

"Stop now, Amy," Jo warned.

"Beth also has delusions about werewolves. Did you know that? She thinks Laurie to be one!"

Jo felt the blood drain from her face, and she prayed her sister would not notice. Her heart lurched in her chest at the thought of Amy spilling Laurie and his grandfather's secret and their two dear neighbors then being dragged off to be cruelly executed by the Brigade.

"Her fever was high," Jo said in a shaky voice. "But her delusions harm nobody, and she and Father now have a creative and very positive outlet for their energies, so allow them their project, Amy."

"What will become of this family, with two lunatics among us?" Amy asked, tears beginning to spill from her bright blue eyes.

"It isn't as bad as all that, I tell you," Jo insisted, knowing she should hold and comfort her aggrieved sister, but simply not caring to.

"It is. It is as bad as all that," Amy said, stomping her foot. "I know they will embarrass me. I am finally making something of myself. Laurie's college friends like me. College boys, Jo! And I am taking drawing classes with people from some very important families. But it will all fall to shreds if Father and Beth display that they are odd in the head for all to see."

"You're ashamed of us," Jo said softly, and then louder, "Amy March, you are ashamed of us!"

"Not of you, Jo."

"If you are ashamed of any of us, then you are ashamed of all of us," Jo said. "Well, we don't need you. I have a bit of an artistic hand, and an eye for color. I can happily do both my part and yours for the exhibit."

"Then do it," Amy said, flat nose high in the air.

"I shall. Only if you promise to come nowhere near the preparations, or the event, for that matter."

"I swear," Amy said, raising her hand so her precious turquoise ring glittered in a ray of sunlight that filtered in through the garret window. "I will not so much as look at the designs, or offer one opinion, and I will stay securely home and wander nowhere near the actual event." She turned on her heel and stomped down the stairs.

Jo stared out the window, angry at her sister's pomposity. How dare she bear such shame for her father and sister, who had suffered through so much. She looked down at the Laurence house and saw the movement of a shadow within, which made her think back to the night she and Beth watched Laurie turn from boy to werewolf. She rushed to the window that overlooked the backyard and saw Beth sitting on a bench, covered by a quilt and two cats. She ran down the stairs and out the back door.

"What are you three doing?" she asked breathlessly as she reached the bench.

"Have you been running?" Beth asked. "You breathe so heavily."

"Yes, I just ran all the way down from the garret to talk to you."

Beth shifted so she could curl up her legs and allow Jo room to sit.

"It's about our secret," Jo said, looking around carefully as she lowered herself onto the bench.

"Our secret?"

"Yes. The one only the cats and we two know. About Laurie."

"Oh, that he's a werewolf?"

"Yes. Beth, that's our secret, but you told Amy."

Beth frowned. "Did I?"

"She knew. And she said you told her."

"I'm sorry, Jo. It must have slipped out."

"Promise me you'll be more careful, Beth. Have you any idea how dangerous it could be for Mr. Laurence and Laurie if the word got out? They would be pulled from their homes, hanged, and their hearts cut from their chests and burned."

"You need not worry. I'll ask Amy not to tell anyone else."

"I already did. Forget about Amy. I beg of you, never mention it to her again. I need you, and the cats, to truly understand and always remember that nobody else can ever know this secret. Swear to me, Beth. Swear to me with all your might, and burn your oath into your memory so no word of this ever slips from your mouth again."

"I understand, and I swear it to you, Jo."

As the sisters embraced, Jo wondered if Beth truly did understand how important it was for her to keep the Laurences' secret.

"In return for your silence, I will work as hard as I possibly can on the stage and the posters for your exhibit," Jo promised.

Beth brightened at the mention of the event. "It will be so grand! The most important people from miles and miles around will attend. We have decided to make it a formal occasion, to attract those of greatest wealth. I just know this will offer a great deal of help to so many of those poor men."

"That's a wonderful idea to make it a grand party, rather than a small one. I will plan the stage and posters accordingly."

The sisters kissed lightly, and upon Beth's request, Jo also kissed the two cats, and the doll Beth brought out from under her quilt.

As Jo made her way back to the house, a smile formed on her lips and grew. If this event truly was formal in nature and attended by the wealthiest and most influential citizens, Amy would be absolutely crushed at having to miss it.

CHAPTER 21

Artistic Aptitude

BEING YOUNG AND AMBITIOUS, AMY DID NOT UNDER-stand that, in her art, she possessed talent but wanted for genius. She was learning this distinction through much tribulation, but mistook enthusiasm for inspiration, so allowed herself to veer off from the fine pen-and-ink drawings in which she showed so much skill, and which were both pleasant and profitable, into other genres, where she verged on failing miserably. The most terrifying experiments were her bold attempts at poker sketching, where she used red-hot pokers to burn faces and figures into wood. Smoke issued from the attic and shed with alarming frequency, and hot pokers lay about promiscuously abandoned. During this period of endeavors, Hannah never went to bed without a pail of water and the dinner bell at her door, in case of fire.

Amy, tired of burnt fingers, turned from fire to oil with cast-off palettes, brushes, and colors given to her by a friend. She dabbed away, producing pastoral and marine views such as were never seen on land or sea. Her monstrosities in the way of cattle would have piqued the interest of any scientist of deformities, and the pitching of her vessels would have produced seasickness in the most seasoned of ship captains, if her utter disregard of all known rules of shipbuilding and rigging had not, at first glance, convulsed him with laughter.

Charcoal produced a family of wild and cocky portraits. Softened into crayon sketches, they did better; for the likenesses were good, and Beth's hair, Jo's nose, Meg's mouth, and Laurie's eyes were pronounced "wonderfully fine." A return to clay and plaster produced such ghastly and mysterious ogres that she was soon unable to find a willing model. Not to be daunted by this, she decided to cast her own pretty foot, and the family was one day alarmed by an unearthly bumping and screaming. Running to the rescue, they found Amy hopping wildly about in the shed, her foot held fast in a pan full of plaster, which had hardened with unexpected rapidity. With much difficulty and some danger, she was dug out. Jo was so overcome with laughter while she excavated that her knife went too far, cut the poor foot, and left a lasting and grisly memorial of this artistic attempt.

The family was able to relax a bit when Amy turned to a mania for sketching from nature, and she set out for river, field, and wood. If "genius is eternal patience," as Michelangelo affirms, Amy certainly had some claim to that divine attribute, for she persevered in spite of all obstacles, failures, and discouragements, firmly believing that in time she should do something worthy to be called "high art."

But art was not her single goal, for she resolved to become an attractive and accomplished woman, even if she never did become a great artist, so she was learning, doing, and enjoying a great many things. Here she succeeded better; for she was one of the happily created beings who please without effort, make friends everywhere, and take life so gracefully and easily that less fortunate souls are tempted to believe that such are born under a lucky star. She had an instinctive sense of what was pleasing and proper, always said the right thing to the right person (Jo aside), did just what suited the time and place, and was entirely self-possessed.

One of her weaknesses was a desire to move in "our best society," without being quite sure what the best really was. Money, position, fashionable accomplishments, and elegant manners were the most desirable things in her eyes, and she liked to associate with those who possessed them, often mistaking the false for the true, and admiring what was not admirable. Never forgetting that by birth she was a gentlewoman, she cultivated her aristocratic tastes and feelings, so that when the opportunity came she might be ready to take the place from which poverty now excluded her. Since the wedding, she scraped even harder to rise, for she was nagged by the fear of her own wedding being as simple and sorry as she saw Meg's to have been, and she felt her heart beat fast and desperate in her chest each time she visited the modest Brooke home.

"My lady," as her friends called her, sincerely desired to be a genuine lady, and was so at heart, but had yet to learn that money cannot buy refinement of nature, that rank does not always confer nobility, and that true breeding makes itself felt in spite of external drawbacks.

Gravitating toward the wealthy members of her art class, she tried her best to amuse and entertain them, to be seen as one of their circle. She worried each day that Beth and her father's Exhibit of Amputees would be seen as pure lunacy and erase the progress she felt she was making up the social ladder. She thought of her argument with Jo, and, with relief, of her promise to not attend. But jealousy nipped at her when she watched the three of them, Beth, Jo, and her father, plan the occasion with animated fervor. She was shocked at the names she saw on their list to be specifically invited, for they were the names of families of the highest social standing and greatest holdings.

"Why would you invite these families?" she asked in a confrontational tone.

"Because we need their help," Mr. March explained patiently, holding a hand up to silence Jo, whose mouth stood open and ready to fire. "We need people who can help the amputees. Help them find jobs, and homes. And we have a guest speaker who creates limbs they can wear so they can walk and work again, so we need people who are in a position to buy them for those who can't afford to purchase their own."

Amy understood, but was still infuriated. When nobody was there to see, she stole glances at the stage designs and first drafts of the fliers and posters. They were good, very good, and she felt sorrow fall in a veil around her because she had no hand in their creation. She had overheard sympathetic talk. People wanted to help the men wounded in the war and the families of those who had not returned. Could it be that her father and sisters were actually involved in something that was both fashionable and timely?

She fussed and fumed, stomped and paced, spat and raged, trying to think of what to do. She knew she could not humble herself to Jo and ask to be a part of the exhibit preparations at this point, but after considerable thought, she felt the only course she could possibly take was to host an event of her own. She brightened as the idea took form; she could have a little artistic fête, a grand party, and invite all the influential members of her art class, although there were a few she could exclude, as they came from families of lower social standing. She tallied the students and came up with twelve, counting herself, for whom she could host a luncheon, which would be somewhat less costly than a dinner or evening party. The crowning touch of her plan was that these guests would then owe her a return invitation, which would, at those times, put her directly in the midst of the most elite members of their community.

"Mother, may I ask a favor of you?" Amy asked once her plan was complete.

"Well, little girl, what is it?"

"Our drawing class breaks up next week, and before we all separate for the summer, I thought I could ask the girls out here for a day. I could show them the river, and we could sketch the broken bridge. They have admired so many of the things in my sketchbook; I know they are wild to see them. They have been very kind to me in many ways, even though they are mostly rich and I am poor, so I would very much like to show my gratitude."

"I imagine that is feasible. What do you want for lunch? Cake, sandwiches, fruit, and coffee would be enough, I suppose?"

"Oh, dear, no!" Amy cried. "We must have cold tongue and chicken, French chocolate and ice cream. These girls are used to such things, and I want this lunch to be proper and elegant."

"How many young ladies are there?"

"Twelve or fourteen in class, but I dare say they won't all come," she replied, thinking of the three poorer girls she had decided to not invite.

"And do you plan to charter an omnibus to carry them all here?" Mrs. March asked, beginning to see her daughter's plan for what it truly was.

"I imagine no more than six or eight will come, so I can hire a beach wagon, and borrow Mr. Laurence's cherry-bounce," she said, using Hannah's pronunciation of *char-a-banc* for the open-topped conveyance with rows of benches.

"Amy, all this will be rather expensive."

"Not very. I've calculated the cost, and I'll pay for it all myself."

"But if these girls are used to such things, don't you think a simpler plan that will be novel to them would be better? Why attempt a style not in keeping with our circumstances?"

"If I can't have it as I like, I don't care to have it at all," Amy said, crossing her arms and stomping her little foot on the floor. "You and the girls could help a little, and I said I would pay all costs myself."

Mrs. March knew that experience was an excellent teacher, and whenever possible, she left her children to learn their own lessons. "Very well, Amy. If your heart is set on it, and you see your way with not too much outlay of time, money, and temper, I'll say no more. Talk it over with the girls, and whichever way you decide, I'll do my best to help."

Amy thanked her mother and went to lay out her plan for her sisters.

Meg agreed at once, and promised her aid, gladly offering anything she possessed, from her little house itself, to her very best salt spoons. But Jo frowned upon the project and would have nothing to do with it at first. "Why should you spend your money, worry your family, and turn the house upside down for a parcel of girls who don't care a sixpence for you?" Having been called from the tragic climax of her novel, she was not in the best of moods.

"They do care for me, and I for them," Amy returned indignantly. "There is a great deal of kindness, sense, and talent among them. Just because you don't care to cultivate your manners and tastes doesn't mean that I can't make the most of every chance that comes my way. *You* can go through the world with your elbows out and nose in the air and call it independence, if you like, but that's not my way."

Amy's definition of Jo's idea of independence was such a good hit that both burst out laughing, and the discussion took a more amiable turn. Much against her better judgment, Jo at last consented to sacrifice a day and help her sister through what she regarded as "nonsensical business."

Hannah wound up at her wits' end, for her week's work was deranged. If it was not fair on Monday, the young ladies were to come on Tuesday, an arrangement which thoroughly aggravated Jo and Hannah. On Monday, a smart but quick shower at eleven obviously dampened not just the ground but also the enthusiasm of the girls, for nobody came, and at two the family sat down in a blaze of sunshine to consume the perishable portions of the feast, so that nothing would be lost.

Tuesday morning, Hannah left the chicken on the kitchen counter, and the kittens got at it, eating most of it and ruining the rest. "I am oh so sorry, Amy!" blubbered Beth, the acting patroness of the cats.

Amy insisted on rushing into town to buy lobster, even though a lower-class staple, because the tongue was simply not enough. To her dismay, one of Laurie's most elegant college friends ran into her and caught sight of the lowly lunch in her basket, and then she found her best dress damaged by the trip and had to quickly prepare a new outfit from her few humble choices.

When she heard the rumble of the cherry-bounce, Mrs. March ran to the porch to greet Amy's guests. She saw, from the house, that only one girl had arrived and cried out to everyone to help clear half the table, as it would be far too absurd to put a luncheon for twelve before a single girl.

Amy acted quite calm and cordial to her single guest, and the rest of the family, being of a dramatic turn, played their parts equally well. Amy and her guest gaily partook of the remodeled lunch, visited the studio and garden, discussed art with great enthusiasm, and then Amy drove her friend quietly about the neighborhood till sunset, when "the party went out."

Amy came back looking composed as ever, though very tired. She observed that every vestige of the unfortunate fête had disappeared, except a suspicious pucker around the corners of Jo's mouth.

The family consumed more of the feast for dinner, and then Amy looked on the remaining dishes with disgust. "I'm sick of the sight of it," she declared. "I've been such a fool. It's a pity there's no full moon tonight. I'd throw it all out for the werewolves to clean up."

It was suggested the food be bundled up and sent to the Hummels, where it would be welcomed and appreciated. Amy agreed that seemed fit, as she felt "Germans enjoyed such messes."

"I thought I should have died at the sight of you two girls rattling about in the what-you-call-it, like two little kernels in a very large nutshell, and Marmee waiting in state to receive a throng," sighed Jo, well spent with her laughter.

"I'm so sorry you were disappointed, dear, but we all did our best to satisfy you," Mrs. March said in a tone full of motherly regret.

"I thank you all for helping me," Amy said quite bravely, but with a little quiver in her voice. "But I would thank you all to not allude to this fiasco for a full month, at least."

No one did for several months, but the word *fête* always produced a general smile, and Laurie's birthday gift to Amy was a charm in the shape of a tiny coral lobster for her watch guard.

...

CHAPTER 22

A Successful Exhibition

IT WAS THE DAY AFTER THE FULL MOON THAT A KNOCK came on the door of the March household and was opened to five men standing uncertainly on the porch.

"Good day," a man standing on only one leg said pleasantly to Amy. "We are looking for Chaplain March."

"I'll find him," Amy said, pale and shaken after having surveyed the group. Three of the men were missing arms or legs. Two were not amputees at all; their wounds were facial, and so glaring that she stared hard even while wanting nothing more than to look away. She found her father and waited until she heard him address the men, and then she raced up the stairs, not stopping until she reached the garret.

"What is it now?" Jo asked, glancing up from the book she was reading.

"The men for your event are arriving. There are five here now, wearing various obvious injuries. Two still own all their limbs but have severe facial wounds I can't bear to describe."

Jo stared at her book, knowing her difficult sister would grow even more so, and trying to muster patience and strength. "You will have to learn to adjust. I imagine we will be their hosts, that they will be staying with us."

"Staying here?" Amy gasped. "With us?"

"Yes. Sleeping here and eating here. It's for only a week or two. I'm certain you can manage to cope."

Jo was correct, that had been Mr. March's plan, but when Mr. Laurence learned about the men's arrival, he insisted on housing and feeding them, knowing the March family had limited resources. Although Mr. March tried to refuse, Mr. Laurence won out, for his house was large enough to comfortably host each man in his own room complete with comfortable bed, washstand, and a small selection of books.

Other amputees who arrived for the event found their way first to the church, and there was always someone about who was eager to supply them with a bed and meals, so the March family found themselves without a lodger of their own, but quite attentive to those housed by Mr. Laurence.

Mrs. March gathered her girls together one day and told them they had all been invited to dinner at the Laurence house. "Mr. Laurence has also invited Meg and John, and they will be there."

"Dinner?" Amy said. "How will the men with those facial wounds eat? The one's mouth has no bottom. And the other has a hole in his cheek that is more than large enough for food to escape through. No. I won't go. I couldn't bear it. The other men can hide their injuries under clothes or the table, but I cannot sit with the men whose faces are torn apart."

"Then stay here," Mrs. March said, seemingly calm, except that her cheeks were pink and her nostrils wide. "Better you stay here than insult those men by displaying your disgust in their presence."

"Very well," Amy countered. "I'll be in my chapel staring at my beautiful Madonna."

"See that you pray for patience and empathy," Mrs. March said in an even tone.

Jo, for one, could not wait to meet the men and clandestinely examine their injuries. She still bemoaned the fact that she had been too young to go off to war as a nurse, but she could now prove to herself, by not being affected by scars and missing parts, that she had the mettle it would have taken to serve.

When the Marches arrived at the Laurence house that evening, they saw that the men were all bathed and groomed, and wore fresh clothing, probably given to them by Mr. Laurence. Their hair was combed, mustaches shaped, and they seemed happily rested and refreshed.

Everyone was introduced all around. Rowland was a tall mustached man, who had been struck by a shell fragment and lost the floor of his mouth; Joseph, the other man with a facial injury, looked fine from his left side, but on the right had an eyelid sewn over a ruined eye and a frightfully large hole in his pitted cheek, having been caught by an artillery shell; Henry, a slight, light-haired man, had lost one arm and one leg, both on the left side of his body, so had to hop rather than rely on a cane, as he had no way to hold one; Elias, dark and bearded, had one leg gone entirely, so there was no stump, no piece hanging at all to show a leg had ever been there, and his pant leg was pinned up securely at his hip; and Percival, with his flaming red hair, had no right arm, and his struggles to adapt to using his left were obvious in all he did.

One might think the atmosphere at the dinner table would have been dour and uncomfortable, but these men, who had come so close to death, were not about to allow their precious second chances to slip between their fingers and so embraced life with eager vitality. They accepted questions easily and responded with honesty and openness.

"What did you think of your battlefield doctors?" Mr. Laurence had asked them. "There is much talk about them circulating, much of it negative. It is said their surgical techniques ranged from the barbaric to the barely competent."

"It troubles me to hear them called butchers," said Elias. "Considering the situation and resources, they worked miracles. My being alive, all of our being alive today is proof of that."

"There are rumors that most amputees were offered no anesthetic during their surgery," Mr. Laurence pressed.

"Utter nonsense!" Percival snorted. "Ample doses of chloroform were always administered beforehand. I think we all agree on that, do we not?"

The four other wounded soldiers exclaimed that was absolutely so.

"The chloroform made one awaken with a thirst so rabid that only the pain of the missing limb could compete," Henry contributed.

"Then what of the screams about which John told me?" Meg asked softly. "I thought they were from the soldiers undergoing surgery."

"The screams I still hear in my sleep," John said, nodding. "I told her only about the unholy noises issuing from the medical tents, not that the sources were usually from soldiers who had just been informed they would lose a limb."

"Or those witnessing, for the first time, the plight of the soldiers under the knife," Elias added.

The other men nodded in agreement, and Rowland stuck his spoon far back in the space between the two ghastly flaps of skin hanging below his mustache, and sucked up his dinner. His sad eyes watched the others at the table, as if expecting them to send him away, but the kindhearted diners paid his crude eating no mind as they chatted nonstop, so he was soon able to relax, and his eyes replaced their sorrowful gaze with one of mirth.

The conversation, as expected, soon turned to the exhibit, and the men assured Mr. March that they had more than enough inspiring stories of war and survival to keep the event on a relatively upbeat note and quickly dispel the unease that was certain to accompany those people who had no idea what to expect.

"The focus must be our survival, not our trials," said brave Percival, even as he fought to keep his spoon straight in his left hand and his soup in his bowl.

Jo nearly dropped her own spoon when her father asked, "Did any of you have werewolves fighting with you?"

"Oh, yes," Elias said. "They fought alongside us, and the doctor who took my leg, but saved my life, was himself a werewolf."

"And with all of you sleeping in tents or on the ground, as John had told me, what precautions did you take when the full moon arrived?" Meg asked.

"We never feared the battlefield werewolves," Henry said. "They had piles of amputated limbs to pick at."

"And they had the wounded," Elias said, eyes averted as he told his morbid tale. "It was an unspoken agreement that they would take the men left out for them, not the able-bodied ones who were needed to fight. You could almost call them angels of mercy. The most severely injured and deeply suffering soldiers were left out on the nights of the full moons so the werewolves could bring a close to their trials. It was said they always first tore out the unfortunate men's throats, to end their lives, before devouring them."

Jo noted that Mr. Laurence's expression was even, and re-

"We never feared the battlefield werewolves. They had piles of amputated limbs to pick at."

flected no more or less interest than that of anyone else at the table. She looked at Beth, and her sister returned her stare with a smile, then offered the doll in her lap a bite of her dinner. Jo wondered if Beth understood everything that was being said or even if she was fully listening.

After dinner, the men retired to Mr. Laurence's den, and the women returned home.

"What was it like?" Amy pressed Meg, who had gone to her mother's house rather than to her own empty one.

"It was an interesting and exciting night. I'm very excited for Father's exhibit now," Meg replied.

"But what was it like eating with those men?"

"No different from eating with you!" Jo snapped, thinking fully of Joseph, whose gaping cheek hole had dripped food and saliva throughout the entire meal.

"The men with the facial injuries had to concentrate on the process of eating so had little to say," Meg explained. "But the others had stories that left us absolutely spellbound."

And spellbound was the only way to accurately describe the attendees of the Exhibit of Amputees, who sat before nearly three dozen amputees, and two guest speakers. Every person who had been personally invited was there, as well as a number of people who had viewed the fliers and posters around town. Everyone was dressed in his or her best clothes, and Jo was happy as a lark, certain that Amy would be most sorry for missing an occasion that was certain to remain on everyone's tongues and minds for months to come.

The audience sat quietly attentive as the men exposed the aggrieved areas of their bodies and explained how they had received their injuries, and a retired doctor who had served in the war related how the medical team had most likely attended to them.

"A good surgeon could amputate a limb in under ten minutes," the doctor said. "It was pure luck, and luck alone, that spared soldiers the surgical fevers that took so many lives, for there was nothing we could do to prevent these fevers, rot, or ulceration."

An inquiry arose about how the doctors decided to amputate, and what the process entailed, and the doctor was quick to answer, "If the bone was broken or a major blood vessel torn, it was the best alternative to remove the limb. The worst injuries were the result of the minié ball, a soft lead bullet that can travel over a thousand yards and causes irreparable gaping holes. It fully splinters the bone and makes mush of destroyed muscles, arteries, and tissue. So, to remove a ruined limb, we sawed through the bone until it was completely severed, and tossed the limb into an always-growing pile. We then clipped or scraped off any jagged pieces so they wouldn't work back through the skin, and then tied off the arteries with horsehair, silk, or cotton threads, whatever was at hand. We left a flap of skin to pull across and sew into place, keeping a small space open for drainage. The stump might be covered with plaster and bandaged. Then we hurried on to the next victim."

Although a good many men and women swooned throughout the educational lecture, the first woman fainted dead away when Elias interjected that a large round of skin, the size of one cheek of his buttocks, had been secured there to house his massive injury sufficiently. A few other women also fainted, two when Rowland stepped onto the stage and a third when Joseph put his finger into his cheek and opened his mouth, and she saw the finger wriggling between what remained of his upper and lower teeth. Preparations had been made in advance for just such incidents, and a nurse stood in the back armed with cots, smelling salts, ice, and a bit of brandy. Once the women were carried off and the woozy students led away, those remaining were compelled to listen and observe more closely than ever.

The audience received a quick lesson on amputation kits, which had come complete with saws, knives, tourniquets, scalpels, and Mr. Liston's bone nippers, which efficiently removed the splinters resulting from sawing and could also, in one quick snip, amputate affected fingers or toes.

To everyone's genuine amazement, the genteel and distinguished James Edward Hanger stepped onstage, as surely and swiftly as any able-bodied man, and revealed that he, himself, was an amputee, and that his one leg was strapped on. He further explained that he was the war's first amputee, and that his injury had been his inspiration to invent false limbs to aid the wearer by serving as the missing part. The audience was fraught with emotion by the end of the exhibit and rabid to offer aid in the form of support, jobs, homes, and false limbs for the men who had tugged at their hearts with their valor, candor, and optimism.

...

CHAPTER 23

The Slaughter of the Amputees

EVERY FEW WEEKS, JO WOULD SHUT HERSELF UP IN her room, put on her scribbling suit, and "fall into a vortex" as she expressed it, writing away at her novel with all her heart and soul, for until that was finished, she could find no peace. Her "scribbling suit" consisted of a black woolen pinafore on which she could wipe her pen at will, and a cap of the same material adorned with a cheerful red bow, into which she bundled her hair when the decks were cleared for action. This cap was a beacon to the inquiring eyes of the family, who, during these periods, kept their distance, merely popping in their heads to inquire, if they dared, "Does genius burn, Jo?" If the cap was drawn low upon her forehead, it was a sign that hard work was going on; in exciting moments it was pushed rakishly askew; and when despair seized the author it was plucked wholly off, and cast upon the floor. At such times the intruder silently and swiftly withdrew until the red bow was seen gaily erect once more upon the gifted brow.

She did not think herself a genius by any means, but when the writing fit came on, she gave herself up to it with total abandon and led a blissful life, unconscious of want, care, or bad weather. She left meals untouched, ignored sound, smell, and noise, and fully conquered fatigue while she sat in an imaginary world, full of friends almost as real and dear to her as those in the flesh. The divine afflatus usually lasted a week or two, and then she emerged from her "vortex" hungry, sleepy, cross, or despondent.

She was just emerging from one of these attacks when she read a note that awaited her attention, prevailing upon her to escort an elderly friend of the family to a lecture, which promised to unfold the glories of the Pyramids and the pharaohs. She jotted a quick note of acceptance and sent Beth out to deliver it. She had been struck by inspiration the night of the Exhibit of Amputees, and this was the first affair she would be attending since, so was reminded to inquire about the men.

"Mr. Laurence's guests have been gone for days," Marmee informed her. "I was sorry to see them go, they were such brave and sociable men. I believe Mr. Hanger and his assistant have only just left. They had a great many orders of false limbs, and so had just as many measurements to take. Mr. Hanger said he expected to be busy for a full year filling all the requests. And, just think, Jo, they have all been paid for in full by the kind souls of this town."

"So no amputees remain here?"

"A few hangers-on, perhaps nine or ten. I think they have nowhere to go back to."

The night of the Egyptian lecture, Jo and Miss Crocker arrived early and took their seats. While her companion set the heel of her stocking, Jo scanned the room; two matrons with massive foreheads discussed women's rights, a pair of humble lovers held hands, a somber spinster ate peppermints out of a paper bag, and an old gentleman took a preparatory nap behind a yellow bandana. On her right, her only neighbor was a studious-looking lad absorbed in a newspaper.

It was a pictorial sheet, and Jo examined the work of art nearest her, idly wondering over the melodramatic illustration complete with an Indian in full war costume, tumbling over a precipice with a wolf at his throat, and a disheveled female flying away in the background with her mouth wide open. She found it laughable that this artist made a living wage with his work, as the hands and feet in the picture were unnaturally small in proportion, and the eyes inhumanly large. Pausing to turn a page, the lad saw her looking and, with boyish good nature, offered her half his paper. "Want to read it? That's a first-rate story."

"Is it about a werewolf?" she asked, accepting the paper with a smile.

"No. They never are, not that I've seen. That's just a common wolf in the picture."

The story was one of light literature, swelling with the usual labyrinth of love, mystery, and murder. In Jo's mind, the author's invention failed, but grand catastrophe cleared the stage for one-half the audience to exalt in the character's downfall and the other half to be haunted by it.

"Prime, isn't it?" the boy asked as her eye went down the last paragraph of her portion.

"I think you and I could do just as well if we tried," Jo replied, amused at his admiration of such trash.

"I'd name myself a pretty lucky chap if I could. They say these authors make a fine living out of stories such as this."

Jo looked again, more respectfully, at the agitated words and thickly sprinkled exclamation points that adorned the page.

"I read all this author's stories," the lad continued. "She

knows what folks like, and deserves to be paid as well as she does, in my mind at least."

Jo's eye caught an advertisement for a contest offering a hundred-dollar prize for the best sensational story. She heard bits and pieces of the Professor's introduction, and scraps about the ancient gods, hieroglyphics, and scarabs as she covertly took down the address of the paper. Her mind delved deeper and deeper into the concoction of her story, and by the end of the lecture, she was unable to decide whether the duel should come before the elopement or after the murder.

She said nothing of her plan at home but fell to work the next day, much to the disquiet of her mother, who always looked a little anxious when "genius took to burning." Jo's theatrical experience and miscellaneous reading were of service now, for they gave her some idea of dramatic effect, and supplied plot, language, and costume. Her story was as full of desperation and despair as her limited acquaintance with those uncomfortable emotions enabled her to make it, and having located it in Lisbon, she wound up with an earthquake as a striking and appropriate dénouement. She inserted, for interest, a minor character who was a werewolf, thinking this unique measure might give her story an edge above the other entries. The manuscript was privately dispatched, accompanied by a note, modestly saying that if the tale didn't get the prize, which the writer hardly dared to expect, she would be glad to receive any sum it might be considered worth. Writing the story had been easy for Jo, but waiting for the decision would be long, hard, and torturous.

The full moon hung low in the sky the night after Jo mailed in her story. On the north side of town, the nine amputees who still lingered were at a friendly inn, where they found the owners and their customers alike always cordially offering them a hot meal and one drink after another. Only one of them accepted far more libation than he should have that night, and the others stood ready to escort him back to the barn where they had been sleeping since the end of the exhibit. The largest man leaned the drunken fool against his chest, where he once wore his left arm, and on the other side, the tipsy amputee was held tight around the waist by a man missing only half his arm on the opposite side. The drinker tried to hop on his one leg, but his step was uncertain and his foot turned more often than not. It was slow but steady going for the men who had been warned, numerous times, to be safe inside well before dark.

The men released their load under a tree and sat down to rest.

"Shouldn't we hurry on? We've been told by nearly every man we saw not to dally," one man said.

"I've never feared a werewolf in my life, and I won't start now," the largest man replied with a snort.

"There are nine of us. Surely we can, together, manage one or two werewolves," another added.

"We'll get there soon," a nervous voice cut in. "The moon is barely up, and we're not terribly far away."

A woeful baying sounded and was carried to the men's ears by the wind.

"Sounds like they're rather far off," one said, in a secure tone.

"But they're fast runners."

"We're upwind of that howl, so that batch is nothing to fear. We need to worry about any lingering in this direction." The speaker raised a dirty hand to point to the east.

As the men's eyes followed the erect finger, they spotted the golden glow of watchful eyes in the thick foliage.

"Get him up, now!" a panicked voice called.

Two men stooped to pick up their crony, but the others began to hop, run, or hobble away as fast as they were able. The swiftest of the group found themselves circled by four massive werewolves, dripping, hungry mouths stretched into demonic grins. The men darted in different directions, pushing blindly through brush and brambles while their own frantic breathing echoed in their ears.

Impossibly, after what seemed like hours of chase, all nine men found themselves together again in one spot, herded like mindless cattle into the middle of a circle of twenty or so snarling werewolves, some on all fours and others standing upright like oversized, hirsute men.

"There's got to be a way to escape," one man said, gasping, as the sharp, savage aroma wafting from the beasts' thick gray coats assaulted his nostrils.

"I thought we *were* escaping," another said with little hope left in his voice. "They rounded us up and delivered us straight to perdition."

A cry escaped from the throat of the drunk man, now sobered by bald terror and utter desperation. The men's sobbing formed a low undertone to the deep chorus of growls issuing from the throats of the werewolves. As they stood there, the men could feel the vibrations of the beasts' noise beneath their feet, as if the creatures were sprung from the ground and controlled the entirety of the earth and its inhabitants.

A werewolf ventured forward and ran his nose along the stump of one man's leg. The man trembled, and a wet stain appeared and grew on the fabric of his pants. The werewolf sniffed again, more deeply, and let his tongue run along the shortened leg as his hot breath penetrated the man's pants and settled damply on the flesh of what remained of his leg.

With one lash of a huge, clawed paw, the werewolf sent the man sprawling on the ground. He stood over him, inhaling and savoring the scent of his victim's fear. The other werewolves stood watching, as if awaiting their cue, while the prone man cried out in protest as the back of his head was ripped neatly from the bone of his skull. The werewolf raised his massive head and chewed hair, tissue, and veins before swallowing the mess in one forceful gulp. The man twitched, noise still spouting from his mouth like steam from a teakettle.

The other men stood stock-still, wide-eyed, and trembling, waiting. They hoped, in vain, to escape, and then hoped to die quickly, but that was not to be. It wasn't often that a large group of werewolves had at their command a healthy number of humans all at once, so for such occasions, they had invented games, which extended the hunt as well as their pleasure. Unfortunately, it also extended the intense fear and unspeakable suffering of their prey.

The werewolves backed away and feigned interest elsewhere just long enough for one of the men to seize the opportunity to flee. He broke away, legs pedaling wildly as one arm and one stump flailed with lunatic exertion. The mouse was loose, but the cats were quick on its tail, for two werewolves followed, loping playfully, and flanked him in a matter of seconds. The amputee's concentration remained straight ahead of him, and it was impossible to tell if he saw or simply sensed his pursuers. His gasps rang out in the moon-brightened night air, soon turning to cries and then to weeping as he admitted defeat and fell to his knees. One werewolf nudged him, and he understood and drew himself up to his feet. The two walked on either side of him and led him back to the game circle, where he was deposited as a lesson to the rest; attempts to escape were futile.

The game continued for hours as the men were liberated and pursued, taken and slowly ripped apart, piece by tiny piece. It was hard to say if it was more painful for the men to watch a fillet of flesh torn from one of their colleagues or to know it was being stripped from their own bones, they were so numbed by the despairing hopelessness of their situation. Occasionally, one or two of them broke out in maddened laughter as jocular disbelief replaced reason.

When the men were too weakened, either mentally or physically, to continue the game, the werewolves tore into them, gorging on the viscous organs hiding in the innermost recesses of their bodies.

With only nine men but twenty werewolves, there was little left when the remains were discovered the next day. Mr. March, hearing of the attack, rushed to the site. His heart ached, as he felt responsible for the men being there, and so he rounded up the eight skulls, which had been licked clean of skin and cartilage, and the few bone fragments he found, and brought them back to his church. With tears falling freely, he set up a special altar on one side of the church and spent all day painting and lettering a magnificent sign.

When Jo went to find her father and bring him home for dinner, she stopped short at the sight of the miscellaneous well-chewed bones and eight skulls that were neatly lined up behind a glowing row of candles and beneath a sign that read, SKULLS AND ASSORTED BONES OF THE FALLEN. PLEASE PRAY FOR THEM. Having heard about the slaughter of the amputees, she fell immediately to her knees and whispered a passionate prayer for the poor men who had outwitted war but not werewolves.

Although the new altar was a somewhat eccentric veneration, the church patrons were now accustomed to the well-respected Mr. March's exceptional thoughts and perceptions; they managed to look beyond the grisly display to the intended homage, and the coffer on the altarpiece was perpetually filled to overflowing.

...

CHAPTER 24

Father's Big Change

SIX WEEKS IS A VERY LONG TIME TO WAIT, AND AN EVEN longer time for a young woman to keep a secret, but Jo did both, and was just beginning to give up hope of ever seeing her manuscript again when a letter arrived that took her breath away. When she opened the envelope, a check for a hundred dollars fell into her lap. For a minute she stared at it with disbelief, then she read the letter and promptly began to cry. Jo valued the letter far more than the money, for it was encouraging, and after years of effort, here was the proof that she had learned to do *something*, though it was only to write a sensation story.

Having composed herself, Jo electrified the family by appearing before them with the letter in one hand and the check in the other, announcing that she had won the first prize. There was, of course, a great jubilee, and when the story came, everyone read and praised it; though after her father told her the language was good, the romance fresh and hearty, the tragedy quite thrilling, and the addition of the werewolf extremely innovative, he said in his unworldly way, "You can do better than this, Jo. Aim at the highest, and never mind the money."

"*I* think the money is the best part!" Amy exclaimed, regarding the magic slip of paper with a reverential eye. "What *will* you do with such a fortune?"

"Send Beth and Marmee to the seaside for two or three months," answered Jo promptly.

"Oh, how splendid! But I simply can't do it, dear, it would be too selfish," cried Beth, who had clapped her thin hands and taken a long breath, as if pining for fresh ocean breezes, then stopped herself and motioned away the check her sister waved before her.

"Ah, but you shall go; I've set my heart on it. You see, I never succeed when I think of myself alone, so it will help me to work for you. Don't you see? Besides, Marmee so sorely needs the change, Beth, and she won't leave you, so you simply *must* go. Won't it be fun for us all to see you come home plump and rosy again? Hurrah for Dr. Jo, who always cures her patients!"

And so, after much discussion, off to the seaside they went. Jo was satisfied with the investment of her prize money, and fell to work with a cheery spirit, bent on earning more of those delightful checks. Little notice was taken of her dark, romantic werewolf stories, but they found a market, and by the time her mother returned, by the magic of her pen, her "rubbish" turned into comforts for them all. "The Werewolf's Daughter" paid the butcher's bill, "A Phantom Paw" put down new carpet, and the promised payment for "Curse of the Moon" would prove a blessing in the way of keeping them in groceries and gowns.

Wealth is certainly a most desirable thing, but poverty has its sunny side, and one of the sweet uses of adversity is the genuine satisfaction that comes from hearty work of head or hand; and to the inspiration of necessity, Jo owed half the wise, beautiful, and useful blessings of her world. She enjoyed a taste of this satisfaction and ceased to envy richer girls, taking great comfort in the knowledge that she could supply her own wants, and need ask no one for a penny. She resolved to make a bold stroke for fame and fortune and copied her novel for a fourth time before submitting it, with fear and trembling, to three publishers. She then, as before, sat back to wait.

Amy was busy with boys and her art and could not be counted on to help, and Meg was in her own house with her own duties, even though she promised to look in on the family often for her mother, so it was Jo's constant challenge to keep track of her father, to be sure he ate and shaved and wore fresh clothes. Marmee had, some time past, released him of any promise to return to the house at night, and it was common for him to spend occasional nights at the church, where he had a room with a cot on which he often collapsed, exhausted, after having forgotten to sleep for days in a row. The man was aflame, growing more feral in faith and in his conviction to honor the dead; seeing this, the family felt it was preferable that he stay there, close to his work.

One night, Jo was lost in her own world again, red-bowed cap pulled far down on her head as she cavorted with her romantic characters. The high-pitched howl of a werewolf slapped her back to reality, and she ran down the stairs to find her father.

"Is he here?" she asked Amy, who sat idly thumbing through an art book.

"Is who here?" she asked without looking up.

"Father! Is he here?"

"I don't think he is. I haven't seen him for days."

"Hannah!" Jo yelled.

"What is it?" Hannah asked, wiping her hands on her apron and leaving a small trail of flour behind her.

"Has Father come home?"

"No."

"The moon is full!" Jo cried. "What if he left the church late and is walking home now?"

"He wouldn't do that. He knows better, as do we all. I'm certain he will simply stay there the night."

"Hannah, this is Father we're talking about. You know he is altered of mind since the war, and his thinking is not always clear as it once was. I sense deeply in my bones that he could be out there! I must go."

"Jo, you can't!" Hannah exclaimed.

"I promise I'll be careful. I must follow my instinct, Hannah, I must."

Jo chose the darkest shawl she could find and wrapped it around her head so it draped lightly over her face to hide its white sheen in the moonlight, while Hannah stood watching, wringing her poor work-ravaged hands in distress. Without a backward glance, Jo made her way out of the house. She stood outside and turned her head, listening for any noise she might be able to attribute to a werewolf, but it was deathly quiet, save for the slight rustlings and callings of small woodland creatures.

She walked slowly and stealthily, keeping to the shadows. With every few feet of progress made, she stopped anew to look and listen for any signs of danger. Suddenly, just ahead of her, she saw her father. Relief flooded her as she rushed toward him, but a looming form jumped out unexpectedly, blocking the sight of him. The enormous figure shifted slightly to one side, and she again caught sight of Mr. March, who stood frozen in midstep with an expression of horror; he was facing a werewolf. Jo could not move or breathe or cry out. She could only stand statue-still and take in the fierce and massive creature that stood adroitly displayed before her astonished eyes.

The beast was raised up on its hind legs, standing a full head and shoulders above her panting father as it stared down at him. It inched toward him, tail raised high against its towering back. Mr. March raised one arm across his face, as if to protect it as the creature fell onto him, and he cried out only once as the werewolf tore away a fragment of his shoulder. Jo tried to make her legs move so she could run and thrash the colossus, distract it so her father could escape, but before she could force her leaden limbs to obey, the beast stopped. It stared down at Mr. March, turned its head from side to side as Jo had seen dogs do when confronted with something puzzling, and then bounded off on four legs as fast as it had appeared.

"Father!" Jo cried out, rushing to him.

"Jo. Come away. Hurry," he croaked, holding a hand up against his wounded shoulder as he stumbled to right himself.

Even as she ran toward the safety of her home, pure terror coursing through her body and her heart pounding against her rib cage, Jo knew for certain that this would always stand out in her mind as one of the most exciting nights of her life.

The pair tore madly across the landscape, not watching out for werewolves or any other threat. Their sights were set directly on the haven of their humble little home, and they would not stop until they reached it. They burst into the house, scaring Hannah into a screaming fit and bringing Amy to tears when she saw her father's injuries.

With care and tenderness, the three women dressed Mr. March's wound, which was nowhere near as severe as Jo had feared. Everyone spoke at once for some time, so when Hannah

*He cried out only once as the werewolf tore away
a fragment of his shoulder.*

and Amy eventually firmly expected an answer to their question of what had happened, Jo spoke over her father and explained that he had received the gash when he tripped over a fallen tree and fell on a small outcropping of sharp rocks.

"It's a wonder you didn't break your neck!" Hannah exclaimed, bandaging the wound with the skilled hands of a nurse. "We're lucky not to be dressing a corpse as we speak."

Jo and Mr. March exchanged a glance, each knowing how true Hannah's statement was.

"Oh, Jo!" Amy said later, when their father was settled and calmed. "How terrifying that he was out there among the werewolves!"

"Yes, but he's all right now, Amy. You can relax. I know the werewolves are your greatest fear."

Amy considered this. "They once were, but now there is one thing I fear above werewolves, dear sister. And that is being poor for the rest of my life."

Jo studied her sister's face, not knowing how to respond.

"Those old nightmares of werewolves have been replaced with new ones where I marry the poorest man in the area, and I jolt awake with a scream lodged in my throat," Amy explained.

Later, when Mr. March was resting and Hannah and Amy had gone to bed, Jo, after having thought long and hard, went to speak with her father. "You do know that you will now become a werewolf, do you not?"

"I do. I can leave, Jo," he said, laying a hand on his injured shoulder. "I will protect this household and this community and leave."

"No. You can't. There is nowhere you can go to completely get away from people. And there are others among us who function fully as respected members of this community despite the burden of their full-moon curse. It is only one night each month that you are a danger to anyone, and you can learn to cope with that night, as many others have done before you, and will do after you. Every other day and night of the month, you are still our beloved father, and we will not lose you."

"How will I learn? How will I cope?" he asked, and Jo saw that he struggled hard to contain the tears that had welled up in his eyes. "It must take years to learn to tame these urges. I will be flailing blindly in an all-new form when the next full moon comes."

"Then you need a mentor, a teacher who can lead you."

"And where do I find such a savior? Be realistic, Jo."

"I am realistic, Father. I want you to rest and heal, but not to worry. Marmee and Beth have only left days ago, so you have two moons under which to take lessons. Before the next full moon, I will take you where you will be taught well. Please believe your daughter that she knows how to help you."

Mr. March locked eyes with her and saw in her face a fierce determination and total honesty. He sensed that she did, indeed, know what to do, and decided to place his fate in her able hands.

"That werewolf," Mr. March said, lying back on his pillow with a ragged sigh. "I don't understand why it stopped. Why was I not slain and eaten out there?"

"For the moment, this is all I will say," said Jo with a grim expression on her young face. "You are alive at this moment because that werewolf recognized you. He knows you, and he is your friend. This is something you must keep foremost in your mind in the upcoming months as you are guided into your new life as a werewolf."

When her father was finally sleeping quietly, Jo entered her bedroom and sat down heavily on her bed. The burden of her father's secret was now added to the pilgrim's bundle she bore on her back. She feared she could now never leave him on his own; she could never move away, never marry, and never have the gay and lively home filled with children of which she had secretly dreamed. She lay back and her weary eyes stared through the window, up to the brilliant constellations in the sky.

CHAPTER 25

Learning to Feed

*J*O SPENT THE NEXT MONTH WAVERING BETWEEN FEEL-
ings of gratitude for the werewolf sparing her father's life and
intense rage, when she longed to stalk to the Laurence mansion
and set it aflame with both werewolves locked securely inside.
She finally concluded that what had been done was done, and the
importance was now in the future, in her father's ability to adapt
to his new condition. When the next full moon was approaching,
Jo did the only thing she could think of to help her father: she
walked him through the garden to the Laurence house and sat
both men down together in the privacy of Mr. Laurence's study.

"Mr. Laurence," she began, reminding herself to remain civil
and avoid accusations and angry outbursts, for they could bear
no fruit. "I have, for some time, known of the condition that you
and your grandson share. I have been careful to not reveal your
secret to anyone, not to one friend or family member, although I
do admit that Beth also knows your secret. She loves you like a
daughter, and you surely realize that she would never put you in
harm's way by saying a word of this any sooner than I would."

Mr. Laurence looked from daughter to father, then back to
daughter.

"You are our friend and neighbor, and I believe it was you,

during the last full moon, who bit my father, suddenly realized who he was, and so released him. I can't say how, but I recognized the wolf. I recognized you."

Mr. Laurence ran his hand over his hair and rubbed his eyes. With a deep sigh, he nodded.

"Thank you for sparing me. I know werewolves feel a hunger that is hard to contain. It couldn't have been easy for you to stop when you did," Mr. March said softly, standing up and reaching out his hand. Mr. Laurence also rose; the men shook hands, gripping each other for a long moment before sitting back down.

Jo sighed. How did her father, under all conditions, consistently manage to show only compassion and forgiveness? Had he no rage for being thrust into this life of a hunted werewolf?

"Had I been younger," Mr. Laurence said, "the hunger could have easily overcome me, but one learns to control himself in wolf form through practice. I must constantly force my grandson to rein in his desires so he may better control his urges. I am proud of what a quick study the youth has proven to be." He stopped and looked into Mr. March's face. "So you are certain that you harbor no anger against me?"

"No. I was a fool for being out when I was. I imagine I'll prove an even greater fool when the moon rises full and I have no idea what to do to protect my family and myself."

"That's why we're here," Jo said.

"Then you didn't come here only to thank me?" Mr. Laurence asked, smiling at his weak joke.

"We came here to ask that you tutor Father in the ways of the werewolf, Mr. Laurence. He won't know what to expect, or what to do. Will you take him with you during the full moon and initiate him properly?"

Mr. Laurence nodded and rose. He stood before Mr. March until he, too, rose, and the men embraced and fell to weeping, for they were now bonded forever as the hapless victims of an ancient curse. Through the heartache, each man realized that he also felt deliriously happy to be alive, despite his monthly burden.

"I must begin by telling you that I suspect this will be harder for you than it ever was for me," said Mr. Laurence. "I am a pure werewolf, as were my parents; in my family, we are born to the role. But being pure also means there is a greater urge to consume human flesh and organs; you, as a convert, will be more satisfied with eating animals than either Laurie or I could ever be. However, you will, I assure you, never forget your first taste of human meat. The thrill of the hunt becomes a passion. I must admit, there are months that pass where I feel I spend my every day merely waiting for the next full moon. It is not an easy life."

"What of the Brigade? I worry that Father will err in their sight and be taken from us," said Jo.

"In that instance, we march down, immediately, to the courthouse and sign testimonials that he was with us the entire night of the full moon, and in human form. They will accept a sworn statement from someone in my position."

"You mean someone in a position of wealth?" Jo asked.

"That's a part of it, Jo. I know it sounds unfair, but yes, money and stature keep many accusations at bay, although I admit it is becoming quite perilous for all werewolves with the new Brigade in force. Nothing proved that so strongly as when I lost my dear, lifelong friend, Harrison Adams."

Jo nervously shifted in her chair.

"I cannot imagine I will excel at being a predator," said Mr. March.

"Instincts step in, and you'll be fine. Do you fear viewing yourself in that way, as a predator, or as a werewolf?"

"Yes, but there are times that the acts men perform make me reluctant to admit to being their kind, also. Do you view yourself in that way, as a predator?"

"My dear man, I am rich, so although I don't feel it, I am constantly seen as one who gnaws on the bones of the humble. I once said, jokingly, of course, that wealth is as heavy a cross to bear as being a werewolf, but I then had a room full of werewolves agree, and thus discovered the unabashed truth of my own statement. One has to constantly guard wealth as carefully as full-moon secrets."

"I once had wealth, but I did not guard it, and my family suffers accordingly. That is a curse I must watch as it plays out day after day. I do not regret helping others, but I very much regret not helping my own," Mr. March said sadly, running his hands through his hair.

Jo turned her face away so her father could not see the single tear that streamed down her cheek. She wanted to tell him the money didn't matter, but the sorry fact was—it did.

"What if I don't hunt?" Mr. March asked suddenly.

"It's important to eat while a wolf to nourish that body. Sickness will result from hunger. And it is an unfortunate reality that you will need to consume human flesh and drink human blood in order to live."

"We have all heard that, but there are so many werewolf legends, one has a hard time separating truth from lore," Mr. March said. "I am sorry to hear that this is, in fact, truth."

And so Mr. March resigned himself to his new situation and was prepared to learn to hunt in order to survive. Before the men's transvection began on the night of the full moon, Mr.

Laurence explained the importance of fully assessing each situation, explaining that, as with any hunt, to attack blindly greatly increased the risk of making a fatal mistake.

When the transvection came, Mr. March did not expect to live through it, so distressing and intolerable was the accompanying pain; he first thought his skin was burning off his bones as it flared with heat. Next, he suffered through the lengthening and twisting of bones, skin, muscles, tendons, and veins as they altered from the human male form to that of a massive, hirsute beast. He stood panting and drooling with a lusty hunger he had never before experienced—not even during his battlefield deprivations. Unexpectedly, he found he knew these new legs and feet well, and bounded easily and steadily out the door behind Mr. Laurence as soon as he was fully transformed.

A few dozen feet away from the house, Mr. Laurence sniffed the air, then looked back to Mr. March, who was hurriedly inhaling a wealth of odors, each more tempting than the last. How did one pluck out the ripest and sweetest to follow? The scent of a deer suddenly overwhelmed the others, and Mr. March turned to face the animal. Mr. Laurence growled for him to follow, to redirect his sense of smell to those aromas wafting from his leader.

Farther out, Mr. March picked up another scent, one that caused him to lap up the saliva on his lips. Mr. Laurence informed him it was a woman he smelled, but that they would not take her, as both the time and the place were wrong.

Finally, they came upon a field where rabbits ran, and Mr. Laurence told Mr. March to try to capture one. Mr. March leapt out even before his neighbor had finished his thought and concentrated on just one of the small animals running amok in terror. In two great leaps, he had the rabbit pinned, and surprise and ecstasy washed over him as his teeth sank into the moist meat. Submitting to his bodily urges, he gave his full attention to his meal. He felt his body pulse with nourishment as his teeth ripped tissue and crushed bone. He coughed and gagged; famished, he was trying to swallow pieces much too large, but the mesmerizing allure of flesh and blood still warm with life made him frantic for the next bite.

He made short work of the rodent, then licked the viscera and blood from his paws. Wanting more, he spread his toes and with one sharp, jutting tooth, scraped the back of each claw, harvesting one last decent mouthful.

When they returned to the bodies of men, Mr. Laurence congratulated Mr. March. "You truly are a man of God. Your self-control is exemplary, and it is well, for that woman we came upon early in the night was a trap set by the Brigade, a new idea being tested by the group. We werewolves must now be more vigilant than ever."

"I imagine it is younger werewolves than I who need to learn to control themselves."

"At any age, resisting those desires is difficult. It will be even more so once you have tasted human flesh," Mr. Laurence reminded him.

"What if I choose to only eat animals?"

"You cannot live on animals alone. It's the human blood that enriches our systems. We will work you up to that, though. You will have another animal, perhaps a larger one, such as a deer, next month, and then . . ." He left the rest unsaid.

Jo had sat up nervously the entire night of the full moon, ears perked to catch any noise or disturbance. She had run to the window again and again, and finally had gone to her writing space in the garret and pulled her chair over to the window where she could stare out at the greatest distance. The next morning, she awoke with a start, cold and cross. When she went downstairs, her father sat wide-eyed at the table. With a small cry, she ran to him and threw her arms about him.

"It was fine," he whispered into her neck. "Mr. Laurence is an admirable teacher. It is a more bearable life than I had imagined." He looked around the kitchen to be certain Hannah and Amy were both well out of earshot. "And I made a kill. A rabbit."

"Did . . . did you eat it?"

"Every morsel," he said with a wide smile.

Amy entered the kitchen at that moment, chattering on about what she would be wearing that day to her drawing class, as opposed to what she wished she would be wearing. Jo excused herself and went outside, hoping the fresh air would calm her nerves. It didn't, and she lost the contents of her pitching stomach in the bushes behind the house.

Soon after, Jo at last got word on her book. One of the three publishers offered to take it, on condition that she would cut it down one-third. Harsher words, that Jo saw as bad, accompanied this good news, however, for the parts the publisher wanted cut were all the ones she particularly admired.

"Now I must either bundle it up anew into a presentable manuscript and pay for printing it myself, or chop it up to suit purchasers, and get what I can for it," Jo said, calling a family meeting. "Fame is a very good thing to have in the house, but cash is more convenient; so I wish to take your wise counsel on this important subject."

"Don't spoil your book, my girl, for there is more in it than you know, and you have worked the idea out well and diligently. Perhaps allowing more time for it to ripen is a good course of action," Mr. March advised, and he practiced what he preached, having waited thirty years for fruit of his own to ripen, and being in no haste to gather it, even now, when it was sweet and mellow.

"But criticism is said to be the best test of such works, for I cannot always see the true merits and faults of the piece," said Jo, knitting her brow. "I've been fussing over the thing for so long, I really don't know whether it's good, bad, or indifferent. I realize the need for cool, impartial people to look at it and tell me what they think."

"I wouldn't leave out one word of it; you'll spoil it if you do, for the interest of the story is more in the minds than in the actions of the people, and it will be all a muddle if you don't explain as you go on," said Meg, who firmly believed that this book was the most remarkable novel ever written.

"But Mr. Allen says, 'Leave out the explanations, make it brief and dramatic, and let the characters tell the story,'" interrupted Jo, turning to the publisher's note.

"Do as he tells you. He knows what will sell, and we don't. Make a good, popular book, and get as much money as you can. By and by, when you've got a name, you can afford to digress, and have philosophical and metaphysical people in your novels," said Amy, who took a strict, practical view of the subject.

"Well," said Jo, laughing, "If my people *are* 'philosophical and metaphysical,' it isn't my fault, for I know nothing about such things, except what I sometimes hear Father say. If I have some of his wise ideas jumbled up with my romance, so much the better for me. Now, what do we think Beth and Marmee would say?"

"I think Beth would only care that it was printed soon, and

Mother's concern would be that there was a lesson in this by which you will learn, and be a better writer for it," said Meg with the vast wisdom of the oldest child.

So, with Spartan firmness, the young authoress laid her first-born on her table, and chopped it up as ruthlessly as any ogre. In the hope of suiting everyone, she took everyone's advice, which resulted in her pleasing no one.

Her father had liked the metaphysical streak, which had unconsciously gotten into it, so although she doubted doing so, she left it in. The editor had mentioned that there was far too much description, so out came nearly all of it, and with it, many necessary links in the story. Meg admired the tragedy, so Jo piled more atop that which already existed. Amy objected to the fun, so with the best of intentions, Jo quenched the sprightly scenes. Then, to complete the ruin, she cut it down one-third and sent the poor little romance, like a plucked robin, out into the big, busy world to try its fate.

Marmee and Beth returned from the seaside, and Jo told them all about her book before they even had time to remove their bonnets.

"I can't tell you how proud I am of you, for I don't know the words to use. I imagine your writing talent comes from your father, not me," Mrs. March said, tears of joy running down her cheeks.

"But keep in mind, Marmee, it isn't yet accepted. But someone who knows books, who truly knows books, saw hope in my work. It took the entire family to advise me and convince me to cut it and rework it, but I have a firm and staunch faith in my novel, and I just know it will be worth every ink stain and hour."

Beth did not look as plump or as rosy as Jo had hoped, but she said she felt much better, and seemed to have renewed spirit and energy. Mrs. March declared that she felt ten years younger, and Jo dreamed of making enough money from her novel to buy a seaside cottage where they could all live out their lives in vigorous health and happiness.

Well, Jo's novel was printed, and she received three hundred dollars for it; likewise, plenty of praise and blame, both so much greater than she expected that she was thrown into a state of utter bewilderment, from which it took her some time to recover.

"I no longer know if I have written a promising book or broken all ten commandments," she said to Marmee. "You've always told me criticism would help, but I'm filled with joy and pride one minute and with wrath and dismay the next. It has been called 'an exquisite book full of truth, beauty, earnestness,' 'all that is sweet, pure and healthy,' and 'a book filled with morbid fancies, spiritualistic ideas, and unnatural characters.' The theory of the book has been criticized, but I had no theory of any kind. It has been called 'the best American novel to have emerged in years,' although I know better than that, and the next critic asserts that 'although it is original and written with great force and feeling, it is a dangerous book.' Dangerous! Of all the things it could be called, I find that the most fanciful. Some make fun of it, some overpraise it, and all insist it has issued forth from some great theory when I only wrote it for pleasure and the money. I do wish I had printed it whole or not at all, for I do hate to be so misjudged."

Her family and friends administered comfort and commendation liberally; yet it was a hard time for sensitive, high-spirited Jo, who meant it so well, but apparently had done so ill. But it did her good, for criticism truly is an author's best education. Once the soreness was over, she would be able to laugh at her poor little book, yet believe in it still, and feel much stronger and wiser for the buffeting she had received. Her greatest comfort was that she knew there were more books inside her, and she drew great happiness and relief from knowing that when she was ready, she'd sit up tall again in her familiar little chair in the garret and write another.

...

CHAPTER 26

Domestic Disaster

LIKE MOST OTHER YOUNG MATRONS, MEG BEGAN HER married life with a determination to be a model housekeeper. She felt that John should see his home as a haven and a paradise; he should always be greeted by a smiling face, should fare sumptuously every day, and never know the loss of a button. She brought so much love, energy, and cheerfulness to the work that she could not but succeed, in spite of some obstacles. Her paradise was not a tranquil one; for the little woman had more energy than discretion, and fussed, was overanxious to please, and bustled about cumbered with so many cares that she was sometimes too tired even to smile. John grew dyspeptic after a course of dainty dishes, and ungratefully demanded plain fare. As for buttons, she soon learned to wonder where they went, to shake her head over the carelessness of men, and to threaten to make him sew them on himself to see if *his* work would withstand impatient tugs and clumsy fingers any better than hers.

Overall, the pair was very happy, even after discovering the harsh reality that they couldn't live on love alone. John did not find Meg's beauty diminished in the least as she beamed at him from behind the familiar coffeepot. Their daily parting was romantic, and John always followed up his kiss with the tender inquiry, "Shall I send home veal or mutton for dinner, darling?" Their little house had truly become a home, though they ceased to frolic over it like children, as John felt the cares of the head of a family fall firmly upon his shoulders.

Meg labored through *Mrs. Cornelius's Receipt Book* as if it was a mathematical exercise, working out each problem with patience and care. Sometimes her family was invited to help eat up too bounteous a feast of successes, or a batch of failures would be secretly dispatched and concealed in the convenient stomachs of the little Hummels. An evening with John over the account books usually produced a temporary lull in the culinary enthusiasm, and a frugal fit would ensue, during which the poor man was put through a course of bread pudding, hash, and warmed-over coffee, which tried his soul, although he bore it with praise-worthy fortitude.

Fired with a housewifely wish to see her storeroom stocked with homemade preserves, Meg undertook to put up her own currant jelly. She asked John to please order home a dozen or so little pots and a quantity of extra sugar, for their currants were ripe and needed to be attended to at once. John took a natural pride in his wife's skills and gratified her request with four dozen delightful little pots, half a barrel of sugar, and a small boy to pick currants for her, anticipating their only crop of fruit laid up in a most pleasing form for winter use.

With her pretty hair tucked into a cap, sleeves rolled up past her elbows, and a coquettishly checked bibbed apron, the young housewife fell to work, feeling no doubts about her success, for she had seen Hannah perform this task hundreds of times. The array of pots rather amazed her at first, but John was so fond of jelly, and the nice little jars would look so pleasing lined up along the top shelf of the pantry, that she resolved to fill them all, and spent a long day picking, boiling, straining, and fussing over her jelly. She did her best, consulted Mrs. Cornelius's book, and racked her brain to remember what Hannah had done that she had forgotten. She reboiled, resugared, and re-strained it all, but the dreadful stuff simply would not jell.

She longed to run home, apron and all, to ask her mother to lend a hand, but she and John had agreed that they would never annoy anyone with their private worries, experiments, or quarrels. They had laughed over that last word, as if the idea it suggested was preposterous. So Meg wrestled alone with the refractory sweetmeats all that hot summer day, and at five o'clock sat down in her topsy-turvy kitchen, wrung her stained, abused hands, lifted her voice, and wept.

Now, in the first flush of their married life, she had often said, "My husband shall always be free to bring a friend home whenever he likes. I shall always be prepared; there shall be no flurry, no scolding, and no discomfort, nothing save a neat house, a cheerful wife, and a good dinner. John, dear, you need never stop to ask. Invite whom you please, and be sure of a warm welcome from me. Invite them all at once, or one at a time. Bring home an entire pack of werewolves under the full moon, and if you call them your friends, I will feed them uncooked meat and animal organs."

A charming idea, to be sure, and John glowed with pride to hear her say it, and felt what a blessed thing it was to have a superior wife. They did have company from time to time, but it had never been unexpected. It can only be called inevitable that during this vale of tears such a thing would happen at last.

If John had not forgotten about the jelly, it really would have been unpardonable of him to choose that day, of all days in the year, to bring a friend home to dinner unexpectedly. Congratulating himself that a handsome repast had been ordered that morning and feeling certain it would be ready the moment they walked in, he had only to indulge in the pleasant anticipation of the charming effect it would produce when his pretty wife came running out to meet and welcome them to his mansion.

It is a world of disappointments, as John discovered when he reached his house. The front door usually stood hospitably open; now it was not only shut but also locked, and yesterday's mud still adorned the steps. The parlour windows were closed and curtained, and no picture of the pretty wife sewing on the piazza, in white, with a distracting little bow in her hair, presented itself. Nothing of the sort, for not a soul appeared except a sanguinary-looking boy asleep under the bare currant bushes.

"I fear something has happened. Step into the garden, Scott, while I look up Mrs. Brooke," said John, alarmed at the silence and solitude.

Around the house he rushed, led by a pungent smell of burnt sugar, and Mr. Scott strolled after him with a queer look on his face. He paused discreetly at a distance when Mr. Brooke disappeared, but he could both see and hear the confusion reigning in the kitchen where one edition of jelly was trickled from pot to pot, another lay on the floor, and a third was burning gaily on the stove. Little Lotty Hummel sat calmly eating bread and currant wine, for the jelly was still in a hopelessly liquid state. Mrs. Brooke, with her apron over her head, sat in a corner crying dismally.

"My dearest girl, whatever is the matter?" cried John, rushing in with awful visions of scalded hands, sudden news of affliction, and secret consternation at the thought of the guest in the garden.

"Oh, John! I am so tired, and hot, and cross, and worried. I've been at it till I'm all worn out. Do come and help me, or I shall die!" And the exhausted housewife cast herself upon his breast, giving him a sweet welcome in every sense of the word, for the pinafore she held against him had been baptized in sugar and berries.

"What worries you, dear? Has anything dreadful happened?" asked the anxious John, tenderly kissing the crown of the little cap that sat crooked on her mussed tumble of hair.

"Yes," sobbed Meg despairingly.

"Tell me quick, then; don't cry. I can bear anything better than that. Out with it, love."

"The . . . the jelly won't jell—and I don't know what to do!"

John Brooke laughed then as he never dared to laugh afterward; and the derisive Scott smiled involuntarily as he heard the hearty peal, which put the finishing stroke to poor Meg's woe.

"Is that all?" he asked. "Fling it all out the window and let werewolves eat every bit, and don't bother any more about it. I'll buy you quarts if you want it, but for heaven's sake, don't have hysterics. I've brought Jack Scott home to dinner, and—"

John got no further, for Meg cast him off, and clasped her hands with a tragic gesture as she fell into a chair, exclaiming in a tone of mingled indignation, reproach, and dismay, "A man to dinner with everything in a mess! John Brooke, how *could* you do such a thing?"

"Hush! He's in the garden! I forgot about the confounded jelly, but it can't be helped now," said John, surveying the slim prospect for a decent dinner with an anxious eye.

"You ought to have sent word, or told me this morning. Or you ought to have remembered how busy I was," continued Meg petulantly; proving even turtledoves will peck when ruffled.

"I didn't know it this morning, and there was no time to send word, for I met him on the way out. I never thought of asking leave, when you have always told me to do as I liked. I never tried it before, and hang me if I ever try again!" John added with a dramatic and aggrieved air.

"I should hope not! Take him away at once; I can't see him and there isn't any dinner."

"Well, I like that! Where's the beef and vegetables I sent home, and the pudding you promised? I had every reason to expect an exceptional dinner this evening."

"I had no time to cook anything. I meant to dine at my mother's. I'm sorry, but I was *so* busy the whole of the day," and Meg's tears began again.

John was a mild man, but he was human; and after a long day's work, to come home tired, hungry, and hopeful and find a chaotic house, an empty table, and a cross wife was not exactly conducive to repose of mind or manner. He restrained himself, however, and the whole thing would have blown over, but for one unlucky word.

"It's a scrape, I acknowledge," he said. "But if you will lend a hand, we will pull through and have a good time yet. Don't cry, dear, but just exert yourself a bit, and knock us up something to eat. We're both hungry as hunters, so anything will serve to please us. Give us cold meat, bread, and cheese. We promise not to ask for jelly."

He meant it as a good-natured joke; but that one word sealed his fate. Meg thought it far too cruel for him to joke about her sad failure, and the last atom of her patience vanished.

"You get yourself out of the scrape the best you can; I'm too used up to exert myself for anyone. So like a man to propose a bone and vulgar bread and cheese for company. I won't have anything of the sort in my house. Take that Scott up to Mother's, and tell him I'm away—sick, dead, anything. I won't see him, and you two can laugh at me and my jelly as much as you like." Having delivered her defiance all in one breath, she flung aside her apron and left to bemoan her situation in the privacy of her own room.

What those two creatures did in her absence, she never knew, but Mr. Scott was not taken up to her mother's. When they had strolled away together and she descended, she found traces of a promiscuous lunch, which filled her with horror. Lotty, the kitchen help, reported that they had "eaten much and laughed even more," and the master bid her throw away all the sweet stuff and hide the pots.

Meg longed to run, crying, to her mother, but a sense of shame at her own shortcomings, and of loyalty to John, restrained her. He might be cruel, but nobody should know of it. After a summary cleaning up, she dressed herself prettily and sat down to wait for John to return home and be forgiven.

Unfortunately, John did not return home for some time. He had carried off the incident as a good joke with Scott, and played the host so hospitably that his friend not only enjoyed the impromptu dinner, but also promised to visit again. But John was actually quite angry. He felt Meg had gotten him into a scrape and deserted him in his hour of need. It simply was unfair to tell a man to bring his friends home anytime, with perfect freedom, and when he took you at your word, to flame up and blame him, and leave him in the lurch to be laughed at or pitied. It was, in fact, so unfair; he felt his wife ought know it. He had fumed inwardly during the feast, but while strolling around for some time, and then finally aimed for home, a milder mood came over him and he told himself he must be patient and try to see Meg's side. He wished he had run the entire way home when he happened upon an assemblage of the Brigade, who walked the streets under the guise of protecting them, the studs pushed into the heavy leather of their breastplates and their helmets winking in the dying sunlight's last weak beams. One of the members stopped him and pushed him roughly up against a wall.

"Why do you walk the streets, man?"

"I was escorting a friend home. He had dinner with us."

"On what did you dine? Anything of liking to a werewolf?"

"There was meat, sir," John said, trying to keep his voice assured and his lips from trembling. "But it was not to the liking of a werewolf, for it was too fully cooked. To a crisp, as a matter of fact."

"Do you know any werewolves?" the man asked, lowering his head so his eyes, from within the dark leather helmet, pierced John's.

"Certainly not!" He shifted his weight slightly to relieve the weakness of his knees, and clenched himself to keep his bladder from releasing.

"Come along," another member of the Brigade said to his crony. "This is obviously some dull clerk who can only dream of a life as exciting as a werewolf's. I'd wager he and his friend were fed by his mother."

The men roared with laughter, and John was torn between protesting that he didn't live with his mother, but with a handsome and loyal wife, and keeping his mouth sealed in the hopes that he would be sooner released.

He chose well, for he remained silent and the group walked on to find more interesting prey.

He realized that he was being swallowed up by the dusk, and imagined Meg worried and crying herself sick. He thought of only her in order to dissolve the memories of his harrowing incident with the Brigade, and those singular thoughts softened his heart and sent him on at a quicker pace. He was now resolved to be kind but firm, quite firm, and show her where she had failed in her duty as a spouse.

Meg, likewise, resolved to be the same, kind but firm, and to show *him* his duty. She longed to run to meet him, and beg pardon, and be kissed and comforted, but instead, when she saw him coming, she began to rock in her chair, humming and sewing like a lady of leisure.

Although he was relieved and thankful upon returning to the safe haven of his home, John was disappointed to be ignored, and felt he deserved the first apology to preserve his dignity. He laid himself upon the sofa and remarked that they were going to have a new moon.

Meg agreed lightly, and a few other topics were introduced by Mr. Brooke and wet-blanketed by Mrs. Brooke. Conversation languished, and John went to one window, unfolded his paper, and immersed himself in it. Meg went to the other window and sewed as if new rosettes on her slippers were among the necessities of life. Neither spoke, although both looked quite calm and firm while feeling desperately uncomfortable.

Meg thought about the difficulties of marriage, realizing that John was a good man but, like any other man, had his faults. He was decided but not obstinate, accurate and particular about the truth. She saw that his temper was not like hers, one flash and then all over, but rather a white, still anger that was seldom stirred but, once kindled, hard to quench. She worried that she had woken that anger against herself, and lost peace and happiness by losing his respect. Her mother had told her and her sisters, more than once, that hasty words often pave the way for bitter sorrow and regret.

She thought back to her hasty speech, her childish anger, and the memory of poor John arriving home to a messy house and a cross wife, and her heart melted. She glanced at him with tears in her eyes, but he did not see them. She put down her work and got up, intent to be the first to say she was sorry. She stood by him, but he did not turn his head, so she stooped down and softly kissed her husband on his forehead. That settled it, as the penitent kiss was better than a world of words, and John had her on his knee in a minute.

"It was too bad to laugh at the poor little jelly pots who had expected to perform such an important task. Forgive me. I will never do so again," he said, but he did. Oh, yes. Hundreds of times, as did Meg, both declaring that it was the sweetest jelly ever made.

Meg soon had Mr. Scott to dinner by special invitation and served him up such a wondrous feast, and was so gay and charming and warm, that Mr. Scott shook his head over the hardships of bachelorhood all the way home.

In the autumn, new trials and experiences came to Meg. Sallie Moffat renewed their friendship and was always running to the little house with dishes of gossip, or inviting Meg to spend a day at her big house. With John absent until night, Meg was lonely and happy for the company, and fell easily into the way of gadding and gossiping with her friend. Seeing Sallie's pretty things made her long for such, and pity herself for not having them. Sallie was kind and often offered her the coveted trifles, but Meg declined them, knowing John wouldn't like it. But then, this foolish woman went and did what John liked infinitely worse.

She knew her husband's income, and loved that he trusted

her. She was free to take what she liked, and he asked only that she keep a full accounting of every penny, pay the bills once a month, and remember that she was a poor man's wife. Thus far, she had done well; she had been prudent and exact and kept her account book neatly, showing it to him monthly without fear. But that autumn, the serpent got into Meg's paradise and tempted her like a modern Eve, not with apples, but with a dress. Meg didn't like to be pitied and be made to feel poor; it irritated and shamed her. So now and then she bought herself something pretty, as much to console herself as to show Sallie that she had no need to economize. She always felt wicked after, for these pretty things were not necessities, but they cost so little that it was hardly worth worrying about. But the trifles increased unconsciously, and she became too active in the shopping excursions.

When she cast up her accounts at the end of the month, the total rather scared her. John was busy that month, and left the bills to her. The next month he was absent, but the third month he had a grand quarterly settling up to do that she never forgot. Sallie had been buying silks, and Meg longed for a lightweight one for parties, as her black silk was so common and old. She felt she couldn't wait another month for Aunt March's twenty-five-dollar New Year gift, especially when she saw a lovely violet silk going away at a bargain, and she had the cash, in the form of the household savings, at her fingertips. Sallie had urged her to buy it, even offering to lend her the money, so despite her best intentions, Meg was tempted beyond her strength. In an evil moment, the shop man held up the lovely, shimmering folds and said, "A bargain, I assure you, ma'am."

She answered, "I'll take it."

When she got home, she felt pangs of remorse while spreading forth the lovely silk that now looked less silvery. She put it away but was haunted by it, and the words "fifty dollars" seemed stamped like a pattern everywhere she looked. When John got out his books that night, Meg's heart sank, and, for the first time in her married life, she was afraid of her husband. The house bills had all been paid and the books were in order, so John praised her, but when he began undoing the old pocketbook, which they called "the bank," she stopped his hand, saying nervously, "You haven't seen my expense book yet." She explained that she was ashamed to show it to him, that she had been dreadfully extravagant lately. "I can replace twenty-five dollars with my New Year money from Aunt March," she promised, exhibiting her deep shame in her every move and word.

John laughed. "I won't kill you for buying a pair of boots for eight or nine dollars, so long as they are good ones in which to put those pretty feet."

"It's worse than boots. It's a silk dress."

"Well, dear, what is the dreaded total?"

She turned the page and her head at the same time, pointing to the sum, which would have been bad enough without the fifty for the dress, and was outright appalling with it added.

"Well, I suppose fifty isn't all that much for a dress, considering all the furbelows and notions it takes to trim it and finish it off these days," he said softly.

"It isn't made or trimmed," Meg sighed.

"Twenty-five yards of silk seems a good deal to cover one small woman, but I'm sure my wife will look as good as Ned Moffat's when she gets it on," John said dryly.

"I know you're angry, John. I don't mean to waste your

money, and I was foolish not to realize all those small things would add up into a great sum. I see Sallie buying all she wants and pitying me because I can't. I try to be contented, but it's hard, and I'm tired of being poor."

Her last words, though spoken quite low, wounded John deeply, for he denied himself many pleasures for Meg's sake. She saw the expression on his face, and could have bitten out her own tongue if that would have taken the words back. He did not utter one reproach, and forgave her readily but he was so quiet, and she suffered through a full week of remorse that made her sick, especially once she realized that he had canceled the order for his new greatcoat on the grounds that they simply could not afford it.

He found her in the hallway, crying into the old greatcoat, and they had a long talk that made Meg love her husband better for his poverty, because it seemed to have made a man of him, given him the strength and courage to fight his own way, and also gave him tender patience.

The next day she put her pride in her pocket, went to Sallie, told her the truth, and asked her to buy the silk as a favor. The good-natured Mrs. Moffat did so readily, and had the delicacy not to make a present of it to her immediately afterward. Then Meg ordered home the greatcoat, making John a very happy husband, and a very warm man during that long, cold winter.

So the year rolled around, and at midsummer, there came to Meg and John the gift of not one child, but two. Meg was greatly relieved in that both children thrived, so there would be no visits by the Brigade to investigate ailing children who could possibly be of werewolf lineage.

Jo pronounced it the greatest joke of the season when Laurie returned home one weekend and the twin babies, of whom he knew nothing, were laid, wrapped tightly in flannel, in his lap.

The boy was named John Laurence, and the girl Margaret, after mother and grandmother, but everyone took to calling the boy Demijohn, which was soon shortened to Demi, and the girl was known and loved as Daisy.

...

CHAPTER 27

Maddening Social Responsibilities

"COME, JO. IT'S TIME," AMY ANNOUNCED.

"For what?"

"You don't mean to say that you forgot your promise to make half a dozen calls with me today?"

"I've done a good many rash and foolish things in my life, but I don't think I was ever mad enough to say I'd make six calls in one day, when a single one upsets me for a week."

"You did. It was a bargain between us in exchange for my finishing the crayon drawing of Beth for you. Come on, we must be honorable and return our neighbors' visits."

"There is a pile of clouds to the east, so I don't think I'll go."

"That's shirking! It's a lovely day with no prospect of rain. Pride yourself on keeping promises, Jo, do your duty, and then be free for six months."

There was no escape, even though Jo wanted desperately to work on her dressmaking. She hated calls of the social sort, and never made any till Amy cornered her with a bargain, bribe, or promise. She clashed her scissors rebelliously but gave in and took up her hat and gloves with an air of resignation.

"I hope you don't intend to make calls in that state of dress!" Amy said, falling into a chair as if fainting at the sight of Jo in such disreputable condition.

"Why not? I'm neat, cool, and comfortable, quite proper for a dusty walk on a warm day. Why don't you just dress for the both of us? I've learned it doesn't pay for me to be elegant."

Amy knew the formal visits, during Jo's contrary fit, would be without pleasure, but saw it as a debt they owed society. Amy thought a moment, and then said, "Jo, do come to take care of me. I want your comfort, of course, but you talk so well, and you look so aristocratic in your good things. I didn't want to say, but I'm afraid to go alone."

"You're an artful little puss to flatter and wheedle your cross old sister. I don't know which is more absurd: the idea of me being aristocratic and well bred, or your being afraid to go out alone." Jo stopped and let out a deep sigh. "I'll go, blindly obey, and hope it pleases you."

"You're a perfect cherub!" Amy cried, and then began issuing orders of what Jo should wear, how to do her hair, which color rose to add to her bonnet, and even which handkerchief to bring. "Come with me. I have the perfect gloves to go with your dress."

Jo followed Amy into the little closet where her prayer altar was set up. She looked at the assembled articles, and then picked up the tuft of fur cut from the coat in Aunt March's wardrobe and inquired about it.

"It's werewolf fur."

"It isn't!" Jo said, examining it carefully.

"No, I don't believe it is. It represents it, though, on my altar."

· "For what purpose?"

"Why, to ask for protection against werewolves, of course. Now turn about and let me fix the way your skirt falls in back. There. We're ready. Let's be on our way."

So Jo frowned darkly, wrestled viciously with bonnet and collar pins, and stuffed her hands into tight gloves with three buttons and a tassel.

"I'm perfectly miserable!" Jo remarked. "But if you find me presentable, I die happy."

Amy pronounced her highly satisfactory, and remarked, as Jo revolved, upon her sorry posture and her need for a shawl. In fact, their walk proved to be one lesson from Amy after another. "Now, Jo dear, the Lambs are very elegant people, and I don't want you to make any of your abrupt remarks or do anything odd, will you? Just be calm, cool, and quiet."

"Let me see—'calm, cool, and quiet'! Yes, I think I can promise that." Amy looked relieved, but naughty Jo took her at her word; for during the first call, being tired of trying to remember all the lessons, Jo decided to simply play the role of a quiet, prim young lady onstage. She sat with limbs gracefully composed, every fold correctly draped, calm as a summer sea, cool as a snowbank, and as silent as a sphinx.

"There seems to have been an absence of werewolf attacks for some time," someone offered by way of conversation.

"Yes, there have been none to speak of since that mass ambush of the visiting amputees, and that's been, what, well over a year?"

At the mention of the amputees, Jo opened her mouth to speak but remembered herself, so sat back in her chair again and remained mute.

"Not so. I believe one fellow was taken in early spring, and a child at the height of summer."

"Yes, yes, that's right. What was I thinking? That baker was found guilty and hanged just two months past. I fear I misspoke. All is as it has always been after all. One person here, another there."

That remark led to a sputtering of comments, and then the room grew quiet once more.

Minutes dragged by like weeks, but Amy finally pronounced it time to leave.

As they bid their farewell, their host audibly remarked as the door closed, "What a haughty, uninteresting creature that oldest March is! One would think the writer of novels would be more animated."

Amy looked disgusted at the failure of her instructions and laid the blame, of course, on Jo.

"I merely gave you what you wanted—properly dignified and controlled."

"How could you mistake me so? You made yourself a perfect stone. Be sociable at this next house, gossip as the other girls do, show interest in dress and flirtations and whatever other nonsense comes up. These Chesters are valuable people for us to know. They move in the best society."

But Jo allowed her spirit of mischief to take over, and talked away as volubly as an old deaf lady, going on and on with an unsavory story about one of Amy's horseback-riding disasters. Worse than any story she told that day, though, was her reply when someone commented on a pastel green hat they had once seen her wear to a picnic. In earshot of everyone there she said, "You can't buy hats in those soft shades, so we paint them any color we like. It's such fun having an artist for a sister," she added.

Smiles that were too wide and eyes that stared out insincere accompanied all the comments.

"How interesting."

"What an original idea."

"Quite different."

When the talk turned to Jo's writing, she took Amy's arm and said, "We really *must* go." To her hosts, she called in a perfect imitation of Mrs. Chester, "*Do* come and see us; we are absolutely *pining* for a visit. *Good*bye."

Amy was so angry with Jo, she could only sputter, her words being as disobedient as Jo and refusing to line up in proper order.

At the next house, they received an enthusiastic greeting from three big boys and several pretty children, and Jo devoted herself to this group, leaving Amy to attend to the hostess. She listened to college stories with deep interest, and caressed poodles and pointers while Amy enjoyed herself surrounded by distant connections of actual British nobility.

Some time later, Amy found Jo sitting on the grass, with an encampment of boys around her and a dirty-footed dog reposing on the skirt of her state-and-festival dress as she related one of Laurie's pranks to her admiring audience. One small child was poking in the pond for turtles with Amy's cherished parasol, a second was eating gingerbread over Jo's best bonnet, and a third was playing ball with her gloves.

"But they were all enjoying themselves," Jo argued after being scolded while they walked to the next visit.

The next family was evidently out, so they gratefully dropped the family card case to do their duty. At the stop after that, Jo uttered another thanksgiving when they were informed that the young ladies were presently engaged.

"Let's go home now, and never mind Aunt March today," Jo begged.

"We're going. You might as well, being already dressed. I hardly think you would want to suffer through preparing yourself again next week. Besides, Aunt likes the call; it gives her so much pleasure. Do stoop down so I can get those crumbs off your bonnet." Amy brushed the hat clean with her handkerchief and said, "Women should learn to be agreeable, particularly poor ones; for they have no other way of repaying the kindnesses they receive."

"I can't help how I am. It would be far easier for me to risk my life for a person than to be pleasant to him when I don't feel like it," Jo complained.

They found Aunt Carrol visiting the old lady when they arrived. The two had been absorbed in an interesting conversation but dropped it the moment the girls walked in, and their temporarily cool countenances suggested they had been discussing their nieces. Jo was in poor humor and her perverse fit returned, but Amy kept her temper and pleased the aunts so much with her angelic manners that the old women were certain the child improved a bit every day.

But Jo, on the other hand, acted so cross that Aunt March finally said to her, "My goodness, child, you are so out of sorts, I wouldn't be the least surprised if you fell down onto the floor like a werewolf and began tearing up my carpet with your teeth."

"I'm not that bad, Aunt," Jo said with an angry sigh.

Amy promised meanwhile to help Aunt Carrol with the upcoming fair, saying that she was happy to donate her time to help others, as it was all she had to give. "Quite right and proper," observed Aunt March. "I like your grateful spirit, my dear; it's a pleasure to help people who appreciate our efforts. Some don't, and that is trying," she said, looking over her spectacles at Jo, who sat apart rocking herself with a somewhat morose expression.

Had Jo known what great happiness was wavering in the balance for one of the March girls, she would have turned dove-like in an instant. Instead, by her next speech, Jo deprived herself of several years of pleasure and received a timely lesson in the art of holding her tongue.

"I don't like favors; they oppress and make me feel a slave. I'd much rather do everything myself and be perfectly independent."

"I told you so," Aunt March said with a decided nod to Aunt Carrol.

"Do you speak French, dear?" Aunt Carrol asked, laying her hand on Amy's.

"Pretty well, thanks to Aunt March. She lets Esther talk to me in her native language as often as I like," Amy replied, shooting Aunt March a grateful look, which caused the old lady to smile affably.

"And how are you at languages?" Aunt Carrol asked of Jo.

"Don't know a word. I'm very stupid about studying anything. I can't bear French, it being such a silly, slippery sort of language, and hard for my tongue to form those words," came Jo's brusque reply.

Polly bent down from his perch on the back of Jo's chair and peeped into her face with a comical air of impertinent inquiry that finally forced a gust of laughter out of Jo.

"Come and take a walk, my dear?" said Polly, hopping toward the china cabinet.

"Thank you, Polly. I will. Come, Amy," said Jo, ending the visit by shaking hands with each old woman and standing back while Amy kissed and hugged them each in turn.

As soon as they left, Aunt March said to Aunt Carrol, "You'd better do it, Mary; I'll supply the money."

"I certainly will," Aunt Carrol replied, "if her mother and father consent."

CHAPTER 28

True Art Prevails

MRS. CHESTER'S FAIR WAS SO VERY ELEGANT AND select that the young ladies of the neighborhood invited to take a table considered it a great honor. Amy was asked but Jo was not, which was fortunate for all parties involved. Mrs. Chester complimented Amy's talent and taste, even offering her the fair's art table. Amy accepted eagerly, and worked hard to build a beautiful and elegant display, not realizing that her dainty pen-and-ink work absolutely eclipsed May Chester's painted vases. May had a list of reasons to be jealous of Amy: boys, talent, popularity, and looks, but attention given to Amy at a recent party by the boy May liked best was the greatest and most painful thorn, so Amy shouldn't have been so surprised when, the evening before the fair, Mrs. Chester declared that she was sorry, but the table had to be reassigned to one of her girls due to its prominence and attractiveness. She added that, so as not to totally disappoint Amy, she was assigning her another table.

Amy's hurt, unsuspicious eyes haunted the woman when the young girl asked, "Would you rather I took no table at all?"

"Please don't have ill feelings, dear, I beg. It's a matter of expediency. You see, my girls naturally take the lead, and this table is their proper place. Everyone is saying so. *I* am grateful for all the work you did to make it so lovely, but there is a good place for you elsewhere. You may have the flower table. I can't imagine what charming things you will be able to do with that! The flower table is always so attractive."

"Especially to the gentlemen," May added, enlightening Amy as to the cause of her sudden fall from favor. She was glad to know the true reason for this change, for she had been absolutely certain the blame for her disgraced position rested on Jo's accurate imitation of Mrs. Chester, and she had planned to deal severely with her sister when she returned home.

Amy colored angrily but turned her back to the girl's sarcasm and answered, with unexpected amiability, "It shall be as you please, Mrs. Chester. I shall give up my place here at once and go where I am most needed."

"You can put your things on your own table if you prefer," began May, a little conscience-stricken, as she looked at the pretty racks, the painted shells, and quaint illuminations Amy had so carefully made and arranged.

She meant it kindly, but Amy mistook her meaning and said quickly, "Oh, certainly, if they are in your way," and sweeping her contributions into her apron pell-mell, she walked off, feeling that herself and her works of art had been insulted beyond forgiveness.

"Oh, dear. Now she's mad. I wish I hadn't asked you to do that, Mama," said May, looking disconsolately at the empty spaces on her table.

"Girls' quarrels are soon over," returned the mother, feeling a trifle ashamed of her own part in this one, as well she might.

The little girls helping at the affair hailed Amy and her treasures with delight, and their cordial reception somewhat soothed her perturbed spirit, so she fell back to work, determined to succeed florally, if she couldn't artistically. But everything seemed against her: it was late, she was tired, and everyone was too busy with her own affairs to help her. Her head soon ached listening to the magpie chattering of the other girls, who made a great deal of confusion with their artless efforts. Their evergreen arch wouldn't stay firm once she got it up, but wiggled and threatened to tumble down on her head once the hanging baskets were filled; her best tile was splashed with water, leaving a sepia tear on Cupid's cheek; she bruised her hands with hammering, and got so cold working in a draft, that she found herself apprehensive for the morrow.

There was great indignation at home when she told her story that evening. Her mother said it was a shame but told her she had done right; Beth declared she wouldn't go to the fair at all in protest; and Jo demanded to know why Amy didn't take all her pretty things and leave those mean people to get on without her.

"Because they are mean is no reason I should be. I hate such things, and though I feel I have a right to be hurt, I don't intend to show it. They will feel that more than angry speeches and huffy actions, won't they, Marmee?"

"That's the right spirit, my dear. A kiss for a blow is always best, though it's often not easy," said her mother with the air of one who had learned of such matters by practice.

"I'd much rather see an entire pack of werewolves tear through the fair and leave it in shreds," Jo said decidedly.

Despite very natural temptations to resent and retaliate, Amy adhered to her resolution all the next day, bent on conquering her enemy by kindness. Her father had left her a reminder to help her through her day, one of his beautiful books next to her breakfast plate opened to a magnificent framed verse written in scarlet, blue, and gold that said, "Thou shalt love thy neighbor as thyself."

"I ought, but I don't," Amy whispered to herself. But the phrase stayed with her throughout the day as she watched May's discontented face behind the big vases that could not hide the vacancies her pretty work had once filled.

A group of girls stood around May's table, and their shrill voices dropped when the change of saleswomen was mentioned, so Amy knew they were now talking about her.

May was sniffing, saying it was too bad there was no time to make other things.

"I dare say, she'd put them back if you asked her," suggested one of the girls.

"How could I, after all the fuss?" began May, but she did not finish, for Amy's voice came across the hall, saying pleasantly, "You are welcome to them, without asking, if you want them. I was just thinking I'd offer to put them back, for they belong on your table, not mine. Please take them, and forgive me if I was hasty in removing them last night."

Amy walked over to return her contributions with a nod and a smile, and hurried away again, feeling that it was easier to flee than stand there and be thanked with gushes and grins.

"How very lovely of her," one girl said.

May's answer was inaudible, but another girl, whose temper was evidently soured by making lemonade, added with a disagreeable laugh, "Very lovely, for she knew she certainly wouldn't sell them at her table."

For a minute, Amy was sorry she had been so nice, as this proved virtue was not its own reward. But her spirits soon began to rise, and her table to blossom under her skillful hands. But it was still a long and hard day for Amy, and by the end of it, she was as wilted as her poor bouquets.

The art table was the most attractive in the room, and there was a crowd about it all day long. Money boxes rattled and important faces moored in front of it, forcing Amy to stare wistfully, wishing she were over there, where she could feel at home and happy, instead of in a desolate corner with nothing to do. The thought of being seen there that evening by her family, and Laurie and his friends, made her feel absolutely martyred.

When she went home for dinner, she didn't report on her dismal day to her family, but she quietly suggested they might consider staying home. She was so pale that they could see her day had been a trying one, so gave her tea and helped her dress. Beth made a charming little wreath for her hair while Jo hinted darkly that the tables were about to be turned.

"Don't do anything rude, pray, Jo. I want no fuss made, so let it pass and behave yourself," begged Amy as she departed early to find reinforcements of flowers to refresh her sorry little table. "The Brigade made a brief appearance this morning, forcefully stomping around the entire room, as if to remind our little fair of their existence. I fear any coarse behavior could lead to an accusation. Their expressions were hungry, so you really must be good."

"I merely intend to keep Laurie and his boys in your corner for as long as possible, and simply want us all to have a good time," Jo said, leaning over the gate to watch for Laurie. Presently, the familiar tramp was heard in the dusk, and she ran out to meet him.

As Laurie tucked her hand under his arm, Jo told him about the wrongs done Amy with sisterly zeal.

"A flock of our fellows are going to drive over by and by, and I'll be hanged if I won't make them buy every flower she's got, and camp down before her table afterward," Laurie said warmly.

"You don't want to make them buy these flowers," Amy said.

"They're not at all nice. I don't think the fresh ones will arrive in time. I don't wish to be unjust or suspicious, but I shall not be surprised if they never arrive at all. Oh, I really must get back. Goodbye for now."

"When people do one mean thing, they likely follow it up with another," Jo observed in a disgusted tone as she watched her sister walk away.

"Didn't Amy get the best flowers from Grandfather's garden?" Laurie asked.

"I think he completely forgot. And he was feeling poorly, so we didn't want to worry him by asking."

"How could you think there was any need of asking?" Laurie said with disbelief. "They are every bit as much yours as they are ours. Don't we always go halves on everything?"

"I would hope not!" Jo interjected. "Half of your silly things would not suit me at all, and you would find most of mine useless. Come, we must go and see what flowers we can find to save Amy's table. For this, I will bless you forever."

"Couldn't you do it now?" Laurie asked, so suggestively that Jo shut the gate in his face with inhospitable haste and told him to be on his way. She leaned against the wall, allowing her heart time to slow its beat and her cheeks to lose their blush.

Thanks to the conspirators, the tables were turned that night, for the Laurence garden donated a wilderness of beautiful and fragrant flowers. The March family turned out en masse, and Jo exerted herself to some purpose, for people not only came to the table but also stayed to laugh at her nonsense, admiring Amy's taste and seeming to enjoy themselves very much. Laurie and his friends gallantly bought up the bouquets and camped around the table, turning that corner into the liveliest in the room. Amy was in her element now, and out of gratitude was as sprightly and gracious as possible. Perhaps virtue *was* its own reward, after all.

Jo circulated about the hall, pretending to look at the wares but actually listening for bits of gossip. When she reached the art table, she saw no signs of her sister's things; imagining that they had been tucked away out of sight, she resented the insult as one against her entire family.

"Good evening, Miss Jo. How does Amy get on?" asked May kindly.

"She has sold everything she had worth selling, and is now quite busy with the business of enjoying herself."

Jo *couldn't* resist giving that little slap, but May took it so meekly that she instantly regretted it and, after a minute, took to praising the great vases, which remained unsold. "Is Amy's illumination anywhere about?" she asked, determined to learn the fate of her sister's work. "I thought I might buy it for Father."

"Everything of Amy's sold long ago. I took care that the right people saw them, and they made a tidy little sum of money for us," said May.

Much gratified, Jo rushed back to tell Amy the good news; and Amy looked both touched and surprised by the report of May's words and manner.

"Now, gentlemen," Amy said, a magnificent idea alight in her lovely head, "I want you to go and do your duty by the other tables as generously as you have at mine, especially at the art table, where you will find vases for your flowers."

"To hear is to obey, but March is fairer than May," said little Parker, making a frantic effort to be witty and tender in the presence of Amy.

To May's delight, the vases all sold, and the boys milled

about carrying them filled with bunches and bunches of Amy's lovely flowers, and drawing constant attention.

Aunt Carrol was there, heard the story in its entirety, looked pleased, and said something to Aunt March in the corner, which made the latter lady beam with satisfaction and watch Amy with a face full of mingled pride and anxiety.

The fair was pronounced a success, and when May bade Amy good night, she gave her an affectionate little kiss and a look that said all was forgiven and forgotten. That satisfied Amy, and when she got home, she was delighted to find every one of the vases paraded on the parlour chimneypiece, with a great bouquet in each.

"It must have been dreadfully hard to sit at the flower table, after working so long, and setting your heart on selling your own pretty things," Beth said that night as the three sisters sat brushing their hair before bed.

"You've a great deal more principle and generosity than I ever gave you credit for," Jo added.

"I only did as I'd be done by," Amy said with a shrug. "I can't explain exactly, but I want to be above the meanness and follies and faults that spoil so many women."

"And for that, one day you will be rewarded, and I will be delighted for you," Jo mused.

A week later, Amy did get her reward, and Jo found it hard to be delighted. A letter came from Aunt Carrol, and Mrs. March's face was illuminated as she read it. "Aunt Carrol is going abroad next month, and wants—"

"Me to go with her!" burst in Jo, flying out of her chair in an uncontrollable rapture. "I will need so many things; I hardly know where to begin."

"No, dear. Not you. She wants Amy."

"Oh Mother, no! You must have misread," Jo said, color draining from her face.

"Aunt Carroll asked specifically, and quite clearly, if Amy might be free to accompany her."

"She's far too young; it's my turn first. I've wanted it for so long. It would be so splendid and do me so much good."

"I'm afraid it's impossible, Jo. Aunt says Amy, decidedly, and it's not for us to dictate when she offers such a favor."

"It's always so; Amy has all the fun, and I have all the work. It isn't fair, oh, it isn't fair!" cried Jo passionately.

"I'm afraid it's partly your own fault," Mrs. March said. "Aunt had originally thought to ask you, but she said your manners were too blunt and your spirit too independent. You told her you hated French and didn't care to learn another language. She feels Amy, being more docile, would be a better companion for cousin Flo."

"Oh, my tongue. My abominable tongue! Why can't I learn to keep it quiet?" Jo groaned, remembering the words that had been her undoing.

"I wish you could have gone," Mrs. March said. "But there is no hope of that, so bear it cheerfully, and don't sadden Amy's pleasure by reproach or regret."

"I'll try my best," Jo said; "I'll take a leaf out of her book, and try not only to seem glad, but to be so, and not grudge her one minute of happiness; but it won't be easy, for it is a dreadful disappointment." She quickly left the room so her mother would not see her bitter tears. She retreated to her garret and wept over the missed opportunity and her own idiocy.

By the time Amy came in, Jo was able to take her part in the family jubilation, not quite as heartily as the others, perhaps, but without repining about Amy's good fortune. She sat, red-eyed, and sewed collars to be handed over to Amy, and helped sort and pack while Amy babbled on about her art career and her aspirations for fame.

"You'll marry some rich man and come back home to sit in the lap of luxury," Jo said.

Amy sensed her sister's envy, and so said, "In a year or so, I can send for you, and we'll dig in the Forum for relics, and carry out all the plans we've made so many times."

"Thank you. And I will be sure to remind you of your promise when the time comes."

There was not much time for preparation, and the house was in a ferment till Amy was off. Jo bore up very well till the last flutter of blue ribbon vanished, when she retired to her refuge, the garret, and cried till she couldn't cry any more. Amy likewise bore up stoutly till the steamer sailed; then, just as the gangway was about to be withdrawn, it suddenly came over her that a whole ocean was soon to roll between her and those who loved her best, and she clung to Laurie, the last lingerer, saying with a sob, "Oh, take care of them for me, for I so fear something will happen in my absence."

"I will, dear, I will; and if anything happens, I'll come and comfort you," whispered Laurie, little dreaming how soon he would be called upon to keep his word.

So Amy sailed away to find the old world, which is always new and beautiful to young eyes, while her father and friend watched her from the shore, fervently hoping that none but gentle fortunes would befall the happy-hearted girl, who waved her hand to them until they could see nothing but the summer sunshine dazzling on the sea.

CHAPTER 29

Foreign Correspondence

.

Dearest People,

Here I really sit at a front window of the Bath Hotel,
Piccadilly. It's not a fashionable place, but Uncle stopped
here years ago, and won't go anywhere else. However,
we don't mean to stay long, so it's no great matter. Oh, I
can't begin to tell you how I enjoy it all! I never can, so
I'll only give you bits out of my notebook, for I've done
nothing but sketch and scribble since I started.

I sent a line from Halifax, when I felt pretty
miserable, but after that I got on delightfully, seldom ill,
on deck all day, with plenty of pleasant people to amuse
me. Everyone was very kind to me, especially the
officers. Don't laugh, Jo, gentlemen really are very
necessary aboard ship, to hold on to, or to wait upon
one, and as they have nothing to do, it's a mercy to make
them useful, otherwise they would smoke themselves to
death, I'm afraid.

Aunt and Flo were poorly all the way, and liked to be
let alone, so when I had done what I could for them, I
went and enjoyed myself. Such walks on deck, such

sunsets, such splendid air and waves! It was almost as exciting as riding a fast horse, when we went rushing on so grandly. I wish Beth could have come; it would have done her so much good. As for Jo, she would have gone up and sat on the maintop jib, or whatever the high thing is called, made friends with the engineers, and tooted on the captain's speaking trumpet, she'd have been in such a state of rapture.

It was all heavenly, but I was glad to see the Irish coast, and found it very lovely, so green and sunny, with brown cabins here and there, ruins on some of the hills, and gentlemen's country seats in the valleys, with deer feeding in the parks. It was early in the morning, but I didn't regret getting up to see it, for the bay was full of little boats, the shore *so* picturesque, and a rosy sky overhead. I never shall forget it.

At Queenstown one of my new acquaintances left us—Mr. Lennox—and when I said something about the Lakes of Killarney, he sighed, and sung, with a look at me—

"Oh, have you e'er heard of Kate Kearney?
She lives on the banks of Killarney;
From the glance of her eye,
Shun danger and fly,
For fatal's the glance of Kate Kearney."

Wasn't that nonsensical?
We only stopped at Liverpool a few hours. It's a dirty, noisy place, and I was glad to leave it. Uncle rushed out and bought a pair of dogskin gloves, some

ugly, thick shoes, and an umbrella, and got shaved à la mutton chop, the first thing. Then he flattered himself that he looked like a true Briton, but the first time he had the mud cleaned off his shoes, the little bootblack knew that an American stood in them, and said, with a grin, "There yer har, sir. I've given 'em the latest Yankee shine." It amused Uncle immensely. Oh, I *must* tell you what that absurd Lennox did! He got his friend Ward, who came on with us, to order a bouquet for me, and the first thing I saw in my room was a lovely one, with "Robert Lennox's compliments" on the card. Wasn't that fun, girls? I like traveling.

I never *shall* get to London if I don't hurry. The trip was like riding through a long picture gallery, full of lovely landscapes. The farmhouses were my delight, with thatched roofs, ivy up to the eaves, latticed windows, and stout women with rosy children at the doors. The very cattle looked more tranquil than ours, as they stood knee-deep in clover, and the hens had a contented cluck, as if they never got nervous like Yankee biddies. Such perfect color I never saw—the grass so green, sky so blue, grain so yellow, woods so dark—I was in a rapture all the way. So was Flo, and we kept bouncing from one side to the other, trying to see everything while we were whisking along at the rate of sixty miles an hour. Aunt was tired, and went to sleep, but Uncle read his guidebook, and wouldn't be astonished at anything. This is the way we went on: Amy flying up—"Oh, that must be Kenilworth, that gray place among the trees!" Flo darting to my window—"How sweet! We must go there sometime, won't we, Pa?" Uncle calmly admiring his boots—"No, my dear, not unless you want beer; that's a brewery."

A pause, then Flo cried out, "Bless me, there's a gallows and a man going up." "Where, where!" shrieks Amy, staring out at two tall posts with a crossbeam and some dangling chains. "A colliery," remarks Uncle, with a twinkle of the eye. "Here's a lovely flock of lambs all lying down," says Amy. "See, Pa, aren't they pretty!" added Flo sentimentally. "Geese, young ladies," returns Uncle, in a tone that keeps us quiet till Flo settles down to enjoy "The Flirtations of Captain Cavendish," and I have the scenery all to myself.

Of course it rained when we got to London, and there was nothing to be seen but fog and umbrellas. We rested, unpacked, and shopped a little between the showers. Aunt Mary got me some new things; for I came off in such a hurry I wasn't half ready. A sweet white hat and blue feather, a distracting muslin dress to match, and the loveliest mantle you ever saw. Shopping in Regent Street is perfectly splendid. Things seem so cheap—nice ribbons only sixpence a yard. I laid in a stock, but shall get my gloves in Paris. Don't that sound sort of elegant and rich?

Flo and I, for the fun of it, ordered a hansom cab, while Aunt and Uncle were out, and went for a drive, though we learned afterward that it wasn't the thing for young ladies to ride in them alone. It was so droll! For when we were shut in by the wooden apron, the man drove so fast that Flo was frightened, and told me to stop him. But he was up outside behind somewhere, and I couldn't get at him. He didn't hear me call, nor see me flap my parasol in front, and there we were, quite helpless, rattling away, and whirling round corners at a breakneck pace. At last, in my despair, I saw a little door in the roof, and on poking it open, a red eye appeared, and a beery voice said—

"Now, then, mum?"

I gave my order as soberly as I could, and slamming down the door, with an "Aye, aye, mum," the old thing made his horse walk, as if going to a funeral. I poked again and said, "A little faster," then off he went, helter-skelter, as before, and we resigned ourselves to our fate.

Today was fair, and we went to Hyde Park, close by, for we are more aristocratic than we look. The Duke of Devonshire lives near. I often see his footmen lounging at the back gate, and the Duke of Wellington's house is not far off. Such sights as I saw, my dear! It was as good as Punch, for there were fat dowagers rolling about in their red and yellow coaches, with gorgeous Jeameses in silk stockings and velvet coats, up behind, and powdered coachmen in front. Smart maids, with the rosiest children I ever saw, handsome girls, looking half asleep, dandies in queer English hats and lavender kids lounging about, and tall soldiers, in short red jackets and muffin caps stuck on one side, looking so funny I longed to sketch them.

"Rotten Row" means "*Route de Roi*," or the king's way, but now it's more like a riding school than anything else. The horses are splendid, and the men, especially the grooms, ride well, but the women are stiff, and bounce, which isn't according to our rules. I longed to show them a tearing American gallop, for they trotted solemnly up and down in their scant habits and high hats, looking like the women in a toy Noah's Ark. Everyone rides—old men, stout ladies, little children—and the young folks do a deal of flirting here; I saw a pair exchange rosebuds, for it's the thing to wear one in the buttonhole, and I thought it rather a nice little idea.

In the P.M. to Westminster Abbey; but don't expect me to describe it, that's impossible, so I'll only say it was sublime! This evening we are going to see Fechter, which will be an appropriate end to the happiest day of my life.

MIDNIGHT

It's very late, but I can't let my letter go in the morning without telling you what happened last evening. Who do you think came in, as we were at tea? Laurie's English friends, Fred and Frank Vaughn! I was *so* surprised, for I shouldn't have known them but for the cards. Both are tall fellows, with whiskers, Fred handsome in the English style, and Frank much better, for he only limps slightly, and now uses no crutches. They had heard from Laurie where we were to be, and came to ask us to their house, but Uncle won't go, so we shall return the call, and see them as we can. They went to the theater with

us, and we did have *such* a good time, for Frank devoted
himself to Flo, and Fred and I talked over past, present,
and future fun as if we had known each other all our
days. Tell Beth Frank asked for her, and was sorry to
hear of her ill health. Fred laughed when I spoke of Jo,
and sent his "respectful compliments to the big hat."
Neither of them had forgotten Camp Laurence, or the
fun we had there. What ages ago it seems, don't it?

I haven't seen or heard a werewolf since arriving in
Europe, although I still can't force myself to go out on
nights with full moons, no matter how great a party is
promised. While on the topic of parties, Aunt Carrol and
Flo sometimes attend grand affairs where I am not
permitted. They wear red ribbons laced through their
dresses as a sort of coat of arms, for I am told they
belong to a historic society, which only allows members
due to primogeniture, and the birthright does not fall on
our half of the family.

Happily, I have seen no sign of the Brigade anywhere.
Europe seems quite accepting of its werewolves. Do you
feel that's a good or a bad thing? I know Father's answer
to that but wonder what the rest of you think.

Aunt is tapping on the wall for the third time, so I
must stop. I really feel like a dissipated London fine lady,
writing here so late, with my room full of pretty things,
and my head a jumble of parks, theaters, new gowns, and
gallant creatures, who say "Ah!" and twirl their blond
mustaches with the true English lordliness. I long to see
you all, and in spite of my nonsense am, as ever, your
loving

Amy

Dear girls,

In my last I told you about our London visit—how kind the Vaughns were, and what pleasant parties they made for us. I enjoyed the trips to Hampton Court and the Kensington Museum more than anything else, for at Hampton I saw Raphael's cartoons, and at the museum, rooms full of pictures by Turner, Lawrence, Reynolds, Hogarth, and the other great creatures. The day in Richmond Park was charming, for we had a regular English picnic, and I had more splendid oaks and groups of deer than I could copy, also heard a nightingale, and saw larks go up. We "did" London to our hearts' content—thanks to Fred and Frank—and were sorry to go away, for though English people are slow to take you in, when they once make up their minds to do it they cannot be outdone in hospitality, *I* think. The Vaughns hope to meet us in Rome next winter, and I shall be dreadfully disappointed if they don't, for Grace and I are great friends, and the boys very nice fellows, especially Fred.

Well, we were hardly settled here when he turned up again, saying he had come for a holiday, and was going to Switzerland. Aunt looked sober at first, but he was so cool about it she couldn't say a word. And now we get on nicely, and are very glad he came, for he speaks French like a native, and I don't know what we should do without him. Uncle don't know ten words, and insists on talking English very loud, as if that would make people understand him. Aunt's pronunciation is old-fashioned, and Flo and I, though we flattered ourselves that we knew a good deal, find we don't, and are very grateful to have Fred do the "*parley vooing*," as Uncle calls it.

Such delightful times as we are having! Sightseeing from morning till night! Stopping for nice lunches in the gay *cafés*, and meeting with all sorts of droll adventures. Rainy days I spend in the Louvre, reveling in pictures. Jo would turn up her naughty nose at some of the finest, because she has no soul for art, but *I* have, and I'm cultivating eye and taste as fast as I can. She would like the relics of great people better, for I've seen here Napoleon's cocked hat and gray coat, his baby's cradle and his old toothbrush, also Marie Antoinette's little shoe, the ring of Saint Denis, Charlemagne's sword, and many other interesting things. I'll talk for hours about them when I come, but haven't time to write.

The Palais Royale is a heavenly place, so full of *bijouterie* and lovely things that I'm nearly distracted because I can't buy them. Fred wanted to get me some, but of course I didn't allow it. Then the Bois and Champs Elysées are *trés magnifique.* I've seen the imperial family several times, the emperor an ugly, hard-looking man, the empress pale and pretty, but dressed in horrid taste, *I* thought—purple dress, green hat, and yellow gloves. Little Nap is a handsome boy, who sits chatting to his tutor, and kisses his hand to the people as he passes in his four-horse barouche, with postilions in red satin jackets and a mounted guard before and behind.

We often walk in the Tuileries gardens, for they are lovely, though the antique Luxembourg gardens suit me better. Père la Chaise is very curious, for many of the tombs are like small rooms, and looking in, one sees a table, with images or pictures of the dead, and chairs for the mourners to sit in when they come to lament. That is so Frenchy—*n'est pas?*

Our rooms are on the Rue de Rivoli, and sitting on the balcony, we look up and down the long, brilliant street. It is so pleasant that we spend our evenings talking there when too tired with our day's work to go out. Fred is very entertaining, and is altogether the most agreeable young man I ever knew—except Laurie, whose manners are more charming. I wish Fred was dark, for I don't fancy light men, however, the Vaughns are very rich and come of an excellent family, so I won't find fault with their yellow hair, as my own is yellower.

Next week we are off to Germany and Switzerland, and as we shall travel fast, I shall only be able to give you hasty letters. I keep my diary, and try to "remember correctly and describe clearly all that I see and admire," as Father advised. It is good practice for me, and with my sketchbook, will give you a better idea of my tour than these scribbles.

Adieu; I embrace you tenderly.

"Votre Amie"

HEIDELBERG

My dear Mamma,

Having a quiet hour before we leave for Berne, I'll try to tell you what has happened, for some of it is very important, as you will see.

The sail up the Rhine was perfect, and I just sat and enjoyed it with all my might. Get Father's old guidebooks and read about it; I haven't words beautiful enough to describe it. At Coblentz we had a lovely time, for some students from Bonn, with whom Fred got acquainted on the boat, gave us a serenade. It was a moonlight night, and about one o'clock, Flo and I were waked by the most delicious music under our windows. We flew up, and hid behind the curtains, but sly peeps showed us Fred and the students singing away down below. It was the most romantic thing I ever saw—the river, the bridge of boats, the great fortress opposite, moonlight everywhere, and music fit to melt a heart of stone.

When they were done we threw down some flowers, and saw them scramble for them, kiss their hands to the invisible ladies, and go laughing away, to smoke and drink beer, I suppose. Next morning Fred showed me one of the crumpled flowers in his vest pocket, and looked very sentimental. I laughed at him, and said I didn't throw it, but Flo, which seemed to disgust him, for he tossed it out of the window, and turned sensible again. I'm afraid I'm going to have trouble with that boy—it begins to look like it.

The baths at Nassau were very gay, so was Baden-Baden, where Fred lost some money, and I scolded him. He needs someone to look after him when Frank is not with him. Kate said once she hoped he'd marry soon, and I quite agree with her that it would be well for him. Frankfurt was delightful. I saw Goethe's house, Schiller's statue, and Dannecker's famous

"Ariadne." It was very lovely, but I should have enjoyed
it more if I had known the story better. I didn't like to
ask, as everyone knew it, or pretended they did. I wish
Jo would tell me all about it. I ought to have read more,
for I find I don't know anything, and it mortifies me.

Now comes the serious part, for it happened here,
and Fred is just gone. He has been so kind and jolly that
we all got quite fond of him. I never thought of anything
but a traveling friendship, till the serenade night. Since
then I've begun to feel that the moonlight walks,
balcony talks, and daily adventures were something
more to him than fun. I haven't flirted, Mother, truly, but
remembered what you said to me, and have done my
very best. I can't help it if people like me. I don't try to
make them, and it worries me if I don't care for them,
though Jo says I haven't got any heart. Now I know
Mother will shake her head, and the girls say, "Oh, the
mercenary little wretch!" But I've made up my mind, and
if Fred asks me, I shall accept him, though I'm not
madly in love. I like him, and we get on comfortably
together. He is handsome, young, clever enough, and
very rich—ever so much richer than the Laurences. I
don't think his family would object, and I should be very
happy, for they are all kind, well-bred, generous people,
and they like me. I had opportunity to note that they
also belong to Aunt Carrol's elite historical society who
wear red ribbons, so I imagine one could marry their
way into attending those grand balls. (Did I
mention—there are also some fabulous games I cannot
attend. I refer to them as such because they are games of
a sort that excite Aunt Carrol and the rest for days, and

sometimes weeks, before they attend them. They speak
in whispers about them, while their cheeks grow scarlet
with anticipation. It is quite hard to try to act dignified
and composed about being left out of such thrilling
events, but I maintain calm and act happy for them.)

Fred, as the eldest twin, will have the estate, I
suppose—and such a splendid one it is! A city house, in a
fashionable street, not so showy as our big houses, but
twice as comfortable and full of solid luxury, such as
English people believe in. I like it, for it's genuine. I've
seen the plate, the family jewels, the old servants, and
pictures of the country place, with its park, great house,
lovely grounds, and fine horses. Oh, it would be all I
should ask! And I'd rather have it than any title such as
girls snap up so readily, and find nothing behind. I may
be mercenary, but I hate poverty, and don't mean to bear
it a minute longer than I can help. One of us *must* marry
well. Meg didn't, Jo won't, Beth can't yet, so I shall, and
make everything cosy all around. I wouldn't marry a
man I hated or despised. You may be sure of that, and
though Fred is not my model hero, he does very well,
and in time I should get fond enough of him if he was
very fond of me, and let me do just as I liked. So I've
been turning the matter over in my mind the last week,
for it was impossible to help seeing that Fred liked me.
He said nothing, but little things showed it. He never
goes with Flo, always gets on my side of the carriage,
table, or promenade, looks sentimental when we are
alone, and frowns at anyone else who ventures to speak
to me. Yesterday at dinner, when an Austrian officer
stared at us and then said something to his friend, a

rakish-looking baron, about *"ein wonderschönes
Blöndchen,"* Fred looked as fierce as a lion, and cut his
meat so savagely it nearly flew off his plate. He isn't one
of the cool, stiff Englishmen, but is rather peppery, for
he has Scotch blood in him, as one might guess from his
bonnie blue eyes.

Well, last evening we went up to the castle about
sunset, at least all of us but Fred, who was to meet us
there after going to the Post Restante for letters. We had
a charming time poking about the ruins, the vaults
where the monster tun is, and the beautiful gardens
made by the elector, long ago, for his English wife. I
liked the great terrace best, for the view was divine, so
while the rest went to see the rooms inside, I sat there
trying to sketch the gray stone lion's head on the wall,
with scarlet woodbine sprays hanging round it. I felt as
if I'd got into a romance, sitting there, watching the
Neckar rolling through the valley, listening to the music
of the Austrian band below, and waiting for my lover,
like a real storybook girl. I had a feeling that something
was going to happen, and I was ready for it. I didn't feel
blushy or quakey, but quite cool, and only a little excited.

By and by I heard Fred's voice, and then he came
hurrying through the great arch to find me. He looked
so troubled that I forgot all about myself, and asked
what the matter was. He said he'd just got a letter
begging him to come home, for Frank was very ill. So he
was going at once, on the night train, and only had time
to say goodbye. I was very sorry for him, and
disappointed for myself, but only for a minute because he
said, as he shook hands, and said it in a way that I could

not mistake, "I shall soon come back, and you won't forget me, Amy?"

I didn't promise, but I looked at him, and he seemed satisfied, and there was no time for anything but messages and goodbyes, for he was off in an hour, and we all miss him very much. I know he wanted to speak, but I think, from something he once hinted, that he had promised his father not to do anything of the sort yet a while, for he is a rash boy, and the old gentleman dreads a foreign daughter-in-law. We shall soon meet in Rome, and then, if I don't change my mind, I'll say "Yes, thank you," when he says, "Will you, please?"

Of course this is all very private, but I wished you to know what was going on. Don't be anxious about me, remember I am your "prudent Amy," and be sure I will do nothing rashly. Send me as much advice as you like. I'll use it if I can. I wish I could see you for a good talk, Marmee. Love and trust me, for I feel I grow much braver and stronger the more I see.

Ever your
Amy

...

CHAPTER 30

The Suitor

"JO, I'M ANXIOUS ABOUT BETH."

"Why, Mother? She has seemed unusually well since Meg's babies came."

"It isn't her health that troubles me, it's her spirits. She sits alone a good deal, and doesn't talk to her father as much as she used to. I found her crying over the babies the other day. When she sings, the songs are always sad ones, and there is often a look on her face that I can't understand. I'm sure there is something on her mind. I want you to try to discover what it is."

"Have you asked her about it?"

"I have tried once or twice, but she either evaded my questions or looked so sad I couldn't bear to interrogate her."

"I think she is growing up, and so begins to dream dreams, and have hopes and fears and fidgets, without knowing why or being able to explain them. She is so like a child, we forget she is eighteen."

"So she is; dear heart, how fast you do grow up," returned her mother with a sigh and a smile. "You are a great comfort, Jo; I always feel strong when you are at home, now Meg is gone. Beth is too feeble, and Amy too young to depend upon; but when the tug comes, you are always ready."

"Why, you know I don't mind hard jobs much. If anything is amiss at home, I'm your man."

"I leave Beth to your hands then," Mrs. March said. "If only she would get quite strong and cheerful again, I shouldn't have a wish in the world."

"Happy woman! I've got heaps."

"My dear, what are they?"

"I'll settle Bethy's troubles, and then I'll tell you mine. They are not very wearing, so they'll keep." And Jo stitched away with a wise nod, which set her mother's heart at rest about her, for the present at least.

While acting as though absorbed in her own affairs, Jo watched Beth; and after many conflicting conjectures, finally settled on one that explained things after seeing her watch Laurie out the window one day. Beth was leaning her head upon her hand in a dejected attitude and staring out at the dull autumnal landscape, when suddenly her expression brightened and she sat up and leaned forward.

"How strong, and well, and happy that boy looks," Beth said, pointing out the window at Laurie.

Jo could only stare at her sister, and saw the bright color of her cheeks fade, the smile vanish, and a tear fall onto the window ledge.

"Mercy on me; Beth loves Laurie!" she said, sitting down in her own room, pale with the shock of the discovery she believed she had just made. She did not feel the competitive jealousy that had once surfaced at the thought of Beth and Laurie together; rather, she cared only for her sister's happiness, even though the union of those two who she loved so mightily would surely break her own heart into pieces. She at first thought it could not be, and then, once convinced it was true, felt determined that she would force the boy to love her sister even while ignoring the aching in her own heart at that very idea. She did, however, worry that the boy would now break both her heart and Beth's, as he seemed to fall in love once a month at college, even though the flames were as brief as they were ardent. Her hope was lodged in Beth being so very different, for when she took one into her caring hands, it was impossible to not simply melt and allow her full access to one's heart. She was not at all like Jo, who with one word or vicious stare sent people shrinking away from her. Beth was lovable, and Jo was certain that Laurie could and would love her.

Jo went outside and called to Laurie to come visit, then quickly boiled water for tea and found whole biscuits among the crumbs and broken pieces to set out. When Laurie did arrive, his grandfather stood at his side holding a huge bouquet of fall flowers. Beth's face brightened when she saw the pair, and she accepted the flowers with quiet, graceful gratitude.

When Jo saw how animated Beth was, she felt certain she had discovered her sister's secret.

"Beth tells me you have a new stage created upstairs. May I see it?" Laurie asked; pressing his hands together in false begging, as he knew Jo would just as likely beg him to see it.

While the two dashed upstairs to look at Jo's latest work of art, Mr. Laurence sat down next to Beth.

"You look tired," he said.

"I am heavy, leaden from holding a weighty secret," she said, cheeks coloring as she glanced down so as not to meet his eyes.

"Such a heavy secret should be shared," he suggested. "I have more than ample room in this drafty old head to hold something for a friend."

"A friend? Is that how you see me, as a friend?"

"A friend, a daughter, a granddaughter."

"A wife?"

The old man stopped and examined the girl's anxious expression, then decided to reply with sincerity and honesty. "Yes, dear Beth, I love you as dearly as I did my wife. What is this about, my girl?"

"I love you."

"I know you do."

"No, you don't. I love you. Passionately. Not as a father, or a grandfather, but rather as a suitor. My thoughts are all on you, and I dread each long minute I'm away from you. I know nothing can ever come of this; society would scorn us because our ages differ so vastly, and I am so ill."

Mr. Laurence sat stunned. Was he worthy of a girl like Beth? Did a man who ate so well and slept so comfortably while others starved and froze on the streets deserve such a prize? Did a werewolf merit such happiness? Did any man?

"I'm flattered, my dear, dear Beth. And so honored. But are you certain you don't confuse our shared passion for music with love for me?"

"No. My only confusion is that society would frown on us being joined. I know what I feel. I know my love for others, and I also know what it feels to be grateful toward someone. This is more, it is a consuming passion, a feeling I have never before had, one that keeps you with me every moment of my day and makes me want to sing your praises at all hours."

"Beth, you thrill me, and you fill me with a joy and hope I never expected to know again! And you very much surprise me."

"Do I leave you too surprised to tell me you love me, too?"

Mr. Laurence trembled as he leaned in and kissed Beth on the corner of her mouth, not daring to set his lips firmly on hers as he hungered to do. "I love you, too, my dear. I dreamed many times of our being together in the ways you have described, feeling foolish because, deep down, I never believed it could ever happen."

"It cannot happen. That is why this is so painful."

"Who says we can't have a private love affair? I can woo with the best of them, my little lady, and nobody else need ever know."

Beth laughed but then turned sober and solemn. "It would not be fair to you. I haven't long to live."

"Old as I am, you yet have a fair chance of outliving me. Don't you see? We're perfect for each other, my girl."

The two embraced, their hearts singing as one with pure joy. While their love would never be consummated, due to Beth's frail condition, they would freely give their hearts and their time to each other.

"Tea!" Jo yelled, spilling onto the tray she carried into the parlour, Laurie running in behind her.

As the four sat and sipped their tea, Laurie started in with tales of his college life. Jo watched, and fancied that Beth's eyes rested on the dark, lively face with a peculiar pleasure as she listened to his stories with intense interest, and Jo saw absolutely that her sister looked nearly as happy and lively as she had before her illness struck. When they had drunk their tea, Beth and Mr. Laurence sat together, humming. Jo suggested Laurie help her clean up the tea mess, and once finished with that loathsome task, she threw herself onto the sofa. He threw himself down next to her, and leaned toward her with both arms spread over the sofa back and his long legs spread out before him. Jo rushed to deposit a pillow between them, but Laurie left no room. She pushed him roughly away and slammed the pillow into place.

"Don't be so thorny, Jo!" Laurie scolded. "After studying myself to a skeleton all the week, a fellow deserves petting, and ought to get it."

"Beth will pet you. I'm busy."

"She looks busier than you," Laurie pointed out, looking at the couple who sat flipping through the pages of a songbook. "She's not to be bothered with me; but you like that sort of thing, unless you've suddenly lost your taste for it. Have you? Do you hate your boy, and want to fire pillows at him?"

Anything more wheedlesome than that touching appeal was seldom seen, but Jo quenched "her boy" by turning on him with the stern query, "How many bouquets have you sent Miss Randal this week?"

"Not one, upon my word! She's engaged. Now then."

"I'm glad of it; that's one of your foolish extravagances, sending flowers and things to girls for whom you don't care two pins," continued Jo reprovingly.

"Sensible girls, for whom I care whole papers full of pins, won't let me send them 'flowers and things,' so what can I do? My feelings must have a *vent*."

"Mother doesn't approve of flirting, even in fun; and you do flirt desperately, Teddy."

"I'd give anything if I could answer, 'So do you.' As I can't, I'll merely say that I don't see any harm in that pleasant little game, if all parties understand that it's only play."

"Well, flirting does look pleasant, but it's a game at which I fail," Jo said, scowling.

"Take lessons from Amy. She has a regular talent for it."

"Yes, she does do so very prettily."

"I'm glad you can't flirt. It's nice to see a sensible girl who can be jolly and kind without making a fool of herself," he said, then went to the piano to play a happy song for Beth.

Jo was just dropping off to sleep that night when she heard stifled sobbing that made her fly to Beth's bedside. "What is it, dear?"

"I thought you were asleep," Beth sniffed.

"Is it the old pain, my precious?"

"No, it's a new one."

"Tell me about it and I'll see if I can cure it."

"You can't. There is no cure, and I have no want of one. It's a pain composed of pure joy. Just lie down here with me."

So cheek to cheek, the sisters fell asleep, and on the morrow, Beth seemed quite herself again, chattering to her cats as she pulled the nightgowns off her dolls and dressed them for the day.

But Jo had made up her mind, and after pondering over a project for some days, she confided it to her mother.

"You asked me the other day what my wishes were. I'll tell you one of them, Marmee," she began, as they sat alone together. "I want a change. I feel restless, and I'm anxious to be seeing, doing, and learning more than I am. I brood too much over my own small affairs, and need stirring up, so, as I can be spared this winter I'd like to hop a little way and try my wings."

"Where will you hop?"

"To New York. I had a bright idea yesterday. You know Mrs. Kirke wrote to you for some respectable young person to teach her children and sew. It's rather hard to find just the thing, but I think I should suit if I tried."

"My dear! To go into service in that great boardinghouse!" Mrs. March looked surprised but not displeased.

"You yourself said Mrs. Kirke is one of the kindest souls who ever lived. It's honest work, and I know I can do it well."

"But your writing?"

"All the better for a change. Seeing and hearing new things

will give me new ideas. I imagine I'll bring home quantities of material to use for my rubbish."

"Are there other reasons for this sudden fancy?"

"Yes, Mother."

"May I know the others?"

"It may be wrong of me to say, but I fear Laurie is growing too fond of me," Jo said with color rising in her cheeks.

"Then you don't care for him in the way it's evident he cares for you?" Mrs. March looked anxious as she put the question.

"Mercy, no! I love the dear boy as I always have, and am immensely proud of him, but anything beyond that is out of the question."

"I'm glad of that, Jo!"

"Why, please?"

"Because, dear, I don't feel you are suited to each other. You are happy friends, but mated for life, I fear you would both rebel. You're too alike and both too fond of freedom. Your hot tempers and strong wills would not survive in a relation that needs infinite patience and forbearance, as well as love."

Jo felt as if the happy hand of her heart had clenched itself into a tight fist, but she forced her face to exhibit happiness and relief for the sake of her mother. She knew she was doing the right thing; once she was gone, Beth could pet and comfort Laurie, and rebuild his romantic notion while it switched from Jo to her.

The women agreed to say nothing of Jo's plan to go to New York until all was settled. When Mrs. Kirke gladly accepted Jo, a family council readily agreed upon the plan, everyone feeling the teaching assignment would render Jo independent and the experience would vastly profit her writing.

"I have something to leave in your especial care," Jo told Beth soon before she left.

"Your papers?"

"No. My boy. Be very good to him, won't you?"

"I'll do my best, for your sake," promised Beth. She opened her mouth to tell her that she would care for him as she cared for her cats and her dolls, as she would care for her own child or grandson, for if the world was kinder, she would be able to step into the position of being his grandmother by marrying his grandfather, the man she loved. But words failed her, so she smiled at her sister and picked up the doll's brush while her kittens looked on. "I have to comb everyone's hair. Mr. Laurence is coming over for a visit, so we must all look nice."

"How will you keep busy with me away, Beth?"

"I have my cats, my dolls, and my dreams. Of course, the cats flee when Mr. Laurence visits, but they return the moment he leaves, so I always have company."

"Tell me about your dreams."

"I like to pretend I have a lover," she said, a blush covering her cheeks as she pulled the brush through one doll's black hair. She looked up to meet Jo's eyes and added, "A werewolf lover."

Jo forced herself to smile. "Any werewolf in particular?"

She merely shrugged with a melancholy smile and far-staring eyes. "Yes. The one destined to end my suffering when the time comes."

Jo studied her sister's face. The poor thing was obviously wracked with delusions and having fantasies about those angels who would guide her to her Celestial City. She briefly wondered if she should question her further but was too distressed with her thoughts of Laurie to give her sister's silly ramblings more thought. She was almost afraid to tell Laurie that she was leaving; but he took the news well and cheerfully.

On the day she left, Laurie leaned in close and whispered significantly, "It won't do a bit of good, Jo. My eye is on you; so mind what you do, or I'll come and bring you home."

...

CHAPTER 31

Jo Spreads Her Wings

J O, ONCE IN NEW YORK, MISSED HER FATHER BITTERLY, and worried for him, mostly that he wasn't clever enough in a way to hide his werewolf side, or that he'd fall while working on his ossuary. It had become years now that Mr. March had been collecting bones; after a war, bones make their way up as soil makes it way down, and all those bones that Mr. March found were treated with proper respect and mounted in the church into a fabulous arch that emanated upward and out from the altar that had originally held merely eight skulls and a handful of bone fragments. Word spread, and people who found bones in their yards or along the road brought him exactly what Marmee dreaded most—more bones—and the display grew so large and awe-inspiring that Mr. March and a team of volunteers picked up all the massive, bulky stretches of pews and turned them away from the front altar to face the altar of bones.

People felt good seeing the found bones put to such magnanimous use, and baskets lay here and there in the church, overflowing at all times with orphaned, unearthed bones deposited there anonymously and with, Mr. March was absolutely certain, God's full blessing. He was possessed by his project, and while he knew his home was changing and his daughters were growing away, he couldn't tear himself free of the waiting bones. He

He couldn't tear himself free of the waiting bones.

believed it to be presently true, and prayed that each daughter's life would follow its proper path, and that his girls would always know they were his second-best fascination—and understand that he had little control over the first, as it was of divine origin.

He did tear himself away from his haven long enough to escort Jo to the train station when she left for the city, and she was so touched by this telling act that she could barely keep her voice steady to speak. She hugged her father to her breast so hard and long that one of the conductors had to call to her to board the train before it huffed off down the tracks.

Upon arriving in New York and being assigned her room, Jo sat immediately to write home, for she knew her letters would be as great a comfort to Marmee and Beth as they were to her as she penned them.

Dear Marmee and Beth,

This letter may turn into a regular volume, for I've got heaps to tell, though I'm not a fine young lady traveling on the Continent.

The moment I lost sight of Father's dear old face at the train station, I began to feel blue, and might have shed a briny drop or two if an Irish lady with four small children, all crying and whining, hadn't diverted my mind; for I amused myself by dropping gingerbread nuts over the seat each time they opened their wide mouths to roar. Soon the sun came out, and I cleared as well, taking the brightness as a good omen, and then enjoying the remainder of the journey with all my heart.

After unpacking, I ventured out my front door, just moments ago, for a breath of fresh air, and turned tail and rushed back inside, so invasive is the hustle and bustle of this city. Will the day ever arrive when I grow accustomed to it all? With each step is a new distraction, a new wonder, or a new abomination—the mightiest being that the Brigade here wears armor. Yes, armor, not leather, breastplates and helmets, so in day's high peak they reflect the sun's light and assault eyes as well as bodies. I don't see why they don't also don the original ancient chain mail for additional drama if they go this far in keeping their appearance fierce!

On my way here, I saw a young lady walking along the street, and I forgot myself and rushed toward her, thinking with her well-dressed hair and beautiful blue dress that she was our Amy. It is proof that I already severely miss you all, and that not one of you will ever leave my mind for even one brief moment.

I received a warm welcome, and do feel at home here in the little sky-blue parlour that is my room. It is all Mrs. Kirke had to give me, but there is a stove in it, and a nice table in a sunny window where I can write my adventure tales and daydream about werewolves. The view is fine, with a church tower opposite and the complexities of the main street below. The nursery, where I am to teach and sew, is an entirely pleasant room, and the two little girls who are now in my charge are pretty children, though rather spoiled. I have chosen to take my meals with them, as I prefer being saved from having to converse with the other boarders and risk saying the wrong thing; also, though none of you believe it, I *am* bashful.

There is the tea bell; I must run and change my cap. This first letter is short, I admit, but I want to rush it on so you know I am safe and sheltered. I shall write constantly and hope you do likewise.

Bless you all!

Ever your loving

Jo

On one of Jo's first days there, as she walked down one of the long flights of stairs, a little servant girl lumbered up the stairs with difficulty, carrying a heavy hod of coal. A gentleman, of perhaps forty years, swept up from behind her, took her burden in hand, carried it all the way up for her, and tipped his hat to her as he set it down at the door. Jo felt that very kind of him and asked Mrs. Kirke about him.

"That must have been Professor Bhaer; he's always doing things of that sort."

With very little prodding, Mrs. Kirke informed Jo that he was from Berlin; very learned and good, but poor as a church mouse. Mrs. Kirke allowed him free use of the parlour to give lessons to help support his two orphaned nephews whom he was educating, according to the last wishes of his sister and her American husband.

Jo controlled Kitty and Minnie, the little girls in her keep, rather well; having learned early on to employ gymnastics until they were glad to sit down and keep still, and then tell the two captives stories, or perhaps recite a lesson or two. Often Jo was almost as tired as they by the time she tucked them in for their naps, but she still forced herself to sit up and get some sewing completed, rather than taking to her own bed and napping, which would have been heavenly.

One afternoon, rocking in her chair and making what she felt were the most precise buttonholes in the world, she heard humming in the parlour, as if a huge bumblebee had been loosed in the house. She couldn't resist the temptation to peek in, and, spotting Professor Bhaer engaged in arranging his books, she took a good long look. He looked like a regular German: rather stout, with brown hair tumbled all over his head, a bushy beard, a good nose, and the kindest eyes she had ever seen. She felt his loud and strong voice splendid, and was convinced it did her ears good, as she enjoyed his accent and the mystery of the German words he sometimes uttered in the middle of his sentences. His clothes were rusty and his hands were large, and he hadn't a really handsome feature in his face, except for his beautiful teeth. She liked him. He had a fine head; his linen was very nice, and he looked like a gentleman, though two buttons were off his coat and there was a patch on one shoe. An unnamed thing in her made Laurie stalk swiftly through her mind while she stared at the Professor.

Professor Bhaer looked sober, in spite of his humming, until he went to the window to turn the hyacinth bulbs toward the sun, and stroke the cat, which received him like an old friend. He smiled, then a tap sounded at the door and a small girl toting a ridiculously large book appeared for her lesson and went to him for a hug, so Jo got back to her own business, although she left her door open in the hopes she might absorb some of the German language lesson.

Mrs. Kirke had asked Jo to go down to the five o'clock dinner, and feeling homesick, she accepted. The long table was full, everyone intent on getting their dinner, the gentlemen especially, who *bolted*, in every sense of the word, for they vanished as soon as they shoveled the food down their throats. There was also the usual assortment of young men who seemed mostly interested in themselves, married ladies and their babies, and old gentlemen who made no secret of their political views. One sweet-faced maiden lady smiled at Jo a number of times, and Jo made a mental note to meet her.

Cast away at the very bottom of the table was the Professor, looking every bit the werewolf with his unruly hair and beard as he shouted answers to the questions of an inquisitive deaf old man on one side and discussed philosophy with a Frenchman on his other. If Amy had been there, she would have turned her back on him forever, because, sad as it is to relate, he had a great appetite and transferred his food from plate to mouth with lightning speed that would have horrified "her ladyship." But Jo didn't mind, for she liked "to see folks eat with a relish," as Hannah always said, and she imagined the poor man must have needed a great deal of food after teaching idiots all day.

On her way up the stairs after dinner, Jo heard herself being discussed by two young men who were settling their hats before the hall mirror.

"Who's the new party?" one inquired.

"Governess, or something of that sort."

"What the deuce is she at our table for?"

"Friend of the old lady's."

"Handsome enough head, but no style."

"Not a bit. Here, give us a light and come on."

At first Jo felt angry, and then she decided not to care, for a governess was every bit as good as a clerk, and she had oceans of good sense even if she didn't have style. Judging from the remarks of the elegant beings who chattered away, smoking like overworked chimneys, she had more than her share of the sense allotted to the houseguests. Oh, how she hated ordinary people!

Jo noticed, the next day as she sat writing in her room, that a small child, a girl named Tina, who was the daughter of the

Frenchwoman who did laundry and ironing for the house, was in the habit of following Professor Bhaer about like a dog. The little thing had lost her heart to him, which delighted the man, as he was quite fond of children, though a bachelor. The women of the house regarded him with affection and went to him to hear stories, and the young men liked to quiz him, as he seldom failed to produce the correct answers. They made all manners of jokes on his name, calling him such things as Old Fritz and Lager Beer. The Professor enjoyed it all like a boy, and took it all so good-naturedly, that he was well liked, in spite of his ways.

The young sweet-faced woman spoke to Jo at dinner, and asked her to come to her room afterward. She was rich, culti-vated, and kind, owned many fine books and pictures, knew in-teresting people, and seemed friendly and warm, so Jo made herself agreeable, hoping to get into good society, only not the same sort that Amy liked.

The women went together on a short stroll, and Miss Nor-ton thrilled Jo by asking if she would sometimes like to attend lectures and concerts with her, as her escort. Jo readily agreed, and the two fell to talking and laughing so easily that Jo almost felt accompanied by one of her own dear sisters. But the outing was dampened when they happened upon a sorrowful sight in the streets.

Jo gasped, bringing gloved hand up to cover the shameless-ness of her open mouth. A man's body lay among clotted bits of skin, hair, and sticky red rocks, obviously a werewolf stoned to death, as his chest bore the gaping wound of the accused. The Brigade here hunted by night, and had done their job right this time, for there were thick tufts of scattered gray hair surround-ing the body, which revealed the man to be a true werewolf. Jo could see, even though they were well bloodied, that his hands wore thick, distinct calluses and his shoulders bore a defeated hunch. She looked at his eyes, closed in repose, and his face, yet determined to flee as it stretched away from his neck. And now he was escaped, although his poor body didn't know it; he was escaped from both his life of poverty and his werewolf curse.

Miss Norton pulled at Jo's sleeve and led her gently away from the grisly sight. "You'll soon grow used to seeing such things and learn to not let them affect your day," Miss Norton said brightly, as if they had been forced to step around a fallen cart of flowers, not a dead body.

As Jo was returning to her room, she accidentally knocked against Professor Bhaer's door with her umbrella and it flew open. There he stood in his dressing gown, with a big blue sock on one hand and a darning needle in the other. Jo stammered and backed away, but he was not at all embarrassed and waved his hand, sock and all, as he wished her a good evening in his loud, cheerful way. Jo could not release from her mind the image of the poor man having to mend his own clothes, and although she knew German gentlemen did embroider, she felt darning hose was another matter entirely; and so privately, she asked Mrs. Kirke if she might take his socks to mend them.

She thought, after that, she would never catch the man in a more embarrassing situation, but when she arrived at the nursery the next day, she found him down on all fours and Kitty leading him with a jump rope as Tina rode his back. Two small boys ate seed cakes as they roared and romped in cages built of chairs. She discovered that the Professor's nephews, Franz and Emil, visited on Saturdays and the children were allowed to frolic as they pleased, so all Saturdays were riotous times, whether spent in the house or out. Jo and the Professor took to leading the children about together, trying their best to keep order when they, themselves, were often the rowdiest of the bunch, and had every bit as much fun as the little girls and boys. The Professor's nephews proved to be jolly little lads; for the mixture of American and German spirit in them produced a constant state of effervescence.

Saturday night in her room, Jo wrote home about her day, adding in a P.S.: "On reading over my letter, it strikes me as rather Bhaery; but I have always sought out exceptional and uncommon people, and simply had nothing more interesting about which to write."

Jo began to leave her door open and pulled her rocking chair up so she might listen in as the Professor gave lessons, thinking she might surprise him one day with a German exclamation when he least expected it, but she was caught in the act.

"So!" Professor Bhaer said as Jo stopped rocking and stared at him like a goose, "You peep at me, I peep at you, and that is not bad; but I think you peep to learn, too. Haf you a wish for German?"

"Yes, I do. But you are so busy, and I am too stupid to learn," she said, blushing as red as a beet.

"Prut! We will make the time, and we fail not to find the sense. I shall gif you little lesson with much gladness, for I haf debt to pay you. These so kind ladies say to one another, 'He is a stupid old fellow, he will not see what we do. He will never opserve that his sock heels go not in holes anymore. He will think his buttons grow out new when they fall, and believe that strings make theirselves.' Ah! But I haf an eye, and I see much. I haf a heart and I feel the thanks for this. Come—a little lesson then and now, or no more good fairy works for me and mine."

Jo couldn't say anything after that. It was a splendid opportunity, and she nodded to seal the bargain. The Professor was very patient with her, but she took four lessons and then found herself stuck fast in a grammatical bog. One day, when Jo had just released a sniff of utter mortification and woe, he threw the grammar book to the floor.

"Now we shall try a new way. You and I will read these pleasant little folktales together, and dig no more in that dry book. It goes in the corner for making us trouble."

Jo opened the Hans Christian Andersen book that he had set before her, forgot her bashfulness, and went at the lesson with a neck-or-nothing style that seemed to amuse him. When she finished reading the first page and paused for a breath, he clapped his hands and cried out in his hearty way.

"*Das ist gut!* Now we go well. My turn. Gif me your ear." And away he went, rumbling out words with his strong voice and a hearty relish.

Jo got to where she could read her lessons pretty well, and felt that way of studying suited her, for she could see that the man carefully tucked grammar lessons into the tales and poetry, much as one gives needed pills in a sweet spoonful of jelly.

She very much missed being home for Christmas but felt almost there when she opened her Christmas parcel and began to look, read, and eat. Beth had made her an "ink bib" that she thought was capital; Hannah sent a box of hard gingerbreads; Marmee sent nice warm flannels; Meg sent a beautiful scarf and matching hat bow she had made from a startling violet fabric; and her father, of course, sent books he carefully adorned with his usual flourished designs. Professor Bhaer gave her a fine Shakespeare, as he felt nothing could help an aspiring writer more than reading the Bard and studying his genius at creating characters and plot.

Not knowing what the Professor would like, and not having

much money, Jo bought several little things and put them about his room, where he would find them unrepentantly: a new inkstand, a small vase of flowers, and the silliest of all, a fat butterfly she made herself and gave worsted feelers and bead eyes. He fancied it immensely and put it on his mantelpiece as if an article of the finest art.

She noted that the good Professor didn't forget one servant or child in the house, gifting everyone from the French laundrywoman to Miss Norton; and neither did they forget him. She was so glad of that.

On New Year's Eve, Mrs. Kirke had a masquerade party for the house and would not allow Jo to pass on the event with the excuse of having no costume. She took her to the garret and pulled out some old brocade dresses for her to choose among, and Miss Norton lent her lace and feathers. She decided to do something daring, and remembering Meg's ball from long ago, she made a red mask, and then laced red ribbons through the dress, so she could go as a female werewolf. She donned all the trimmings she always fought Amy to keep off her, not knowing exactly why she suddenly wanted to look alluring but not stopping her hand.

She took a last look at herself in the mirror. The dress made her stand taller, and she was amazed at the image in the looking glass, for the fine form of a woman stood there, a mysterious, timeless, ageless woman frozen in one instant, like one of those new miraculous photographs or one of Amy's sketches.

As she walked, masked, through the house, she didn't speak, and all heads turned as she passed so they might catch one more glance of the beguiling creature. She savored the event, being someone that night that she had never before allowed herself to be. She suddenly wished Laurie was there to see her, and all night she wondered what the sight of her would make him say or do.

She was shaken from her thoughts as midnight arrived and everyone unmasked. Some were shocked to see it was she behind the red mask, and all continued to stare and flock around her for the rest of the night. She saw this all as great fun, and felt like a heroine, a femme fatale, smiling the slightest bit and forcing her eyes past the interested soul who stood talking in front of her, as if she was forever scanning the room for a more entertaining companion. She even overheard one young man tell another that he thought he'd seen her at one of the small theaters.

"You haf on a very gut and daring disguise, Miss March," the Professor said, lifting her hand and brushing it lightly with his lips. "But I like you better wif the mask off and your own beautiful face showing."

Jo lifted that beautiful face and stared at him.

"Did you mean to be so daring, with the red ribbons?"

"So daring?"

"Do you know the meaning behind the red ribbons?"

"Do you?" She smiled.

"Of course. The custom is in Europe widespread. I was taken much by surprise to see a handsome girl werewolf here tonight."

Jo wondered if he hoped she truly was a werewolf, so quickly said, "It's merely a costume."

"On you it is not merely a costume, and you prove to be more creative and, um, innovative, yes, that is the right word, than I thought. To look at you makes me feel years younger."

"Professor, you are already the youngest person I know. I wouldn't want you younger, as I have never savored changing diapers."

"A quick mind, but a quicker tongue," he observed with a small thundering of laughter. "Am I right?"

The man knew her so well already! "I fear you are," she confessed. "My tongue has always lashed quicker than my brain."

She hated that the party ended and the night was over. She undressed, feeling somehow changed inside, as the sun began its ascent to light the way for the glorious New Year. She decided to continue playing the part of the mysterious writer; she would redo some of her hats into more unusual shapes, and perhaps sew buttons and charms on her gloves and collars to set her apart just enough to remind her that she was a unique experience for those she met along the way.

She was cheerful all the time, worked with a will, and took more interest in other people than she used to, which she found quite satisfactory. That night in bed she decided she had had a very happy New Year, and she felt she was getting on quite well in spite of her many failures.

...

CHAPTER 32

Sensational Writing

THOUGH VERY HAPPY IN THE SOCIAL ATMOSPHERE AND quite busy with the daily work that earned her bread, Jo still found time for her literary labors. The purpose that now took possession of her was a natural one to a poor and ambitious girl. She saw that money conferred power; money and power, therefore, she resolved to have—to be used not for herself alone but for those she loved more than herself.

The dream of filling her home with comforts, giving Beth everything she wanted, from strawberries in winter to an organ in her bedroom; going abroad herself, and always having more than enough, so that she might indulge in the luxury of charity, had for years been Jo's most cherished castle in the air.

The prize-story experience had opened a way that might, she hoped, after long traveling and much uphill work, lead her to her castle, but the novel disaster had quenched her courage for a time. Public opinion is a giant that has frightened stouterhearted Jacks on bigger beanstalks than hers.

She took to writing sensation stories, for in those dark ages, even an all-perfect American reads rubbish. She told no one but concocted a "thrilling tale," and boldly carried it herself to Mr. Dashwood, editor of the *Weekly Volcano*. She had a womanly instinct that clothes possess an influence more powerful over many than the worth of character or the magic of manners, so she dressed herself in her best and topped off her appeal by donning Meg's lovely violet scarf and adding the matching bow to her bonnet.

Walking along to the editor's office, she wondered when she would grow used to the city. She thought the Brigade here, wearing armored breastplates and helmets, to be even more fearsome and daunting than the members back home who wore leather, and their numbers seemed enormous, for she couldn't walk around the block without seeing at least two or three of them, as they never walked alone. It was also common to see, in certain sections of town, hanged werewolves with gaping, exposed holes in their chests, and unlucky werewolf sympathizers who hung just as dead, but with chests intact.

She turned a corner and stepped aside as more of the Brigade passed, led by giant men who stood so tall and wide that their breastplates, hanging in the middle of their chests, looked more like ornamentation than protection. One of the huge men bared his teeth to her as he passed, but she could not decipher if it was a grin or a growl so did not return a greeting. Trailing behind them walked a woman, utterly consumed by her breastplate, which fell to below her hips, so that she was forced to stagger as she walked. Jo watched her pass and, glimpsing the flank of her body inside the armor, thought she looked like a frail insect encased in a massive web of metal. The woman was smaller than Jo, and she thought, "Why, I could be an able protector if she is, although I would not battle werewolves, as Father would strongly disapprove." This insight gave her courage to propel herself forward and to face her fears, so she took a deep breath and forged onward.

She tried to persuade herself that she was neither excited nor nervous, and bravely climbed two pairs of dark and dirty stairs to find herself in a disorderly room, a cloud of cigar smoke, and the presence of three gentlemen, sitting with their heels rather higher than their hats, which articles of dress none of them took the trouble to remove on her appearance. Somewhat daunted by this reception, Jo hesitated on the threshold. She threw her scarf's end over her shoulder, raised her head and her voice, and announced, "I was looking for the *Weekly Volcano* office; I wished to see Mr. Dashwood."

Down went the highest pair of heels, up rose the smokiest gentleman, and carefully cherishing his cigar between his fingers, he advanced with a nod and a countenance expressive of nothing but sleep. Feeling compelled to get through the matter somehow, Jo produced her manuscript, and blushing redder and redder with each sentence, blundered out fragments of the little speech carefully prepared for the occasion.

"A friend desired me to offer—a story—simply as an experiment—would like your opinion—be glad to write more if it suits."

While she blushed and blundered, Mr. Dashwood had taken up the manuscript and was turning over the leaves with a pair of rather dirty fingers, and casting critical glances up and down the neat pages.

"Not a first attempt, I take it?" he said, observing that the pages were numbered, covered only one side, and were *not* tied up with a ribbon, which was a sure sign of a novice.

"No sir. She has had some experience, and got a prize for a tale in the *Blarneystone Banner.*"

"Oh, did she?" Mr. Dashwood gave Jo a quick look, which seemed to take note of everything she had on, from the violet bow in her bonnet to the buttons on her boots. "Well, you can leave it, if you like. We've more of this sort of thing on hand than we know what to do with at present; but I'll run my eye over it and give you an answer next week."

Jo did *not* care to leave it, for Mr. Dashwood didn't suit her at all, but under the circumstances, there was nothing for her to do but bow and walk away, pulling herself up so she looked particularly tall and dignified, as she was apt to do when nettled or abashed. Just then she was both; for it was perfectly evident, from the knowing glances exchanged among the gentlemen, that her little fiction of "a friend" was considered a good joke; and a laugh, produced by some inaudible remark of the editor, as he closed the door, completed her discomfiture. She frowned at the thought of those savage men, who were rougher and fouler than any werewolf she had ever met, laughing at her and at the work she had slaved over with such dedication. Half resolving to never return, she went home and worked off her irritation by stitching pinafores vigorously, and an hour or two later was cool enough to laugh over the scene.

When she went back, she rejoiced to find Mr. Dashwood alone, and much wider awake than before.

"We'll take this if you don't object to a few alterations," he said straight off in a very businesslike tone. "It's too long, but omitting the passages I've marked will make it just the right length."

Jo hardly knew her own manuscript, so crumpled and underscored were its pages and paragraphs. She felt like a parent, asked to cut off her baby's legs in order that it might fit into a new cradle, as she looked at the marked passages, those that had been carefully put in as ballast for much romance, which had also been stricken out.

"But, sir, I thought every story should have some sort of moral, so I took care to have some of my sinners repent."

Mr. Dashwood's editorial gravity relaxed into a smile, for Jo had forgotten her "friend," and spoken as only an author could.

"People want to be amused, not preached at. Morals don't sell nowadays."

"You think it will do with these alterations, then?"

"Yes. It's a new plot. I like the werewolf, and it's pretty well worked up, with good language."

"How do you, that is, um, what compensation . . . ," Jo stammered, not knowing how to ask the most important of questions.

"Oh, yes. We give from twenty-five to thirty for things of this sort. Pay when it comes out, not before," returned Mr. Dashwood, as if that point had escaped him; such trifles do often escape the editorial mind, it is said.

"Very well. You can have it," said Jo, handing back the story with a satisfied air. After the dollar-a-column work, twenty-five seemed good pay. "Shall I tell my friend you'll take another if she has one better than this?"

"We'll look at it. Can't promise to take it. Tell her to keep it short and spicy. Lose the moral and keep the werewolf. What name would, uh, your friend like to put to it?"

"None at all, if you please; she doesn't wish for her name to appear, and owns no nom de plume," said Jo, realizing her error, as the editor obviously knew her to be the author.

"Just as she likes, then. The tale will be out next week. Shall I send the money, or will you call for it?"

"I'll call. Good morning, sir."

Following Mr. Dashwood's directions, and making the werewolves coarser and far more common and low-born than those

she knew, Jo rashly took a plunge into the frothy sea of sensational literature. Like most young scribblers, she went abroad
for her characters and scenery; and bandits, gypsies, counts,
nuns, duchesses, and werewolves with foreign accents appeared
upon her stage and played their parts with as much accuracy and
spirit as could be expected. Her readers were not particular
about such trifles as grammar, punctuation, and probability, and
Mr. Dashwood graciously permitted her to fill his columns at
the lowest prices, not thinking it necessary to tell her that the
real cause of his hospitality was the fact that one of his hacks, on
being offered higher wages, had just left him in the lurch.

She soon became interested in her work, for her emaciated
purse grew stout, and the little hoard she was making to take
Beth to the mountains next summer grew slowly but surely as
the weeks passed. Fearing her parents might not approve, she
kept her writing career a secret from her family. She had sincerely meant to write nothing that would make her ashamed, but
Mr. Dashwood rejected all but the most thrilling tales, and
thrills could not be produced except by harrowing up the souls
of the readers with history and romance, land and sea, science
and art. She was becoming, by way of her research, quite a
learned person, and soon found that her innocent experience
had given her but few glimpses of the tragic world that under-
lies society. So she set out to find material to keep her stories
original in plot and masterly in execution. She grew more adventurous, venturing out to ransack police stations and lunatic
asylums for the purpose of keeping fresh meat in the fascinating
picnic hamper of her stories. She searched newspapers for accidents, incidents, and crimes; she excited the suspicions of public
librarians by asking for works on poisons. Delving in the dust of
ancient times for fact or fiction so old they were as good as new,

she introduced herself to folly, sin, and misery as much as her limited opportunities allowed, and acquired an acquaintance with the darker side of life, which comes soon enough to us all.

Jo was also discovering a live hero who was neither rich nor great, young nor handsome, in no respect what is called fascinating, imposing, or brilliant; and yet he was as attractive as a genial fire, and people seemed to gather around him as about a warm hearth. Professor Bhaer was poor, yet always appeared to be giving something away; a stranger, yet everyone was his friend; no longer young, yet as happy-hearted as a boy; plain and peculiar. His benevolence was always on display as he turned his sunny side to the world, and any sorrow he had kept its head carefully tucked under its wing.

She went to his room for her lesson one day, and he sat reading with a soldier cap folded out of newspaper on his head. Jo knew she would never get through the lesson without laughing while he wore it, so she reminded him. He felt for it atop his head, looked at it, threw back his head, and laughed merrily. "Ach, that Tina. Always dressing me up." As he put it on the table, he noticed one of the illustrations on it, and unfolded it with a sigh. "I wish these papers did not come into the house; they are not for children to see, nor young people to read. I haf no patience with those who make this harm."

Jo glanced at the sheet and saw a pleasing illustration composed of a lunatic, a corpse, a villain, and a viper. Her heart jumped when, for a moment, she fancied it was the *Volcano*, but it wasn't. She pushed it aside.

"You are right to put it from you. I do not think that good young girls should see such things. This is nothing but bad trash."

"Many respectable people make an honest living from writing sensation stories."

"If these respectable people knew what harm they did, they would not think the living *was* honest. They haf no right to put poison in the sugarplum, and let the small ones eat it. No, they should think a little. Better they sweep mud into the street before they do this thing!" He went to the fire and placed the paper on top of the blazing logs. "I should like much to send all the rest after this one."

Jo thought what a large blaze her pile of papers would make, but thought to herself that her stories were not like that; they were silly, never bad. But she read some of them anew, and saw in the stories not the stuff that she had thought she might write to champion the cause of the werewolves, but rather the stuff that promoted them as dangerous beings on the outskirts of society. She was so disturbed at what she had done, and by the thought of falling in Professor Bhaer's esteem, that she stopped writing the stories and spent her time penning, instead, a lively, fancy, and girlish romance. She felt as ill at ease in the new style as she would have done masquerading in the stiff and cumbrous costume of the last century. She sent this didactic gem to several markets regardless, but it found no purchaser; and she was finally inclined to agree with Mr. Dashwood that morals didn't sell.

But all the same, despite her wishing that she hadn't such an inconvenient conscience, Jo had learned a valuable lesson, and saw that writing shaped not only the writer but the reader as well. She and her sisters had been lucky to have their parents and *Pilgrim's Progress* to hedge them around with principles, which might have seemed like prison walls to impatient youth but which would prove sure foundations to build character upon in womanhood. So, morals or not, her stories had to somehow lead her readers down the right path.

It was a long winter, and her pen lay idle while she thought about her life and worked hard at her German lessons. She tried her hand at tales for children but didn't care for all her naughty boys to be eaten by bears or tossed by mad bulls as was expected. She actually thought it might be great fun to place a bad boy as hero of a piece, and knew children would love the concept, but she also knew she would want for a buyer, as adults were the ones who purchased books for children.

Spring finally arrived and Jo was packing for her return trip home, planning to be there in time for Laurie's graduation.

"Going home? Ah, be happy you haf a home to go in," Professor Bhaer said, pulling his beard and rumpling his hair wildly so that it stuck straight up all over.

"I would love for you to see my home and meet my family. You should come next month. My friend Laurie graduates then, and we could go to the commencement."

"This is your best friend of whom you speak?"

"Yes, my boy Teddy. I'm very proud of him and would like you to meet him."

Jo looked up then, quite unconscious of anything but her own pleasure in the prospect of introducing the two men to each other. Something in Mr. Bhaer's face suddenly recalled the fact that she might find Laurie more than a best friend, and simply because she particularly wished not to look as if anything was the matter, she involuntarily began to blush, and the more she tried not to, the redder she grew. She hid her face, but the Professor saw it, and his own changed again from that momentary anxiety to its usual expression, as he said cordially, "I fear I shall not make the time for that, but I wish the friend much success, and you all happiness. Gott bless you!" With that, he shook hands warmly and went away.

But after the boys were abed, he sat for a long time before the fire nursing the ache in his heart and feeling keenly the difference in his age and Jo's. His thoughts were on only Jo as he remembered first seeing her, watching her with the children, cringing as she barked out German phrases in a horrid accent, and taking away his breath simply by walking into the room at the masquerade party.

"It is not for me; I must not hope it now," he said to himself with a sigh that was almost a groan; then, as if reproaching himself for the longing that he could not repress, he went and kissed the two tousled heads upon the pillow, took down his seldom used meerschaum, and opened his Plato. He did his best, and did it manfully; but he didn't find that a pair of rampant boys, a pipe, or even the divine Plato were very satisfactory substitutes for a wife and child, and home.

Early as it was, he was at the station the next morning to see Jo off; and thanks to him, she began her solitary journey with the pleasant memory of a friendly face smiling its farewell, two nostrils filled with the familiar musky scent of him, a bunch of violets to keep her company, and best of all, the happy thought that although the winter had gone and she had been unsuccessful in her writing, she had been very successful in making a friend worth having. She vowed to try to keep him all her life.

...

CHAPTER 33

A Werewolf's Broken Heart

AURIE, PERHAPS IN AN ATTEMPT TO IMPRESS JO, STUDIED with some purpose, graduated with honors, and gave the Latin oration with both grace and elegance. His proud grandfather and all the Marches, except Amy, were there, but Laurie had eyes only on Jo, whom he had missed terribly, for she left a hole in his life that could not be filled by a full dozen less interesting people.

The next day she saw a stalwart figure looming in the distance as she was walking back home from Meg's, and she somehow sensed that he was about to do something that would cause her to hurt his feelings.

"I suppose you will now take a nice, long vacation," she said by way of greeting.

"I intend to."

Something in his resolute tone made Jo look up quickly, to find him looking down at her with an expression that assured her that the moment she had been both living for and dreading had come.

"You must hear me, Jo. I've loved you since I've known you, Jo—couldn't help it, you've been so good to me. I've tried to show it, but you wouldn't let me; now I'm going to make you hear, and give me an answer, for I *can't* go on so any longer."

"Do I know you well enough to answer your question?" she asked, having expected him to first reveal to her that he was a werewolf.

"Know me? Jo, you know me better than I know myself."

Her heart sank with the realization that he expected her to commit to him while not being wholly honest with her. She had always maintained a tiny shred of hope that, despite his being a werewolf, despite Beth and her needs, and despite the Professor's attentions, she and Laurie would still find themselves together always. But if he didn't confess to her, before they were engaged, that he was a werewolf, then she knew he would not be her partner, not as she needed a husband to be.

"I am desperately sorry, Teddy."

"Your answer is no," he said slowly and softly.

"Please, let me tell you—"

"*Don't* tell me that, Jo; I can't bear it now!"

"Tell you what?" she asked, wondering at his violent attitude.

"That you love that old man."

"What old man?" demanded Jo, thinking he must mean his grandfather.

"That devilish Professor you were always writing about. If you say you love him, I know I shall do something desperate," and he looked as if he would keep his word as he clenched his hands with a wrathful spark in his eyes.

"Don't swear, Teddy! He isn't old!" she lashed back. "Nor is he anything bad, but good and kind, and the best friend I've got—next to you. Pray don't fly into a passion; I want to be kind, but I know I shall get angry if you abuse my Professor. I haven't the least idea of loving him, or anybody else."

"But you will after a while, and then what will become of me?"

"You'll love someone else, too, like a sensible boy, and forget all this trouble."

"I *can't* love anyone else; and I'll never forget you, Jo, never! Never!" he cried, sinking down until he sat on the grass. "I'll never marry another, Jo. You've spoiled me for good." He felt as if he had been found to be a werewolf and his heart had been torn from his chest. All hope was lost; Jo would never marry him. What would he do, and, especially, what would he think about? How could he ever erase her smile from his thoughts when, for so many years of his life, it had dominated them?

Jo looked down at Laurie, not knowing what to say or do, but then she realized that he would find another; the Professor would not, and she could not leave that kind man alone for all his life. She wished she could know if she was truly refusing Teddy because he was a werewolf or because he hadn't been completely honest with her, but she was not able to be any more frank with herself than he had been with her. All she knew for certain was that she could not marry him.

As she walked into the house and caught sight of Beth, she was struck anew with the change in her. No one spoke of it, or seemed aware of it, for it had come on too gradually to startle those who saw her daily; but to eyes sharpened by absence, it was very plain; and a heavy weight fell on Jo's heart when she looked into her sister's face. It was no paler, and but a little thinner than it had been in the autumn; yet there was a strange, transparent look about it, as if the mortal was being slowly refined away and the immortal was shining through the frail flesh with an indescribable pathetic beauty. But Beth seemed happier than ever, and she shone with special radiance whenever Mr. Laurence paid her one of his numerous visits. Marmee stated she didn't know what to do with the time she had on her hands, as Mr. Laurence attended to Beth completely, from shopping for special treats, to teasing her into eating more heartily, to taking her into the yard to breathe in fresh air whenever the weather was fair.

Mr. Laurence came to the house one day with a worried expression. "My dearest Beth," he said, taking her hand. "I don't know how to tell you this. I have business in London to which I must attend. My grandson is suffering greatly from having lost the woman of his dreams, and I am taking him with me, hoping, of course, that he will also find interest in the business. The unfortunate lad feels his heart is broken and the world is a howling wilderness, and I can't be comfortable letting him go off on his own, which he was ready to do this very afternoon. So with both the boy and the business demands on my shoulders, I fear I must go. I hope, I pray, that you understand."

"Of course I do. Completely. Although I will miss you more than I can say."

Jo walked in as the old man pecked her sister on the cheek. When they told Jo of Mr. Laurence's plan, she smiled. "Then what would you think, Beth, of you and I taking this opportunity to go to the mountains?"

"Oh, no, Jo. Please, not so far from home, I beg you."

"Well, then, is there anywhere where you would want to go?"

"Perhaps to the seashore again. It is so quiet, there is so much open air, and the sea breezes smell of eternity."

Jo agreed, recalling how those sea breezes had blown color into Beth's cheeks the last time she was there.

So off they went, and one day, Beth lay on the warm rocks with her head in Jo's lap, while the winds blew healthfully over her, and the sea made music at her feet. Jo looked down at her, wondering if her sister guessed the hard truth that confronted her so aggressively. She put down her book and looked out to the sea, her eyes filled with tears, and her arms instinctively tightened their hold on her dearest treasure as she bitterly acknowledged that her sister was drifting away from her.

"Jo, I'm glad you know it. I've tried to tell you, but I couldn't," Beth said, turning to look up at her.

Suddenly their roles were changed, for Jo was the weaker of the two, and the one who had to be comforted.

"I've known for a good while, and now I'm used to it. Don't be so troubled. It's all for the best, you see."

"Is knowing this what made you so unhappy in the autumn, Beth?"

"Yes. My illness was the reason for my melancholy. I was exhausted from the knowledge that I would soon die."

"Did you feel it then and keep it to yourself all this time?"

"No. James knows."

"James?"

"Mr. Laurence. He has been a great comfort, and I am over the feelings I had in the fall of being angry that I would never be strong and full of happy plans like you."

"I thought you were unhappy because you were in love."

"I am in love."

"With Laurie?"

"Laurie? Wherever did you dream up such a notion? No, not with Laurie."

"But you said you were in love with a werewolf."

"And I am. With Mr. Laurence. With my loving James."

Jo smiled in spite of her pain, not realizing the true depth of the love Beth and Mr. Laurence had, but certainly being happy they were able to bring some joy to each other.

"I could never have loved Laurie, Jo. He is so fond of you, and you two are so happy together. He is like a brother to me, and I hope you will truly make him my brother one day."

"Not through me," Jo said decidedly. "Although Amy would suit him excellently." This was, indeed, a rare instance where Jo felt a wealthy werewolf was a superior match to a poor, dull man, for Amy's letters indicated that she thrived on the excitement offered by upper society. "But I have no heart for such things now. I don't care what becomes of anybody but you, Beth. You must get well."

"I try, I swear to you, I try. But I lose a little every day, and feel sure I won't get it back. It's like the tide, Jo. When it turns, it goes slowly, but it can't be stopped. I don't know how to express myself as you do, but I will try to explain. I have a feeling that it was never intended that I should live long. I'm not like the rest of you. I never made plans about what I'd do when I grew up; I never thought of myself as being married, as you all did. I never imagined myself as anything other than stupid little Beth, trotting about at home, of no use anywhere but there. I don't want to leave you all, but I'm not afraid, even though it seems as if I should be homesick for you even in heaven."

"Nineteen is too young. There must be ways. God cannot be so cruel."

Beth was too weak to reason with Jo, to explain that she had the courage and patience to give up life and cheerfully wait for death. She worried more for the sorrow of her family than the passing of her life, and seeing her sister so distraught over her made her begin to sob. A great pain passed between the sisters, breaking over them and soaking them so they could only sit clinging to each other and to this fragile thing we call life.

Jo didn't hear all the words as Beth rambled on about missing her cats, and the dolls she had left behind. She prattled on about the birds, how she liked the peeps more than the gulls. She likened Jo to a gull, strong and wild, fond of storms and wind, flying far out to sea, and happy all alone. At the end of the day, she asked Jo to stop hoping, explaining that she simply wanted everyone to be happy, enjoying their time together, until the tide went out for her.

When the sisters arrived back home again, everyone could see plainly what they had prayed so fervently to be saved from seeing. Tired from her short journey, Beth went at once to bed, saying how glad she was to be home, and asking when Mr. Laurence was returning. When Jo went back downstairs from settling her sister comfortably on her pillows, she found she would be spared the hard task of telling Beth's secret. Her father stood leaning his head on the mantelpiece and did not turn as she came in; but her mother stretched out her arms as if for help, and Jo went to comfort her without a word.

CHAPTER 34

A Rekindled Relationship

AT THREE O'CLOCK IN THE AFTERNOON, THE ENTIRE fashionable world at Nice may be seen on the Promenade des Anglais, a charming place; for the wide walk, bordered with palms, flowers, and tropical shrubs, is bounded on one side by the sea, on the other by the grand drive, lined with hotels and villas, while beyond lie orange orchards and the hills. Many nations are represented, many languages spoken, many costumes worn; and on a sunny day, the spectacle is as gay and brilliant as a carnival. Haughty English, lively French, sober Germans, handsome Spaniards, ugly Russians, meek Jews, free-and-easy Americans—all drive, sit, or saunter here, chatting over the latest news and criticizing whichever celebrity has arrived, be it Ristori, Dickens, Victor Emanuel, or the Queen of the Sandwich Islands. The equipages are as varied as the company, and attract as much attention, especially the low-basket barouches in which ladies drive themselves, with a pair of dashing ponies, gay nets to keep their voluminous flounces from overflowing the diminutive vehicles, and little grooms on the perch behind.

Laurie walked slowly along on Christmas Day, with his hands behind him and a somewhat absent expression. He looked like an Italian, was dressed like an Englishman, and had the independence of an American—a combination that caused sundry pairs of feminine eyes to look approvingly after him, and sundry dandies in black velvet suits, with rose-colored neckties, buff gloves, and orange flowers in their buttonholes, to shrug their shoulders, and then envy him his inches. There were plenty of pretty faces to admire, but Laurie took no notice of them, glancing now and then at some blond girl, or some lady in blue, until the quick trot of ponies' feet made him look up at one of the little carriages coming rapidly down the street. There sat Amy, young, blond, and dressed in blue, as promised.

"Oh, Laurie, is it really you?" Amy cried, dropping the reins and holding out both hands, to the great scandalization of a French mamma, who hastened her daughter's steps, lest beholding that the free manners of these "mad English" should demoralize her. "I am so happy we shall be spending Christmas together!"

"I called at your hotel, but you were out," he said, climbing up into the passenger seat of her quaint little carriage.

"I have so much to tell you. There is a Christmas party tonight at our hotel, and Aunt insisted I force you to be there."

Laurie paled a bit, but not enough for Amy to notice. His eyebrows drew together and he asked, "Your aunt said you could be there?"

"Where?"

"The party at your hotel."

"Absolutely. Now, tell me what you've been doing. The last I heard, I believe your grandfather wrote that he expected you from Berlin," she said, jiggling the reins so the ponies began to trot.

"Yes, I spent a month there. I wanted him to join me, but he won't leave Beth's side. He goes home now only long enough to bathe and change clothes, and often sleeps on a cot at your mother's house. I hear meals are carried across the garden to him and Beth, so he may offer her delicacies in the hopes of tempting her to eat an extra bite or two of food."

"He is such a dear! I thought of going home, but Mother says I shall never have another chance like this, and besides, I can't do any more for Beth than anyone else. I do better staying here to work at the soldiers' hospital."

"How long have you been doing that?"

"Oh, forever. I never forgot that I refused to be in the same room with the war amputees from Father's exhibit, as if they wore their wounds only to annoy me. Now it is nothing to me to see and smell the sores and scabs of the inmates. I have a need to make up for my rudeness, now that I see myself clearly: I burnt Jo's book after she toiled over it for years, I've had more temper tantrums than anyone else on this promenade, and I have, generally, been extremely naughty and selfish my entire life. I've been cloistered and protected from all that is ugly; someone else always dealt with the unsightly things in my stead, as I happily stepped back. Enough."

"Your mother was right in advising you to stay here. All that can be done for Beth's comfort is being done," Laurie said, and then braced himself, as Amy stopped suddenly to avoid running into a passing procession.

They sat silently, watching the priests, white-veiled nuns holding tapers, and some brotherhood in blue, chanting as they walked. Amy glanced at Laurie out of the side of her eye and felt a new sort of shyness steal over her, for he had changed; he was greatly improved, handsomer than ever, but she could not find the merry-faced boy in the moody-looking man beside her. They sat watching the procession until it wound away across the arches of the Paglioni Bridge and vanished in the church.

They stopped shortly at a picnic to which Laurie had been invited, and he introduced Amy around. She found herself entirely pleased with the gracious nature of the people Laurie had claimed as friends, although she thought their choice of food— entire birds, rabbits, and squirrels offered with feet and heads in- tact—to be quite odd. But she had seen a variety of odd things devoured since her arrival in Europe, so thought no more of it, and concentrated instead on the pleasant company. "That meat owns a terrible smell," she whispered to Laurie as they surveyed the feast together. "I don't think I'll have any."

"I wouldn't advise it," he returned. "It is an acquired taste— very fresh, cooked ever so slightly, and with all organs still intact."

Amy took his advice and tried not even one bite, satisfying herself with an orange, although the others ate the meat with great relish and commented on its wonderful flavor.

Far too swiftly, time passed and they were forced to leave the merry gathering and continue on their way.

When they arrived at Avigdor's, Amy found precious letters from home, and gave Laurie the reins as she read, reporting snippets to him occasionally, but mostly laughing or sighing. She showed him a silly sketch of Jo in her scribbling suit, with the bow rampantly erect on her head, and issuing from her mouth the words "Genius burns!"

Laurie glanced over at her continuously as she read, pleased by her natural elegance in dress and bearing. She finished read- ing, folded the letter, and said, "This will be a regular merry Christmas to me, with presents in the morning, you and letters in the afternoon, and a party at night."

"And you're absolutely certain your aunt invited you to this party?"

"What is it that so disturbs you? Of course I am invited. She said to also invite you."

"I had already been invited, thank you, but the other invitation was nowhere near as cordial or welcome as yours. It would be my honor to escort you," he said as they alighted at the ruins of the old fort and a flock of splendid peacocks came trooping about to see if they had anything to eat. Amy stood laughing and scattering bread crumbs, so Laurie took the opportunity to assess her completely, to see what changes time and absence had wrought. He saw much to admire and approve; she was sprightly, elegant, and graceful, had gained certain aplomb in both carriage and conversation, and simply seemed more of a woman of the world. But her old petulance now and then showed itself, her strong will still held its own, and her native frankness was unspoiled by foreign polish.

When she dropped him at his hotel, he stood watching the carriage pulling up the hill, wondering how he could stand to not see her again for hours.

Amy had discovered that tarlatan and tulle were cheap in Nice, and so had been enveloping herself in them on such occasions, accessorizing old garments with fresh flowers and a few trinkets, to great effect. That night, she was taking special care to dress, having seen her old friend in a new light, as a handsome and agreeable man. She put on Flo's old white silk ball gown and covered it with a cloud of fresh illusion, out of which her white shoulders and golden head emerged with a most artistic effect. She gathered the thick waves and curls of her hair up into a Hebe-like knot in the back of her head, as it was becoming, although not in style. Not having ornaments fine enough for this important occasion, Amy looped her fleecy skirts with rosy clusters of azalea and framed her white shoulders in delicate green vines. She surveyed her new white satin slippers with girlish satisfaction and *chasséed* down the room, admiring her aristocratic feet.

"My new fan just matches the flowers, my gloves fit to a charm, and the real lace on Aunt's handkerchief gives an air to my whole dress. If I only had a classical nose and mouth, I should be perfectly happy," she told her reflection, surveying herself with a critical eye.

She looked unusually gay and graceful as she glided down the stairs to wait for Laurie. She walked up and down the long saloon, arranging herself here and there, but always thinking better of it and moving to another place. Laurie came in so quietly she did not hear him as she stood at a distant window with her head half turned and one hand gathering up her dress. The slender white figure against the red curtain was as effective as a well-placed statue, and Laurie felt an ember warm the stone coldness that Jo had left in his heart when she refused him.

He pushed the red handkerchief into the depths of his pocket as he walked up to her, and they stood looking at each other until he startled himself by saying, "I arranged these flowers for you myself, remembering that you are particular about them." He handed her a delicate nosegay in a holder she had coveted since seeing it in Cardiglia's window.

"How kind you are!" were the only words she could bring herself to say, for her tongue was heavy and cumbersome behind her little pink lips.

The company assembled in the long *salle à manger* that evening was such as one sees nowhere but on the Continent. The hospitable Americans had invited every acquaintance they had in Nice. A Russian prince sat in a corner for an hour and talked with a massive lady dressed like Hamlet's mother in black velvet; a Polish count, aged eighteen, devoted himself to the ladies; a hungry-looking German roamed about alone; a stout Frenchman looked for a dancing partner; and a British matron at-

304 LOUISA MAY ALCOTT AND PORTER GRAND

tended with her full flock of eight finely dressed children. There were also scatterings of shrill-voiced American girls, handsome, lifeless Englishmen, traveling young gentlemen, French demoi-selles, and others from all nations, lined against the walls and smiling benignly.

Amy took the stage that night leaning on Laurie's arm, and realizing she looked well. She loved to dance, and after dancing a few times with Laurie, a count asked her to the floor and she accepted, but she could not forgive the look of relief on Laurie's face when he sat down next to her aunt. She avoided him for some time, accepting other opportunities to chat or dance, but found her anger melted and readily accepted when he asked her for another dance.

"I wish I had thought to lace red ribbons through my dress as I see so many of; it is a lovely idea for Christmas, but would it not be more festive to also use green?" she said as they came upon empty chairs and sat down.

"You don't understand the meaning of the ribbons," he said, stiffening.

"No, I do. I know Aunt belongs to an elite society and that the ribbons show who she is to her peers."

"What more do you know about it?"

"Nothing."

"I suppose she will next invite you to attend the games!"

"Games? What games?"

"I doubt she would want you there, Amy. I never should have said anything."

"I am going to ask, first, if she planned to go, and second, if I can."

Laurie melted into the crowd to watch as Amy found her

aunt and asked her about the games the next night. Aunt Carrol's expression revealed nothing as she answered Amy's query.

"She asked if you explained the games to me," Amy said, finding Laurie.

"I hope you told her the truth, that I had not."

"Of course. She also gave her word that if you explained everything to me, and I still wanted to, then I could go."

"I don't want to explain it, and you don't want to go."

"I do," she said, stomping her foot as she had when a child. "I want to know all about this society, and I want to go to its functions."

"They are nothing that you expect."

"Then tell me."

"I will not!"

"You must!"

"They're werewolf games, Amy." He kept his voice low and stern. "Do you care to see a werewolf tear a person to pieces? That is the game."

"You joke!" she cried, expecting to see the familiar mischievous grin spread across that dark, handsome face.

He sat her down and explained the details of the game. She became flustered, so he took the red handkerchief from his pocket and handed it to her; their eyes met as she took it and brought it to her face.

"Now, do you still care to attend?" he asked once his description was finished.

She stood up, stunned, with her mind darting to varied scenes from "werewolf hunting" with Esther: Polly hiding deep in the wardrobe, her own hands cutting gray fur from the pelt of the coat, the werewolf pack lounging and grooming in the moonlight, the delicious haunting wail of their howl, two fierce males battling to win a mate, the decidedly sweet palpitating fear that ran through her as she knelt at the window to watch them.

"Yes," she said, secure that she had thought long and well. "I do very much want to go. I have had a lifelong fear of were-wolves, so feel compelled to attend."

He looked at her evenly, staring deep into her eyes as steadily as if reading her mind. "Amy, you do not have the strength and fortitude to witness such a thing. Your aunt was wrong to approve your going."

"Please see, Laurie, that I must do this to face my fears, so I might become a better person. One of the books I found here speaks of developing munificent strength by literally standing before demons. I will try anything to not be so weak."

"You are not weak, Amy, you're quite brave." Laurie saw clearly now that he had always loved Jo for her adventurous valor, but she was simply mischievous, not courageous. Amy was the valiant one, fighting her fears, staring into the face of terror in order to redeem herself, and it seemed nothing short of epic to him. He felt his body warm as he caressed the little blond girl who housed a backbone of steel in her dainty body.

"Do you play a role in this game?" she finally asked.

"Yes, I have participated in them, but only once," said Laurie, shaking himself out from his daydreams. "I never wanted to do so again, and Grandfather disapproves of them quite adamantly."

"What is your role?"

"I cannot say. Please, no more talk of this, or my temper may show. I have only just found you, and this is a certain way to lose you just as quickly."

"You worry over losing me? Me? In my cheap tulle and little

posies that can be had for nothing? Me, who knows nothing better than how to make the most of all my poor little things?"

Amy rather regretted that last sentence, fearing it wasn't in
good taste; but Laurie replied, "I admire that very same brave
patience that makes the most of opportunity, and the cheerful
spirit with which you cover your poverty in flowers. I have always thought of you as one who looks ahead with fresh eyes and
easily accepts the delights that life has to offer. Not all of us are
so fortunate." And he filled up her dance book with his own
name and devoted himself solely to her for the rest of the
evening.

CHAPTER 35

Werewolf Games

ALTHOUGH LAURIE DID EVERYTHING IN HIS POWER TO try to convince Amy not to attend the Lycanthrope Society games, she was certain she must. He then begged and cajoled Aunt Carrol to forbid her to witness the event, but the woman was adamant that all must, at long last, be revealed to the girl, and as Laurie had explained the games, she was determined to keep her word. "You are an adult now, Amy," Aunt Carrol explained. "If you are going to live here, I think you should have your eyes opened for you. I, for one, am tired of hiding."

"Hiding? In what way do you hide? Do you also play the games?"

"No more questions. You will see everything. You will see more than you ever expected to in this lifetime. I know this will be a frightening experience for you, but remember, through it all, that you are quite safely tucked away. Stay where you are put, and no harm can befall you."

Amy shook her head, thinking Jo's thespian bent must have come from Aunt Carrol's side of the family, as the woman was certainly waxing dramatic. She kept reciting to herself, as she dressed for the event, the comforting thought that everyone was being overly cautious, and that the games were nowhere near as frightening as they wanted her to think they were, but her hands quaked as she fastened her necklace in place.

She went to the window and pulled the drape aside. The sun was burning itself out to make space for the night, and she hoped the coach would come soon. Since arriving, she had been out before on full-moon nights, without incident, but she still felt uncomfortable and had devoted a great deal of time during those nights to peering back over her shoulder.

She had been told they had to be "in place" that night by the time the moon rose in the sky, so she tucked in her handkerchief and picked up her bag. Aunt Carrol, Flo, and a few others were assembled downstairs waiting for the carriage, which she could hear rumbling up the street. She gripped her bag tightly the entire ride to hide the tremor in her hands.

Amy was deposited with a groomsman, and everyone else continued on in the carriage. "What is this? Where are they going? Why have I been left alone?" she asked, but she could have received equally scant reply from the gloves he wore as he recited, over and over, only that she must follow him to the belvedere.

"Belvedere," said Amy, rolling the odd word about on her tongue.

She was mounted on the back of a horse, and although riding was an activity she had sadly failed to master, she was pleased, at least, that there was a lady's sidesaddle on the animal, so she could ride in a dignified manner, rather than astride like a field peasant. She was driven through the woods for what seemed days in the dim dankness of the twilight forest. At long last, they reached an enormous clearing, and in the middle of it, standing quite solitary, was the immense belvedere, made entirely of glass panes set in a lovely iron spiderweb of designs, and containing a small cluster of men.

As she was led over to the massive structure, she admired the lacy metalwork designs reinforcing the thick glass panes that reflected the dwindling sunlight.

"In America, we would call this a gazebo, although this is the largest gazebo I have ever seen," she told the groomsman, who nodded once in response and then proceeded to open an enormous lock on the belvedere. She was led in and left standing looking at the men with whom she now shared her cage as the door was locked securely behind her.

The men were friendly enough but looked her over in a curious manner, as if she really shouldn't be there. She began to worry that the descriptions of the games were more accurate than she had allowed herself to believe. A couple was let into the belvedere with them, the door was decisively shut, and an additional lock was secured over the first. Amy smiled at the girl, relieved to see another female, but the girl only half-smiled in reply, then turned her plain face away and showed Amy her back.

They didn't wait long; the moon rose full and high in the sky, and a howl rang out nearby, shaking the panes of the belvedere with its mighty fury. The people inside began to act very excited, and Amy suddenly noticed that there were people outside as well. She looked up at the glow of the moon through the glass ceiling and could feel her heart beating in her throat. She prayed to the Madonna to help her get through the night, and to make her stronger for what she was about to witness. She pressed her hands and face to the glass; she could easily envision herself out there, for she had been tutored well by Laurie, and knew those people were the poor, who had been considered someone else's property, who had been bought and sold and, quite unluckily, had wound up here. She counted two men and a woman with light skin like hers, and two men and two women with mocha or brown skin. One man had skin near to the color of Laurie's, reminding her of him, so she craned her neck to find him and discover his and Aunt Carrol's roles in this event.

One man in the belvedere called out, and all the little caged creatures ran to the west, watching two enormous werewolves stalking one of the women. Amy cried out to warn her, and the others laughed and turned to glance at her, so she pressed her lips together and allowed the tears to fall from her eyes as the burly, magnificent monsters fell upon two of the people and tore their limbs and heads from their bodies. Amy's stomach turned over, and she was glad her nerves had squelched her hunger that day. She fell to the floor of the belvedere and sat there, staring out, breathing deeply to settle the roiling of her belly.

"First time here, is it?" one of the men spat at her, then turned back to watch the carnage before she could find breath to answer.

One of the fierce, hellish creatures bounced its prey against the glass precisely where her face looked out, and the man's cold, glazed eyes were directly before her own. She shuddered but whispered a prayer of thanks that she had not been forced to meet the eyes of a living man.

She cowered there on the floor, wishing she had not been so insistent on witnessing these games. She had been a fool; how could watching such horrifying acts cure her fear, when these images were now burnt into the deepest recesses of her brain, where her nightmares lurked? And why could Laurie not have stayed with her to assure her with his strong arms and comforting words?

The others exclaimed when blood or tissue splashed the

*She cowered there on the floor, wishing she had not been
so insistent on witnessing these games.*

glass panes of their safe harbor, and Amy watched, eyes frozen open and intent on one werewolf whose long tongue protruded to lick the brain, bit by bit, from one of the skulls. Once the people were torn apart enough to look like any other meat, it was easier to watch, as one could imagine it was a wild animal, a sick or injured one, being hunted and felled, according to the natural order of the world.

After the first group of people had been killed, new ones were sent in, causing everyone in the belvedere, except Amy, to cheer, and it took the werewolves the whole of the night to kill those poor souls. They seemed to be injuring them only enough to contain them, and then taking their time nibbling flesh from bone and retrieving dripping organs from the cavities of their poor abused bodies. Amy felt some relief in that once they delved in for the organs, the victim was dead, or nearly so.

At day's first light the spectators were released from their glass prison. They chatted and laughed amiably among themselves, but Amy was silent, concentrating on forcing one foot before the other and then remaining upright on her horse. She nearly fell into the carriage, and then stared out, unseeing, as she was driven back to the hotel alone. Nobody else was there when she arrived. She ran about pulling curtains open so the rooms were flooded with daylight, and she undressed, washed, and curled up in her bed, pulling the covers up all the way to her flat little nose. Somehow, her exhausted body relaxed and she fell asleep; blessedly, she did not dream.

Laurie had come to Nice intending to stay a mere week but had remained there an entire month. He was tired of wandering about alone, and Amy's presence enlivened everything, making the sunshine brighter, the music more lively, the art more heart-wrenchingly beautiful, and his reason to get out of bed each morning of lofty importance. The two took comfort in each other's company, and were much together—riding, walking, dancing, or dawdling—for in Nice no one can be very industrious during the gay season. Amy was grateful for the many little pleasures he gave her and tried to repay him with little services and attentive companionship.

The next day as they rode Amy's little pair of ponies and carriage to Valrosa so she could sketch, she was the first to speak of the hunt.

"Will you tell me your part in it?"

"After you tell me your opinion of it. After all, it took a great deal of money and connections to buy you a spot."

"People pay to witness that?"

"Dearly," he said with a laugh. "As with a great many other things, nobody would ever bother with producing them unless there was a profit. There was a very small audience the night you were there, because it was right after the holidays. Normally, you never would have gained entrance in so short a time."

"Dear Laurie, I must know your part in this. Do you trade in this unwholesome market that barters human beings like sacks of grain?"

"No. I would never . . ."

"Then what?" She stopped the carriage and the two sat looking at each other. "I didn't see you for one moment that night."

"Yes, you did."

She stared at him, a tiny crease forming between her eyes as she pondered. Then the crease disappeared and the color washed from her face in a wave of nausea. "Are you . . ."

"Yes. I am a werewolf. My grandfather is a werewolf. Your Aunt Carrol and Flo are werewolves, and a great many of the people you have met here and professed to like are werewolves."

A million questions flooded her mind as she drove along. "How long have you and your grandfather been werewolves? And Aunt Carrol and Flo?" she finally asked.

"You have never known any of us when we were not."

The memory of the dead man thrown up against the belvedere surfaced, and she asked, "Was it you who rubbed my nose in that dead man's face; pushed it on the glass where I sat?"

"No. That was Flo."

Flo? That horrendous, looming beast was the quiet and meek little Flo?

"Is that the end of your questions?" he asked, his temper obviously inflamed.

"I should say not! Why would you take part in such an event?"

"For you. I told you, I did it once and did not care to ever do it again, but as you were watching, I participated. I would never do so otherwise. I did it so you could know full well the man before you. Realize, Amy, that these games satisfy our need for human flesh and blood, for it is absolutely necessary for our survival. These games actually stop innocents on the streets from being slain."

"Those people were not innocents?"

"Those people were slated for this purpose. The reason they were chosen is not ours to dissect; I have no knowledge of or input in the process, for it is the duty of only the loftiest officials of the Lycanthrope Society to acquire those unfortunate people. There are things we, as werewolves, simply must accept, just as there are things you do not like but must view as necessary evils."

She looked up into the softness of his eyes and saw his sincerity. "Does anyone else in my family know about you?" she inquired after some thought.

"Jo and Beth."

"You told them and not me?"

"I never told them. I cannot say what they saw, or when, but somehow they know, and they have kept my secret safe."

Amy sat thinking. She had always feared werewolves above all, but she had also always believed her father when he reminded them that werewolves, every day of the month save one, were exactly like everyone else—kind or cruel, cross or happy, content or miserable. As children, they had never been permitted to make negative remarks about werewolves, or to play games, such as pretending to be members of the Brigade, that caused undue hysteria toward them, but Jo had often whispered a quick, inventive werewolf tale in her ear, firing her imagination and scaring her out of her pretty blond curls.

"One more question. How do you live with the killing? How do you look at yourself in a mirror, knowing you have murdered someone under the light of the full moon?"

"I suppose that's hardest for those who are bitten and turn into werewolves during their life. When you are born a werewolf, as I was, when it is all you know, you must, as everyone else, learn to love yourself as you are, and forgive yourself your faulty acts."

As horrific as Amy knew those acts must have been, she saw sense, clarity, and wisdom in his words. She thought for a moment and then launched another question. "There is no Brigade here to accuse and punish?"

"There is, but mostly for ritual, except in the most modest neighborhoods where society's worst reside. I imagine in those areas they exist for a purpose and, no doubt, see little repose."

"So the rich protect the rich, and the Brigade is not needed in the nicer areas."

"Think on it, Amy. A poor man sees purpose in earning his family's supper, and can be bought to accuse another. The ritual of the Brigade is faulty."

"And wealthy men cannot be bought?" Amy exclaimed at the absurdity of Laurie's presumption.

"All I am saying, Amy, is that we cannot speak for all men. Human or werewolf, saint or sinner, rich or poor, we must each, individually, come to terms with our own ethics based on our personal morals and life experiences. Not all men have the heart and stomach to be butchers or morticians."

"Are there any commandments by which you live as a wolf?"

"A great many. Grandfather taught me to be cautious and discreet, and to try, when possible, to slay only those deserving," he said, looking away. "However, that is not always possible. But we do show restraint when we hunt, if that's what you ask. Humans have the tastiest flesh and the sweetest blood, but there would be no people left in your hometown if the werewolves there had accepted every opportunity for a kill. But we must accept some of those opportunities, you see, for it is the human flesh and blood that best sustains us."

She looked up at Laurie but did not see one of the fanged, wicked, golden-eyed beasts; rather, she saw a lonely little boy, a joking lad, and the dour, confused man he had grown into—he who owned such a serious affliction that every cent of his grandfather's money could not cure it.

Pale hands picked up the reins, and Amy watched the picturesque scenes as they drove silently along winding roads, past an ancient monastery where the chanting of the monks reached their ears. A bare-legged shepherd in wooden shoes, pointed hat, and rough jacket over one shoulder sat piping on a stone, while his goats skipped among the rocks or lay at his feet. Meek, mouse-colored little donkeys, laden with panniers of freshly cut grass, passed by, with a pretty girl in a straw hat or an old woman sitting between the green piles. Brown, soft-eyed children ran out from the quaint stone hovels to offer nosegays or bunches of oranges still on the bough. Gnarled olive trees covered the hills with their dusky foliage, and fruit hung golden in the orchard, while beyond green slopes and craggy heights, the Maritime Alps rose sharp and white against the blue Italian sky.

Valrosa well deserved its name, for in that climate of perpetual summer, roses blossomed everywhere. They overhung archways, thrust themselves between the bars of the great gate with a sweet welcome, wound through lemon trees and feathery palms, and invaded every shadowy nook, cool grotto, fountain, house wall, pillar, and balustrade.

"This is a regular honeymoon paradise, isn't it?" Amy exclaimed, enjoying the view and the luxurious whiff of perfume that came her way. "Have you ever seen such roses?"

"No, nor felt such thorns," returned Laurie, with his thumb in his mouth after a vain attempt to capture a solitary scarlet flower.

"Try lower down, and pick those that have no thorns," said Amy, gathering three tiny cream-colored ones and putting them in his buttonhole with slightly trembling fingers. She inhaled deeply but caught only the attractive fragrance of a man, not the feral scent she had expected.

He stood a minute, looking down at them. In the Italian part of him there was a touch of superstition, and he wondered if this small act was of any significance. He had thought of Jo in reaching for the thorny red rose, for vivid flowers became her, and they were the sort she grew to wear in the greenhouse at home. The pale roses Amy gave him were the sort that Italians laid in dead hands, never in bridal wreaths, and he wondered how to make sense of the omen. Was it true physical harm or his heart's loss of one, or both, sisters that was being revealed to him? In the next instant, his American common sense again ruled his head, and he forgot the nonsense and admired the view of the sunny Mediterranean.

"When are you going to go see your grandfather again?"

"Very soon."

"He expects you, and you really ought to. He could benefit greatly from the diversion and the company."

"I know it."

"Then why don't you go?"

"Natural depravity, I suppose."

"Natural indolence, you mean. You are altogether too dreadful," she said severely, unpacking her sketchbook and pencils. "I need a figure in my sketch. Do you mind if I use you?"

"So long as I can remain indolent and not trouble myself too much."

"No need to be so sour with me."

"You are the sour one. I don't know what you may think of me. You have practiced hiding your disgust with the inmates at the hospital too well, for your hatred of who and what I am does not reveal itself in the least."

"You know my family has always accepted werewolves, even lazy ones."

"But do you?" He walked up to her, and she flinched as he took her by the shoulders. He smiled, excited by the fear he could smell emanating from her soft white skin. He sniffed her neck loudly, and she pulled away. He pulled her back up against him roughly, and he felt her relax and lean into him.

"I need some time, Laurie, to understand what I feel," she

said, stepping away from him so she could look full into his eyes. "My old love for you has altered, but not in the way you think. It has sharpened, and grown from a sisterly love to a mature, romantic love. Oh, I know I am a fool to voice this to you before I know how you feel about me, especially as I suspect you are merely being kind by spending this time with me. If you are asking if I will remain your friend, then I can say absolutely yes. If you are asking if I can be more, I must be honest and say that I need time to think."

"So do I," he said, pulling her to him so she couldn't see his face. "I have never cared for anyone but Jo in that way. Now I have much to question."

"I was sure she loved you dearly."

"She did, just not in the right way. It's lucky for her she didn't love me; I'm nothing more than a murdering good-for-nothing werewolf who doesn't even earn his own way." The hard, bitter look came back to his face, and it troubled Amy.

"We both have to think about what we feel for each other, and what we mean to each other, Laurie."

She looked up at him, and in his black eyes she was startled to see the longing stare with which he used to look at Jo, the stare she had begun to pray would, one day, be aimed at her. She felt a joyous tear escape one blue eye and course down her cheek. Laurie caught it with his fingertip and deposited it on his tongue. Amy swooned, thinking that the most romantic act she had ever seen.

They laughed and chatted easily all the way home but actually felt ill at ease; the friendly frankness was disturbed, the sunshine had a shadow over it, and despite their apparent gaiety, there was a secret discontent in the heart of each, as they prepared to be rejected by the other.

As they parted at Aunt Carrol's door, Amy asked with pounding heart, "Shall we see you this evening?"

Laurie thought for a moment, her words concerning his grandfather still circling his head. He sorely missed hunting with the man, for it was the one activity the two enjoyed pursuing together. They shared many fond memories of their moonlight slaughters of both men and beasts, and of guardian and heir lying down to savor their prey and bask in victory. "Please make my adieux to your aunt. I am going, on your advice, back to see my grandfather. I believe, as you said, that we need this time apart—to think. Goodbye, dear." And with these words, uttered in a tone she liked, Laurie left her, after a handshake almost painful in its heartiness.

Amy sat looking down at her lap, already feeling the pain of missing the handsome werewolf. She ached for his touch the moment his hand left her arm, and his scent clung in her memory like a skittish cat, jumping out often to remind her how well she loved him.

...

CHAPTER 36

On the Dusty Shelf

*I*N FRANCE THE YOUNG GIRLS HAVE A DULL TIME OF IT till they are married, when *"Vive la liberté!"* becomes their motto. In America, as everyone knows, girls early sign a declaration of independence, and enjoy their freedom with republican zest, but the young matrons usually abdicate with the first heir to the throne and go into a seclusion almost as close as a French nunnery, though by no means as quiet. Whether they like it or not, they are virtually put upon the shelf as soon as the wedding excitement is over, and most of them might exclaim, as did a very pretty woman the other day, "I'm as handsome as ever, but no one takes any notice of me because I'm married."

Not being a belle or even a fashionable lady, Meg did not experience this affliction till her babies were a year old, for in her little world primitive customs prevailed, and she found herself more admired and beloved than ever.

As she was a womanly little woman, the maternal instinct was very strong, and she was entirely absorbed in her children, to the utter exclusion of everything and everybody else. Day and night she brooded over them with tireless devotion and anxiety, leaving John to the tender mercies of the help, for an Irish lady now presided over the kitchen department. Being a domestic man, John decidedly missed the wifely attentions he had been accustomed to receive, but as he adored his babies, he cheerfully relinquished his comfort for a time, supposing, with masculine ignorance, that peace would soon be restored. But three months passed, and there was no return of repose. Meg looked worn and nervous, the babies absorbed every minute of her time, the house was neglected, and Kitty, the cook, who took life "aisy," kept him on short commons. When he went out in the morning he was bewildered by small commissions for the captive mamma; if he came gaily in at night, eager to embrace his family, he was quenched by a "Hush! They are just asleep after worrying all day." If he proposed a little amusement at home, "No, it would disturb the babies." If he hinted at a lecture or a concert, he was answered with a reproachful look and a decided "Leave my children for pleasure, never!" His sleep was broken by infant wails and visions of a phantom figure pacing noiselessly to and fro in the watches of the night. His meals were interrupted by the frequent flight of the presiding genius, who deserted him, half-helped, if a muffled chirp sounded from the nest above. And when he read his paper of an evening, Demi's colic got into the shipping list and Daisy's fall affected the price of stocks, for Mrs. Brooke was only interested in domestic news.

The poor man was very uncomfortable, for the children had bereft him of his wife, home was merely a nursery, and the perpetual hushing made him feel like a brutal intruder whenever he entered the sacred precincts of Babydom. He bore it very patiently for six months, and when no signs of amendment appeared, he did what other paternal exiles do—tried to get a little comfort elsewhere. Scott had married and gone to housekeeping not far off, and John fell into the way of running over for an hour or two of an evening, when his own parlour was empty, and his own wife singing lullabies that seemed to have no end. Mrs. Scott was a lively, pretty girl, with nothing to do but be agreeable, and she performed her mission most successfully. The parlour was always bright and attractive, the chessboard ready, the piano in tune, plenty of gay gossip, and a nice little supper set forth in tempting style.

John would have preferred his own fireside if it had not been so lonely, but as it was he gratefully took the next best thing and enjoyed his neighbors' society.

Meg rather approved of the new arrangement at first, and found it a relief to know that John was having a good time instead of dozing in the parlour or tramping about the house and waking the children. But by and by, when the teething worry was over and the idols went to sleep at proper hours, leaving Mamma time to rest, she began to miss John, and find her work-basket dull company, when he was not sitting opposite in his old dressing gown, comfortably scorching his slippers on the fender. She would not ask him to stay at home but felt injured because he did not know that she wanted him without being told, entirely forgetting the many evenings he had waited for her in vain. She was nervous and worn out with watching and worry, and in that unreasonable frame of mind that the best of mothers occasionally experience when domestic cares oppress them. Want of exercise robs them of cheerfulness, and too much devotion to that idol of American women, the teapot, makes them feel as if they were all nerve and no muscle.

"Yes," she would say, looking in the glass, "I'm getting old and ugly. John doesn't find me interesting any longer, so he leaves his faded wife and goes to see his pretty neighbor, who has no encumbrances. Well, the babies love me; they don't care if I am thin and pale and haven't time to crimp my hair; they are

my comfort, and someday John will see what I've gladly sacrificed for them, won't he, my precious?"

To which pathetic appeal Daisy would answer with a coo, or
Demi with a crow, and Meg would put by her lamentations for a
maternal revel, which soothed her solitude for the time being.
But the pain increased as politics absorbed John, who was always
running over to discuss interesting points with Scott, quite unconscious that Meg missed him. Not a word did she say, however, till her mother found her in tears one day, and insisted on
knowing what the matter was, for Meg's drooping spirits had
not escaped her observation.

"I wouldn't tell anyone except you, Mother, but I really do
need advice, for if John goes on much longer, I might as well be
widowed," replied Mrs. Brooke, drying her tears on Daisy's bib
with an injured air.

"Goes on how, my dear?" asked her mother anxiously.

"He's away all day, and at night when I want to see him, he is
continually going over to the Scotts'. It isn't fair that I should
have the hardest work, and never any amusement. Men are very
selfish, even the best of them."

"So are women. Don't blame John till you see where you are
wrong yourself."

"But it can't be right for him to neglect me."

"Don't you neglect him?"

"Why, Mother, I thought you'd take my part!"

"So I do, as far as sympathizing goes, but I think the fault is
yours, Meg."

"I don't see how."

"Let me show you. Did John ever neglect you, as you call it,
while you made it a point to give him your society of an evening,
his only leisure time?"

"No, but I can't do it now, with two babies to tend."

"I think you could, dear, and I think you ought. May I speak quite freely, and will you remember that it's Mother who blames as well as Mother who sympathizes?"

"Indeed I will! Speak to me as if I were little Meg again. I often feel as if I needed teaching more than ever since these babies look to me for everything." Meg drew her low chair beside her mother's, and with a little interruption in either lap, the two women rocked and talked lovingly together, feeling that the tie of motherhood made them more one than ever.

"You have only made the mistake that most young wives make—forgotten your duty to your husband in your love for your children. A very natural and forgivable mistake, Meg, but one that had better be remedied before you take to different ways, for children should draw you nearer than ever, not separate you, as if they were all yours, and John had nothing to do but support them. I've seen it for some weeks, but have not spoken, feeling sure it would come right in time."

"I'm afraid it won't. If I ask him to stay, he'll think I'm jealous, and I wouldn't insult him by such an idea. He doesn't see that I want him, and I don't know how to tell him without words."

"Make it so pleasant he won't want to go away. My dear, he's longing for his little home, but it isn't home without you, and you are always in the nursery."

"Oughtn't I to be there?"

"Not all the time; too much confinement makes you nervous, and then you are unfitted for everything. Besides, you owe something to John as well as to the babies. Don't neglect husband for children; don't shut him out of the nursery, but teach him how to help in it. His place is there as well as yours, and the children need him. Let him feel that he has a part to do, and he will do it gladly and faithfully, and it will be better for you all."

"You really think so, Mother?"

"I know it, Meg, for I've tried it, and I seldom give advice unless I've proved its practicability. When you and Jo were little, I went on just as you are, feeling as if I didn't do my duty unless I devoted myself wholly to you. Poor Father took to his books, after I had refused all offers of help, and left me to try my experiment alone. I struggled along as well as I could, but Jo was too much for me. I nearly spoiled her by indulgence. You were poorly, and I worried about you till I fell sick myself. Then Father came to the rescue, quietly managed everything, and made himself so helpful that I saw my mistake, and never have been able to get on without him since. That is the secret of our home happiness. He did not let business wean him from the little cares and duties that affected us all when you girls were young, and I try not to let domestic worries destroy my interest in his pursuits. Each do our part alone in many things, but at home we work together, always."

"It is so, Mother, and my great wish is to be to my husband and children what you have been to yours. Show me how; I'll do anything you say."

"You were always my docile daughter. Well, dear, if I were you, I'd let John have more to do with the management of Demi, for the boy needs training, and it's none too soon to begin. Then I'd do what I have often proposed, let Hannah come and help you. She is a capital nurse, and you may trust the precious babies to her while you do more housework. You need the exercise, Hannah would enjoy the rest, and John would find his wife again. Go out more, keep cheerful as well as busy, for you are the sunshine maker of the family, and if you get dismal, there is no fair weather. Then I'd try to take an interest in whatever John likes—talk with him, let him read to you, exchange ideas, and help each other in that way. Don't shut yourself up in a bandbox because you are a woman, but understand what is going on, and educate yourself to take your part in the world's work, for it all affects you and yours."

"John is so sensible, I'm afraid he will think I'm stupid if I ask questions about politics and things."

"I don't believe he would. Love covers a multitude of sins, and of whom could you ask more freely than of him? Try it, and see if he doesn't find your society far more agreeable than Mrs. Scott's suppers."

"I will. Poor John! I'm afraid I *have* neglected him sadly, but I thought I was right, and he never said anything."

"He tried not to be selfish, but he *has* felt rather forlorn, I fancy. This is just the time, Meg, when young married people are apt to grow apart, and the very time when they ought to be most together, for the first tenderness soon wears off, unless care is taken to preserve it. And no time is so beautiful and precious to parents as the first years of the little lives given to them to train. Don't let John be a stranger to the babies, for they will do more to keep him safe and happy in this world of trial and temptation than anything else, and through them you will learn to know and love one another as you should. Now, dear, goodbye. Think over Mother's preachment, act upon it if it seems good, and God bless you all."

Meg did think it over, found it good, and acted upon it, though the first attempt was not made exactly as she planned to have it. Of course the children tyrannized over her, and ruled the house as soon as they found out that kicking and squalling brought them whatever they wanted. Mamma was an abject slave to their caprices, but Papa was not so easily subjugated, and occasionally afflicted his tender spouse by an attempt at paternal discipline with his obstreperous son. For Demi inherited a trifle of his sire's firmness of character—we won't call it obstinacy—and when he made up his little mind to have or to do anything, all the king's horses and all the king's men could not change that pertinacious little mind. Mamma thought the dear too young to be taught to conquer his prejudices, but Papa believed that it never was too soon to learn obedience. So Master Demi early discovered that when he undertook to "wrastle" with "Parpar," he always got the worst of it, yet like the Englishman, baby respected the man who conquered him, and loved the father whose grave "No, no," was more impressive than all Mamma's love pats.

A few days after the talk with her mother, Meg resolved to try a social evening with John, so she ordered a nice supper, set the parlour in order, dressed herself prettily, and put the children to bed early, that nothing should interfere with her experiment. But unfortunately Demi's most unconquerable prejudice was against going to bed, and that night he decided to go on a rampage. So poor Meg sang and rocked, told stories and tried every sleep-provoking wile she could devise, but all in vain; the big eyes wouldn't shut, and long after Daisy had gone to sleep, like the chubby little bunch of good nature she was, naughty Demi lay staring at the light, with the most discouragingly wide-awake expression of countenance.

"Will Demi lie still like a good boy, while Mamma runs down and gives poor Papa his tea?" asked Meg, as the hall door softly closed, and the well-known step went tiptoeing into the dining room.

"Me has tea!" said Demi, preparing to join in the revel.

"No, but I'll save you some little cakies for breakfast, if you'll go by-by like Daisy. Will you, love?"

"Iss!" And Demi shut his eyes tight, as if to catch sleep and hurry the desired day.

Taking advantage of the propitious moment, Meg slipped away and ran down to greet her husband with a smiling face and the little blue bow in her hair, which was his especial admiration. He saw it at once and said with pleased surprise, "Why, little Mother, how gay we are tonight. Do you expect company?"

"Only you, dear. I'm tired of being dowdy, so I dressed up as a change. You always make yourself nice for table, no matter how tired you are, so why shouldn't I when I have the time?'

"I do it out of respect for you, my dear," said old-fashioned John.

"Ditto, ditto, Mr. Brooke," laughed Meg, looking young and pretty again, as she nodded to him over the teapot.

"Well, it's altogether delightful, and like old times. This tastes right. I drink to your health, dear!" And John sipped his tea with an air of reposeful rapture, which was of very short duration, however, for as he put down his cup, the door handle rattled mysteriously, and a little voice was heard, saying impatiently, "Me's tummin!"

"It's that naughty boy. I told him to go to sleep alone, and here he is, downstairs, getting his death a-cold pattering over that canvas," said Meg, answering the call.

"Mornin' now," announced Demi in a joyful tone as he entered, with his long nightgown gracefully festooned over his arm and every curl bobbing gaily as he pranced about the table, eyeing the "cakies" with loving glances.

"No, it isn't morning yet. You must go to bed, and not trouble poor Mamma. Then you can have the little cake with sugar on it."

"Me loves Parpar," said the artful one, preparing to climb the paternal knee and revel in forbidden joys.

But John shook his head, and said to Meg, "If you told him to stay up there, and go to sleep alone, make him do it, or he will never learn to mind you."

"Yes, of course. Come, Demi." And Meg led her son away, feeling a strong desire to spank the little marplot who hopped beside her, laboring under the delusion that the bribe was to be administered as soon as they reached the nursery.

Nor was he disappointed, for that shortsighted woman actually gave him a lump of sugar, tucked him into his bed, and forbade any more promenades till morning.

"Wowoof!" said Demi the perjured, blissfully sucking his sugar and regarding his first attempt as eminently successful.

"No, dear, there are no werewolves in here. Now please go to sleep."

Meg returned to her place, and supper was progressing pleasantly, when the little ghost walked again and exposed the maternal delinquencies by boldly declaring, "Wowoof!" His eyes were widened for effect.

"Now this won't do," said John, hardening his heart against the engaging little sinner. "We shall never know any peace till that child learns to go to bed properly. You have made a slave of yourself long enough. Give him one lesson, and then there will be an end of it. Put him in his bed and leave him, Meg."

"He won't stay there; he never does unless I sit by him."

"I'll manage him. Demi, go upstairs, and get into your bed, as Mamma bids you."

"S'ant! Wowoof," replied the young rebel, helping himself to the coveted cake and beginning to eat the same with calm audacity.

"You must never say that when it isn't true, and we all know it isn't. I shall carry you if you don't go yourself."

"Go 'way; me don't love Parpar," said Demi, and retired to his mother's skirts for protection.

But even that refuge proved unavailing, for he was delivered over to the enemy, with a "Be gentle with him, John," which struck the culprit with dismay, for when Mamma deserted him, then the judgment day was at hand. Bereft of his cake, defrauded of his frolic, and borne away by a strong hand to that detested bed, poor Demi could not restrain his wrath, but openly defied Papa, and kicked and screamed lustily all the way upstairs. The minute he was put into bed on one side, he rolled out on the other and made for the door, only to be ignominiously caught up by the tail of his little toga and put back again, which lively performance was kept up till the young man's strength gave out, when he devoted himself to roaring at the top of his voice. This vocal exercise usually conquered Meg, but John sat as unmoved as the post that is popularly believed to be deaf. No coaxing, no sugar, no lullaby, no story—even the light was put out, and only the red glow of the fire enlivened the "big dark," which Demi had always regarded with curiosity rather than fear. This new order of things disgusted him, and he howled dismally for "Marmar," as his angry passions subsided, and recollections of his tender bondwoman returned to the captive autocrat. The plaintive wail, which succeeded the passionate roar, went to Meg's heart, and she ran up to say beseechingly, "Let me stay with him; he'll be good now, John."

"No, my dear. I've told him he must go to sleep, as you bid him, and he must, if I stay here all night."

"But he'll cry himself sick," pleaded Meg, reproaching herself for deserting her boy.

"No, he won't; he's so tired he will soon drop off, and then the matter is settled, for he will understand that he has got to mind. Don't interfere; I'll manage him."

"He's my child, and I can't have his spirit broken by harshness."

"He's my child, and I won't have his temper spoiled by indulgence. Go down, my dear, and leave the boy to me."

When John spoke in that masterful tone, Meg always obeyed, and never regretted her docility.

"Please let me kiss him once, John?"

"Certainly. Demi, say good night to Mamma, and let her go and rest, for she is very tired with taking care of you all day."

Meg always insisted that the kiss won the victory, for after it was given, Demi sobbed more quietly, and lay quite still at the bottom of the bed, whither he had wriggled in his anguish of mind.

"Poor little man! He's worn out with sleep and crying. I'll cover him up, and then go and set Meg's heart at rest," thought John, creeping to the bedside, hoping to find his rebellious heir asleep.

But he wasn't, for the moment his father peeped at him, Demi's eyes opened, his little chin began to quiver, and he put up his arms, saying with a penitent hiccough, "Wowoof!"

"No, son," said John. "I know you are too smart to believe there is a werewolf in here."

"Wowoof!" said Demi again, this time louder.

John walked through the room, checking every inch, even under toys and bed and atop the looming wardrobe, and then carefully, and with great display, latched the windows securely. "Now you can see that no werewolf is in here, and none can get in." He rattled the window shutter. "And beyond this thick wood is a very strong glass pane, so you are perfectly safe."

Sitting on the stairs outside, Meg wondered at the long silence that followed the uproar, and after imagining all sorts of impossible accidents, she slipped into the room to set her fears at rest. Demi lay fast asleep, not in his usual spread-eagle attitude, but in a subdued bunch, cuddled close in the circle of his father's arm, and holding his father's finger, as if he felt that justice was tempered with mercy, and had gone to sleep a sadder and wiser baby. So held, John had waited with a womanly patience till the little hand relaxed its hold, and while waiting had fallen asleep, more tired by that tussle with his son than with his whole day's work.

As Meg stood watching the two faces on the pillow, she smiled to herself, then slipped away again, saying in a satisfied tone, "I never need fear that John will be too harsh with my babies. He does know how to manage them, and will be a great help, for Demi is getting too much for me."

When John came down at last, expecting to find a pensive or reproachful wife, he was agreeably surprised to find Meg placidly trimming a bonnet, and to be greeted with the request to read something about the election, if he was not too tired. John saw in a minute that a revolution of some kind was going on, but wisely asked no questions, knowing that Meg was such a transparent little person, she couldn't keep a secret to save her life, and therefore the clue would soon appear. He read a long debate with the most amiable readiness and then explained it in his most lucid manner, while Meg tried to look deeply interested, to ask intelligent questions, and keep her thoughts from wandering from the state of the nation to the state of her bonnet. In her secret soul, however, she decided that politics were as bad as mathematics, and the mission of politicians seemed to be calling each other names; but she kept these feminine ideas to herself, and when John paused, shook her head and said with what she thought diplomatic ambiguity, "Well, I really don't see what we are coming to."

John laughed, and watched her for a minute, as she poised a pretty little preparation of lace and flowers on her hand and regarded it with the genuine interest that his harangue had failed to waken.

"She is trying to like politics for my sake, so I'll try and like millinery for hers—that's only fair," thought John the Just, adding aloud, "That's very pretty. Is it what you call a breakfast cap?"

"My dear man, it's a bonnet! My very best go-to-concert-and-theater bonnet."

"I beg your pardon; it was so small, and I naturally mistook it for one of the flyaway things you sometimes wear. How do you keep it on?"

"These bits of lace are fastened under the chin with a rosebud, so." And Meg illustrated by putting on the bonnet and regarding him with an air of calm satisfaction that was irresistible.

"It's a love of a bonnet, but I prefer the face inside, for it looks young and happy again." And John kissed the smiling face, to the great detriment of the rosebud under the chin.

"I'm glad you like it, for I want you to take me to one of the new concerts some night. I really need some music to put me in tune. Will you, please?"

"Of course I will, with all my heart, or anywhere else you like. You have been shut up so long, it will do you no end of good, and I shall enjoy it, of all things. What put it into your head, little mother?"

"Well, I had a talk with Marmee the other day, and told her how nervous and cross and out of sorts I felt, and she said I needed change and less care, so Hannah is to help me with the children, and I'm to see to things about the house more, and now and then have a little fun, just to keep me from getting to be a fidgety, broken-down old woman before my time. It's only an experiment, John, and I want to try it for your sake as much as for mine, because I've neglected you shamefully lately, and I'm going to make home what it used to be, if I can. You don't object, I hope?"

Never mind what John said, or what a very narrow escape the little bonnet had from utter ruin. All that we have any business to know is that John did not appear to object, judging from the changes that gradually took place in the house and its inmates. It was not all paradise by any means, but everyone was better for the division-of-labor system. The children throve under the paternal rule, for accurate, steadfast John brought order and obedience into Babydom, while Meg recovered her spirits and composed her nerves by plenty of wholesome exercise, a little pleasure, and much confidential conversation with her sensible husband. Home grew homelike again, and John had no wish to leave it, unless he took Meg with him. The Scotts came to the Brookes now, and everyone found the little house a cheerful place, full of happiness, content, and family love. Even Sallie Moffat liked to go there. "It is always so quiet and pleasant here, it does me good, Meg," she used to say, looking about her with wistful eyes, as if trying to discover the charm, that she might use it in her great house, full of splendid loneliness, for there were no riotous, sunny-faced babies there, and Ned lived in a world of his own, where there was no place for her.

This household happiness did not come all at once, but John and Meg had found the key to it, and each year of married life taught them how to use it, unlocking the treasuries of real home love and mutual helpfulness, which the poorest may possess and the richest cannot buy. This is the sort of shelf on which young wives and mothers may consent to be laid, safe from the restless fret and fever of the world, finding loyal lovers in the little sons and daughters who cling to them, undaunted by sorrow, poverty, or age, walking side by side, through fair and stormy weather, with a faithful friend, and learning, as Meg learned, that a woman's happiest kingdom is home, her highest honor the art of ruling it not as a queen but as a wise wife and mother.

...

CHAPTER 37

Beth's Bones

THE MARCH FAMILY SADLY ACCEPTED THE INEVITABLE and tried to bear it cheerfully, each doing their part toward making Beth's last year a happy one. The pleasantest room of the house was set apart for her downstairs, and in it was gathered everything that she most loved: flowers, pictures, her piano, the little worktable, her dolls and all their things, and the beloved clutter of cats. Father's best books found their way in there, as well as Mother's easy chair, Jo's desk, and Amy's finest sketches; and every day Meg brought her babies there on a pilgrimage to make sunshine for Aunty Beth.

The first few months were tranquil and happy, for cherished like a household saint in its shrine, Beth enjoyed crafts, poetry, and company all the day long. Meg, Jo, and her mother sat together in the sunny room, Meg's little ones bleating and whooping with joy on the floor as the women read aloud, or chatted while their needles mended old garments and created new ones.

Beth watched as each person who loved her saved, sacrificed, and put great energy into her keeping, so talked frankly about it one day to Mr. Laurence.

"This has gone on long enough. I cannot bear to watch these loving people as they set aside everything that is important to them so they can nurse me. It is their very lives they are putting up to wait on a shelf in order to play dutiful servant to me."

"I will happily pay for a nurse, or move you to my house and install a nurse there," Mr. Laurence said, stroking the brow of his beloved Beth.

"No, James, I know them too well. If you did that, they would simply, bit by bit, move themselves to your house to be by my side. Besides, I could not bear to be without my cats, and they will not venture anywhere near your home." She looked up at the kindly old werewolf and saw his wounded expression. "You, too, my love, have sacrificed far too much for me. I have taken you too long away from your business and your grandson. The two of you should be off in Europe, enjoying every day you have been given together."

"But I want to be here with you."

"That is the greatest of my concerns. I know that all this effort is expended with love, and that each of you is doing just what you wish to do. But I say you have all done enough. I have no chance of recovering. I can only look forward to becoming an even emptier bag of bones, and of suffering through greater and greater pain as my poor heart struggles to keep me alive. This is a wretched existence, even with your loving presence at my side."

"What, then, may I do for you, my dear? Just ask."

"The full moon is upon us. I want you, as the animal you become, to take me that night, devour me, nourish yourself—so my death and my infirm body can be of some use to life on this earth."

"You can't mean that."

"I do."

The old man loved her very much and thought he would do anything she asked of him, but he had to absolutely refuse her this request. Beth's tired eyes looked up at him and he saw the pain in them; he knew this was likely the kindest and most loving thing he could do for her, but he also knew he was incapable of destroying that which he most loved. He put his head in her lap and wept. Mrs. March almost entered the room at that moment, but upon seeing the touching scene, she retreated, distressed, to release a few more of her own carefully pent tears.

"It is what I want," Beth said, trying one last time to convince him. "I am so weary of it all: pitying looks, false cheerfulness, throbbing pain, a weak and frail body that refuses to obey a mind that is yet sharp, the guilt of taking those I love from other pursuits. I want that peaceful, eternal sleep that is promised to those who do kind deeds on this earth, for I do not fear where I will go. I know that only good awaits me. I can only hope, though, that in the next world I will be of more use than I was here, for I have accomplished nothing during my stay."

"Your worth is far greater than you know, and you are much loved. I would do anything for you, but it is not an ethical deed you ask. I fear my hands would be forever bloodstained and my heart filled with regret."

"I understand," she said, allowing her hand to drop from his and turning her face away. "It was far too bold of me to ask. Forgive me, James, please."

"Don't. Don't apologize," the old man said, allowing all the tears he had in him to fall and splash onto Beth's bedclothes.

Once he left, Beth fretted, fearing she had gone too far with what she asked of him; simply because he became a beast once a month, it did not make him a monster capable of killing his own lover.

That evening, Beth asked Jo to help her bathe. The warmth of the water was heavenly as her sister and mother lowered her into the tub, and she almost dozed off as they gently washed her every inch.

Jo got out her nightgown, but Beth waved it away. "I want to wear my beautiful new gown."

Jo felt her heart catch. The gown had been made to give Beth something lovely in which to be buried; but she could see no way to refuse her. After all, was it not best that Beth be given this fleeting opportunity to enjoy it?

With trembling hands, Jo dressed her sister, and Beth looked chaste and ethereal in the gown; her skin was almost as white as the soft material, and the pink in her cheeks from the warmth of the bath matched perfectly the delicate rosettes scattered on the sleeves and bodice.

Jo helped her into her bed and tried to give her the nighttime dose of her medicine, but Beth refused to take it. "Please, Jo, it makes me so tired, and I want to be awake for a little while yet to admire the ripeness of the moon. I promise to take it before I go to sleep."

"Of course," Jo said, stretching her lips up in a poor imitation of a smile.

Beth sat up watching the few wispy clouds drift across the face of the moon until she felt secure that everyone else was asleep. She could hear Marmee snoring, and Jo was somewhere upstairs. Father was out for the night, as he never came home on nights with full moons anymore. In the distance she heard a baying, so prepared to rise from her bed. She tried to find purchase with her feet, but her defeated legs would not support her weight, so she tucked the medicine into the bow at her waist, dropped to the ground, and crawled slowly through the house.

It took every ounce of the vigor remaining in her feeble body to pull herself up and turn the doorknob. She breathed slowly and deeply for a time, then crawled through the doorway and pulled the door closed behind her. She had to lie on the porch for a moment to regain strength.

As she moved slowly across the lawn, the moonlight caught the whiteness of her skin and gown and made her look otherworldly, as if she was a fairy princess thrust up from the ground, or an angel descended from heaven. She wound her way around, finding her favorite tree in Mr. Laurence's yard and positioning herself on the side that would hide her from the windows of her house in case Jo should look out. She lay against the tree, breathing hard from the exertion, and trembled slightly from the chill of the perspiration that coated her skin in a gelid layer.

She raised the medicine bottle and looked at it. Decisively, she pulled the cork out with her teeth and spat it aside. She raised her head and poured nearly half the bottle down her throat. She coughed, gagged, and then tossed the bottle away into the bushes.

It did not take long for her to nod off. She awoke once, feeling warm breath on the side of her face. Her eyes could not focus as she turned her head and looked into the wide mouth and sharp teeth before her. Her last thought was, "Is it you, darling?" It was not him, but she was asleep before she could realize as much. When the taste of her blood filled the werewolf's mouth, the beast could not stop, so it ate what little meat there was on her bones, her weak heart, her failing organs and flaccid muscles.

It was some time later that a second werewolf happened onto the gruesome remains. Mr. Laurence whined. Had he known she meant absolutely her words, he could have been there sooner; he could have resisted hurting her, and he could have protected her.

He knew, as he sniffed and tasted the pile, that there was one small thing he could yet do for her. Mournfully, he settled down and chewed the bones, leaving them and the skull in a pile licked clean and white, so the morning sunlight would catch them and draw all eyes to the brightness that had been Beth.

When the discovery was made the next morning, Jo ran to Meg's little house, said, "It's Beth!" and ran to the church to find her father. She said the same to him that she had said to Meg, nothing more, nothing less, because she doubted he could make the run home without collapsing if he knew she was already gone.

When they entered the house, they found Meg sitting with Marmee and Hannah and weeping, while her children cried at her feet. Mr. March ran outside immediately, understanding, upon not seeing her body, and found the pile of stark, gleaming bones. He threw himself on them, crying until he gasped for breath.

Mr. Laurence must have seen Mr. March from his window, for he walked slowly outside. Jo saw him from her own window, and a scarlet cloud of rage engulfed her. She stormed from the house and stopped the old werewolf. "Did you take my sister's life?"

"Jo!" Mr. Laurence cried out. "How could you believe I would do such a thing?"

"Because you're a . . ."

"Please, speak the word. A werewolf. Because I'm a werewolf, you blame me."

Jo's mind shuddered with images of Mr. Laurence's many generous acts and his days of sitting contentedly with Beth, and her anger fell off her in flakes, like the old paint from the sides of the house.

The distraught men gathered
the bones reverently.

"She may have asked you to do it," she said in a low, ashamed tone.

"She did ask me. And I refused," he spat, wrinkled cheeks red with indignation. "I was not there when she died. Had I been, I would have protected her. Don't judge me as a werewolf, Jo, but as a neighbor." And then he turned to see to Mr. March.

Jo reddened as the old werewolf went over to give her father a comforting embrace. Mr. Laurence then lifted one of Beth's bones and held it to his cheek for a moment before stooping to retrieve another, and as Jo watched the men, she understood that neither of the two had slain her sister. The distraught men gathered the bones reverently and, cradling them in their arms, walked silently to the church, tears streaming down their faces. They spent the day working with some younger volunteers, who climbed the walls to place Beth's skull and bones in prominent spots along the ossuary, so the Marches could always look up and immediately see their dear Beth among the other fallen.

Everyone understood what Beth had done, because it was what she had always done; she wanted not to be a burden, or a bother, or a trial to anyone else, and so offered herself to the werewolves. It was not to end her misery, but to end theirs. The family was relieved that her suffering was ended, but each had to find a way to come to terms with her sacrifice. Jo and Mr. March came to enfold Mr. Laurence into their grief, and they comforted one another the best they could.

The next morning, when Mr. March woke up in his church, he stumbled out of his room and rushed to lay eyes on his dear Beth. Spring sunshine streamed in like a benediction and landed directly on Beth's skull so it glowed among the others, as if specially blessed. The other skulls grimaced and leered from on high, but hers smiled down softly with a gentle, benign expression.

...

CHAPTER 38

Converting for Love

LAURIE SPENT HIS TIME BACK HOME BEING DUTIFUL
to his grandfather and wondering if he had erred in telling Amy
his secret. He couldn't imagine a woman like her being willing
to devote herself to a werewolf. As the great Goethe, whenever
he had a joy or a grief, put it into a song, so Laurie resolved to
embalm his love-sorrow in music, and compose a requiem, which
should harrow up Amy's soul and melt the heart of every hearer.
He had musical friends in Vienna, in whom he found much inspiration, so when he left his grandfather again, he went there
and fell to work with the firm determination to distinguish himself. But whether the sorrow was too vast to be embodied in
music or music too ethereal to uplift a mortal woe, he soon discovered that, at present, a requiem was beyond him. His mind
worked poorly, his ideas needed clarifying, and he kept finding
himself humming the lively dancing tunes to which he had trotted with Amy at the Christmas ball, putting an effectual stop to
tragic composition for the time being.

His next attempt was at opera, for nothing seemed impossible in the beginning, but here again, unforeseen difficulties beset
him. He wanted Jo for his heroine, and called upon his memory
to supply him with tender recollections and romantic visions.
But memory turned traitor and, as if possessed by the perverse

spirit of the girl, could only recall Jo's oddities, faults, and freaks, and she would only appear in his head beating rugs with her hair tied up in a bandana, barricading herself with a sofa pillow, or throwing cold water over his passion. So he turned to his memory's golden-haired phantom, who was enveloped in a diaphanous cloud, floating airily before his mind's eye in a pleasing chaos of roses, peacocks, white ponies, and blue ribbons. But this heroine did not possess the fire and intensity needed for an operatic heroine, so the work gradually lost its charm and he forgot to compose and sat musing, pen in hand, or roaming about the gay city to find new ideas to refresh his mind.

"If this is genius simmering, I'll let it simmer and see what comes of it," he said, all the while with a secret suspicion that it wasn't genius but something far more common. Whatever it was, it cooked down into a hardened ball of discontent, and he found his thoughts always on Amy.

He reread letters from her and from Jo, realizing his fickle heart had changed its mind and ached now for the fairest, youngest March sister alone. He rummaged among his letters, some from America, which were yet unopened, and was stricken, upon reading them, to discover that Beth was gone. The only thought in his mind was that Amy needed him, and he rushed immediately from Germany to the shore of La Tour, where he knew the Carrols were presently living. When he arrived, he was informed that the family had gone to take a promenade on the lake, but that Mademoiselle Amy might be in the château garden, so in the middle of the servant's speech, Laurie departed to find her.

He found her in one corner of the pleasant old garden where chestnuts rustled overhead, ivy climbed everywhere, and the nearby water glistened and shone, ignited by the sun. She was sitting on a seat built into the wall, leaning her head on her hand, with a homesick heart and heavy eyes, thinking of Beth and, unbeknownst to Laurie, wondering why he had not come to see her in so long a time. He stood a minute, looking upon her with new eyes, seeing the tender side of her character that he had never before witnessed. Everything about her mutely suggested love and sorrow—the blotted letters in her lap, the black ribbon that tied up her hair, the womanly pain and patience in her face, even the little ebony cross at her throat seemed pathetic to Laurie, for he had given it to her, and she wore it as her only ornament. If he had any doubts about the reception she would give him, they were laid to rest the minute she looked up and saw him; for, dropping everything, she ran to him, and in a tone of unmistakable love and longing, cried out, "Oh, Laurie, Laurie! I knew you'd come!"

Everything was said and settled then; for in that moment, Amy felt that no one else in the world could comfort and sustain her so well as Laurie, and Laurie decided that Amy was the only woman in the world who could fill Jo's place and make him happy. Neither told the other as much, but both felt the truth, were satisfied, and gladly left the rest to silence.

Fred Vaughn returned, and putting his proposal of marriage to Amy, was decidedly but kindly told "No thank you," for Amy had firmly decided, while Laurie was away, that his being a werewolf could not matter to her. She refused to feel guilt for making the choice to not marry into poverty and, in cold rooms, raise lean children with empty stomachs. Laurie had money, and wit, and humor, and he was extremely skilled and generous in choosing the perfect gift. She could think of no other person who had ever made her so happy with his presence, and so miserable with his absence, and her greatest fear had altered from that of werewolves to the harrowing thought of living without him. She had watched great brutes of men in the market who slaughtered animals, and they had appeared more vulgar and cruel to her than either the gentle Mr. Laurence or Laurie with his quiet dignity and gentle manners ever could. And now, seeing him again and feeling the sudden lightness in her heart and the fresh joy coursing through her, she knew absolutely that he was the man with whom she wanted, more than anything, to share the rest of her life. She knew absolutely that should she find herself without him, her heart would not continue to beat. No, it would still within her chest and shrivel, over time, to a hard little stone that would rattle within her as she walked through the rest of her lonely life.

In spite of their new sorrow, the loss of Beth, it was a happy time for the two. Neither planned on going home immediately, even as they clung to each other in homesickness and grief, as nothing could be done for Beth, and they had been told they could visit her remains in the ossuary anytime they wished. Laurie let the days pass, enjoying every hour, and leaving to chance the moment when he would ask Amy to be his bride.

The matter was settled on the lake, at noonday. They had been floating about all morning, from gloomy St. Gingolf to sunny Montreaux, with the Alps of Savoy on one side, Mont St. Bernard and the Dent de Midi on the other, pretty Vevey in the valley, and Lausanne upon the hill beyond, a cloudless blue sky overhead, and the bluer lake below, dotted with picturesque boats that looked like white-winged gulls.

Amy was dabbling her hand in the water, and when she looked up, Laurie was bent over, leaning on the oars.

"You must be tired. Rest a little and let me row. You spoil me, and I have been altogether too lazy and luxurious."

"I'm not tired, but you may take an oar, if you like."

Amy moved next to him, and though she used both hands, and Laurie only one, the boat went smoothly through the water.

"How well we pull together, don't we?" she said.

"So well that I wish we might always pull in the same boat. Will you, Amy? Can you love me, knowing who and what I am?"

"I will. Yes, I will."

They embraced happily, but she broke away from him.

"I do have a condition."

"A condition?"

"Yes. I think we need to be partners in all ways if we are to marry, do you not agree?"

"Absolutely."

"Then you must make me your equal."

"I don't understand."

"The full moon will soon be upon us. You must bite me, infect me so I am made to be like you."

"Amy, do you know what you ask?"

"My eyes are open. I see people from all walks of life who alter when the moon shines full in the sky. I have also met those married to werewolves, and it is a trial, but one with which they are able to live. But I am prepared to become a werewolf, because it will unite us in a bond even more powerful than marriage. I spoke to Aunt Carrol, and she explained everything to me, down to the tiniest detail."

"I don't know if I can, Amy. It is a great responsibility you ask me to take on."

"It is I who take on the responsibility—gladly."

"Here, it is an easy life for a werewolf, but back home, were-wolves are hunted. I hear constantly that the Brigade gains strength and members consistently. Now even the wealthiest and most influential people are being accused and dealt with, and I worry for Grandfather every day, especially as he has written to tell me the Brigade now hunts by night. There is increasing madness in their fervor. I couldn't allow you to risk life and limb for the love of me."

"By merely associating with you, I could be accused of being a sympathizer, and be dealt with just as severely. Perhaps we can live here if you will rest easier, but we must do whatever being a couple demands, Laurie, and one demand can only be satisfied with both of us being werewolves, for we must be equal partners."

"I don't know, Amy. I don't know if I can."

"If you cannot, then I cannot marry you. Laurie, I know that this is what I want. We two can always be together, no matter if the moon wanes or waxes, or hangs low and full, but I demand a complete and perfect partnership."

"My dear, have you any idea how much you would be altered?" Laurie gasped.

"I've thought it through well, and I don't believe I would be altered so much. We exist in a chain of slaughter; we are each of us a link that kills or is killed. I would merely become a carnivore of modified appetites."

Time did not change Amy's mind, although Laurie launched one argument after another. There was no way to refuse his little bride, despite the pictures he planted in her mind of her having to avoid the Brigade once they returned home, and how her tastes for food and drink would alter. They talked and they talked, and she finally convinced him. And so, reluctantly, pushed to his limit both by Amy and Aunt Carrol, he agreed to infect her under the next full moon.

They spent the next few days peacefully, wrapped in the

gratifying company and delightful comfort of each other's presence.

On the night the moon was full, Amy carefully prepared herself according to Aunt Carrol's suggestions and sat in the garden to await her betrothed. Everyone else was out, Aunt Carrol and Flo at another event, and the servants dismissed for the evening. She sat, shivering in her cape, and suddenly heard a stirring to her left. She turned and had to look up to meet the stare of the huge, fearsome werewolf that stood before her. A whimper escaped her throat, and the beast backed off, but she steeled herself and stood up. She dropped the cape from her shoulders and pulled open the bow on the bodice of her gown; the garment fell open so far that her entire chest was exposed to the golden eyes, as Laurie had promised to bite her where the wound would not show. From the waist up, she wore only his little ebony cross on a ribbon tied about her throat, and the moonlight played upon her porcelain skin so she appeared lit from within. Trembling, she lay down on the bench, so inflamed with passion and disbelieving of the reality swirling about her that she was not even aware of the stone's coldness against the bare flesh of her milky back.

The werewolf's entire body was quaking with the anticipation of biting into that pale body, and his hearty lungs took in excited bursts of air and released them slowly in a low and steady growl.

Amy fought to keep her mind blank, for if she allowed one thought to intrude, it would twist itself into her terrible memories of the night in the belvedere.

Laurie stepped toward her, and her blood ran cold as the thick, wild smell of the beast reached her, so dense that she both smelled and tasted his feral, woodsy musk; the breath was a thick cloud on her face made thicker with each pant the were-wolf exhaled. She stared at the teeth, long and sharp and capable of grave harm, and she nearly leapt up and ran, and began to turn to do so, but he caught her eyes with his and she was unable to flee, or to even move one pretty little finger as she fell into the vortex of his stare, spinning madly as her supine body lay stretched out, vulnerable, and completely at his mercy. She gasped and cried, a few tears escaping her wide blue eyes, as the teeth penetrated the flesh on the underside of her breast. He had meant to pull his teeth out slowly and carefully, so as to leave the smallest of scars, but having the sweet blood in his mouth made the thought of her flesh irresistible, so he tore out the bite of meat caught between his teeth. She might rave angry for a time, but Amy would understand fully his appetite, and forgive gener-ously, after her first transvection from woman to wolf. Her fin-gers found the top of the gray head, and her small, soft hand stroked the tangle of knurled fur, while the beast licked and licked, devouring every drop of the blood that escaped her rav-aged breast.

...

CHAPTER 39

A Cure for Regret

J
O WAS FACED WITH DARK DAYS, PINING FOR HER SISTER
as she tried to concentrate on cheering her father and mother,
hoping it would quiet the ache in her own heart. Well after the
black crepe and bunting had been removed from the house, she
yet felt aggrieved and sore. She tried in a blind, hopeless way to
do her duty, secretly rebelling against it all the while, for it
seemed unjust that her few joys should be lessened, her burdens
made heavier, and life harder and harder as she toiled along.
Some people seemed to get all the sunshine, and some all the
shadow; it was not fair, for she tried more than Amy to be good
but never got any reward, only disappointment, trouble, and
hard work, while her sister played, carefree, somewhere in the
faraway fairyland of Europe. She saw her dismal world only in
shades of gray, feeling that life's colorful benevolence was reserved for others, with no bright yellow hope or rosy pink cheer
allotted to her.

She often went to the church to find her father, and together
they sat, she in his lap as if a child, staring up at Beth's skull,
speaking to her as if she still ate her meals at home and tended
to her dolls and cats. Jo called herself the "church of one member," for her father devoted to her time enough to put into con-

soling an entire flock of lost sheep, but never before had he nursed such a sad little lamb that needed so much tender care.

Jo took over the housecleaning duties, for how could she hate brooms and dusters that had been held in Beth's hands, or dishcloths the dear girl had made herself and embroidered with happy little creatures and sayings to brighten one's day and mood? Jo found herself humming the songs Beth used to, even though, once recognized, the tunes brought tears to Hannah's and her mother's eyes.

One day as she sat sewing with Meg, she noticed that her sister was much improved, so said, "It looks like marriage is an excellent thing after all. I wonder if I should ever blossom out half as well as you have."

"You are like a chestnut burr, Jo, prickly outside but silky soft within, and a sweet kernel, if one can get at it. Love will make you show your heart someday, and then the rough burr will fall off."

"Frost opens chestnut burrs, and it takes a good shake to bring them down. Boys go nutting, and I don't care to be bagged by them," returned Jo.

Meg laughed, seeing a glimmer of Jo's old spirit. "Why don't you write? That always used to make you happy and soothe you."

"I've no heart to write, and if I had, nobody cares for my things."

"We all do, and you know that well. Never mind the rest of the world. Try it, to do yourself some good, and to please us all."

"Don't believe I can," Jo said, but she got out her desk and papers.

An hour afterward, her mother peeped in and found Jo scratching away, wearing her black pinafore and an absorbed expression. Jo never knew what happened, but something got into that story that went straight to the hearts of her family, causing them to laugh and cry over it. Her father, against her will, sent it into one of the popular magazines, and it was not only paid for, but others were requested. They wanted her to do a series with the same characters—the handsome, wealthy, lonely werewolf and the woman who loved him with all her heart—but insisted she could not marry him. There were a number of romantic scenes, and she was asked to keep those, and to build on the complications of their relationship while keeping their love keen and strong. She felt an ember of happiness ignite within her, for she had portrayed the werewolf protagonist in a positive light—as a sensitive, caring being, much like the werewolves she knew, but she still could not fully dissect from the flurry of words exactly what made these stories good.

"I don't understand," Jo said. "This is such a simple little story. Why would everyone praise it so?"

"There is truth in it," said her mother. "That's the secret; humor and pathos make it alive, and you have found your style at last. You have had the bitter long enough; now comes the sweet. Do your best, my girl, put your heart into it, and grow as happy as we are in your success."

By and by, Jo roamed away upstairs and tried to write, but she was restless, for it was rainy and she could not go for a walk. She stood in the garret, looking around, as if something would leap out and guide her to the one thing that would soothe her soul. Against one wall stood four little wooden chests in a row, each marked with its owner's name and each filled with girlhood relics. She opened her own and stared down into the chaotic collection, until a bundle of exercise books caught her eye. She drew them out, turned them over, and relived that pleasant winter at kind Mrs. Kirke's. She looked thoughtful at first, next sad, and when she came to a little message written in the Professor's hand, her lips began to tremble and the books slid off of her lap.

"Wait for me, my friend," the Professor wrote. "I may be a little late, but I will surely come."

"Oh, if he only would!" Jo thought. "My dear old Friedrich was so kind, so good, and so patient with me always. I didn't value him half enough when I had him. Everyone has gone from me and I am so alone. Soon I'll be twenty-five, with nothing to show for my years! An old maid, a literary spinster with a pen for a spouse and a family of stories for children."

And holding the little paper fast, as if it was a promise yet to be fulfilled, Jo laid her head down on a comfortable ragbag and cried, as if in opposition to the rain pattering on the roof.

Jo must have fallen asleep, for suddenly Laurie's ghost seemed to stand before her.

"Oh, my Teddy!"

"Dear Jo, you are glad to see me, then?"

"Glad?" she shrieked, getting up in one mighty leap when she realized it truly was he who stood before her. "Words can't express my gladness! Where is Amy?"

"Your mother's got my wife down at Meg's."

"Your what?" The joy she had felt at seeing him fell from her and landed at her feet.

"Oh, the dickens! Now I've done it." And he looked so guilty that Jo was down upon him like a flash.

"You've gone and got married?"

"Yes, please, but I never will again." And he went down upon his knees with a penitent clasping of hands and a face full of mischief, mirth, and triumph.

"Actually married?"

"Very much so. Don't I look like a married man and the head of a family?"

"Not one bit, and you never will. So tell me, when, how, where?" She held her breath, allowing her lungs to empty slowly, to prevent herself from raging, and cursing Amy, who had once again stolen the ripest plum from the tree.

"Six weeks ago, at the American consul's in Paris—a very quiet wedding, of course, for even in our happiness, we could not forget dear Beth. We said nothing, so as to surprise you."

"And how do the two of you get on?" she asked as she led him down the stairs and back into the heart of the house. Her thoughts were jumbled as she realized that she was actually happy for her sister, and then wondered if Amy was aware of Laurie's secret; perhaps her concern was also needed.

"Like angels."

"I fear Amy will rule you all the days of your life," she laughed, trying to keep her voice light and carefree.

"She is the sort of woman who knows how to rule well; in fact, I rather like it, for she winds one round her finger as softly and prettily as a skein of silk, and makes you feel as if she was doing you a favor all the while. But we respect ourselves and one another too much ever to tyrannize or quarrel."

"Well, should she abuse you, come to me, and I will defend you."

Amy walked in just then, her face full of the soft brightness that betokens a happy heart. Her voice had a new tenderness in it, and the cool, prim carriage was changed to a gentle dignity, both womanly and winning. She was now stamped with the unmistakable sign of the true gentlewoman she had hoped to become, and Jo saw in her all the wonderful dreams and expectations that could be realized in life; all those glimmering things that had so adroitly and cleverly eluded Jo March. She envisioned her sister's future, driving white horses, eating off gold plate, and wearing diamonds and point lace every day, for Teddy thought nothing too good for her. An ache shot through her heart at the realization that it was Teddy, not the jewelry or finery, that was the greatest treasure.

"Love has done much good for our little girl," said Marmee softly.

Mr. Laurence arrived soon after, arms filled with the loveliest flowers, and he took Jo aside and said, "You must be my girl now," and glanced at the empty corner by the fire while stroking her arm.

"I'll try to fill her place, sir," Jo whispered back with trembling lips, desperately missing even the ill, disposed version of her sister, and grateful that the one whom Beth had loved so dearly forgave her the horrible accusations she had made against him.

Amy called a family council, and with grave face and wringing hands, stood, as if onstage, before them all.

"I wish to announce that I have . . . converted . . . for love."

"Converted?" Meg asked. "To which religion?"

"Not to a religion. To lycanthropy."

"I know that word," Meg said, eyes narrowed and boring into her sister's, and then her face altering considerably as she realized its meaning. "A werewolf? Amy! You have become a werewolf?"

For one moment the group was silent, and as still as a roomful of statues, only eyes moving as each glanced at the others, and a single tear coursed down Marmee's red cheek. Jo, who realized with a quick and fleeting stab of envy and excitement that she had somehow been expecting this announcement, coughed, and as if that was his cue, Mr. Laurence rose and hugged Amy to him.

"Please know, everyone," Amy continued, "that this was my choice alone; an informed decision made after much study and thought. Laurie tried his best, for some time, to convince me otherwise, but for us to be true partners, to be equals, it was, in my mind, an essential conversion."

"I understand. I have considered it myself," Marmee said, wearing a sad smile. "But I decided, finally, no. I have, however, learned to live with a werewolf mate."

Amy's brow furrowed and then smoothed, and she stepped over to her father and took his hands in hers.

"Is it true? Are you also a werewolf, Father?"

"It is. I am."

"Father!" Meg cried.

John rushed to gather his wife in his arms, realizing what a startling blow this was to her, but she pushed him away and rose to her feet.

"Whoever in this room is a werewolf, please raise your hand," she demanded in a scandalized tone.

Amy's little pink hand was the first to rise, followed by Mr. March's, Laurie's, and Mr. Laurence's.

"For how long has it been that this family has been dwelling next to werewolves?" Meg asked nobody in particular.

Mr. Laurence answered her. "My grandson and I were both born werewolves."

Meg moved to sit back down, John catching her to center her on her seat, as the poor woman was virtually paralyzed from this thunderclap of information. The two sat for a short while, John whispering into her ear. She nodded finally and then rose, woodenly, to hug her father, Amy, Mr. Laurence, and Laurie in turn, but Jo saw clearly in her sister's eyes that it was with resignation, not acceptance.

Jo watched Amy smile and chat, trying to find something in the swish of her skirts or the blinking of her eyelashes to suggest that she was a werewolf. There suddenly pounded into her the undeniable loss of Laurie, and the loss of her own chance to become a werewolf for love, and she worked hard to keep her tears back as she reluctantly released her most cherished wish, the one she had held tenderly in one corner of her heart for years.

"Are you not scared to death of being a werewolf?" Jo asked Amy when they happened to be alone together in the kitchen.

Amy's little titter tinkled from her mouth, "I am scared to death of being married! I am Mrs. Theodore Laurence, and I barely feel capable of half the talents that position demands."

"You shouldn't worry. You've always been talented, Amy. In your way."

"In my way?" Amy asked.

"Yes. In your way."

"Are we in harmony, sister? About Laurie?"

"Of course."

"Jo, I watched for years as your eyes danced the moment he walked into the room, and his did the same for you."

"I didn't cede my chance for happiness," Jo insisted, "but only my chance to, for once, fit in. I imagine Laurie and I could have caused quite a stir overseas."

"Yes, I could see you, Jo, wearing something outrageous, such as men's trousers or tails, and having all of Paris mimic the famous American writer's outlandish style."

The sisters embraced, but Amy felt stiffness in Jo and suspected she had not stepped aside so willingly after all.

The family sat and ate and talked while the day ended and night began, Meg's little imps stealing sips of tea and ginger-bread, and vying for the attention of their pretty blond aunt and her playful, grinning husband as they demanded that Laurie, again and again, hold them upside down.

A knock came upon the door, and Jo, being closest to it, heard it over all the hearty laughter and chatting. She opened it with hospitable haste, and started with surprise; for there stood a stout, bearded gentleman, beaming in at her from the darkness like a midnight sun.

"Oh, Mr. Bhaer, I *am* so glad to see you!" cried Jo, with a clutch, fearing the night would swallow him up before she could get him inside.

"And I to see Miss March—but no, you haf a party." And the Professor paused at the sound of voices and the tap of dancing feet.

"No, it's just the family. My sisters and friends have just come back home, so we are all very happy. Come in and make one more of us."

"I will, gladly," he said as Jo hung up his coat, and then he looked carefully at her face and asked, "Have you been ill, my friend?"

"Not ill. Tired and sorrowful."

"Ah, yes, I know! My heart was sore for you when I heard." He took her hand in his big, warm paws, and Jo felt as if no comfort could equal the look in his kind eyes.

Before anyone knew it, Mr. Bhaer was drawn into the circle, and he talked loudly and well. Jo watched him as she knit, and noticed that his bushy hair had been cut and smoothly brushed, and that he actually had gold sleeve buttons in his immaculate wristbands. She smiled, thinking the dear old fellow couldn't have gotten himself up with more care if he had been going a-wooing. That thought hit her so hard and made her blush so dreadfully that she had to drop her ball of yarn and go down after it to hide her face.

Once the party broke up, and Mr. Bhaer had asked her parents' permission to visit again, Jo wondered what the business was that had brought the Professor to the city, and finally decided it must have been an appointment of great honor somewhere but that he had been too modest to mention the fact.

Safe in his own room, the Professor looked at the picture he had discovered nestled in a bookshelf's clutter at Christmastime; it still donned the merry green bow, now crushed and soiled. The young woman in it, who appeared to be gazing darkly into futurity, would have been astonished to see that before retiring, he kissed the picture in the dark.

When Laurie and Amy returned home that night, Laurie said quite suddenly, "That man intends to marry our Jo!"

"I hope so. Don't you?" Amy said with a laugh.

"I do like the man, but I wish he was a little younger and a good deal richer."

"If they love one another, it doesn't matter one particle how old or how poor. Women *never* should marry for money."

"If my memory serves me," Laurie said in a serious tone, "you once thought it your duty, for the sake of your family, to make a rich match, which would explain your marrying a good-for-nothing like me."

"I'd have married you if you didn't have a penny. I thought, for a time, that I would marry for money, but what matters in the end is that I married purely for love."

Laurie merely smiled in reply as he searched through their luggage, feeling unable to find a single thing he needed.

"Whatever is this?" asked Laurie, pulling out the swatch of gray fur that Amy had cut from the coat in Aunt March's closet.

"Werewolf fur." She laughed. "It was part of a game Esther and I played." She briefly explained the game, the coat in the wardrobe, and even poor little Polly hiding deep inside behind the coat.

"A game?" He sniffed the fur, drew a serious face, and held it out to her. "Come over here and smell it, Amy."

She took a whiff and smelled a familiar, woodsy scent. "Is it, is it really werewolf fur?" She found herself surprised, yet again, by the heightened acuteness of her senses, which she was only slowly learning to heed. "How could it possibly be when a werewolf, in wolf form, reverts back to a person at death?"

"Nearly killed in wolf form, and quickly skinned. Stripped of their skin before their last breath."

"Oh!" Amy cried, skin crawling in nauseating spasms. "Who could possibly perform such an act? How terrible!"

He nodded, and she looked down. "That is how I know many innocent people are being killed by the Brigade. When true werewolves are found, they are contained until the next full moon and then skinned alive to harvest their pelts, as that is the only way to claim the valuable hides. With the prices offered for such a pelt, you can be certain true werewolves are not being hanged and then ripped open to rot."

"I am ashamed at the ridiculous game I played, pretending to hunt werewolves, and imagining I had, myself, claimed a hide."

"It isn't your fault," said Laurie, taking his wife's small, pale hand in his. "It was an innocent game, and you were a mere child, but I do wonder where old lady March got the coat. One day I will find out."

"I doubt you could," Amy argued. "It looked and smelled of the ages. It could be older than your grandfather, and it could have come from anywhere."

"Of course, I stand corrected, my bride. We cannot dwell on the past and must simply be content that such practices are far less common than they once were. But for now I see no reason to further upset you, my dear, so I beg you to allow the distraction of my kiss to alter your thoughts." He laid his lips on the soft pink petals of her mouth and encircled her with his arms. "Do you feel better, and can we talk about something else now?" he asked.

"I have a topic ready," Amy declared quickly. "Should you care if Jo marries Professor Bhaer?"

"I assure you I can dance at Jo's wedding with a heart as light as my heels. But I wish we could do something for that capital old professor. Perhaps we could say some relation died in Germany and left him a tidy fortune."

"Jo would find us out and spoil it all," said Amy with a shake of her head. "She loves him immensely just as he is, and is quite proud of him. I owe Jo for my education, and she believes in settling debts, so we'll get to her that way one day soon."

"How delightful it is to be able to help others. I have always dreamed of having the power to give freely. Out-and-out beggars get taken care of, but poor gentlefolk fare poorly within their little hovels, because they won't ask for help. There must be a thousand ways to help them, though, delicately, so it does not offend."

"I also want to put out my hand and help, in return for all the kindness others have done for me," she agreed.

"And so you shall, little angel that you are!" cried Laurie, resolving with a glow of philanthropic zeal to found and endow helpful institutions to feed and educate those in need, and so at last make good use of his life.

"Do you feel we give from the guilt of being werewolves, or are we as kind as we hope to believe we are?" Amy asked.

"We give for the same reasons Grandfather does—guilt. But we cannot apologize for who we are, so our guilt is embedded in our having more than others."

"And that excess is what we shall share!" Amy exclaimed happily.

So the young pair shook hands upon it, then paced happily on again, feeling that their pleasant home was more homelike because they hoped to brighten other homes, believing their feet would walk more easily along the flowery path before them, if they smoothed rough ways for other feet, and feeling that their hearts were more closely knit together by a love that could tenderly remember those less blessed than they were.

CHAPTER 40

...

The
Dilapidated Umbrella

WHILE LAURIE AND AMY WERE STROLLING COMFORT-
ably over velvet carpets and blissfully setting their house in
order, Jo and Mr. Bhaer were enjoying promenades of a different
sort, along muddy roads and sodden fields.

It had always been Jo's habit to take a walk toward evening,
and she saw no reason to give them up simply because she might
happen onto the Professor either coming or going. By the second week, after uncountable impromptu visits where Jo returned
home with the man on her arm, everyone knew perfectly well
what was going on, and they even took to having coffee for dinner, as "Friedrich, or rather, Professor Bhaer, didn't like tea."
The family acted stone-blind to the changes in Jo's face, her
singing while she worked, and doing up her hair three times a
day, yet it was quite clear that, while the Professor talked philosophy with the father, he was also giving lessons on love to the
daughter.

After a fortnight of coming and going with lover-like regu-
larity, he stayed away for three whole days, causing Jo to turn
cross and disgusted, for if he had gone home as suddenly as he

had come, he should have, at the very least, stopped by to bid the family goodbye, like a gentleman. She fought to beat down painful thoughts that those forces that blew happiness and fulfillment into lives, and flew off with loneliness, discontent, and sorrow, were once again eluding her, leaving her to wallow alone in drab melancholy.

One dull afternoon she put on her things for her customary walk. Her mother bade her take her umbrella and put on warm boots, and asked her to pick up some twilled silesia, a paper of number-nine needles, and two yards of narrow lavender ribbon.

Jo agreed absently, walking until she found herself in the part of town down among the countinghouses, banks, and wholesale warerooms, where gentlemen congregated. She loitered casually, examining engineering instruments in one window, samples of wool in another, and thinking back to what wonderful ends and discards she and her sisters used to find in this area for their stage decorations.

She stopped short, having pushed through a group of men, to find the hanged remains of two people in threadbare clothes dangling from an open warehouse door. Around the neck of the one whose chest had been torn open in order to remove his heart was a sign declaring the corpse a werewolf, and the other wore a sign denoting him a sympathizer. Jo stared, for far too long, at the drooping faces of the dead men, and then, as she tried to hurry on her way, two soldiers from the Brigade dragged along another shabbily clad man. Jo looked away from the man's bloodied face, pretending to adjust her bonnet. She looked up once more at the dangling dead men and realized suddenly that some things changed very little. It was from this very doorway that she had seen her first body hanged as a werewolf when she was a mere child venturing to the pickle factory to find shiny remnants with which to bespangle her stage.

A drop of rain made her remember that she was wearing a new bonnet, and as the drops continued to fall, she thought the ruined ribbons would be of little matter next to that of her ruined heart.

"It serves me right, " she muttered to herself. "What business had I to put on all my best things and come philandering down here, hoping to see the Professor? Now go do your errands in the rain; if you catch your death of cold and ruin your bonnet, it's no less than you deserve."

She rushed across the street so impetuously that she narrowly escaped annihilation from a passing truck, and precipitated herself into the arms of a stately old gentleman who acted mortally offended. Jo righted herself, spread her handkerchief over her bonnet, and hurried on, with increasing dampness about the ankles, and much clashing of umbrellas overhead. The fact that a somewhat dilapidated blue one remained stationary above her head attracted her attention; and, looking up, she saw Mr. Bhaer looking down on her.

"I feel to know the strong-minded lady who goes so bravely under many horse-noses, and so fast through much mud. What brings you down here, my friend?"

"I'm shopping."

Mr. Bhaer smiled, glancing on one side to the pickle factory and on the other to the wholesale leather-and-hide building. "You haf no umbrella. May I also go, and take for you the bundles?"

"Yes, thank you." Jo's cheeks were as red as her ribbon, and she wondered what he thought of her; but she didn't care, for in a minute she found herself walking arm in arm with her Professor, feeling as if the sun had suddenly burst out with uncommon brilliance, and that all was right in the world again. There was no happier woman paddling through the wet that day.

"We thought you had gone," Jo said hastily, for she felt him looking at her.

"Do you believe I should go with no farewell to those who haf been so heavenly kind to me?"

"No, I didn't. I knew you were busy with your own affairs, but we all rather missed you, Father and Mother especially."

"And you?"

"I am always glad to see you, sir." In her anxiety to keep her voice calm, she succeeded in making it rather cool, so that the Professor seemed chilled by her frosty little monosyllables, and his smile vanished.

"I thank you. And come one more time before I go."

"You *are* going, then?"

"I haf no longer any business here; it is done."

"Successfully, I hope."

"I think so, for I haf a way opened to me by which I can make my bread and gif my nephews much help."

"Tell me, please."

"That is so kind you care to know. My friends find for me place in a college, where I teach as at home, but earn enough to make the way smooth for Franz and Emil. For this I should be grateful, should I not?"

"Indeed, you should! How splendid it will be to have you doing what you like, and where I will be able to see you and the boys often."

"Ah, but we shall not meet often. I fear this place is in the West."

"So far away!" said Jo, dropping her skirts and leaving them to their fate, for it now no longer mattered what became of her clothes or herself.

Mr. Bhaer could read several languages, but he had not yet learned to read women, and was mystified by the many moods Jo had seemed to drift through during their conversation.

Jo rather prided herself on her shopping capabilities, and particularly wanted to impress her escort with the neatness and dispatch with which she would accomplish the business. But owing to the flutter she was in, she upset the tray of needles, forgot the silesia was to be twilled until after it was cut off, gave the wrong change, and covered herself with confusion by asking for lavender ribbon at the calico counter. Mr. Bhaer stood by watching her blush and blunder; and as he watched, his own bewilderment subsided. Once outside again, he splashed happily through the puddles and insisted on stopping to purchase a farewell feast to bring to her house that night.

Jo frowned at his extravagance, for he ordered oranges, figs, nuts, grapes, daisies, and honey. Then, distorting his pockets with the knobby bundles, and giving her the daisies to hold, he put up the old umbrella, and they traveled on again.

"Miss March, I haf a great favor to ask of you," he said after they walked half a block.

"Yes, sir," she said, hoping she had sounded casual, and that he could not hear the rapid beating of her nervous heart.

"I need to get a dress for my little Tina, and am too stupid to go alone. Will you kindly gif me a word of taste and help?"

"Of course, yes."

"Perhaps also a warm shawl for her mother, she is so poor and sick."

The Professor left it all to her, and she chose a pretty gown for Tina, and then ordered out the shawls. They realized the clerk mistook them for a couple shopping for their family, so playfully launched into their roles.

"Does this suit you, Mr. Bhaer?" Jo asked, turning her back to him so he could see the comfortable gray shawl she modeled.

"Excellent! We will haf it!" the delighted man replied.

It was time for them to part, and Jo was flustered enough to, in a hasty gesture, fling the poor daisies from the pot in her hand, badly damaging them. Mr. Bhaer stooped to help her pick them up, and saw that the drops on her cheeks were tears, not rain.

"Heart's dearest, why do you cry?" he asked.

"Because you are going away."

"Ach, my Gott, that is *so* good!" cried Mr. Bhaer. "Jo, I haf nothing but much love to gif you. I came to see if you could care for me, and if you wanted me for more than a friend. Can you make a little place in your heart for old Fritz?"

"Oh, yes!" said Jo, and he was quite satisfied, for she folded both hands over his arm, and looked up at him with an expression that plainly showed how happy she would be to walk through life beside him, even if she had no better shelter than the old umbrella.

Even if he had desired to do so, the Professor could not go down on his knee, on account of the mud; neither could he offer his hand, except figuratively, for his were both full; much less could he indulge in tender demonstrations in the open street, and so he expressed his rapture with such a happy expression on his face that his joy seemed to create little rainbows in the drops of rain that sparkled on his beard.

Jo looked far from lovely during this momentous event; her skirts were in a deplorable state, her rubber boots splashed to the ankles, and her bonnet a ruin, but Mr. Bhaer considered her the most beautiful woman living. She thought the same of him, even though his hat brim was quite limp and every finger of his gloves needed mending.

Passersby probably thought them a pair of harmless lunatics as they strolled leisurely along. The Professor looked as if he had conquered a kingdom, and Jo trudged alongside him, as if her place had always been there.

"Friedrich—" she began.

"Ah, heaven!" he interrupted, pausing in a puddle to regard her with grateful delight. "She gif me the name that no one speaks since my dear mother died!"

"It's just that I think of little Fritz as Fritz, but I think of you as Friedrich. Of course, I won't call you that unless you like it," she added quickly.

"Like it? It is more sweet to me than I can say."

It was quite obvious that Jo would never learn to be proper; for as they stood on the steps of her house, she stooped down and kissed her Friedrich under the umbrella, for she was so far gone, she was mindless of everything but her own happiness.

"It's like kissing a werewolf, delving into that beard," she said, laughing.

As he joined her in mirth, this simple moment became a crowning one of their lives as they turned from the night, storm, and loneliness to the household light, warmth, and peace waiting to receive them, and with a glad "Welcome home!" Jo led her love in and shut the door.

...

CHAPTER 41

New Life for Plumfield

OR A YEAR JO AND HER PROFESSOR WORKED AND WAITED, hoped and loved, met whenever he was able to leave his obligations out west, and wrote such voluminous letters that Laurie joked that the rise in the price of paper was easily accounted for. The second year began rather soberly, for their prospects did not brighten, and Aunt March died suddenly. But when their first sorrow was over, for they loved the old lady in spite of her sharp tongue, they found they had cause for rejoicing, for she had left Plumfield to Jo, which made all sorts of joyful things possible.

"It's a fine old place, and will bring a handsome sum, for of course you intend to sell it," said Laurie, as they were all talking the matter over some weeks later.

"No, I don't," was Jo's decided answer as she petted the fat poodle, whom she had adopted out of respect to his former mistress.

"You don't mean to live there?"

"Yes, I do."

"But, my dear girl, it's an immense house, and will take the power of money to keep it in order. The garden and orchard alone need two or three men, and farming isn't in Bhaer's line, I take it."

"He'll try his hand at it there, if I propose it."

"And you expect to live on the produce of the place? Well, that sounds paradisiacal, but you'll find it desperate hard work."

"Fear not. The crop we are going to raise is a profitable one," Jo said, and laughed.

"Of what is this fine crop to consist?"

"Boys. I want to open a good, happy, homelike school for little lads, with me to take care of them and Friedrich to teach them."

"Isn't that just like her?" cried Laurie, appealing to the family, who looked as much surprised as he.

"I like it," said Mrs. March decidedly.

"So do I," added her husband, who welcomed the thought of a chance for trying the Socratic method of education on modern youth.

"It will be an immense care for Jo," said Meg, stroking the head of her one all-absorbing son.

"Jo can do it, and be happy in it. It's a splendid idea. Tell us all about it," cried Mr. Laurence, who had been longing to lend the lovers a hand but knew that they would refuse his help, so now recognized his opportunity.

"I knew you'd stand by me, sir. Just understand that this isn't a new idea of mine, but a long-cherished plan. Before my Friedrich came, I used to think how, when I'd made my fortune, and no one needed me at home, I'd hire a big house, and pick up some poor, forlorn little lads who hadn't any mothers, and take care of them, and make life jolly for them before it was too late. I see so many going to ruin for want of help at the right minute, and I seem to feel their wants, and sympathize with their troubles."

Mrs. March held out her hand to Jo, who took it, smiling, with tears in her eyes, and went on in the old enthusiastic way, which they had not seen for a long while. "I told my plan to Friedrich once, and he said it was just what he would like, and agreed to try it when we got rich. Bless his dear heart; he's been helping poor boys, well, poor people of all sorts, all his life. Money doesn't stay in his pocket long enough to lay up any, but now, thanks to my good old aunt, who loved me better than I ever deserved, I'm rich, at least I feel so, and we can live at Plumfield perfectly well, if we have a flourishing school. It's just the place for boys; the house is big, and the furniture strong and plain, there's plenty of room for dozens inside, splendid grounds outside, and they could help in the garden and orchard. Such work is healthy, isn't it, sir? Then Friedrich could train and teach in his own way, and Father will help him. I can feed and nurse and pet and scold them, and Mother will be my stand-by. I've always longed for lots of boys, and never had enough; now I can fill the house full and revel in the little dears to my heart's content."

As Jo waved her hands and gave a sigh of rapture, the family went off into a gale of merriment, and Mr. Laurence laughed till they thought he'd have an apoplectic fit.

"Nothing could be more natural and proper than for my Professor to open a school, and for me to prefer to reside in my own estate."

"She is putting on airs already," said Laurie, who regarded the idea in the light of a capital joke. "But may I inquire how you intend to support the establishment? If all the pupils are little ragamuffins, I'm afraid your crop won't be profitable in a worldly sense, Mrs. Bhaer."

"Now don't be a wet blanket, Teddy. Of course I shall have rich pupils; I imagine I will be forced to begin with such, and then, when I've got a start, I can take in a ragamuffin or two, just for a relish. Rich people's children often need care and comfort, as well as poor. I've seen unfortunate little creatures left to servants, or backward ones pushed forward, when it's real cruelty. Some are naughty through mismanagement or neglect, and some lose their mothers. Besides, the best have to get through the hobbledehoy age, and that's the very time they need most patience and kindness."

"You certainly showed patience and kindness to me when I most needed it," Laurie said.

"And you've succeeded beyond my hopes, for here you are, a steady, sensible businessman, doing heaps of good with your money, and laying up the blessings of the poor, instead of dollars. But you are not merely a businessman; you love good and beautiful things, and enjoy them yourself. I am proud of you, Teddy, for you get better every year, and everyone feels it, though you won't let them say so."

"I say, Jo, that's rather too much," he began, in his old boyish way. "You have all done more for me than I can ever thank you for, except by doing my best not to disappoint you. So, if I've got on at all, you may thank these two for it." And he laid one hand gently on his grandfather's head and the other on Amy's golden one, for the three were never far apart, whatever the cycle of the moon.

"I do think that families are the most beautiful things in all the world!" burst out Jo, who was in an unusually uplifted frame of mind just then. "When I have one of my own, I hope it will be as happy as the three I know and love the best. If John and my Friedrich were only here, it would be quite a little heaven on earth," she added more quietly. And that night when she went to her room after a blissful evening of family counsels, hopes, and plans, her heart was so full of happiness that she could only calm it by kneeling beside the empty bed always near her own, and thinking tender thoughts of dear Beth.

It was an astonishing year altogether, for things seemed to happen in an unusually rapid and delightful manner. Almost before she knew where she was, Jo found herself married and settled at Plumfield. Then a family of six or seven boys sprang up like mushrooms, and flourished surprisingly—poor boys as well as rich, for Mr. Laurence was continually finding some touching case of destitution, and begging the Bhaers to take pity on the child, and he would gladly pay a trifle for its support. In this way, the sly old gentleman got around proud Jo, and furnished her with the style of boy in which she most delighted.

Of course it was uphill work at first, and Jo made queer mistakes, but the wise Professor steered her safely into calmer waters, and the most rampant ragamuffin was conquered in the end. How Jo did enjoy her "wilderness of boys," and how poor, dear Aunt March would have lamented had she been there to see the sacred precincts of prim, well-ordered Plumfield overrun with Toms, Dicks, and Harrys! There was a sort of poetic justice about it, after all, for the old lady had been the terror of the boys for miles around, and now the exiles feasted freely on forbidden plums, kicked up the gravel with profane boots, and played cricket in the big field where the irritable cow with a crumpled horn used to invite rash youths to come and be tossed. It became a sort of boys' paradise, and Laurie suggested that it should be called the "Bhaer-garten," as a compliment to its master.

It never was a fashionable school, and the Professor did not lay up a fortune, but it was just what Jo intended it to be, "a happy, homelike place for boys who needed teaching, care, and kindness." Every room in the big house was soon full; every little plot in the garden soon had its owner, and a regular menag-

erie appeared in barn and shed, for pet animals were both allowed and welcomed. And three times a day, Jo smiled from the
head of a long table lined on either side with rows of happy young
faces, which all turned to her with affectionate eyes, confiding
words, and grateful hearts, full of love for "Mother Bhaer." She
had boys enough now, and did not tire of them, though they were
not angels, by any means, and some of them caused much trouble
and anxiety. But her faith, inherited from her father, in the good
spot that exists in the heart of the naughtiest, sauciest, most tan-
talizing little ragamuffin gave her patience, skill, and, in time,
success.

Very precious to Jo was the friendship of the lads, their penitent sniffs and whispers after wrongdoing, their droll or touching little confidences, their pleasant enthusiasms, hopes, and
plans, even their misfortunes, for they only endeared them to her
all the more. There were slow boys and bashful boys, feeble boys
and riotous boys, boys that lisped and boys that stuttered, one or
two lame ones, and a merry little quadroon, who could not be
taken in elsewhere, but who was welcome to the "Bhaer-garten,"
though some people predicted that his admission would ruin the
school. Despite their differences, these boys all had in common
their love and admiration of Jo. They looked up to her as a
mother, in one way, but quite differently in another; for she was
the exact model for the girl that they all hoped to marry; and
they couldn't help but think of her as a girl, for she seemed every
bit as young as them as she expertly chased balls, flew kites, won
all their marbles from them, or courageously explored the dark
interiors of caves right alongside them.

Yes, Jo was a very happy woman there, in spite of hard work,
much anxiety, and a perpetual racket. As the years went on, two
little lads of her own came to increase her happiness: Rob,

named for Grandpa, and Teddy, a happy-go-lucky baby, who seemed to have inherited his papa's sunshiny temper as well as his mother's lively spirit. How they ever grew up alive in that whirlpool of boys was a mystery to their grandma and aunts, but they flourished like dandelions in spring, and their rough nurses loved and served them well.

Amy looked with awe upon Jo, for whom a broken vase or spilled bowl was of little concern. Jo breezed through her castle, kicking aside clutter and putting the joy and leisure of her husband and the boys above all material things. Amy thought of her own precise, pristine environment and doubted she would ever learn to do the same.

Jo used her experience, and her writing skills, to produce a series of delightful stories about a boarding school for boy werewolves. She needed only a bit of imagination to elaborate on the realities of her life, as the boys were such a constant source of amusing anecdotes and maddening idiocy that she often worried a few of the more daring ones would cut themselves short and never see adulthood. Her adventurous yarns were loved by young boys across America and Europe, where her books were sold, so much so that she was constantly receiving letters telling her about one of her books' capers that had proven itself too irresistible for one or more daring lad to boldly attempt himself.

...

CHAPTER 42

A Family Harvest

THERE WERE A GREAT MANY HOLIDAYS AT PLUMFIELD, and one of the most delightful was the yearly apple picking. For then the Marches, Laurences, Brookes, and Bhaers turned out in full force and made a day of it. Five years after Jo's wedding, one of these fruitful festivals occurred, a mellow October day, when the air was full of an exhilarating freshness, which made the spirits rise and the blood dance healthily in the veins.

Jo almost had everything ready when she rounded the corner into the kitchen and found six tall and muscled soldiers from the Brigade there among the obviously awed lads. The men's horrific tunics and helmets and the sharp silver daggers they wore at their waists made them look like a band of barbarians, and as she inhaled, she learned that they smelled the part as well.

"May I help you gentlemen?" Jo called out loudly so her voice would rise above the excited exclamations of the boys. "I'm afraid I didn't hear you ring."

"The boys let us in," one of the men snarled, exposing a nasty grin.

"You are the woman who writes about werewolves?"

"Yes."

"Where do you get your information to put in your books?"

"They are books for children, sir. Fantasy, amusing and gay, but with a moral, I assure you."

"I know your books," one of the men said unkindly. "I discovered my own son reading one."

"How nice—"

"No. I had not approved the book for him."

Jo was astounded at the thought of censoring all the books her collection of boys owned and hid and coveted, so said, "So long as your son reads, sir, you should be quite satisfied."

The man snorted and scowled in reply.

"It leads us to believe you may harbor a werewolf here," the largest man said. "Or at very least sympathize and abet them in other ways, if you know enough of them to write such things."

"I assure you, the tales in my books are manufactured in my mind only, and these creatures assembled before you turn wolfish only at the dinner table, not under the light of the moon," Jo said.

"Perhaps we should question a few of these young men, " one soldier said.

"I got my eye on this one," another said, grasping Tommy Bangs by the thin meat of his upper arm, which scared the incorrigible boy into behaving completely for a full month afterward.

With a nod from the largest of them, the obvious leader, the men began to search the house, shoving crockery to the floor and storming on to upend other rooms. The one soldier still had Tommy Bangs entrapped, and he dragged the tearful little imp along with him as he spilled cushions and books onto the floor.

"You'll find no gnawed bones, if that's what you seek," Jo called out, feeling the temper that she long thought she had completely under control rising into her throat. She paced from room to room, ordering the boys to get the baby and go outside, and nervously following the soldiers to right things as they upset them.

"I think we will need you, great writer of werewolf tales, to come away with us," the leader of the group said with a guffaw. "To answer some questions."

Jo saw that one soldier now had clutched, in the thick meat of his fist, a burlap bag that bulged, but with what, she couldn't imagine. What had they found? Through her mind flashed images of the hanged and beaten werewolves and werewolf sympathizers she had seen throughout her life, followed by the inane comfort that as a mere sympathizer, she would not have her chest torn open and her heart extracted.

"I cannot leave the boys, sir . . . ," she began, but was seized roughly and dragged outside.

"The boys are coming too," she was informed by the leader, who had taken Tommy Bangs to free the other soldier to round up the other boys.

Jo tried to think up a reply, an excuse, or anything to spare herself and her brood, when a voice rose up behind her.

"Is that you, Charles?"

The leader's eyes widened and he released Tommy's arm, reached up, as if to remove his helmet, but checked himself and merely stood straighter. "Chaplain March, sir, I never expected to find you here." He stressed the *here* as if it was a dirty thing.

The other soldiers, flustered, released Jo, and she stood rubbing her sore arm where their rough fingers had grasped her.

"I'm happy to see you!" Charles said heartily, stepping over to Mr. March and hugging him to his breastplate with one massive arm. His bright blue eyes twinkled out gleefully from between the cut leather of his helmet. The man loomed so high over him that Mr. March looked like a youth in comparison.

"As I am to see you," Mr. March said with a warm smile.

"I didn't know if you had made it home alive," Charles said, examining the older man's face. "I lost news of everyone once I was sent home."

"This is my daughter," Mr. March said, stepping over and putting a protective hand on Jo's shoulder. Silence prevailed for a few moments. "I am very grateful to God to see you so well recovered from your war injuries, Charles."

"Yes. I harbor a limp, but it does not prevent me from fulfilling my duties."

"Your duties of accusing werewolves?"

"My duties of feeding my family," Charles replied. "I am in charge of the Brigade now, and I have reassembled members and am improving their skills. We are reverting to older practices, such as hunting not only by day but also under the light of the full moon, so we may rest assured we have found true werewolves. I am in the business of protecting all families."

"Feeding and protecting one's family is of utmost importance," Mr. March said, meeting the man's eyes firmly. "My family will all be here soon for our annual apple-picking festivities."

"We . . . we received a report, sir."

"I assure you, neither my daughter nor son-in-law are werewolves."

"We had a report of a sympathizer."

Mr. March walked a short distance away from Jo to take the man aside, and she had to step forward to gain balance, so fully had she allowed herself to be supported by her father.

After a few moments of hushed conversation, Charles called

loudly to the other men to assemble, and when they did, he ordered them to take their leave.

"Tomorrow, then, Charles," Mr. March said as the men retreated. "I will see you at the church."

The soldiers left wordlessly and clearly, grudgingly, as if not fully believing their raid had ended, and Jo saw that the filled burlap bag would be leaving with them. One yelled back by way of a farewell, "We'll be watching you and yours, missus."

"If you find yourself able to keep up with these ruffians well enough to watch them, then I applaud you," Jo returned in a voice every bit as loud and stern as the man's.

The boys had run over to find Jo when they saw the soldiers leaving, and their eyes widened and their jaws dropped with admiration at the woman's pluck.

"Don't worry, Jo. I'll do everything in my power to see to it that Plumfield is always protected," Mr. March promised. "I will speak to Charles. I served in the war with the man, and I believe his intentions to be pure, although his actions sorely lack empathy and compassion. God will guide me through, so I am certain I can speak with him and arrange that something like this will never again happen to you."

Jo nodded and fell again into the comfort and safety of her father's arms. "I thank God you came here when you did. Friedrich is out in the fields."

"I slept at the church, so thought I would come early to help you. It's over, Jo. You can relax now."

"I was so frightened, Father."

"As was I. But Jo, we must not tell your mother about this."

"I know. I don't even want to worry Friedrich with it, if I can help it. Especially if you feel it won't happen again."

"There is certain to be some way I can assure that. For now, we must attend to our preparations. We have a joyous day ahead of us, and we cannot allow this to dampen it. Set your mind on family and celebration, and put aside all else. We must be strong and forge ahead, my girl."

"Father, I won't let those evil men ruin this occasion for me, for you, or for anyone in this family."

"The men are merely misguided, dear, not evil. The war got in their blood, and they seek to make war their way of life. We must pray for them, harder than ever."

"Even though they will hunt you under the light of the moon?" she asked quietly enough that the boys would not hear. She looked into her father's face, saw his answer there, and sighed. "Very well, I will try my best to be as forgiving as you are, Father. I will include that troop of men in my prayers."

"And God will bless you."

Jo breathed deeply, steadied herself, took a moment to gather her wits. Then she called all the dirty faces around her and cautioned the boys to say nothing of the soldiers' visit. "My mother, as do most, worries terribly, so please spare her and everyone else, and don't say anything about those men coming here, for it would ruin this happy occasion."

The boys all agreed and turned to leave, but Jo stopped them. "I know those men look quite daring in their thick cocoon of leather, but beneath, they are just men. Men like Papa, Uncle Teddy, Mr. Laurence, and Grandfather here. They are, however, not kind men. Kindness is the greatest gift one can give the world, kindness to each and every creature with which we share this earth. We all share the struggle to survive." She stopped short, having heard both her mother's and her father's voices in her own. "Now, I want all of you to march into that house and straighten everything that has been knocked askew. I want everything in place and suitable for visitors, and wish to see no sign, anywhere within, of those diabolical men who stormed through this house." Tommy Bangs was the first to run toward the house to do his part.

Jo saw, from across the road, a curious sprinkling of people. They would probably be shunned now, for the Brigade had sent six of their own to investigate them, a number that suggested undeniable guilt. The neighbors, seeing Jo looking their way, turned aside, and she knew for certain then that the label had been stitched on tight, and with strong thread, and that the congenial relationships she had with those people, and with her community, were now spoiled. She took a deep breath, gathered her skirts, and turned toward the house to finish her preparations.

The old orchard wore its holiday attire. Goldenrod and asters fringed the mossy walls. Grasshoppers skipped briskly in the sere grass, and crickets chirped like fairy pipers at a feast. Squirrels were busy with their small harvesting. Birds twittered their adieux from the alders in the lane, and every tree stood ready to send down its shower of red or yellow apples at the first shake. Everybody was there. Everybody laughed and sang, climbed up and tumbled down. Everybody declared that there never had been such a perfect day or such a jolly set to enjoy it, and everyone gave themselves up to the simple pleasures of the hour as freely as if there was no such things as care or sorrow in the world. It was so bright and altogether gay that Jo nearly forgot her fright of the morning.

Laurie and Amy arrived late, and Laurie instantly began sniffing the air and giving Jo a questioning look, so she knew he smelled the recent danger and threat of the Brigade.

"It's passed," she assured him softly. "Father handled it all admirably."

The matter was dropped, as Marmee and Meg were upon them then, having rushed to have their first glance at Amy and Laurie's darling baby girl, who had been named for Beth. Having full werewolf blood, the baby was weak and ailing, but when the women gathered together to coo over her, the thin, pale baby lifted her delicate arms and uttered soft, adorable syllables in reply to their chirping.

Mr. March strolled placidly about, quoting Tusser, Cowley, and Columella to Mr. Laurence, while enjoying "the gentle apple's winey juice." The Professor charged up and down the green aisles like a stout Teutonic knight, with a pole for a lance, leading on the boys, who made a hook-and-ladder company of themselves and performed wonders in the way of ground and lofty tumbling. Laurie devoted himself to the little ones, rode his small daughter in a bushel basket, took Daisy up among the bird's nests, and kept adventurous Rob from breaking his neck. Mrs. March and Meg sat among the apple piles like a pair of Pomonas, sorting the contributions that kept pouring in, while Amy, with a beautiful motherly expression on her face, sketched the various groups and watched over one pale lad, who sat adoring her with his little crutch beside him.

Jo was in her element that day, and the activity cleared her mind of the morning's trauma. She rushed about with her gown pinned up, her hat anywhere but on her head, and her baby tucked under her arm, ready for any lively adventure that might turn up. Little Teddy bore a charmed life, for nothing ever happened to him, and Jo never felt any anxiety when he was whisked up into a tree by one lad, galloped off on the back of another, or supplied with sour russets by his indulgent papa, who labored under the Germanic delusion that babies could digest anything, from pickled cabbage to buttons, nails, and their own small shoes. She knew that little Ted would turn up again in time, safe and rosy, dirty and serene, and she always received him back with a hearty welcome, for Jo loved her babies tenderly.

At four o'clock a lull took place, and baskets remained empty, while the apple pickers rested and compared rents and bruises. Then Jo and Meg, with a detachment of the bigger boys, set forth the supper on the grass, for an out-of-door tea was always the crowning joy of the day. The land literally flowed with milk and honey on such occasions, for the lads were not required to sit at table but allowed to partake of refreshment as they liked, freedom being the sauce best beloved by the boyish soul. They availed themselves of the rare privilege to the fullest extent, for some tried the pleasing experiment of drinking milk while standing on their heads, others lent a charm to leapfrog by eating pie during the pauses of the game, cookies were sown broadcast over the field, and apple turnovers roosted in the trees like a new style of bird. The little girls had a private tea party, and Ted roved among the edibles at his own sweet will.

Jo was certain to include a vast array of meats, and she noted happily that her father, Mr. Laurence, Laurie, Amy, and their little daughter, Beth, had their plates heaping with the beef, mutton, pork, squirrel, rabbit, chicken, brains, hearts, and livers she had specially prepared, as well as Friedrich's special old-world sausages, bratwurst, and headcheese, which he made in bulk and stored in the coldest reaches of the cellar. A shiver shook her spine as she wondered what accusations would have come to light if her father had not appeared when he did and the soldiers had found their meat cellar.

When no one could eat any more, the Professor proposed the first regular toast, which was always drunk at such times. "Aunt March, God bless her! Here is a toast heartily given by the good man, who never forgot how much he owed her, and quietly drunk by the boys, who had been taught to keep her memory green."

"Now, to Grandma's sixtieth birthday! Long life to her, with three times three!"

The cheering, once begun, was hard to stop. Everybody's health was proposed, from Mr. Laurence, who was considered their special patron, to the astonished guinea pig, who had strayed from its proper sphere in search of its young master. Demi, as the oldest grandchild, then presented the queen of the day with various gifts, so numerous that they were transported to the festive scene in a wheelbarrow.

During the ceremony, the boys had mysteriously disappeared, and when Mrs. March had tried to thank her children, and broken down, while Teddy wiped her eyes on his pinafore, the Professor suddenly began to sing. Then, from above him, voice after voice took up the words, and from tree to tree echoed the music of the unseen choir, as the boys sang with all their hearts the little song that Jo had written, Laurie had set to music, and the Professor had trained his lads to give with the best effect. This was something altogether new, and it proved a grand success, for Mrs. March couldn't get over her surprise and insisted on shaking hands with every one of the featherless birds once they had descended from their tree limbs.

After this, the boys dispersed for a final lark, leaving Mrs. March and her daughters under the festival tree.

"I don't think I ever ought to call myself 'Unlucky Jo' again, when my greatest wish has been so beautifully gratified," said Mrs. Bhaer, taking Teddy's little fist out of the milk pitcher, in which he was rapturously churning.

"And yet your life is very different from the one you pictured so long ago. Do you remember our castles in the air?" asked

Amy, smiling as she watched Laurie and John playing cricket with the boys. She glanced at Jo's bear of a man and wondered if her sister truly was happy with having lost Laurie and gained Bhaer. She didn't see how it could possibly be so.

"Yes, I remember, but the life I wanted then seems selfish, lonely, and cold to me now," Jo said, looking from the lively lads in the distance to her father, leaning on the Professor's arm, as they walked to and fro in the sunshine, deep in one of the conversations that both enjoyed so much, and then to her mother, sitting enthroned among her daughters, with their children in her lap and at her feet, as if all found help and happiness in the face that never could grow old to them.

"My castle was the most nearly realized of all," said Meg. "I asked for splendid things, to be sure, but in my heart I knew I should be satisfied if I had a little home, and John, and some dear children like these. I've got them all, thank God, and am the happiest woman in the world." She laid her hand on her tall boy's head, with a face full of tender and devout content.

"My castle is not so very different from what I planned," said Amy. "Happily, I found I do not have to relinquish all my artistic hopes, or confine myself only to helping others fulfill their dreams of beauty. I've begun to model a figure of my baby daughter, and Laurie says it is the best thing I've ever done. I think so, myself, and mean to do it in marble, so that, whatever happens, I may at least keep the image of my little angel. But many pure werewolf young are born weak, and strengthen suddenly and quickly within a couple of years. We can only believe she will be one of them as we face each new day."

As Amy spoke, a great tear dropped on the golden hair of the sleeping child in her arms, for her one well-beloved daughter was a terribly frail little creature, and the dread of losing her was the shadow over Amy's sunshine. But the burden was doing much for both father and mother, for one love and sorrow bound them closely together. Amy's nature was growing sweeter, deeper, and more tender. Laurie was growing more serious, strong, and firm, and both were learning that beauty, youth, good fortune, even love itself, cannot keep care and pain, loss and sorrow, from the most blessed.

"She is growing better, I am sure of it, my dear. Don't despair, but hope and keep happy," said Mrs. March, as tenderhearted Daisy stooped from her knee to lay her rosy cheek against her little cousin's pale one.

"I never ought to, while I have you to cheer me up, Marmee, and Laurie to take more than half of every burden," replied Amy warmly. "He never lets me see his anxiety, but is so sweet and patient with me, so devoted to Beth, and such a stay and comfort to me always that I can't love him enough. So, in spite of my one cross, I can say with Meg, 'Thank God, I'm a happy woman.' "

"There's no need for me to say it, for everyone can see that I'm far happier than I deserve," added Jo, glancing from her good husband to her chubby children, tumbling on the grass beside her. "Friedrich is getting gray and stout. I'm growing as thin as a shadow, and am thirty, and Plumfield may burn up any night, for that incorrigible Tommy Bangs *will* smoke sweet-fern cigars under the bedclothes, though he's set himself afire three times already. But in spite of these unromantic facts, I have nothing to complain of, and never was so jolly in my life. Excuse the remark, but living among boys, I can't help using their expressions now and then."

"Yes, Jo, I think your harvest will be a good one," began Mrs. March, frightening away a big black cricket that was staring Teddy out of countenance.

"Not half so good as yours, Mother. Here it is, and we never can thank you enough for the patient sowing and reaping you have done," cried Jo, with the loving impetuosity that she never could outgrow.

"I hope there will be more wheat and fewer tares every year," said Amy softly.

"A large sheaf, but I know there's room in your heart for it, Marmee dear," added Meg's tender voice.

"Thank God for all the people assembled here today," Jo said. "Four generations of precious people."

"Woowuf!" sang baby Teddy from her lap.

"Yes, darling," she said with a laugh, folding his dimpled little hands in hers as she gave silent thanksgiving that all these members of their family were yet together to enjoy another apple harvest. "Thank God for all the werewolves here today, too. Four generations of beloved werewolves."

Touched to the heart, Mrs. March could only stretch out her arms, as if to gather children and grandchildren to herself, and say, with face and voice full of motherly love, gratitude, and humility, "Oh, my girls, however long you may live, I never can wish you a greater happiness than this!"

The End

Acknowledgments

...

One million, five hundred and twenty-three thank-yous to Adam Chromy, my energetic and amazing agent, who recognized that there is a place in this wide and wonderful world for my unusual books. Also, thank you to Artists and Artisans' Jamie Brenner who has consistently been positive and supportive, and to Gwendolyn Heasley whose incredibly keen perception has been a gigantic help and a true marvel.

Thank you to Betsy Mitchell, editor in chief of Del Rey, for choosing to acquire this book from among the vast legion of manuscripts, and to my editor, Kaitlin Heller, and copy editor Margaret Wimberger, who helped me navigate the tightrope between Louisa May Alcott's book and my own. Another hearty thank-you to Del Rey art director David Stevenson for designing the fierce and fabulous cover. More thanks must be strewn out to all the talented people at Del Rey and Random House who worked so diligently to bring this manuscript swiftly into print.

Thank you to Linda Bark'karie for sticking by me and taking on the project of illustrating this book with her breathtaking artwork.

Thank you to Ann Slaughter, my Word wizard, who was, with utter calm, able to undo my most grievous errors and helped me format, space, insert, number, and delete.

Thank you, of course, to Louisa May Alcott, a remarkable woman who was very much ahead of her time.

And the last thank-you goes to my two most profound inspirations for the hungry werewolves in this book: my husband, Jeff, who loves to hunt, and my late German Shepherd, Blitzkrieg.

LOUISA MAY ALCOTT was born in Germantown, Pennsylvania, on November 29, 1832, the second of four daughters. Her family was poor, and like the March sisters in *Little Women*, the four Alcott girls entertained themselves by staging amateur theatricals, holding meetings of their Pickwick Club, and putting out a family newspaper. Later, Alcott's brief experience as an army nurse during the Civil War provided material for her first major literary success, *Hospital Sketches*, published in 1863. Five years later, the publication of *Little Women* catapulted Alcott to fame and fortune nearly overnight, and its immense popularity led her to write four sequels: *Little Women and Good Wives, Little Men, Aunt Jo's Scrap Bag,* and *Jo's Boys and How They Turned Out.*

Before *Little Women,* however, Alcott supported herself by writing gothic romances and sensational thrillers that appeared under the pseudonym A. M. Barnard. "I think my natural inclination is for the lurid style," she once admitted. Several volumes of these so-called blood-and-thunder tales, including *Behind a Mask, Plots and Counterplots, A Double Life,* and *Modern Magic,* have been compiled by Madeleine Stern, perhaps Alcott's most distinguished biographer and literary editor.

An active participant in the woman's suffrage and temperance movements in the last decade of her life, Louisa May Alcott died in Roxbury, Massachusetts, on March 6, 1888, and was buried in the Alcott family plot in Sleepy Hollow Cemetery, Concord. She was not, to the best of anyone's knowledge, a werewolf.

. . .

Cleveland, Ohio, native PORTER GRAND holds an A.S. in liberal arts and a Bachelor's degree and Doctoral in theology. She has worked, among other jobs, as a waitress, bartender, carnival barker, go-go dancer, shampoo girl, welfare caseworker, and reference librarian, and now writes daily in her Huntsburg, Ohio, farmhouse.

ABOUT THE TYPE

This book was set in Bell, a typeface that was introduced by John Bell in England in 1788. The typeface was cut for Bell's foundry by the notable British punch cutter Richard Austin. Bell had a resurgence in 1931, when it was recut by the English Monotype Company. It was brought to America in 1932, where it was cut by the Lanston Monotype Machine Company of Philadelphia.